The Confession of Lucifer, Fallen Angel

Chuck A. Maier

Cover Artist:
St. Wolfgang and the Devil by Michael Pacher 1483.
Munich, Alt Pinakothek

ISBN: 978-1-4834-6684-2 (sc)
ISBN: 978-0-578-19038-9 (hc)
ISBN: 978-1-4834-6685-9 (e)

Library of Congress Control Number: 2017903756

Lulu Publishing Services rev. date: 05/17/2017

For Tammy, Brittany and Charlie,

who were my beginning

And

For my father, Charles Albert Maier

And

For my BellaStrega

who will be at my end

The Confession of Lucifer, Fallen Angel

To which is added

A faithful account of the Devil's fall from heaven, his view of mankind, and the rightful compilation and construction of his testimony

To which is included

The adventure of Sean Wilde, book scout.

G. Doré
J. GAUCHARD SC.

"One day the angels came to present themselves before the Lord, and Satan also came with them. The Lord said to Satan, "Where have you come from?"

Satan answered the Lord, "From roaming through the earth and going back and forth in it."

Job 1: 6,7

"Books delight us, when prosperity smiles upon us; They comfort us inseparably when stormy fortune frowns on us. They lend validity to human compacts, and no serious judgments are propounded without their help. How highly must we estimate the wondrous power of books, since through them we survey the utmost bounds of the world and time, and contemplate the things that are as well as those that are not, as it were the mirror of eternity."

The Philobiblion of Richard de Bury, 1345 a.d.

PROLOGUE

Leaf One,

The Manuscripta Diabolica

In the beginning, God created the heavens and the earth.

Before the beginning, God created ***Me****.*

I was the beginning.

I was the first of His angels. I was the first of His beings. It was I who was present before anything…

From His lips He bequeathed to me the name 'Lucifer' – a title of great recognition. Know you that my name defined means 'Bringer of Light.'

Pity.

How unenviable it is that I have come to be recognized as little more than the complete embodiment of darkness. All that is evil. The very author of sin itself.

Father Thomas Chrysostomus quickly closed the book. He could not control the flood of guilt nor the surmounting tension that enveloped him for having opened the infernal testament. Yet neither could he toss the book aside. What rested in his hands was the most frightening thing he had ever seen. Within this manuscript lay the account of the Satan. It was engaging him as if it were the very nature of temptation itself.

Reluctantly, the monk pulled the book close to himself and mumbled a solitary prayer. Perhaps he wished God to forgive him for what he was about to do. Perhaps he wished to forgive himself. At this point he allowed neither to matter.

He then looked down at the volumous work and drew it from where he had embedded it in the cavity of his chest. His fingers shook as they fumbled at the cover and peeled it back, forcing it open once more.

I am weary of man. I am weary of the separation from my Creator and the realm I once knew as my home.

Long have I walked the earth. Longer still have I been alone.

Now, I wish to lay forth my confession.

I wish to rid myself of this realm and all those that claim humanity.

I wish to find the compact of forgiveness.

I wish to exist no longer in this diabolical form to which I have been interred.

Here and now, before you, I, Lucifer lay forth my confession.

I wish to know if I can be forgiven for my very self...

In the dark pervading solace of the library, the monk collapsed to his knees. Somewhere in his heart he knew better than to continue reading.

But what choice did he have? Who could resist the temptation of such knowledge as this?

There is always a choice.

The monk's wrinkled fingers struggled to turn the leaf of blood-smeared parchment. A shiver followed. And then, the confession of the fallen angel Lucifer began to unfold as his eyes fell upon the very next page...

Contents

> "The devil was sick, the devil a monk would be:
> The devil was well, the devil a monk was he."
>
> Rabelais

Docheiariou

Mount Athos, Greece
1496 A.D.

The storm had finally arrived.

Torrents of rain pounded violently against the outer walls of Docheiariou as a northeasterly wind swelled the Aegean Sea, aggravating the salty body of water and forcing it to strike repeatedly at the land mass spread out before it. The small monastery stood firm though, nestled safely on the western side of the island, but it's close proximity to the waters' edge made escape from seasonal outbursts such as this one, futile. The thunderous crash of waves, breaking just outside, seemed to have little effect on the community of monks living and working just inside its walls. It was now November, and winter had finally come to the Orthodox island republic of Athos.

Forty-two monks resided within the walled monastery. It was for them, a place of uninterrupted absolution, each man allowing himself complete focus and concentrated worship of God. The men, as an edict had long been established forbidding women to set foot on the island, lived a life chaste in the stringent moral demands for both the daily labors they carried out, and the means by which they worshipped. The monks would spend early morning in prayer, sometimes for hours on end. When not fasting, the men would assemble for meals in the refectory, always dining in silence, ·save the prayers that would always be spoken by one of their own during the meal. Daily labors would find division between fishing or cultivation of the land that surrounded them. The afternoon would be filled with scripture reading and more time in prayer. Assembled worship, work, and private meditational devotion made up the formula for the life of a monk on Athos. Here, in the monastic confines of Docheiariou, materialistic concerns of the world did not exist, nor had they ever.

Between the loud aggravated claps of thunder, pensive footsteps could be heard of a small elder figure walking ever so silently down a cobblestone corridor within the monastery. He had, outstretched before him, an iron lantern the contents of which illuminated the abbey and allowed him safe passage through the dark winding hallway. The figure was making his way towards the chapel, shifting his frail, cloaked frame from side to side as he walked. A small girdle book bound in leather swayed upside down, tied by a topknot, from his waist. The bottom of his robe shuffled along the flooring as he now could see the sanctuary door a few feet before him. He mused at how massive the door was in comparison to himself, his eyes studying the oaken structure. The old monk bowed his head, which lay tucked deeply behind a large cloaked hood, or cowl, whispering a silent prayer to himself before turning the iron handle and entering the place of worship.

Four monks, his spiritual brothers, were on their knees before an effigy of the crucifixion, having already assembled sometime earlier for the daily confession. They turned instinctively towards the little man as he removed his hood.

It was the abbot of Docheiariou, Father Andreas Koutrakos.

He smiled, acknowledging them as the cowl came to rest on his slightly hunched shoulders. He had become an old man now. His long gray beard and ever thinning hairline served as a reminder of the strain one could expect from a life so ridged in its spiritual demands. Behind his steel blue eyes, it was whispered among the monks, lay the wisdom of a hundred men. His mind had remained sharper than most, although his body had become sorely withered with age. His presence evoked a calming among his fellow monks, a welcoming reassurance that the life they had chosen was not a vain attempt to dissocialize themselves from the rest of humanity, but a human effort to achieve oneness with their creator. The monastery would one day be incomplete with his passing, a time, it did not seem, was looming too far in the distance.

The old man took in his surroundings. The simple beauty of the main chapel, with it's flooring made of small stones neatly assembled together, detailed oak carvings, medieval paintings, iron sconces, and beautiful iconography, made him feel as though this was the closest place in which he could connect with the heavens, and father Koutrakos never tired of being surrounded by its walls.

As abbot, Father Koutrakos maintained complete authority over manners concerning spirituality and worship. He had come to the island forty years earlier, in the fall of his twenty eighth year, abandoning his former life as a scholar in thc grcat city of Constantinople. Wisdom in all facets of life had won him great admiration with the holy men of Docheiariou, and it was he who heard the confessions of the men residing here. Father Koutrakos had a gift of assuring absolution in both the words he spoke and the vigilance of his prayer, and he was loved by all.

The holy man also served a secondary, but equally vital purpose as well. He was the monastery's chief librarian and archivist. Having been a former scholar, the written word and the power of books and their content held for him both profound love and a: passion he could never seem to escape. It was the pride he took as both abbot and librarian that could be seen manifesting his pleasant demeanor. The separation a monk experiences from secular society, welcoming a life void of worldly appetites and so rigorous in its demands spiritually, never seemed to affect his demeanor or the dutiful way he carried out his labors.

Within Docheiariou's library were housed some of the most prized artifacts and valuable manuscripts the world had never seen. To be a bit more specific, the library cataloged some two hundred manuscripts, all illuminated by hand, innumerable works of art, and many sacerdotal vestments. They had been gathered and assembled since the monastery's founding in 1030 A.D. by the anthoinite monk, Daniel of Docheiariou. All of the priceless antiquities were located on the second floor of the main tower and it was the dear old abbot who had been entrusted to care and preserve them. He himself had fantastic skills as an expert manuscript illuminator, and had illustrated over twenty works on the gospels in his self-imposed exile on Athos. His care for the relics had been as that of a mother to a child, each one finding special favor and deserving individualized attention. They were beloved friends in whom he found much comfort and solace. Their value to him far outweighed any monetary price that could be affixed in the world existing beyond Athos.

The old abbot acknowledged the four monks as he humbly shuffled pass them in the sanctuary, nodding his head in approval of their presence, but saying nothing. He thought to himself how little the place had changed since he first saw it, so very many years ago. The younger monks seemed unnecessarily in awe of the abbot, his piety, though infectious, called no special need for attention. He would hear their confessions before the evening vespers, or lighting of the candles, as he normally did at the close of the day. Compassion was his gift, it had been his only means of confronting his own sins, and he would bestow among the four who gathered presently, the lessons he had learned when he, so many years ago, was among them. He snickered to himself, how fortunate it must be that only four of his brothers sought the necessity of confession, the other thirty-seven must have felt purity enough.

Father Koutrakos made a slight whimpering sound as he approached the ornately carved confessional chamber. The wooden structure, outset in the comer of the chapel, was just large enough to hold two adult men. The chamber had a divisionary wall that would separate the two individuals when inside, save for a small grated window inset within the dividing wall for conversing. A large purple cloak, or curtain hung from the top of the Holy box, draping down and shielding its internal contents from the outer sanctuary. It was the one place where the sins of man could be confronted, purged, and ultimately, forgiven.

The old abbot tugged at the hanging cloak, and pulling it aside, turned towards the men kneeling before him, and motioned with his hand, bidding the first monk to enter. What sins would be in need of forgiveness today he wondered? What absolutions would necessitate penance? These were questions he had come to ask himself at the close of the day, realizing of course, that most sins were never really against God, but against man himself. He smiled at his brother. As the two monks entered the confessional, the abbot noticed the quiet stillness of the room, he could almost hear the flames dancing from the tips of candle wicks held fast to the stone walling by black, wrought iron sconces.

While the two men whispered softly to one another from behind the purple curtain, the stillness of the room was interrupted by a loud crack of thunder from outside. This did nothing to halt the process of what was being done within the confessional, but it did startle the three monks waiting within the sanctuary. As the first man stood, eyes quickly scanning the room, the ferocious winds gathered from outside swelling pressure that blew open a small window perched just above a statue of the Blessed Virgin, to the western corner of the room. Strong gusts of wind billowed in accompanied by rain and as they swept through the altar, the candles were extinguished, rendering the sanctuary black. The monks set out immediately to the task at hand. They scattered, the first monk immediately closing the window, the others tending to the candles. Within moments the window had been shut, a bolt tightly fasting it to the wall ensuring it would not so easily be flung open again, and the room became once again illuminated as the monks had effectively relit all the candles.

The monastery was quiet once more. The abbeys and hallways had been deserted as the monks not attending confession had retired to their cells, or rooms, for a night of intent individual worship, and the reading of scriptures in silence. The close of day had come to Docheiariou.

Time passed within the chapel, the abbot having heard two hours of his brothers sinful woes. The storm still raged outside, but the only evidence of its existence was the small puddle of water that had been left on the floor from the outburst before. Father Koutrakos had now brought the last confession to a close. The old monk made the sign of the cross, pulling his hand from the air and touching each side of his chest, blessing the fourth, and last monk. The two men stepped from the wooden box, exchanging a hug, as Father Koutrakos warmly gave a kind smile to the repentant young monk, assuring the man, whatever his concerns, all would be forgiven.

The younger monk bowed before the abbot, and placing his hood back over his head, turned and proceeded to leave the chapel, mumbling sacred hymns under his breath as he closed the door behind him.

Father Koutrakos was alone now.

He began the task of securing the chapel for the evening, beginning first, by extinguishing the burning candles. He had put out no more than two luminaries, when he noticed, from the comer of his eye, a hooded figure standing next to the confessional entranceway. Could he have possibly overlooked the monk before? Maybe he had miscounted, age would sometimes cause problems with even the simplest of mathematical equations.

“My son,” he called out in a scratchy, solemn voice ripened with age, “Forgive me if l failed in some way to notice you before, my old age and withering eyesight, seem to be getting the better of me,” he paused awaiting a response that never came. “Would it please you that I hear your confession my brother?”

The figure that faced him from across the room shifted slightly, making no effort to reveal what face lay hidden behind the hood tightly enclosing his head. He nodded, saying nothing, and then held out a hand, which the abbot could tell was very pale, and motioned the old monk forward.

Father Koutrakos obeyed, shifting his little frame forward and walking towards the confessional. This was odd. It wasn’t like a fellow monk to not respond to a direct question from an abbot. Maybe the man was guilt ridden with shame for an act of sin that was causing him to feel regressive, not wanting to reveal his identity. This was acceptable to the abbot. Sin was a very powerful thing indeed. If anonymity was required, so be it. As the old man approached, the figure, towering above him by almost a foot, looked down and from within the hood, began to speak.

“If it please you father,” a deep, soft voice began, “I have a great deal to confess.”

The voice seemed to strike deep within the old abbot, causing him to cock his head slightly to the right, it sounded like the voice of someone he had not heard in many years. A loved one perhaps. He shook off the feeling, realizing that the hour was growing late and there would be one more confession he would have to hear before retiring himself to his own cell for the evening. He smiled at the shape standing before him, just the way he had done to every man who had come to repent so many times before. Placing his hand on the shoulder of his fellow monk he guided the cloaked figure inside. He noticed the pale hands of his brother once more, as they were now at his side. They were up close, where he could see the protrusive length of the fingers. They seemed unusually long, possibly having an extra digit at the tips. Outside, the monastery of Docheiariou was being pounded relentlessly by the winter storm.

The sanctuary became deathly quiet, only the sounds of mother nature, far in the distance, could be heard. The two men had now positioned themselves on oaken seats within the confessional. Father Koutrakos reached to his forehead and wiped away the small rivulets of sweat seeping from his brow, then motioned upwards with his hands pulling the heavy curtain closed. A slight chill shot down his spine. He was tired, and for some reason that escaped him, nervous. He could hear no sound from the other side of the partition. He glanced down at his wrinkled fingers, and the scripture book he was holding. Focus on the task at hand. He could still hear nothing, not even the sound of the figure breathing. The old abbot leaned his wrinkled face towards the windowed grate in the center of the partition, and putting his lips to the opening, began speaking in a soft, assuring tone. "Relax my son, and know that you are in the presence of the Lord thy God," the words trailing off, "You may at any time begin your confession."

Silence. He could just see the outlined shape of a cloaked figure through the tiny portal, but it sat unmoving.

A crash of thunder from outside!

The small window that had been locked and secured earlier, was ripped from the wall as wind and rain once again burst through the sanctuary, toppling the statue of the Blessed Virgin and sending it shattering across the stone floor in thousands of marbled pieces. The candles flickered once, before the winter air filled the vestige and enshrouded the room in cold, black darkness.

Father Koutrakos jolted at the noise, dropping his scripture book to the floor. He shivered uncontrollably, his feeble body contorting, his heart racing. Calm yourself He addressed the figure once more. "Brother?" he began calming his body," Do you have need to confess your sins?"

Again, there was no immediate reply. Yet something strange had begun to happen; the thick air inside the confessional was growing cold. The abbot could see his breath in front of his face when he exhaled. The temperature was dropping fast, and he could not wait very long before dealing with whatever damage had occurred outside the confessional. His eyes shifted back to the hooded outline on the other side of the partition as it was now turning, edging closer to the portal. He could now feel an eeriness about him. There was something odd in the breath of his companion as its warm tone danced through the grate. Something is wrong.

"Where am I to begin?" a soft raspy voice returned.

"Begin with the thing that is troubling you most my son."

There was a momentary silence as the temperature seemed to be dropping further. Then, the voice began speaking again. "My very existence is what troubles me, father."

"Go on my son," the abbot stated as he clung tightly to his robe for warmth.

"I am afraid I am beyond redemption."

"All men fear this from time to time brother," the monk said with reassurance in his voice, "but no man is beyond the mercy of God."

"Then help me father," the voice pleaded with heavy contention, "for I am guilty of a great many things." There was deep lamentation in every word the soul conveyed. The old monk humbled himself further. He lowered his head in pity.

"I am here for you my son. Tell me of your sin."

In that very instance, a thunderous roar erupted outside the monastery! The monk jolted in his seat, caught off guard by the sudden noise. He could feel his nails dig into the wooden bench he was seated upon. Somewhere deep within the pit of his bowels he knew something was horribly wrong.

Fighting to gain some control of his percipience, he peered his squinting eyes through the small grate that separated him from the figure which sat on the other side. What he saw through the tiny portal stopped his heart cold. The outline of some otherworldly shape was staring back at him. As the old man stammered to speak, a sound bellowed from the other side.

"I need your blessing, Father," a sinister tone began, "For I am sin!"

Father Koutrakos froze. Merciful God! He was paralyzed, an undeniable dread enveloping him. His heart pounded unmercifully within his chest. It would explode. Yes. He was going to die right then and there, from fright no less. There was no reassurance of God, no calming warmth. Alone. Satan had come for him. A stench of sulfur bled through the dividing wall. The old abbot gathered what little energy he could muster and sprang from the confessional, ripping the curtain away to reveal the horror awaiting him on the other side.

Nothing.

The voice and the figure it had been attached to were gone, if they had ever really been there at all. The moon, shining through the windowed hole, just above the corner where the statue of the Virgin Mary had been, cast a glow of light that illuminated enough of the sanctuary for Father Koutrakos to see the damage caused by the storm still raging outside. He caught sight of the broken statue on the floor and allowed himself the displeasure of viewing the severed head of the virgin still intact and looking up from the floor in his direction.

It was weeping.

The old abbot fell to his knees, hands clenched tight in fear, terrified, as the darkness of the sanctuary and the frigid winter wind enveloped him. The Devil himself had come to Docheiariou. God it seemed had abandoned His most penitent disciple.

"I have known men to hazard their fortunes, go long journeys half way around the world, forge friendships, even lie, cheat, and steal, all for the gain of a book."

A.S. W. Rosenbach

The Proposition

Paris, France

The Present

Sean Wilde was seated at his favorite cafe, the Cafe de Madeline, off the boulevard St-Michel, where it intersects the Rue de la Harpe, near the River Seine. He had occasioned himself to come here often, passing the late afternoon hours with a cafe mocha and a new novel of fiction, himself staring up every few minutes at the bustling tourists and Parisians alike, that could be seen weaving in and out of the market square. The Latin Quarter of Paris was alive with activity, as the late afternoon sun was starting to disappear beyond the horizon. It was a good place to read, to unwind.

Today he sat alone, his sandy blond shoulder-length hair tossed about in the light, afternoon breeze, as he shuffled from page to page of the dramatic work, Torquemada, by his favorite author, Victor Hugo. And how right he should take in the edification of such a work; he was, after all, in

Paris. What better place in all the world to experience Hugo. What better place in all the world to experience life.

His hand wandered up to the thin layer of stubble that had formed some mock beard about his tight jaw line. Such a fantastic writer, he mused, pressing the mocha to his lips, preparing himself for the warm rush of pleasure that would soon follow. He closed his eyes; and unintentionally, his mind began drifting a bit from the pages and from the coffee. How strange it was that, of all the places in the world, he had found himself here. France. This cafe. It all seemed impossible, like one of those dreams a person never realized he had until after it had already come true. No one could have predicted what events would have had to transpire to get Sean here, least of all, himself. No, that was the most incredible part of all.

He caught himself amidst the dream, and quickly pulled back as a lithe Parisian beauty, her long black hair dancing in the breeze, her supple round breasts bouncing beneath a faux silk Versace dress, passed by his table casually giving him an eye, flirtatious, but truthfully he knew, uninterested. Bitch. Still, it was a nice diversion. He closed the book, resting it on the table and bringing the dark sunglasses, lying next to his mocha, to his face. Hugo will have to wait a bit longer.

People were everywhere, there formations like that of a colony of ants all structured in whatever pursuit fancied them. Some were here to shop; some were heading to the riverside nightclubs; and others were on their way to tour the Musee de Cluny for a lesson in medieval art. Sean smiled, taking in the aroma of the city. The numerous cafes lined down the boulevard, smelled of ground coffee and freshly made bread. He stood, cupping the small, but thick, volume of Hugo under the pit of his arm as he tossed a few Euros on the small glass table. It was time to get started, to do that task that had been alluding him for so long. Oh, he had threatened to start on many occasions, but always the same excuses. Tomorrow. They were the excuses made by everyone who has ever been too lazy, too lacking to follow through with a task or a dream. He refused to be classified with such failures that plagued humanity. If for no other reason, that was enough. Tonight, he would find his way to the typewriter and he would begin his story.

Sean Wilde casually strolled along the Rue de la Harpe, his suede oxfords clapping the pavement beneath his feet. His loose hand slid into the inner pocket of his light, cashmere jacket and felt around for the crumpled pack of cigarettes hidden within. He stopped mid stroll, and placing the book between his legs, freed both hands long enough to light the slender fag, and then proceeded merrily along. The sun was slowly melting into the cityscape and soon, very soon, Paris would be aglow. This wasn't called "The City of Light" for nothing.

He had gone no further than half a city block when he came to the entrance of a small shop, his shop. He took in the rush of nicotine.

The wooden sign above the door read: "Ruffled Pages East, Rare Books Bought and Sold, Sean Wilde Proprietor."

He pulled a small key from the outer pocket of his jacket and inserted it into the door, twisting the latch, and ushering himself inside. He was home. The small store was deathly quiet, and very dark. Sean flicked a small switch, lighting the room. The oaken shelves were lined down the outer walls of the store, harboring many fascinating books of both rarity and prestige. There were no more than two thousand volumes housed within the place at any given time. Sean liked it that way, it was much easier to manage a stock of that size. Ruffled Pages East was small, but it was enough. Sean often mused that his establishment was so narrow, that should a customer stand in the middle of the store, arms outstretched, he or she could touch the books resting on either shelf at the same time. This was of course an exaggeration. Still, it was his, the most stable dwelling he had known in the past thirty-eight years.

He lived in the flat, or apartment just above the store. It was a bit of a throwback to a time long ago when an owner of a store lived above the place he worked; but for Sean, this was just his style. He turned, locking the front door behind him, and moved towards a small staircase at the back of the store, dodging a recent acquisition of books he had yet to price and put on his shelves... He then flicked the store's lights off from the back stairwell and proceeded to the loft upstairs, sucking on the last bit of cigarette he had left.

Upon entry into the loft upstairs, Sean made a clumsy effort to tum on a lamp atop a comer end table, tripping over the garbage he had forgotten to dispose of earlier that morning. In the quiet luminescence of the small room, everything was in a neat and orderly fashion, much different from the way he had kept his former dwellings of years past. Life was different now. It was hard for him to even imagine he had lived any other way.

The contents of the room sat upon dark, oak beamed hardwoods, a flooring that Sean believed was probably two hundred years old or more. A fanciful Persian rug adorned the floor of the main sitting area. Two chairs, patterned with a leopard skin design and a wine-colored leather couch were in company as well. A heavily carved coffee table sat in the middle of the furnishings. Upon it were a chess board, small humidor, ashtray, and two volumes of art by the Italian painters Caravaggio and Tintoretto. Pictures, bordered in heavy gilded molding revealed the art that pleased him the most; the Italian masters, Pre-Raphaelite masters, and of course the great Goya with his dark satirical themes. They were all here. Home. His home.

One mahogany book shelf was all that was present in the room of his vocation. It stood seven feet tall and was three feet wide. Upon its shelves lay the books Sean would rather suffer fire and damnation than be parted with. These were his personal books, his divine acquaintances: first editions of Hugo, Dumas, Defoe, and Poe. Who really needed anything more? Well, maybe good wine perhaps. But who needed more than that?

In the comer of his dimly lit quarters sat a desk, and upon that desk, a typewriter. It begins tonight. Sean moved towards the desk, exchanging his keys for a small glass sitting upon the tiled countertops in his kitchen, and proceeded to find his seat at that desk. He turned the iron knob of a very old lamp he had bought a year or so ago in one of the antique stalls on Paris' Left Bank, the Carre Rive Guache, for some outrageous sum.

He wanted to begin at that very moment, lifting his fingers to the keypad, but there was a problem. There was no music. Sean hated the idea that his life had to exist in any way void of the soothing nature made by the ensemble of finely tuned instruments harmonizing together in bombastic resonance. Metallica was fine, Iron Maiden was better still, but Beethoven kicked all their asses.

Sean picked up the remote control of his two hundred CD changer, and pointing it from the desk towards the stereo across the room, chose selection forty-eight, Beethoven's Pathetique Sonata. Perfect. It was now time to begin. He had waited too long already; the story must survive him.

No need to see its publication, just a need to store it in the vault downstairs so that somewhere, at some time, beyond this time, there would be a record, a tale, one that might even rival one of Hugo's. Okay, maybe not Hugo; but his story was true, and that's what made the shit so incredible.

It would be written like a novel; forget the personal memoir crap. Sean Wilde lifted the bottle of twelve-year-old Glenlivit whiskey he had left out the night before and poured the amber liquid into a short fat glass, smelling its aroma as it splashed within. Satisfied that all was as it should be, he took a sip from the glass and raising his hands to the keys, began his tale while Beethoven filled the room with his powerful Sonata.

The call had come one morning in April, the day of no real matter. Sean Wilde lay passed out across a bed of dirty clothes, himself the product of a week-long drinking spell. Scotch Whiskey- his poison; lack of cash flow- his curse.

He was living in Boston at the time, if one could call the roach infested hovel of an apartment he occupied, living. "Existing" would have been a much better word. There was nothing of sustenance or value in the place he was currently calling home. No furniture, no television, no bed. There was however, a pile of books and magazines strewn about the floor. He had managed to, at some time, procure a microwave which worked quite splendidly when he could afford to keep on the electricity used to power the device. Money had at no point in time come easy for him, but now he had hit a particularly rough drought. Any day, he would be kicked out of his apartment, and he would have nowhere to go but the streets of the city. A grim outlook indeed.

Sean had spent the better part of the previous twenty years as a book scout, searching the confines of every bookstall, flea market, garage sale, auction house, or any such place where the prospect of finding some overlooked treasure that came in the form of a book could be turned into a marketable commodity. His chosen career path was nothing he was ashamed of, but it was certainly not the most stable of professions, either.

What choice did he have? Books were in his blood and had been a part of every aspect of his life- his whole life. Besides, he was good at it. Most book scouts can go weeks, months, or even years without finding that proverbial treasure that could be bought for two dollars one day and turned into two thousand the next. Yes, that rarely happened, but it had happened with enough frequency for Sean to eke out a substandard living for the past few years. Oh, he had tried getting into the general job market, but the nine to five routine never quite panned out. Not for him anyway. No real job ever lasted more than six months before he found his way back on the streets of Boston, or maybe New York, hunting his quarry once again.

Unemployed from society, as was now the case, he suffered needlessly in his attempts to surface a single volume of literature that would ease his aching wallet. He had found some patented sympathy from the owner of a small bar located just below his current apartment, and it was this friendship that had kept him in his present state for the past week.

But the phone was now ringing.

Sean woke with a sudden spasm of surprise. How long it had been ringing concerned him very little, that it was ringing at all was the real surprise. He thought the phone had been disconnected weeks ago, and seeing as he had made very little use of it in the weeks before, he sat up a bit shocked at the fact its bothersome ring was filling his apartment.

His head was pounding, his hair matted and greasy. He lifted the receiver from its resting place and grumbled some garbled wording that might have resembled "Hello." But the muffling of Sean's words made even the clarity of that word hard to understand.

Nothing. There was no response on the other end of the phone line. Sean spoke into the phone more clearly a second time, but the line had gone dead. Sean let the receiver drop and fell straight back into the pile of clothes. Another day in hell's kitchen.

He was now staring at the ceiling, his eyes wandering from the various mildew spots dotted in various places to the tiny spider spinning a web about the square lighting fixture. Life at some point had to get better than this. He began to pull himself up, noticing the foul taste that resided in his mouth. Then came the realization that he needed to relieve himself immediately. He thought his kidneys would explode as he began a rather quick approach toward the toilet, emptying his bladder and discharging a sigh of relief. If the apartment looked bad, the bathroom was significantly worse. He slid off his boxers and made for the shower. Roaches scurried down the drain as Sean entered the shower stall. Black mildew outlined the grooves of the tile. He was still groggy, and the coming headache didn't seem to make things much better. He tried to focus. His hands reached for the shower knobs and made the necessary adjustments, his naked form welcoming the rush of warm water as it splashed against his solid frame. He was rubbing his eyes when the unfamiliar noise came again. It was the phone!

Sean wasted no time. He sprang from the shower naked, and sent water in all directions of the house as he ran through the cluttered maze of books and clothes. He approached the phone, feeling his feet still wet from the shower slip from under him sending him, crashing to the floor. The pain of the harsh landing would have to wait. He now thrust a hand forward, pulling the receiver to his face;

"Hello?" he answered with an unsure, suspicious tone.

"Mr. Wilde, I presume?" the voice came back in the most non-threatening of proper English accents.

"Depends who wants to know; who's this?"

"My name, Mr. Wilde, is Sir Nicholas DeBury. I am, shall we say, a rather aggressive collector of rare books and ephemera," he paused allowing Sean to digest his words. "You and I have mutual acquaintances in the world of rare books, and though I am not at liberty to reveal the identity of my contact, your name has come up as a person whose services might provide me with a starting point to acquisition a treasured book, one in which I have been seeking for a very long time."

Sean was already put off by the demeanor of his caller. Pounding the streets, wheeling and dealing constantly with so many collectors and shop owners, he had become weary of strange calls like this one. It smelled of trouble. And there was no denying that this book scout had enough of his own problems to contend with. No need to add more.

Before Sean could inquire further, the Englishman began again, "Mr. Wilde, I've no interest in wasting your time as I'm sure you've no interest in wasting mine, so allow me to get right to the point." He paused again: "I want you to steal a book for me."

Yep. This guy is nuts. Sean responded with very little hesitation,

"Times are tough right now, Mr. DeBury; in fact, I can't remember a time when things were this bad, but I find books, not steal them; so regardless of what you've been told about me, look elsewhere. You got the wrong man." he slammed the phone down hard, angered at the false hope of a turnaround in fortune. It was now time to embrace the depression that was sure to follow.

Sean had been surrounded by books from a very young age. His mother had died when he was only two years old, so his father, Thomas Wilde, became his whole world.

Thomas Wilde was a man of very basic means enjoying no elevated social standing, but his soft hand and love for the written word became paramount in the development of his young son, Sean. The two became inseparable.

Tom Wilde owned a small bookstore in Boston called Ruffled Pages. The store specialized in modem first editions and very general antiquarian stock; and with Sean's development from child to adolescent, it served as his training ground and a source that would come to stake out a lifelong passion.

From his father, Sean learned how to identify first edition books from their later printings. He learned to grade the quality of each volume sold in the shop and to recognize their rarity. He also learned the general nature of all business transactions, which is the art of buying at a low price and selling for a profit. He read voraciously as well, his appetite falling towards every pamphlet, book, and magazine dealing with books and the people who collected them.

His father had always dreamed of dealing in the rare material; Folio Shakespeare's, the Caxton's, incunabula, private presses, and any other priceless books that seemed to always stay in circles of much higher standing than his. Thomas Wilde's problem was that he just lacked the ruthlessness, and finances to play in the same arena with those elitist dealers who always handled the truly rare volumes.

Still, he never stopped fascinating his young son with the idea of having or selling priceless books; and every chance he could, he would take his son to some auction house or book fair, just to chance a glimpse at one of the rare diamonds of his profession.

The two men lived just above Ruffled Pages in a small, but cozy, apartment with good books and good company. Cancer, sudden and quick, took Thomas Wilde from his son just before the child's sixteenth birthday; and having no insurance, much less extended family, Sean was forced to hit the street and begin his talents as a book scout to avoid foster care. Most of Boston's local book dealers were amazed at the frequency with which he could turn up a valuable find. And much to their credit, knowing of the difficult circumstances to which he had fallen, they would always give him a little higher percentage of the books he brought them than they would give other local book scouts. His was a skill not learned in school, but rather by following every lead, regardless of where it led. Garage sales, flea markets, bookstalls, estate sales, and every attic he could convince someone to let him rummage through became his hunting ground. Most scouts met with far more failure than with success, as it was a difficult job for some, impossible for most, and more often than not, very disappointing. When he would hit a drought scouting for books, he would invariably end up in some dead end job of sorts which never lasted very long. He always seemed to get by though, that is, until the last six months.

Sean, drying himself off, mused at the seriousness of his situation. He was broke, the alcohol wasn't helping, and yes, maybe he was desperate enough to steal a book. He slipped into the same clothes he had been wearing the past week, a pair of Levi jeans and a black T-shirt that had a picture of William Shakespeare on the front and a quotation on the back that read: "Titus Andronicus is still better than anything you've ever written." How he loved that shirt. His pants were loose owing to all the meals he had recently been forced to skip, his waist was now a slim thirty inches, down from thirty-two. He reached down to the floor, beside the phone and picked up a crumpled cigarette carton, sliding out an individual pack and unraveling the cellophane. There Always seems to be enough money for these. He pulled out the slim stick of cancer, and lit the end with some matches he had lifted from the downstairs bar. Sean Wilde, with a hard, inhaling breath, took in the morning.

There was no doubt this time. He would have to find a real job. He pondered the word, allowing himself the reflection that both the word job, and the Biblical Job were spelled alike and for a very good reason. He was at the end of his rope. Any future turn of events that might lean towards the positive, seemed bleak. Something had to change. Then, abruptly, it did.

The phone was ringing again.

Sean was determined to ignore the caller. Every sense of right and wrong he had ever felt told him not to answer that phone. On the eighteenth ring, he caved.

"Didn't I say I'm not..."

"Interested? Yes Mr. Wilde, I heard you," the voice broke in, "Forgive my manners in interrupting you, but seeing that it stands as the only way I may be afforded some civility of dialog, please here what it is I have to say."

Sean paced the floor of his apartment with the receiver in one hand the dialing pad in the other, "Listen, I apologize for hanging up on you earlier; but I just gave up my career as a book scout ten minutes ago, and I'm damn sure no fucking thief. So, if books or theft is involved with your request, you can see you've got the wrong man." There was a long pause as the caller allowed Sean to absorb the words he had just spoken. He knew that even though Sean may have wanted to believe these things he said were true, one thing was certain: most men could be bought for the right price, and book scouting wasn't a vocation that could be wished away. He knew it was in Sean's blood. People that loved books, in whatever capacity, were just that way.

"Sean," he had yet to call him by his first name, "I am aware of your recent financial misfortunes, and I can understand fully your reluctance in hearing out what I have to say."

"You have a very eloquent way of stating the obvious, Mr. DeBury," he interrupted.

"Spare me one hour of your time Mr. Wilde- one hour. That's all I ask. I can assure you that I will trouble you no more afterwards. Furthermore, I will deposit ten thousand American dollars into an account of your choosing if you will hear me out. Should you feel, in anyway uncomfortable with me or with the offer which I have to propose, we shall simply part as acquaintances and I will put you on a plane back to Boston. Then you may return to whatever it is that occupies your time.............. I'm sorry what is it that you do?"

Cheap shot. Who does this ass hole think he is? "Sir Nicholas, I really appreciate the lengths you've gone to pick me from the crowd, but as I told you before, I don't-"

"There will be a first-class ticket waiting for you at ten P.M. tomorrow evening at the luggage drop- off for a Delta flight, leaving Logan International and bound for London's Gatwick International. This should afford you ample time for sleep so that you will be refreshed upon arrival to my country. Do the both of us a favor, Mr. Wilde, and be on that flight."

His tone was serious, his confidence obvious. Sean took a long drag from his cigarette, letting the spent ash glide softly to the floor. He looked at his surroundings, books scattered about, clothes so dirty they could practically stand by themselves, and a life- his life- in sore need of repair. What did he really have to lose?

No. This was bullshit. Just tell him, "No!"

"I don't like surprises, Nick," he said mockingly. "You can either tell me the specifics now, or you can kiss my ass and find someone else with more to lose than me." He was brimming with overconfidence.

"Mr. Wilde, be assured that I have told you all I am willing to divulge over the phone, and be also comforted by the fact that I do indeed know of no such person with less to lose than you."

Ouch! He was dipping below the belt and crushing Sean with every verbal blast from his arsenal of semantics. "I don't see how a man in your position can feel so threatened by the mere consideration of discussing with me a very mutually benefiting solution to both our problems, but whether or not you decide to proceed with my initial request and the subsequent offer of ten thousand dollars, it is, of course, your decision."

"I'll sleep on it."

"Ten thousand cash, Mr. Wilde."

"I heard you the first time; I'll give it some thought." Sean's tone was now more aggressive. "Ah, yes, so you did," DeBury stated as if Sean's response was of little concern. "My driver, Mr. William Dodd, will pick you up upon arrival, and will drive you to my home in Chelsea, where we shall continue this conversation in greater detail. My hope, of course, is that you will not waste his time by not showing up. However, if you truly decide not to be on that plane, I will proceed to find a more willing participant to take in the task. Good day to you," his words ending abruptly.

The fact that the phone line immediately fell silent, did in no way quell Sean's vain attempt to practice his profane linguistic skills, "Find someone else, you pompous prick!" he returned in a voice that could be heard down the hall of his apartment complex.

Ten thousand dollars. The figure rolled around his head. It was a lot of money- maybe even enough for a new start. He was at a definite cross road of his life, unsure of which tum to take. Ten thousand dollars. He let the now extinct cigarette butt fall from his mouth and followed it as it came to rest on an empty bag of Doritos, crumpled on the floor. He shuffled to the bathroom and caught the reflection of himself in the mirror as he searched for his toothbrush. The vision staring back wasn't pretty. The caller knew of his current financial problems, and this certainly put him at an unfair advantage. Hell, maybe it was this Sir Nicholas who had his phone turned back on in the first place. It didn't sit right, though. Ten thousand dollars. Damn my soul to hell. Sean Wilde was going to London. And he would be leaving tomorrow.

"Please allow me to introduce myself, I'm a man of wealth and taste. I've been around for a long, long year, laid many a man's soul to waste."

Mick Jagger/Keith Richards

Engagements

Father Koutrakos, still shaken and unnerved from his frightful encounter within the confessional, retired himself to the library located within a small tower outcropping of the Docheiariou monastery. It was here that he felt safer, more peaceful and more protected than anywhere else in the world.

By the standards of an academic library, the dwelling was quite small, no larger than about six hundred square feet in total floor spacing and about fifteen feet in height from the floor to the oak beams overhead. The floor was made from various stones that had been collected on Athos by the monks who had built the structure years earlier, as was almost every central room in Docheiariou. And the walls, like most other significant rooms in the monastery, were made of massive, oak planks, with various Iconography hanging from every blank space the walls would afford. The library's environment was almost as humbling as the sanctuary itself.

Simple wood framed book cases were recessed into the walls as well. Manuscripts, illuminated by many of the skilled artisans that had passed through Docheiariou's hallowed rectory, sat silent on the shelves, awaiting a curious hand to pluck them forth and view their inner contents.

The old man sat bewildered, unable to shake the evil presence that had come to invade his mind and his heart. He wiped his forehead, dismissing his fears. He was just tired, that was all. His old age and the late hour had been unkind, seeking to somehow play tricks with his mind. He glanced up from the small writing desk in which he was seated, surveying the room, his eyes falling on the many volumes around him. He was perspiring uncontrollably. Did his heart know some inner secret that had yet escaped the rations of his mind? He pulled at his snowy white beard. The old monk could not remember a time when he had come to feel this shaken, this afraid.

Something terrible was still with him- watching him, studying him; of this he was sure. Maybe the Angel of Death was coming to claim him. If this was so, why should he be afraid? Had he not dedicated a life, his life, in pursuit of holy measure? Was he momentarily doubting an existence beyond death?

He stood up from his chair, body trembling, in an effort to pull from the book shelves a Latin text of the gospel "John." Surely this would bring some soothing calm to his tattered nerves. Come now O death, hasten thy sting, and claim me if my time should be no more.

The candle on the desk flickered, as rain streamed down the large leaded glass window behind the monk's desk. As the abbot surveyed the text before him, a small spider scurried into view as it trampled lightly across the illuminated page. He allowed the creature uninterrupted passage- watching the tiny intruder hop from the vellum sheet and scamper along the desk until it disappeared from view. The room was now placid, the next few moments passed in silence. Father Koutrakos could hear only the sound of his own heart beating within his chest. Thump, thump. The rain and thunder were dying back a bit, he thought to himself, as he came to rest again at the desk. His eyes took in the room once more. He was alone. Thump, thump. He watched the shadow of himself beyond the bright, burning candle, and finally dispelled all notions that might give way to fear. Relax.

As the abbot turned his eyes from the room, allowing them to fall in the direction of the book laid out before him, there was a crash of thunder; and an immense force of windfall blew the glass window open, extinguishing the candle, and abandoning him to the darkness that followed. Thump, Thump, Thump, Thump.

Momentary paralysis came with the certain recognition that he was not alone. His body froze of its own accord, joints stiffening, as he tried to grapple with a fear he couldn't control. His cloak was dampening with the perspiration seeking to find a means of escape from his body. Father Koutrakos was bathing in his own fevered sweat. On his knees, he began reciting the Lord's Prayer alone to himself in the darkness.

To his utter surprise, the candle re-illuminated itself, as a flame jumped around the wick and brought light to the darkness. Though the uncontrolled trembling in his body simply would not cease, he lifted his fevered brow from the cradled state of prayer. His eyesight was now focusing on the objects surrounding him. On the wall just beyond the candle, there were now the shadows of two figures, his upon the floor, and what looked to be that of a robed monk, like himself, standing on the left. Someone was in the room behind him.

Making a frantic attempt to contain the frozen pangs of fear, he swung his aged frame around to glimpse the figure that was now casting a shadow on the wall in front of him.

There was nothing. No one glanced back. The old man dropped his head, closing his eyes. His wrinkled hands now shielded his face. He could take only so much before his heart was sure to burst. He looked up toward the wooden beams that supported the ceiling structure of the library, and raising his hands in a fit of exhaustive defeat, called out, "Father in Heaven, who art mightier than all kings, in all nations, do not forsake me, I beg of you!"

To his astonishment his prayer was answered. But not by the voice of God. Another called out to him.

"He's heard that request before, Father," a voice resounded in the same tone the monk had heard earlier in the confessional. "Remember Golgotha, place of the skull? He wasn't listening to His own Son then, what makes you think he would listen to you now? Ah.... but that was a long time ago, wasn't it?"

The old man's body turned violently back toward the wall where the shadow had been, the sudden twist causing discomfort in his lower abdomen. He was now facing the robed figure of a monk seated on a small bench across the room.

The visitor sat very still, motioning not the slightest muscle. A hooded cowl was pulled tightly around his head, hiding any facial feature that might give way to his true identity. The abbot's eyes widened as he studied the cloaked personage before him. He was entranced in a hypnotic gaze. His lungs made way for speech, grasping at whatever air he could inhale. His heart was now deliberating with a ceaseless thrashing.

"Who....... forgive me...... I... heard no one enter," the poor man was stammering for relaxed speech, "Y... you would be...?"

"Don't be afraid of me father," the voice came across in a deep, but soft manner. "I mean you no harm." Such an admission from the hooded figure was useless- for the elder man was trembling uncontrollably. Some inner voice was warning the abbot that he was in the presence of some great evil. No amount of self-assurance would dissuade the angst he bore for the visitor.

"I am not of this dwelling; nor am I from your time, nor am I of this earth," the figure then stated. If the uninvited guest was acting to excuse the invasive nature of his sudden entry, he would have to do better.

"You... are a vision, then.... a saint perhaps. Forgive me;.... my fear is beyond my containment," the monk said bowing before the being opposite himself.

It was long understood by the men of Docheiariou, and of the whole republic of Athos, that while not common by any means, saints, even the Virgin Mary herself, had revealed themselves to certain monks who had achieved oneness with the heavens. Why, this very monastery itself had been founded and dedicated to the Archangel, Michael. Was Father Koutrakos witness to a visitation of holy origin? Had he now achieved the higher plane in which he had spent the better part of the past forty years seeking? It could be so. Dare he even think it so?

The figure rose from the chair and moved toward the abbot. The old man held his position, choosing not to rise or greet his uninvited guest. In truth, he could not have moved even if he had wished to.

Hands, their flesh a hue more white than pink, emerged from the sleeves of the approaching intruder's robe and came about his waist to loosen the rope that had been holding the robe in place. The abbot kneeled, flinching not a single limb. His eyes had become saucer- like as he watched the figure come to a halt, ten feet away. Then, before him now, he witnessed the unwelcome visitor move his hands from his waist to his head, taking off the hood, and allowing the robe to fall to the floor beneath his feet.

"I am neither saint, nor vision, Father. I am one of whom the heavens speak no longer and the beings of this world tremble in fear," he began, "Behold the face of one created before the time of man, before the dawn of earth, before the stars glimmered in the night sky. Cast a gaze upon me, Father. Behold the angel, Lucifer! Behold him who fell first from the heavens! Behold the first prince of hell!"

A bright light filled the library as tears began to well in the old monk's eyes, his mind seeking to find reason, even some form of justification, for the event taking place. He could find none. His hands were clammy, and he cowered, unable to move his fingers. Many monks on the island had witnessed miraculous visitations before. This however, was different entirely. Nowhere, not in the annals of any history book, he could recall, save that of the Bible itself, was there a documented appearance from the fallen angel, Lucifer. Had he somehow offended God? What cause should give way to such a horrid visitation? The questions became endless, the fear insurmountable.

Father Koutrakos looked upon the angel, his facial expression turning from fear to wild disbelief. Lucifer, the devil, possessed a beauty that was beyond worldly description.

His frame, muscular yet thin, stood six feet two inches tall; and his head was encased in golden locks that curled and dangled loosely just below his shoulders. His skin looked smooth, and was tanned a deep, golden brown. In the glow of the candle light, his body showed every sinewy indentation of muscular perfecting that was beholden him. His cheekbone was tight at the jaw line. The most distinguishable feature about the figure was his eyes. They, in no way, fit the rest of him. They were black and lifeless, reminding the old man of a time long ago when he had been a small boy and had witnessed a fisherman bring to shore a large shark off the coast of Lavrio. He had thought then the way he did now. How soulless, how void of compassion were the eyes of that shark. He was presently gazing at the likeness of those same eyes.

The angel, naked and proud, confidently standing before the monk began to speak just as soon as he saw the first sign of fear subside within the old man's face.

"I can see I am not at all what you expected," he said smiling, "You may count yourself to be one of very few human beings to witness my true form as it was before I was cast from heaven. I reveal myself to you so that you will calm yourself and find within your heart less room for fear."

The monk lifted his weakened frame to a hunched stance, still shaking, but searching for composure. He could feel the cracking sound of his feeble joints as he backed himself to a wall for added support. He was soaked in his own fear, but managed to force from his lips some verbal offering, "How should it be that I refrain myself from fearing one of whom the heavens speak no more?" his voice elevating to little more than a whisper, "This cannot be happening! You simply cannot be real!" The old man was sure he was in a nightmare, from which the act of waking, seemed impossible.

"I shall never tire in my amazement when confronting you humans," he paused tilting his head slightly, "Tell me, man of faith, why fear one who can do no worse to you than you would do to yourself? You have spent a life in utter chastity, impoverished servitude, and dedicated worship of a God you've never seen. Yet I, Lucifer, His greatest creation, stand here naked before you, clothed in the revelation of brilliance, which is my being. How, then, can you find our meeting so grossly unfathomable?"

A blank stare between the two souls replaced any chance of continued conversation, before the angel turned from the monk as if he were going to leave. Father Koutrakos mentally questioned every scripture, every belief he had ever had. He wanted to respond, to say anything. With his back to the abbot, the Angel formed a wicked smile on his face as he became aware of the realization that the mind of the old monk must be convinced in another way. It was after all, the fifteenth century. The people of Europe were burning old women- tying them to the stake for supposedly being witches. It was time to employ some new guise that would better fit the century he was occupying.

Just as the monk began to speak, his wrinkled lips parting slightly,

Lucifer stopped and hunched his back, calculating every motion and every spasm that was to follow. The old man watched, mouth agape, as the angel's shape began distorting itself horribly.

Two small holes opened at the shoulder blades of the angel's back, small at first, then gaping more and more, until from them emerged two bat-like projections, which, unfurling as would a moth from a cocoon, clearly formed huge, black wings, covered in short black hair, stretching out six feet in each direction. As they flapped lightly the monk cowered, sinking back to the stone floor with his hands pulled up as a useless shield about his face. He would surely go mad. The hunched changeling turned to face the old abbot who was shivering on his knees. The angel was smiling even more sadistically as the skin on his body changed from a golden tan to a darkened sienna. From the corner of his head at each temporal lobe, horn-like projectiles emerged, curling as they came forth, like those of a ram or goat. The angel was now basking in the frightened demeanor of his quarry. The once golden locks had been replaced with strings of black reeds, more closely resembling snakes than hair. Father Koutrakos gaped as he watched the nimble feet being replaced with cloven hooves that clapped against the stone flooring as this creature began walking slowly toward the abbot, basking in the discomfort of his victim.

What stood before the old monk was a grotesque aberration of nature, beyond even the wildest imaginings of the most famous painters of the day. The artist Albrecht Durer would have been impressed.

"I've no doubt, dear man of faith," the beast began to speak, after sharpened fangs had replaced some of his teeth, "that my appearance should now represent a portrayal with which you are more familiar. How do you like me?" The demon bent over, leaning his face only inches from the terrified monk, "Please, be in complete understanding with whom you are dealing. I am not some ghostly apparition set forth to harass the likes of you, but I am the most powerful being you are likely to meet in the whole of your life." The uninvited one was unquestionably forthcoming.

Allowing his hands to fall from his face, Father Koutrakos rose with legs shaking feverishly. As he reached deep within his heart for some manner of strength, he began pleading with his uninvited guest. "Leave this place," the words stumbled out. "I beg of you, in the name of God thy maker; punish me with your presence no more!"

At once, a brilliant light filled the library, temporarily blinding the abbot.

With his vision clearing, he saw that he was alone. Only the light flickering from the wick of a candlestick made any sound; and the window, once shattered by a forceful gale, now appeared whole, entombed in its encasement within the library's stone wall just as it had been earlier. Everything was as it had been before. The old monk, gripping his sanity, made a furious motion toward the refectory table, taking his seat once more in front of the Gospel of John, laid out before him.

He was dreaming, of course, with his eyes open; there could be no doubt. His mind was slipping, but better to lose one's mortal sanity than one's immortal soul. He desperately sought reason that would not come. He felt dizzy, his eyes rolling and blurring slightly. He tried to focus on the manuscript in front of him. A pain shot through his arm, and his body began to list, his brain unable to fight the rest he sorely needed from the night's burgeoning experience.

Father Koutrakos was now giving in to sleep, his body slouching over and his head becoming stationary on the book before him. He would rest for now, welcoming the peace that was overtaking his body and the soft stillness which now was permeating the room.

He had slept no more than an hour when Father Koutrakos lifted his head, wiped the saliva dripping from the corner of his mouth, and adjusted his vision. The sound of tapping had awakened him. His body wanted nothing more than rest, but the incessant noise would not let up. As his eyes began to focus, the old man saw a figure was coming into view.

It had not been a dream, this demon who had spoken earlier, had returned.

The vision that came into view was that of the mythical godlike Adonis he had seen earlier, now clothed and seated across from him. His hair was pulled back and tied with what appeared to be a fine, silk string. He sat with his legs crossed and his arms folded. He was clothed in a white peasant shirt which was frilled about the ends and black pants encasing his lower torso. The abbot noticed that his feet were void of covering and his hands looked nothing like those of any man he had ever met. They seemed to have an extra digit, all of which extended into unusually long fingernails. Gone were the cloven hooves. Absent were the horns. He watched as the uninvited one tapped at his knee.

Gaining some degree of confidence, the monk retorted, "Should I believe you to be the being you claim, what possible truths could exist in anything you might utter forth from your lips? Are you not a priest of falsehoods, a lord of lies? You could not possibly...."

"You know and believe only what you have read. But, does not the very nature of academics, science, and art, involve a need for future understanding? Shall we question only what we have read, no more? History's mysteries fall deaf upon the mind that believes the bias of a single author." The demonic interloper then took to his feet, moving in no particular pattern about the dimly lit room, "I make this request of you, myself being greatly unconcerned as to whether you should place any degree of faith in what I have to say. I am in need of a vehicle, a human, whose respect and piety are paralleled by no other. I shall share with you a most wondrous testament, fit to join the collection of books now resting on this shelf," he said while pointing. "You know so little of the story, Father; hear what it is I have to confess. Listen to the gospel according to Lucifer."

"Should I, for some brief leave of my senses, entertain your request, what hell awaits me? I ask you once again to tell me what offense of mine has brought you here, punishing me with your presence?"

"Look into the depths of your soul, dear man. Do you not wish to have the knowledge that only I can bestow? Be sure that there exists no cause on this earth, nor in the realm of heaven, or the belly of hell, that give reason for my appearance before you now, none save the desire of me alone. In exchange for your time, not. Your soul, I will reveal to you much that is unknown; and I will further give you what has been allowed by no man living. I will give you knowledge and insight such as your mind could fathom not."

Father Koutrakos had now gained a degree of composure, not allowing himself to be tormented, at least, for the moment. He studied the figure, searching for some ingenious vocabulary. He was at a loss at where the conversation should begin.

"Then you are real? A vision, perhaps, or a demon who has been sent to punish me for sin of which I am guilty?"

"On the contrary Father: it is because of your piety, your complete devotion to my Creator that I have chosen to speak with you at all." He cleared his throat, and began again: "In the vast scope of this age, and any other for that matter, you are the only human I have witnessed who is worthy to hear what I have to say."

The abbot noticed the whiteness of Lucifer's teeth and their symmetrical perfection, as he spoke. "That my piety would attract one who calls himself Lucifer can in no way be a sign of spiritual accomplishment on my part. My soul, if heaven should welcome it one day, belongs to God Almighty. What service could I possibly offer the prince of lies?"

The demon meandered about the room, ignoring the monk's response as he sniffed the air. "Centuries fly by, my dear abbot, but the smell of old books, being collected in myriad fashion upon the bookshelves of the conservationist, stays the same, regardless of the library that houses them." He refocused on the monk now, "We all have our little earthly treasures, don't we know?" He was smiling, staring directly at the old man, "I understand you to be both an accomplished wordsmith, and a fine illuminator of considerable skill. This having any validity, I should like to proposition you with the task of documenting a confession I shall willingly lay before you- an account, if you will, of an angel wronged and redemption lost."

The monk lifted his brow, distorting his facial expression, and scoffing the request. "Away with you, foul creature. Have you not caused the downfall of man with similar offers? Knowledge gained at the expense of one's soul is more knowledge than I seek to obtain. Leave me. Find another soul to hear what you have to confess- I am without the eagerness to hear you speak."

The fallen angel began to recount the memory of the Genesis account- the temptation in the Garden of Eden. Of course, this was so very long ago, when the world was young, as was he. The monk was both worried and scared, as he should be. Lucifer would have to approach the abbot a bit differently. "Understand this, I am not about tempting you with any information you do not willingly seek. Has it not occurred to you already that my presence here on Athos could not be if I had not been pardoned by my Creator Himself? This island is a holy place. There are rules..........."

Father Koutrakos, ever wise and cautious, could not help but feel a sense of wonderment at the thought of continuing the conversation; and, as he tried to acquit himself of further speech, his inquisitive nature took hold. Only one word was surfacing, "Rules?"

The demon explored the monk, his eyes wondering up and down the man's elderly little frame. He was so decrepit in stature, so void of physical beauty. How could his Creator love this being more than he? "Come now, Father, and listen to what I have to say. I have assured you that the cost on your part will be nothing; and for me, this could prove quite redemptive."

"What task should I perform that will leave my soul unscathed?"

Lucifer, the angel who evoked war in heaven, the tempter who beckoned Christ in the wilderness, the instigator who was responsible for sin in the world, watched as the rain slid down the library window. For a moment, his angelic compass was someplace else.

He then turned to the monk, staring towards him with an expressionless look.

"I have moved about this world for longer than your books of history can record their events. Time means nothing to me. I have born witness to more wondrous sights and to more disastrous catastrophes than your mind could warrant imagining; yet, still I stand before you, empty and incomplete. My role, my very existence, has left me weary and embittered. It is my wish, if only once, to make an attempt, however vain the circumstance, to seek some form of absolution."

The monk, bewildered and unsteady, parted his lips to speak, "What....... what are you saying?"

"Father Koutrakos, I wish for you to hear my confession. I want to know if I, Lucifer, can be forgiven for sin. I wish to know if I can be forgiven for myself."

The old monk could say nothing. He stood, appalled at the very idea, his mind unwilling to cooperate with the utterance just spoken. Impossible. Unimaginable! The request proved to be more than the old man could bear. The idea that Satan was presenting himself before the elderly abbot, seeking solace and forgiveness for the very act which he had caused, was beyond all moral comprehension. The room was now spinning. Both the presence of Lucifer and the weight of their consultation caused the elderly abbot to become overwhelmed with anxiety. And as his mind would grapple with no more diabolic allusion, the old monk's eyes rolled back in his head and he collapsed to the floor.

"I don't much care if I see another mountain in my life.
I have passed all my days in London."

Charles Lamb

London

Sean's body contorted-yawns coming involuntarily and his arms stretching to relieve the past six hours of sleep- as the large Boeing 747 was now descending from the gray clouds above, revealing the patchwork countryside of glorious England below.

From the sky overhead, Sean, still groggy, noticed the uniqueness of the landscape with its grassy knolls arranged in a chessboard like fashion. It was so beautiful and mysterious amidst the fog.

The flight had been smooth. He pitied those in the two classes behind him with the discomfort of their seating and the lack of service and attention they must have received. On the other hand, he had spent the trip spread out in his chair that had become a ready-made cot. But now he was sitting up admiring the scenery below. The four whiskey sours he had engulfed upon boarding had given him just the necessary ingredients for a good night's rest, and his mind became despondent at the thought of traveling any other way. The in- flight movie hadn't been bad either.

Even though the sun was barely creeping above the horizon, his mind had already begun to paint the picture of this beautiful country. The book scout had come to fashion England as a lovely maiden, timeless in her treasures and bold in her presentation.

This had not been his first trip to London. His father had brought him here once, shortly before his death, when Sean was thirteen. It had been designed as both a vacation and a book-hunting trip. He still cherished the memories of Charring Cross Road, the countless book stalls and book stores, and the fervor in which the two men had spent three weeks, scouring the bustling city streets for volumes that would satiate their appetites. He recalled a volume of Samuel Pepys Diary, accidentally misplaced, he was sure, within the outside contents of a sidewalk bookstall in Cecil Court, the heart of Charring Cross Road. The book had been a first printing, tattered, but complete enough to be sold for a princely sum only moments later to the rare book dealer, Harrington Peters. This allotted them enough money to pay for the entire expense of the trip, minus the cost of books, of course. His father had been so amazed at his son's talents. He caught on very quickly and became a remarkably remorseful book scout. For Sean, the pubs, the theater, the art museums, and the culture radiated from this city in a fashion even New York failed to match. This had been the best vacation he had ever had.

Now he was coming back.

There was a general feeling of quizzical discomfort as the plane approached the runway. He paused to fasten his seat belt, as the pilot was now giving instructions for all passengers to prepare for landing. The Virgin flight 227, from Boston to London, was nearly over. Sean's eyes fell to the pretty flight attendant who was quickly collecting each passenger's used cups and crumpled napkins. Soon, all his questions would be answered. Who was Sir Nicholas DeBury? Why had Sean become such an important necessity to this task of his? And more importantly, how the hell had he found Sean, in the first place? He glanced at the small duffel bag he had packed, now resting at his feet. He thought of how pathetic it was that all the clothing he owned could be crumpled tightly inside. Whatever his next move, he had to procure a life somehow better than the one he now possessed.

The plane had been at rest for twelve minutes when the captain came over the intercom once more, instructing the first class passengers to disembark the plane. Sean removed his only luggage, the duffel bag, and a recent copy of the Antiquarian Book Review held tightly in his left hand. He and stepped from the plane, nodding to a fatigued pilot, and keenly noticing a button that had come loose on the shirt of a very buxom female flight attendant's shirt. Smiling to himself, he then began making his way toward the terminal gate.

Gatwick Airport was lively, aggravated with a multitude of travelers scouring in feverish attempts to map out whatever course of direction deemed necessary: some arriving, some leaving, some lost. He was in London, and already felt more at home than he had felt anywhere since the passing of his father.

"Mr. Wilde?" a voice called from behind, as an elderly hand touched his shoulder. Sean turned to view a staunch little man in a well-tailored suit, maybe five feet six inches tall and displaying a dark receding hairline. He was staring up at Sean with his squinty little eyes, examining this newcomer to London.

"Now how could you have known what I would look like, you've never......."

"My name is William Dodd, Sir," he broke in, "I am Sir Nicholas DeBury's personal chauffeur. It is a pleasure to meet you."

Sean could barely hear the man amid the sounds of human traffic noisily ringing behind him in the bustling airport. "Again, I'm a bit amazed that you knew who I was."

"Sir Nicholas instructed me to seek an individual who least looked as if he belonged in first class seating; and since there were only eleven first class passengers- well, forgive me, Sir, but I....... "

Cheeky bastard, Sean thought to himself. "Well, that's mighty presumptuous, Mr. Dodd, but correct, nonetheless," he hinted at sarcasm. "Any chance I might get a drink before we hit the road?"

"But, Sir it's ten a.m.?

"It's five o'clock somewhere, Mr. Dodd," he joked.

"Might I first suggest you have your passport tended to, while I fetch your luggage?"

"Well, Mr. Dodd......"

"You may call me William, if you like."

"Yes...well...I wish there were luggage for you to grab, but I'm afraid you're lookin' at everything I brought with me," William Dodd was eyeing the distressed leather duffel bag, flung over Sean's shoulder, trying not to make a disdainful smirk. "So if you could just..."

"Very good, Sir, we'll get you checked in, and I will show you to the car. There are plenty of refreshments and spirits awaiting you there. Please Sir, follow me."

Sean began following the little man through the maze of travelers and airport staff, watching how they weaved and interspersed with one another, all with the set purpose of getting to some eventual destination. He too wanted to reach some destination, one of happiness he had so long been deprived. The two men were now approaching the customs area where Sean was greeted by a scruffy haired Briton, who suitably inquired about Sean's reason for entering his country. He thought to find humor by responding that he was being hired for some choice bit of thievery, but decided against it.

After convincing the clerk that he posed no threat to person or state, he resumed his station beside his well-dressed guide and followed him through a sliding glass door that lead to the parking lot outside. He sniffed the air. It was cool and damp. The odor reminded him of his visit long ago to London. He turned to the driver, "So tell me, how long have you worked for Sir Nicholas DeBury?"

The old man looked up at Sean, pulling a handkerchief from his pocket and patting his wrinkled forehead, "I've been in residence with Sir Nicholas for a very long time, Sir- so long in fact, that you might say I've lost track of the time."

Sean returned a skeptical eye, "What can you tell me about him?"

"Well sir, my employer is a bold man, rather blunt and uncompromising at times, but never in such a manner as would seem disrespectful. He is, I believe, a fair man, firm in his demands of the household staff, but as good an employer as one would imagine there to be." He cleared his throat, "I have only worked for one other individual, so my opinions may be a bit limiting."

"But, I mean, what do you know of him personally, outside the house, that sort of thing?"

"As it would be in poor taste to meddle in the affairs of my employers, I refrain myself from any real attention to his duties and those things which are of little concern to me." He paused and began again, "What general information I can tell you is that Sir Nicholas comes from a very distinguished lineage that can be traced back at least as far as the early thirteenth century. Everyone knows of his large publishing firm, DeBury Publishing. I'm told the firm owns the contracts of several high-profile authors from around the world, as well as those of some famous recording artists. I'm not really sure which ones, though; and while I'm certain his publishing firm does quite well financially, I've also heard he has an exhaustive cache of family money as well."

"And his book collection?" Sean probed a little deeper.

"Ah yes, the books." There was a moment of hesitation, not so much from a need to harbor information of a secretive nature, but because it seemed necessary to move the conversation to a new plane of awareness, the books. "It is certainly within the realm of possibility that Sir Nicholas DeBury might have within his possession the greatest book collection in all of Europe. He has the most insatiable appetite when it comes to purchasing and housing great books. I have often heard him ranting, late at night, at his goal of restoring the lost library of Alexandria to its former glory with his acquisitions. Sir Nicholas has forbidden the entire staff from discussing his book collection outside the home, but as I'm sure you will be introduced to its contents soon enough, I see no reason to evade your questions. I've never worked for a man like him before; and I'm afraid I can't tell you much more. I try not to pry, you see," He was pointing towards a long black limousine idling in the parking lot, bringing the conversation to a close. "Ah, here we are, allow me to get the door."

The luxurious vehicle was a welcomed offering when compared to the other modes of transportation parked in various locales in the passenger pick up area of Gatwick International. His host sought to meet every comfort that might be imagined, and Sean felt a little like a movie star when he slid onto the car's leather seats. He mused at how often he had seen these sleek machines with their steel frames exuding wealth and power, slide in dignified grace down the streets of Boston and New York, knowing himself that such a luxury could hardly be afforded by the likes of him. "Now this I can handle, Mr. Dodd............. l mean, William."

The little man secured his passenger, "Please make yourself comfortable, Mr. Wilde. Beside your arm there, upon the armrest, is a remote for the tele; and the bar door just below is fully stocked with almost any beverage you might desire. Our ride to Chelsea will take about fifty minutes, provided traffic is moving along well, so please relax and enjoy the journey."

Sean watched as the chauffeur shut his door and made his way around the back of the limousine, entering the car from the right side, a custom he could not get used to.

Settling in, and gazing about the car's interior, he wondered what it must be like to live life this way. Does having money like this make life that much better, more enjoyable? Sean was quickly deciding that, in fact, it would. He cautiously put his feet upon the seat horizontal to his own, trying not to put enough weight on the spot so that it would not leave an indentation, and opened the door of the small wet bar facing him. Nicholas DeBury had every vice imaginable. Inside were two bottles of 1982 Petrus Pommerol, a 1982 Lafite Rothschild, a 1961 Trotanoy, a 1990 Dom Perignon, and a host of the finest liquors he had ever seen assembled in one place. What caught his eye was a bottle of twenty-five-year-old Macallan Scotch Whisky, unopened. It seemed he would have to do the honor himself. Come ta papa. As he began to pour the clear liquid into a ready-made glass, the phone, attached to his armrest, started ringing.

"H... Hello," he answered slowly.

"Let me start by thanking you for your civility; your phone manners seem to have improved greatly since last we spoke." There was no mistaking the voice of Sir Nicholas DeBury.

"Look Mr. DeBury, you offered me a lot of money for a single conversation. I'm here. I still don't know the first thing about you or what it is you think I can help with."

"There should be no cause for fear or apprehension on your part, Mr. Wilde. We shall be in one another's company soon enough, everything in its own time."

Sean hated all the secrecy. He was here. What was the need for such evasive answers? It was time to end the elusive tete-a-tete, "I should also warn you that...."

"Let me say 'Thank You' for coming Sean," DeBury broke in. "You must forgive my rudeness, but I've an errand of some importance to attend to immediately. I shall see you back at the house shortly," he said as the line went dead.

Fucking high society piece of shit. Who does he think he is? If there had been a growing concern previously for the secretive nature surrounding Sean's little adventure, it was starting to increase in fastidious leaps. What, he would wonder, made this book so unable to be discussed over the phone? Book collectors could be an odd lot, no doubt and in his time he had seen both dealers and collectors do about anything to get their hands on rare editions; but there was some underlying fear to this. A concern of some different nature he could not put his finger on. Hell, the insane sum of ten thousand dollars for idle conversation should have warned him that he was in way over his head; but Sean's skull was a thick one. He sat back in the leather's cushioned embrace, sipping at the whisky. So many questions, so few willing answers. The limousine was now entering onto the motor way, as Sean Wilde peered out the tinted window, taking in the unparalleled scenery of the English countryside.

The city of London was a compressed abstract of signature buildings and age old structures, alive with the furied amassment of people and vehicles in every form and fashion, moving hurriedly in every direction.

Sean could recall only faint memories of the time when he and his father had visited before, staying in the west end of the city, where many of the bookstores, theaters, and restaurants were. Sitting in the back of the limousine, nursing his Macallan' s, the sights he was taking in were a bit different this time, more rural and less of the tourist city he had come to view. People were working, selling goods and produce along the streets, sweeping the doorsteps of their little shops, and greeting one another as they passed along the street.

The car approached the Thames River by way of Albert Bridge, which turned into Oakley Street just over the river. The sleek, black machine then rounded the comer, passing Chelsea Old Town Hall, and glided leisurely down King's Road. They were now in Chelsea, Royal Borough of London's well-to-do. If a person had money, this is where he would live. King's Road was lined with a few individual homes and many high-end apartments, all of which were in some way lavishly decorated with wrought iron gating and old world charm. Large bouquets of petunias had been fashioned in front of every home, their colors radiating every spectral prism of a rainbow. It was odd to see so many flowers in the heart of a city this large, and he couldn't help comparing this part of London to the historic homes of Charleston, South Carolina, back in the states, where he had visited once in his youth.

The limousine stopped in front of one such house. Sean eyed the building's stone exterior, following upwards to a section of criss crossed wooden beams that decorated the upper, Tudor facade. He engulfed the last bit of whiskey, as his driver had now come to open the door of the vehicle.

"We have arrived sir, may I help you out?"

"I'm just fine, thanks," Sean said.

The little man closed the door as Sean exited, and resided himself to moving the vehicle.

Sean started up the flagstone steps, noticing as he ascended toward the home's entrance, the neatly groomed yew hedges and the gold heart ivy that made the short pathway so decidedly English. The home was one of many situated snugly beside one another, making it rather difficult to tell where one residence began and another ended. His nose caught the aroma radiating from a nearby pub. The smell of Chelsea was fantastic. He had been so preoccupied with his surroundings, that he hadn't noticed the figure of a man standing at the home's entrance.

"Mr. Wilde, I presume," the man guarding the doorway inquired.

"That's me. Sean Wilde at your service," he returned.

"My name is Finneas Frakes, I am Sir Nicholas DeBury's resident butler, and I will be in charge of your comfort while you are with us," he began. "Sir Nicholas has entrusted me with making sure your stay with us is a pleasant one."

Sean eyed the man carefully, noticing immediately their differing heights. Finneas Frakes stood about six feet, six inches tall. His grooming was impeccable, his age probably early sixties. He had very little hair, but what he did have was combed to the side, suggesting with no real hope, that he had more. His face was turned upwards; in the snobbish way the butler is often portrayed in film. His frame was thin, and his small beady little eyes rolled slightly as he looked at Sean's bohemian style of dress with a dissatisfying glare. "I noticed Mr. Dodd did not remove your luggage from the car?"

"Yeah, well this is all I brought with me Mr. Frakes," Sean presented his meager offerings. "Finneas. Please call me Finneas."

"Of course, sorry. Anyway, I hadn't planned on staying very long, Finneas; so if we could go inside, maybe I could meet your boss and get this over with. I'm kinda tired from the flight."

"At once sir, right this way."

The towering servant led Sean through the front door, and into a heavily oak paneled entranceway, where the wealth of objects scattered about the place seemed to heighten his sense of awe. What looked like original oil paintings were hanging from every wall, and the main hall way was adorned on either side with statues and busts, most resembling authors and poets of the past. All of the molding fastened to the walls looked of burnished gold, and the furniture looked as if it had been produced centuries ago. To his left, there was a knight's armor in full dress, awaiting a battle that would never come. Behind it, in what Sean imagined was the dining area, contained a large burl table which looked as if it could seat twenty people. The home was clearly larger than it had looked from the outside. The ceiling's overhead was vast, maybe sixteen or seventeen feet to its peak. Sean felt intimidated, overwhelmed by the grandeur and magnificence of the home. He had never been in a private residence this eloquent, and standing in the entrance, he just shook his head. Maybe he was just regretting his own lack of personal accomplishment, devaluing in some way his own self-worth.

"Mr. Wilde?" Finneas said.

Sean shook himself free of the trance like state, "Sorry........ sorry, it's just that this place is so.... so."

"Impressive."

"Yeah, impressive."

"Please Mr. Wilde, follow me."

Finneas led his guest up a long, winding stairway, his neatly polished shoes clapping the hardwood flooring as he walked, climbing to the second floor which overlooked the main drawing room. Sean, looking over the railing, noticed the largest stone fireplace he had ever seen. Tapping his shoulder to get his attention once more, Finneas motioned Sean down the hallway and into a large room that he immediately recognized as a guest bedroom. The room was decorated in oak paneling, oak furniture, and a four-post bed that could probably sleep six. It was a man's room, fit for a king.

"This shall be your room while you are with us," Finneas said. "Relax for a while. The room for bathing is to your right, just beyond that bureau; and I have prepared some tea which I have placed on the night stand by your bed. Perhaps you should lie down for a bit and then join Sir Nicholas in the library a bit later."

Sean had forgotten about seeing the library. "Where is Sir Nicholas now?" he asked.

"He had some business matters that needed tending; he should be along shortly."

Sean knew this would be an excellent time to view the contents of DeBury's library without his presence. "Actually Finneas, I slept pretty well on the plane; so if it wouldn't be too much trouble, I'd like to take a quick leak and pass my wait in the library, if that's okay."

"You have the run of the house, Sir, as you wish. Shall I get you anything else?"

"I'm fine, thank you."

"Very good. You can reach the library from this floor by making a left out of your room and walking down the hall. The upstairs entrance will be the third door on the right. Should you fashion entry from the ground floor, simply follow the stairs back to the bottom floor and proceed down the hallway to the right. You simply cannot miss it. It is the soul of the house."

Sean had come to find Finneas a bit snobbish, but thanked him, none the less, and waited as the butler left the room. He then proceeded to throw is bag on the bed, and set about relieving nature's calling.

Feeling somewhat refreshed, he set out to find the library.

Turning into the hallway, he noticed how unusually long it was, stretching in either direction, as far as he could see. The hard wood flooring was accompanied by Persian carpeting that ran down its center. Making his way a bit further, he noticed the walls covered in more original paintings, not of people, like the one's he had seen downstairs, but somehow oddly themed in macabre, literary pictorials. There was poor Lavinia, from Shakespeare's Titus Andronicus, reaching forward with tree limbs where her hands should have been. Further along was Fortunato, begging for release from the brick-walled tomb that Poe had scripted for his character's untimely demise. Next, were the skeletal remains of Esmeralda and the grotesque Quasimodo, embraced forever within the bowels of the cathedral in Notre Dame. The paintings all seemed to suggest a dark, gothic theme, the worst of each tale they represented; and Sean thought to himself how they made for a very eerie decor. Further along, passing two doors, he came to a third door, its frame encased in glass. That's where his eyes first caught sight of what lay just beyond the glassentine barrier.

The room lying just beyond the door revealed itself in a show of magnificence that Sean could never have imagined in twenty lifetimes. He caught himself holding his breath, nervous, at the thought of entering alone. How could he venture into such hallowed territory? He had to quell the surmounting curiosity.

Sean opened the door carefully, as if he was interrupting some event on the other side. His father would have shit his pants if he could have viewed the contents on the other side.

If there was a heaven on earth, a Garden of Eden for the lover of books, Sean had just found it. The room, if one could call the three- thousand-square- foot area laid out before him a room, was housed upon two floors and was the largest private library he had ever seen. Adorning the rich mahogany bookshelves, inset in the walls from floor to ceiling, were rows upon rows of the finest, gilded leather volumes, each being a striking testament to the individual binder who had been privilege to fasten their pages. Sean stood aghast, trying to sort through the images flooding his brain. The room smelled of puckered vellum, age toned to perfection. A hint of pipe tobacco could be sensed, faint in the distance. Sean moved slowly toward the left, his eyes focusing on some of the titles stacked upright on the shelving. His fingertips came to rest on the raised bands of one particular volume, and he read its embroidered title, The History of the Decline and Fall of the Roman Empire, 1776-1778. Beside it were five volumes of Walter Raleigh's The Historie of the World, 1687. Then came Moliere's The Dramatic Works, 1875-6. The titles went on and on, down the shelves as he mused at their spines, each one decorated in the finest levent morocco he had ever seen. Each volume had extravagant gilt dentelles; and the elaborative designs ingrained on the exterior of each book, would come to leave a lasting impression on anyone viewing their princely state. He was going to puke! Accompanying each volume's spine was a gold, armorial coat of arms, bearing what he assumed was the DeBury family crest. Kings adorned their books this way. What the hell did DeBury want with Sean?

Turning from the volumes lining the upper walls, he slowly proceeded down a short winding staircase, descending to the bottom floor, never shifting his eyes from the surrounding splendor. The first thing that caught his attention was a small rectangle curio, about six feet in length and three feet in height, standing alone in the middle of the floor. It seemed to be made of some type of ornately carved wood, poplar maybe; and its frame was surrounded by glass, for the purpose of display. What items were therein made Sean's heart skip two beats.

Below the glass, safe from a fool's touch, were three books, housed in an orderly fashion, side by side. He recognized them instantly, but doubted his proximity to them, pawning the sight to a dream- like state he was surely in. The volume to the left may well have been the Holy Grail itself, for it was the first book ever to be printed on movable type, the forty- two lined Bible, published in Mainz, Germany in 1454, by Johann Gutenberg. Other than a Bible, autographed by God Himself, no book even came close to holding such value and prestige like that book did. To its right was Recuyell of the Historyes of Troye, the first book ever printed in the English language, by William Caxton in 1474. Further to the right was the last book in the case, a manuscripted copy of a book Sean thought existed in only three copies. He realized now that there existed a fourth. The book was Richard de Bury's Philobiblion, the first treatise on the love of collecting books, written in 1345. Oh shit! Could this guy be somehow related to Nicholas DeBury? The thought played out in his mind, but he shortly dismissed it as coincidence.

Still............

There was a noticeable space next to the Philobiblion that seemed empty, as though there should have been a fourth book present. His mind filled the void space with priceless books that deserved to be there, maybe William Morris' Kelmscott Chaucer; but he dismissed the daydreams and perused the lower contents of the library even more.

Feeling a bit dizzy (from all that had transpired within the compass of his day) he took a seat, coming to rest on a brown leather sofa situated in front of a large fireplace in the center of the room. He thought how odd it was that fireplaces seemed to accompany a library's interior design. One little spark catching a vellum page, and the library would be toast, quite literally.

His eye caught sight of a book, propped upon a stand just across from where he was sitting. It was the First Folio of Shakespeare, one of the most revered works in the English language. His head was spinning; his sense of professionalism was waning. How does one address the owner of such a library? Any words of praise would be decidedly unnecessary, unjustifiable. The-contents housed within this room, their quantity easily approaching the thirty thousand mark by conservative estimates, represented the greatest of man's earthly literary achievements. Forget the machines, the castles, the cities. These volumes symbolized so much more. They represented the thoughts, dreams, and brilliance of the authors who created them. It was an unbelievable sight. His head shook as he looked to a shelf on his right, unmistakably full of Caxton's first editions. Resting on the row below was a shelf containing volumes from Caxton's successor, Wynkin de Worde. He stood, nauseous, imagining the hands that caressed the volumes when they were created. Just as great works of art are formed from the hands of scintillating masters, so it is with words, assembled in such creative fashion as to evoke upon their reader ideas of war, salvation, and the reshaping of thought. These resulting books should achieve no less praise than the greatest paintings of the world. And the authors should be regarded as their irrefutable master.

Sean had lost track of the two hours that had passed since his entry into the library and was startled when two glass doors opened on the library's main floor revealing the butler, Finneas Frakes, accompanied by a silver serving cart.

"I trust you have been enjoying your time with us so far, Mr. Wilde, and that at least some of your curiosity has been relieved."

"This place is beyond incredible. I don't know what to say," he looked bewildered, "These books...... are they real?"

"Indeed, Sir, I believe they are quite genuine."

"No man living could have the financial means to afford such a collection. Whole countries couldn't afford a fifth of what's in this room. How, if you don't mind my asking, did DeBury manage this?"

"Sir Nicholas requests that the staff abstain from discussing the contents of this room with anyone, for obvious reasons; and I am afraid it is not my place to answer questions concerning the business affairs or aquisitional conquests of my employer. I am sorry."

Sean couldn't get a straight answer from anyone, an unfair advantage in his position. Was the evasive nature of DeBury's staff necessary? What were they trying to hold over him? It was bullshit, whatever it was; but there was little he could do. His patience waning, he retorted, "So where's DeBury now?"

"Ah yes," the butler began, "Regrettable though it is, Sir Nicholas will be detained for a bit longer than was previously expected; so I brought some spirits while you wait." He was pointing to the serving cart.

"Any idea how long he'll be, Finneas?" Sean asked, uneasy with referring to the servant by his first name.

"It is difficult to say, perhaps a couple of hours. I shan't hazard a guess."

Sean sought to seize an opportunity. "Finneas, would it be possible for me to step out for a bit, maybe take in some of London's sights?"

"Whatever you desire, Mr. Wilde. I'll have Mr. Dodd bring the car around immediately." Finneas Frakes excused himself and disappeared into the hallway just beyond the glass doors. Sean felt as if he could spend the rest of his life perusing the contents of DeBury's library; but it was time to clear his head, and time alone in a city like London could do just that. Besides, there would be time to dissect the library's contents later.

Finneas now stood in the doorway, and ushered Sean to follow him. The limousine was ready. Sean glanced once more at the room, his mind notating every aspect, every detail. He then followed the butler down the hall. Reaching the front door, the two men exchanged trivial civilities, and Sean descended the stone path, leading to the small figure awaiting him. The car door was already opened.

"Where shall we go today, Mr. Wilde?" the little man inquired.

"Charring Cross Road, William; it's time to allow a book scout a little fun," Sean was smiling.

"Very good, Sir, Charring Cross Road it is." The driver waited for Sean to take his seat, and abruptly shut the door. It was time to visit Sean's favorite part of the city, the street that housed more bookseller's than any other in the world, at least in those areas of the world he had traveled. His mind could recall only vague memories of walking down that street with his father. But, in both a sordid attempt to relive a happy memory and the chance to unveil a real treasure, he would return. He sank down in the cushioned leather once more. As the limousine pulled away from the sidewalk, he noticed Finneas still standing on the steps, watching and smiling in his smug little way. The car sped off down King's Road, heading for the West End of London.

Sean decided then and there, something seemed altogether odd about Finneas Frakes.

"At first be like a modest maiden,
and the enemy will open his door;
Afterward be as swift as a scurrying rabbit,
and the enemy will be too late to resist you."

Sun-Tzu

Constantinople

Father Koutrakos could hear the soft sound of seagulls singing just outside the opened window of the library. Salt sea air entered through the fissured glass, a cool breeze pervading the room. He had awoken only moments before, having found himself cradled upon the hard-stone flooring he had unwittingly chosen to use as a bed the night before.

Last night must have somehow been a dream. He was on his feet now, wiping saliva from the corner of his lips and padding down his robe in a vain attempt to straighten the wrinkled burlap covering. How long had he slept? He was uncertain about that detail, and his vision was a bit blurred. It was out of character for him to take in this much rest; there were duties to attend, responsibilities to God. The room was now coming into focus; everything was as it should be, nothing out of place. He groaned. There were new body aches this morning; age was playing havoc with his elderly muscles. He winced slightly, urging his body to shuffle his sandaled feet towards the open window. The old abbot smiled at the breathtaking view. The beautiful land of Athos, with its brightly colored flora dotting the steppes below, was being softly caressed by the rolling waves of the Aegean Sea. Birds hovered overhead, riding along the cool, oceanic breeze. The storm had passed. Off in the distance, a rainbow, its coloration more intense than any he could remember seeing before, dipped into a far corner of the sea. He tugged at his beard as his thoughts moved elsewhere. For him, life was reaching its apex. Old age was withering his frame, and his body was struggling to fight the inevitable. He knew he would not live much longer. The thought of death frightened him, and he was ashamed that he could not control the feeling. He surveyed the room once more. His only company was the beloved manuscripts resting upon their shelves. He would think no more of the night before; it had been no more than the awakening truth that he was old and his mind was beginning to fail him.

He looked once more at the sea with its shades of blue, varying in the distance. The old man was allowing his mind to travel, taking a journey into a past that he had chosen to suppress for fifty long years. Tears welled in the corners of his eyes; he was there once again. He actually saw the splendor of his former city. For Father Andreas Koutrakos, the past had unfortunately returned.

The year was 1451, forty- five winters ago.

The great Byzantine empire stretched far across the Mediterranean territory, and its proud city of Constantinople was situated at the northeastern tip of Greece. This glorious city was surrounded in the west by three heavily constructed walls, which ran parallel to one another across the whole city, serving as a fortification for invading armies and separating its people from the outside land mass. The remaining city was bordered to the north, south, and east by the Sea of Marmora and the Strait of Bosphorus. From its center, the city was less than five miles in either direction. It served as a capital of advanced learning, blossoming arts, and scholarly thought.

It was here in the great city that a young boy of seventeen, Andreas Koutrakos, was being heralded as one of the great young thinkers of his day, a future courtesan of the Emperor himself. He had come under tutelage of one Joseph Briennius, a University professor and head of the

Patriarchal Academy, a man who stood as the leading Byzantine scholar of the day. He taught his young pupil all manner of languages, western as well as eastern thought, and fueled the student's embracing of the arts in painting and writing, as well as his role of scholar to the Orthodox Church. It was little surprise to anyone that young Andreas, was taking his family's name to the height of cultural and religious status.

For Andreas personally, academics served only part of his fascination with life and the world around him. The underlying element, and what many saw as his greatest source of pride, was the love he had for a young girl of his same age, Helena Mykonos.

He had known her all of his life. The two families had lived a short distance from one another within the city walls. Helena was as headstrong as she was beautiful, and this had become a leading source of the attraction. She stood just over five feet tall, with long auburn curls that draped about a Grecian face of porcelain beauty. Her eyes were dark and mysterious; her lips were the natural color of rose petals. Soft, fragrant skin molded a voluptuous frame and this caused a yearning within young Andreas daily; but he was aware that he would find no fulfillment until they could be wedded. He loved her from the moment he saw her as a child; for each, there was no other.

Fear loomed in Constantinople's uncertain future. It had been widely suspected that Sultan Mehmet II, ruler of the Ottoman Turks, was now setting his desire on the necessity of conquering the great city in an effort to establish a great capital for Ottoman rule. Outside the city's outermost wall, construction had already begun on a castle-like fortification by the Turks.

In an effort to dissuade the rumors, Emperor Constantine XI Paleologus, then ruler of the Byzantine empire, sent ambassadors to the Sultan, in hope of seeking the promise that an invasion was not of prevalent concern. Upon arrival, Constantinople's ambassadors were thrown into prison, and then decapitated a short time later. A virtual declaration of war had been realized.

Warnings had been discussed of the now certain threat of war, but as the elder scholars conveyed their concerns, the Emperor realized that the only chance the city had to defend itself lay in the help of other nations and whatever military aid might be sent. The Islamic warlords were readying themselves to take the city of Constantinople, by whatever means necessary.

The Emperor had great faith in the well-fortified walls that surrounded the city, since they had structurally remained impervious to attack since 323 B.C... True, it had been victimized by the early crusades two hundred and fifty years earlier, but that invasion had occurred within the city walls. In the Emperor's eyes, there was no need to over enforce a fourteen mile stretch of walling that could not reasonably be penetrated.

In the summer of 1452, Andreas, attempting to even the odds in the event a breach was achieved by the Turks, brought before the Emperor a Hungarian cannon builder by the name of Urban, who readily offered his services in the construction of artillery that would properly defend the city should the walls fail. The Emperor refused to pay the engineer the price the man felt was deserved, and sent him away, much to the discomfort and unease of his scholars, who believed in the necessity of Urban's skills. Paleologus would, instead, send dispatches to the outer lands of Europe, seeking armaments and manpower from neighboring countries.

The messengers returned to their city with a grim outlook. England and France had just ended the Hundred Years War, and both countries were too war torn to offer support. Spain and the Germanic countries offered their willingness to send support, but as time passed, little came. Italy had become the only hope left. It was believed that if Constantinople were taken, Italy would have the problem of trading goods with difficult Arabian merchants; and moreover, there would always be the concern for an impending threat of Turkish invasion from the South. The Emperor wasted little time in sending a dispatch to Rome.

The Pope, Nicholas V, was willing to offer support if the Orthodox Greeks would submit to the Papacy. Constantine was reluctant, but being in no position to bargain, he agreed; and for his acceptance, the paltry amassment of two hundred soldiers was sent as aid. Constantinople could only brace itself for the coming attack.

Emperor Constantine began to take count of his existing military force, realizing upon completing the census how dire his situation really was. The men who could be expected to defend the city numbered less than ten thousand. A grim reality was beginning to set into the consciences of the leading government officials.

Andreas feared for the life of his family, especially his beloved Helena, who refused his repeated urgings to flee to Italy where she would be safe until the impending threat had passed. She refused, willing to neither leave his side, nor abandon her family.

In April of 1453, Mehmet II arrived at Constantinople's outer wall with an army of Turkish Janissaries that numbered almost seventy thousand men. War, with the threat of invasion, was now to be realized. Within the employ of the Turkish garrisons were the most vile, barbarous raiders known as the Bashi-Bazouks, numbering some additional twenty thousand men. Their cruelty was legendary, since they were paid not in monetary offerings from those who they fought beside, but in what they could pillage within three days, should the invasion be successful. In addition, was even more for the citizens of Constantinople to fear.

Seventy cannons lay poised at Constantinople's great wall. The engineer Urban, having been turned away by the Emperor Palaeologus, had found a commission with Sultan Mehmet and constructed for the Turks a great cannon spanning twenty-eight feet in length that fired a twelve-hundred-pound ball which, it was believed, could level the protective shielding of the city. In addition, an armada of over a hundred various Turkish vessels had entered the Sea of Marmora and were being positioned for an attack from the ocean. The people of Constantinople braced for the coming battle.

On April 11, Sultan Mehmet, satisfied of his positioning, gave the order for the bombardment to begin.

Andreas Koutrakos gathered with the learned men in the Forum of Theodosius near the city's center and began the arduous task of helping design a scheme for retaliation. There was decidedly little that could be done but to wait out the attack, which had begun swiftly and steadily.

The Turkish army fought consistently for a month. Every time their cannons would deliver a substantial blow to the outer walling, those citizens living just inside would spend the whole of an evening repairing the structure with whatever materials could be found. This worked for a time, but the never ceasing bombardment from the land and a resounding victory from the sea insured that the city would eventually be doomed.

On the morning of May 28th, Emperor Constantine, realizing that the walls would no longer protect his citizens, assembled his scholars and priests and made a final speech of farewell as he would now give the only thing he had left to offer his people- his life, if need be. He then rode from them with his last remaining troops. Young Andreas was devastated, since he had hoped God would defend his people from the invading Islamic militants.

On the 29th of May, 1493, the great Byzantine empire of Constantinople fell, giving way to the Turkish warlords.

Emperor Constantine had perished in battle, along with his last remaining troops, as the last wall crumbled. Chaos reigned. Fire spread throughout the city as the remaining citizens began making a desperate attempt to flee. Young Andreas Koutrakos was among them, but the only existing objective of any real concern to him was to find his beloved.

Every man, woman, and child was being slaughtered as the hoarding marauders entered the city. Blood ran in streams through every avenue and passage of street. Nuns could be seen jumping from rooftops, preferring martyrdom to de-flowerment, as the invaders were now preferring to take captives. The raping and pillaging had only just begun.

Andreas was being pushed and hurried as the mass hysteria of people, deep in the throngs of fear, grasped at some futile attempt for escape. His young eyes could not believe what they were witnessing. His fellow citizens were being systematically butchered, not even allowed the right to surrender. Blades shimmered briefly catching the reflection of the fire that burned wildly, before tasting the flesh of innocents. All around were the sounds of trumpets blaring and Church bells ringing, their sounds deafening. He could not concern himself with escape, having long made peace with the fact that death for him was imminent. All that mattered now was finding Helena and somehow, seeing her to safety.

Helena Mykonos sat shivering, crouched in the corner of her family's home, clinging tightly to her mother, both women terrified and emotionally unsure of what to do. Andreas would come. Just outside, the clashing of weapons and the painful screams of the dying were all the two women could hear. The air was putrid, the smell of acrid smoke and fire permeating the home. Helena, her hair tussled and her dress tom, held her mother tightly, trying in some vain attempt to be strong.

The two women screamed as the door to their home was abruptly smashed in.

Standing before the frightened women was the leader of the Bashi-Bazouks, Abdullah Tas, a most cruel and heartless Turk. To each of his sides were two other soldiers, one brandishing a six-foot spear, the other a curved sword. The women, knowing from the evil smile that had formed on the faces of these men, were now coming to understand terror in a way that they could never have imagined before.

The Turkish outlaw towered above them, his dark skin displaying dirt, and superficial wounds incurred during the battle. His head was encased in a purple turban, and he looked gigantic; his eyes were wild and a coal- black beard was matted to his face. Teeth were missing, and his clothes were a mixture of colors and rags. Helena, unwise to the lack of compassion this Turk possessed, threw herself in front of her mother begging and pleading for mercy.

An act of mercy was not a trait with which Abdullah Tas had familiarized himself. Behind him now, the wailing of human cries could be heard; Byzantium was fading fast.

Andreas was running faster and faster. With his body soaked in sweat, he was dodging what confrontations he could, praying under his breath for his family's safety while trying frantically to find his beloved. A cannon blast exploded just in front of him in the distance as he watched in horror as many of his colleagues from the university, all scholars, were hurled into the air, their limbs detaching from their bodies by violent contusion. Turning briefly, he saw the Janissaries pouring into the city with javelins, swords, and arrows, jutting from the men who had attempted resistance. He would not allow himself to imagine the worst of his beloved. She was assuredly alive. Somewhere, Helena was waiting.

Abdullah Tas clasped his hand tightly around Helena's hair wrenching her violently from the woman she was attempting to shield. Helena screamed, feeling a portion of her hair ripped at the root by her heartless assailant. She looked up, helplessly unable to scream, as she watched the barbarian sink the tip of his spear in the delicate flesh of her mother's abdomen, impaling her on its silvery tip. The men laughed as the older woman writhed in pain, blood gushing from the new opening in her stomach as life began ebbing from her contorted body. For them, victory had long been accomplished; this was simply the sport that followed, no more than a game.

Tears blurred Helena's vision as she clumsily rushed the party of degenerates. Her moves were easily calculated by the seasoned warriors, who promptly threw her to the floor, her head opening on contact with the stone. She was dazed, but could easily make out the intent of her captors. Blood oozed from the back of her head. They would rape her first, one by one, then slit her throat; there could be no doubt. Her beloved Andreas wasn't coming. She was going to be tortured and would die alone. Hope had not seen fit to spare her a life with her beloved, or the promise of a child in future days. She could take no more.

Abdullah Tas moved in slowly, calculating the desired position in which he would experience the joyous, orgasmic sensation of conquest. His captive was weak, barely coherent.

The two raiders at his side smiled, knowing their turn would come soon enough; for now, they would wait and watch excitedly as the helpless female became a victim of their heightened carnality. The one to have her last, they were deciding, would be the one to employ the manner of her death. This would prove fun for all.

The large man was on his knees, preparing to loosen his clothing, just above the helpless woman. Saliva dripped from the corner of his mouth; his brow fevered in the wake of his lustful excitement. The woman underneath could smell his vile stench, her legs fighting to be free from such a state of discomfort. Off to the corner, there was a light moaning resounding from the older woman, a noise too difficult to mistake for coherent speech, as the blood continued to ooze from her contorted body.

It was then that Abdullah Tas took his eyes off his intended victim for a fraction of a second.

Helena Mykonos, battered in body and even weaker in spirit, lifted her frail form from its position for only a moment, rising several inches beneath her assailant. Her hand lunged for a dagger sheathed on a baldric of Abdullah' snow loosened pants, freeing the razor-sharp blade from its holster. The surprised Bashi-Bazouk turned back quickly, his eyes widened by his obvious miscalculation. She was not as incoherent as he had thought.

Wasting not a second, the woman beneath thrust the potent end of the blade deep within her chest, her eyes rolling, the wind leaving her body as she embraced the pain that followed. Better to die a virgin, she thought with a last flicker of reason, than to sacrifice her chastity to a spawn of the devil. Even if she succeeded in cutting the beast atop her, she would meet her fate by the two soldiers behind him. She could not reasonably escape. She would see her beloved on the other side; she could now hope for little more.

The marauder rose in a fit of rage, himself robbed of the lively pleasure of conquest. The woman sprawled on the floor below released the handle of the blade; a dark, maroon colored liquid began soaking her torn dress. She writhed in pain. Her agony was warranted, since she had missed the intended organ, her heart, and was now suffering the torment that lay in her miscalculation. Her eyes flickered, unable to properly focus. Abdullah Tas would now help her find the resolution she had been so eager to seek.

The barbarous warrior fastened his belt and reached down, withdrawing the knife from her chest at a quickening speed that caused Helena to scream with unhampered abandon. The raider smiled, his men laughing from behind, as he wiped the bloodied end of the blade on her dress, sheathing it back in the baldric. He watched as her body listed a bit, seeking some comfortable position until death could claim her. He knew it would not come quickly. Bending down, he lifted her body in a semi-upright position, cupping her head in his hands, admiring how beautiful she still looked. He licked the blood trickling from the corner of her pale lips. Helena could hear him whisper something in her ear, his rough hands parting the mangled hair from her ear. She could not see from behind her back the malicious care with which the invader unsheathed his blade once more.

Abdullah Tas then placed the dagger beside her left ear and caressingly let the blade penetrate her delicate skin, slitting her throat until the knife met the other ear. Helena's eyes rolled one last time as her body's desperate attempt to suck in air became lastingly futile. Her body went cold; the warrior letting it fall lifeless onto the floor. Helena Mykonos was dead.

The marauder then stood frustrated, but temporarily satiated, and ordered his men to take what valuables they could find. They would find more women to fulfill their lustful tasks; it was time for them to move on.

Andreas, now approaching the Mykonos home, took a deep breath, trying to comfort himself and find relief in his assurance that God had indeed seen fit to protect his future bride. He motioned forward, ignoring the screaming from behind, and entered the home with a cautionary hesitation.

Tears welled instantly before his brain could accept the message of reality that lay before his eyes. There, lying half naked in a pool of her own blood, was the person he loved and cherished most in the world. His knees buckled, his body uncontrollably falling to the floor. He opened his mouth to scream, to cry; but no sound emerged. He was outside of himself; thought and reason were damned. His eyes wandered to the disheveled mess that had once been a home. He didn't have to look far before he found the lifeless form of Helena's mother nearby. The two women seemed to be reaching for one another, death's lasting embrace. He began crawling towards the body of the women whom he had once promised everlasting joy.

He shrank before her, cradling her cold torso in his arms. He looked into her eyes, widened, but void of life. Tears poured like rainfall, as all he held dear in the world rested lifeless in his arms. She was the mother of children he would never have; she was the warm passionate fire of love he would never know. He lifted her wrist, her body propped by the strength of his chest, and removed from her arm the only trinket the Bashi-Bazouks had not taken. Why would they? It was a simple band, woven clumsily of silken threading, that Andreas had given Helena the first time he had asked her to marry him- when they had been only six years old. She had never removed it from her wrist. Andreas was removing it now.

He laid her body upon the flooring; sadness was being replaced with rage as the moments passed. He mumbled a Christian offering, covering the two bodies with some linen he had been able to find; then, turning from the horrid scene of waste, he stormed from the small house, gripped with all the rage of a berserker newly born.

When once again he entered the burning street, all that lay before him was the carnage of a failed regime. Once, Constantinople had been the capital of Christian civilization, the glory of an age that had lasted hundreds of years. Proud Byzantium. Now, it lay in ruin with its people unable to defend even themselves. Armageddon had arrived, the slaughtering surmounting with each passing moment. God seemingly had failed to hear his request. He would now ignore God.

On the ground, he noticed a small trace of blood that had trailed from the inside of the home he was now leaving. He followed its broken path to a house some ten yards in the distance. Andreas could not focus his mind properly, but felt deep within him an obsession to fulfill the lust of revenge that had been surmounting with each step he took. He could hear the screaming of a woman coming from inside. His head was swimming as his eyes went searching for some manner of weaponry that might cause a maximum bit of harm. There, in the distance, it called for him. In the flash of a momentary gaze, his eyes fell upon a lone scimitar, the curvature of the blade protruding from the body of a hapless contemporary. This would do. With a determined fervor, Andreas withdrew the weapon from the dead man's back, feeling the skin of its victim release the foreign object. If there was to be an element of surprise, it was now up to him to procure it. He lunged forward, thrusting the door of the small house open and awaiting fate's next revelation.

Surprised by Andrea's sudden entry, three men stared wildly with tunics pulled low, as their perpetrated rapes were seemingly being thwarted once more.

Andreas put no thought into his motion, instinctively swinging the blade forward, willing to accept any limb as prize enough. The soldier closest to him could not pull back fast enough to escape the slicing motion of the blade, as in bit hard, severing his erect penis in one swift motion. Blood began spewing about the small room with explosive combustion. As he fell to his knees while screaming a cry beyond what could be constituted as human, his fellow underling charged Andreas as his spear thrust forward in preparation to impale a new victim.

Andreas, surprised at his own speed, sidestepped the charge; the spear's tip sliced a portion of his robe. He thrust his curved weapon downward, cleaving his assailant just below the knee. The invader dropped his weapon, his hands gripped at a leg that was no longer there. With his body being unbalanced now, he crashed to the floor. Andreas looked at his prey with both surprise and disbelief. He had not imagined himself living this long against seasoned warriors. His victory had been in his surprise, and he now towered above the two ingrates who lay groveling and clamoring to nurse their dejected limbs. He also noticed the woman whose screaming he had heard earlier, was a family friend, Sarina Sardos. She was lying hurt on the floor; but she was alive. Andreas could not help the horrible thought which came into his mind. Why could these bastards not have happened by this house first? Then Helena might still be alive. But then another question came to mind. Where was the third man he saw after he had burst through the door? In the confusion, this man seemed to vanish. Andreas knew in a terrifying moment of realization that hunter had become prey.

Looking down, he saw the point of a blade protruding from his lower abdomen, just to the left of his navel, before he felt the rush of pain that followed. As fast as it appeared, it vanished. In an instant, he felt his legs weakening and his body collapsing to the floor. His mind was horrified at the revelation that he had been stabbed by some weapon from behind. It would soon be over.

As he fell, he twisted his body in the direction of the attack. Seeing a Goliath smiling back, he was certain; that the blood dripping from this giant's outstretched sword was his own. The pain came as soon as he felt the stone floor beneath him, hard and fast. The giant moved in closer. The half-naked female behind him scurried to a corner of the room, where only moments before her attackers entered, she had been cooking a broth soup kettled above a flaming hearth. Abdullah Tas was now readying himself for the kill, with blood from his own men ebbed about the floor and touching the lower soles of his boots. Andreas could see the aggravated motion in which the predator sheathed his sword, and reaching from behind his back,

Abdullah Tas drew forth a small hand ax. Its blade was dull and would provision its recipient with as much pain upon contact as possible.

Andreas stared at the man above him. He thought about his personal desire to live. He thought of his beloved Helena. He had done what he could to exact a proper revenge; he was no match for his oppressor. The sting of death was poised above. May God have mercy!

Without warning the towering giant screamed- the ax falling from his hands, which were now flailing wildly. Andreas shielded himself, not wanting to receive any stray drops of boiling liquid that had just been poured over his attackers upper body. Energy returned for a moment's reprieve as Andreas lifted himself from the ground, cupping his side and trying to stop the profusion of blood seeping from his wound.

Abdullah Tas was on his knees. His face was on fire and swelling welts were rising as his flesh burned. He had once again miscalculated the strength of a woman he had intended to violate; there would be no third chance. Standing behind him, bloodied and bruised, was the woman whom he had ignored when Andreas had broken in. She seemed to be satisfied with her momentary revenge. Andreas kicked the screaming barbarian in the face, feeling the front row of his teeth shatter beneath the thrust of his sandal. He would enjoy this. God help him; he would relish this.

As the Turk removed his hands from his face, trying to focus, Andreas slid a Rondel dagger in each eye socket, enthralled in the misery he was now causing the man who had harmed his Helena. As the raider screamed again, Andreas reached to the ground, his rage quelling his pain, and picked up the ax which had earlier been intended for him. He flew into a rage. His hand swinging again and again, cleaving bits of flesh from the head of Abdullah Tas. Blood flew, splattering the walls, the floor, the Grecian.

When he stopped, Andreas took survey of the surroundings. The woman who had helped him had fled. The two men he had attacked were groveling in pain, bleeding to death. Night had come, and the only light that luminated the room came from the glowing embers of the fireplace behind him. He stood, soaked in the blood of the unidentifiable heap of flesh below him. God had granted him revenge. Now, if only death and the reuniting with his beloved in the afterlife could follow.

He stumbled, dazed, aching, and seemingly dying, from the Grecian home. He could see his city and his people being tom to shreds. "It was a good day to die," he thought to himself.

He would have collapsed then and there, but a group of his fellow statesmen were hurriedly passing, offering assistance to their young colleague. Andreas was alive, but barely recognizable beneath the coat of blood smeared over his body. He wanted to die, but was urged by his friends to run, which he found himself doing with undesired ease. The group was heading to a landing of beach at the Boucoleon Harbour, to the east of the city, at the heart of the Sea of Marmora. It was their only chance of escape from the crumbling city falling in around them.

Constantinople was no more. Helena Mykonos was no more. What then, was there to live for? Andreas stopped, turning with a clumsy effort to return to the city and perish in the fighting. Arrows whizzed about his head; and in the distance he could see a vision that would stay etched in his mind for whatever few moments were left to him. He could see a marching troop of Turks, carrying upon the tip of a spear, the head of Constantinople's great Emperor, Palaeologus VIII.

Before he could react, a cannon blast took out a small area of ground twenty feet from where Andreas was standing, sending bodies of men skyward, and at the same instance, rendering him unconscious.

As the ability to decide for himself was now in the hands of others, his body was loaded aboard a small fishing boat, moored to the shore. The elders with him pushed from the land, rowing with reckless abandon, distancing the small craft from the fallen city. Andreas stirred briefly, but only to watch from a distance, as the glowing fires engulfed what was left of the great Byzantium empire. He fell back in the craft, weeping softly to himself, then giving way once more to unconsciousness.

The small craft would drift for weeks, floating southwest and void of instrumentation, leaving the Sea of Marmora and sliding into the northern Aegean Sea, passing the Isles of Imbros and Lemnos, as if protected by God. The boat urged on to the monastic republic of Mount Athos, where it washed upon the shore.

Father Koutrakos snapped from the daydream, startled by the soft hum of a violin-like instrument. He turned responsively to see the angel Lucifer sitting, legs folded, upon the refectory table, playing the instrument.

"Hell of a dream, Father," he jumped from the table placing the instrument down, "Did it really happen that way? I remember parts of it a little differently, but I guess we all must be allowed a few romantic notions, eh?"

"You are real demon."

"More real than you could possibly imagine."

The monk clasped his hand around the silken bracelet in his hand, having not remembered pulling it from his robe earlier.

"I wouldn't take your little love charm, Father; there is no need to fear me, remember?"

The monk was now remembering the aggression he had embraced when his family was slaughtered forty years past, and aggressively charged the prodding, meddlesome pest, "You will not leave me alone until I have heard you speak, so be quick and reveal to me whatever burdens your mind; then be gone and chastise me no further."

"Answer me this," the demon spoke, prodding a little more. "You have been on this island since the destruction of your city. I wonder, do you not feel as though you have wasted a life worshipping One who, in your greatest time of need, abandoned you?"

"God has never abandoned me, devil!"

"Easy now, Father. Surely we must ration that He has. Did He not take you from a future, one of scholarly promise and hope? No, wait! Maybe He had to have you totally to Himself, allowing the destruction of your city, the death of your beloved, while sparing you, just to have your presence here on Athos. He took from you everything. How could you allow yourself such pragmatic loyalty to One so undeserving?"

"It is His right; it is His will," the abbot paused, "I am not of the stature to question."

"You are too kind, Father, and such a fool. I wonder how you might feel if you knew of His imperfections, that life is so much a game with great fortune smiling on some," he said as he pointed to the monk, "Others, however, have not been so lucky." A vision appeared of the dead Helena, as the demon pointed to the floor.

The monk was caught off guard, but his response came decisively quick: "Confess to me what you will demon; then leave an old man to die in peace. I will no longer tolerate such blasphemy in this, most sacred of places."

Lucifer pulled up a wooden stool and situated himself comfortably in front of the monk. He then fixed his eyes on the old abbot; then crossing his legs, he began to speak.

"Very well, Father, let us begin." the demon dropped his tone lower while calming his pitch and then began to speak, "In the beginning, there was no heaven, and there was no earth. There was, however, Me."

The room was now deathly quiet as Father Andreas Koutrakos readied himself for a confession that he could not possibly have been prepared to hear.

"Wear the old coat and buy the new book."

Austin Phelps

Charring Cross

London is often times portrayed as a gray, foggy, metropolis. But today, nothing could be further from the truth.

The sun was shining brightly, the sky void of over casting clouds, as the limousine glided down Monmouth Street, heading straight for Charring Cross Road. Sean sat in the back of the vehicle, feeling a bit like royalty, digesting the sights of the West End. Hyde Park, Westminster Cathedral, Piccadilly Circus, Buckingham Palace, the list went on and on. There was so much history steeped in every nook of the city. Sure it was the capital of England, but it may have well been the capital of the world. Every country seemed to be equally represented. People were everywhere, and distinguishing between tourists and locals would have been quite a task. Lines formed in every direction, some for food, some for theater tickets, some for cabs. Every nationality illustrated the vast melting pot that was the city, and now Sean was a part of that stew.

The limo came to an abrupt halt, sliding into what must have been a very rare parking vacancy within Trafalgar Square. The driver exited the vehicle, hurrying to open Sean's door, as maniacal cab drivers whizzed by.

"This spot should do nicely, Mr. Wilde," he said pointing, "Charring

Cross begins right there. I shall give you two hours and then meet you further up Charring, in Soho Square."

"Great. I'll meet you there William," Sean yelled above the noise and congestion.

"Very good sir," he nodded, "Two hours then."

Sean waved the little man on, as he watched the limo aggressively pull back into traffic, causing a little brown cab, to veer abruptly, the cabby making a lewd signal with his hand. Hand signs he thought, seemed to convey the same meaning regardless of country one was in.

He turned pausing for a moment at the street sign. He was finally here, God it had been so long. The street of dreams. He took in the smell of London. Some people need a fifty-thousand-dollar sports car, others, a large estate on a faraway island. Sean was different. He needed the constant thrill of the hunt, a chance meeting with some treasure foolishly tossed aside by an unwitting hand. But it had to be a book, for what treasure was greater than that? He had often times wondered. One thousand yards of booksellers and outside book stalls loomed in the distance, his kind of street.

Sean had lost track of time, realizing that he had forgotten to adjust his watch five hours ahead, when the flight had left Boston. He had now already used up thirty minutes in his short perusal of two second hand bookstores, and began moving further up the street. He caught sight of three men dressed in heavy drag, shouting noisily at every passerby, urging for publicity of what sort Sean was unsure. He was then nudged by what looked to be a punk rocker, heading to Piccadilly no doubt. He checked his back pocket. If he had been in New York, the wallet still snugly interred would have surely been lifted, but thankfully, it hadn't been. There were some odd people in this world, but individualism makes the world go around, and the West End had more than its fair share.

Another thirty minutes passed and he had found nothing but junk, a few tattered volumes, dismissing the oasis he had once suspected might still yield a princely book he could tum a dime on back home. He decided he would resume the hunt later, for now he would chase the hour he had left shopping some of the rare book stores, and with any luck, finding a dealer who may know something about the mysterious Sir Nicholas DeBury.

He had walked only a short ways further, entering Cecil Court, when a sign caught his attention; Anthony Taylor-Rare Books, bought and sold.

Having struck out with the scouting process, his time being too limited to do much good anyway, he resigned himself to sift through the contents of Mr. Taylor's store.

The store front looked quaint and inviting, as Sean opened the green door and entered the shop. It was a bit musty, resembling an attic, he thought, more than a business. The room he entered was twelve hundred square feet, at most, dimly lit, and lined on either side with seven foot bookshelves, as they could have fit no other place, and each section had attached to it, a rolling ladder. A globe was seated in the center of the room, behind it, a table with what appeared to be some very old maps laying on top. The floor was made of uneven pine, creaking as he walked across its surface. He had seen no one upon entry, not even when the monotonous clank of the attached bells sounded upon the door's opening. His eyes instinctively began scanning the books lining the shelves. Many had noticeable dust, looking as if they had not been touched by anyone in a long time. He reached for a volume, brushing it softly, it's binding reading; The Common Law, by Oliver Wendell Holmes Jr. 1881. Not a cheap book by any imagining.

"Can I help you with anythin' sonny," a voice called from behind.

Sean almost cost himself a fortune he didn't have, just catching the volume as it leaped from his startled hands. If the binding had cracked against the floor, eight thousand, of his promised ten thousand dollars would have belonged to Anthony Taylor. His chest heaved with relief.

"I'm so sorry," Sean conveyed, "I didn't see anyone when I came in, so I helped myself to having a look around. Your selection, it's quite nice," he was going for flattery.

"Thank you my good man. Yes, well, at least it should be said you know a good book when you see one, eh?" This guy could have sprung directly from any one of Dickens' novels. He was an older man, rather haggard, in comfortable dressings of khaki pants, a soft wool sweater, and what could have been clogs, the kind Birkenstock made, on his feet. He looked to be in his later sixties, and his back was hunched slightly to the right. His skin looked old and wrinkled, and protruding from the left side of his mouth was a wine-colored pipe, it's smoke circling just above his hairless head.

He had large blue eyes that sat just below the bushiest eyebrows Sean had ever seen.

"That's a particularly fine book you've got there," he winked approvingly.

Sean neatly slid the book back into it's empty slot on the shelf. "A tad bit over my price range I'm afraid, but your right, I do know a good book when I see one."

"Splendid, just splendid m'boy," he smiled warmly, "I haven't had a customer all day, weather's unusually nice I suppose," he held out his hand, "Anthony Taylor, bookseller, at your service."

"Sean Wilde, book scout," returning a hand. Unemployed, he had wanted to say, but refrained from the embarrassment. The old man had the softest hands. "Please to meet you Mr. Taylor."

"No, no. We'll have none of that 'Mr.' shit sonny. Come over to the sofa and make yourself comfortable, while I put on a spot of tea. You Americans are so formal." Sean was humored, and he watched the elderly man walk towards the back of the shop, feeling a little odd at the thought of being treated with such hospitality from a bookseller he had never met. It wasn't that booksellers were an unapproachable lot, it was just that rare book dealers were usually very suspicious about customers even handling their goods, let alone inviting them at a first meeting for tea. Sean decided this guy must not get too many visitors.

"I'm a bit curious," Sean was following close behind, "I've never known a dealer to keep such expensive stock so close to the front door of a store. Someone could make off with that book and you'd never know."

The old man chuckled, "You act like that's a first edition of Carrie, by Stephen King. That book you picked up, The Common Law, I think it was, tell me, how many people do you think even know what that book is? A few scholars from a university perhaps, who would never risk their careers trying to steal it, and maybe a couple of well off collectors who would have no trouble purchasing it," he continued, "No, I'm afraid not too much to worry about there. Behind a glass case, as on the open pasture, a sheep is more vulnerable to a wolf because of his high profile, on the shelf he seems less visible, safety in numbers you see."

"But what about desperate book scouts?" Sean joked.

He began filling two cups with tea, "I've got something for them too."

They both laughed as Anthony Taylor pointed to the high tech-security cameras located in various crevices about the store. Sean took to the old man instantly, likening him to a grandfather he wished he had. Book hunting would be postponed, for the company of his new friend.

The two men sat, each sipping tea and swapping stories, some of books lost, some of books gained, passing the time in an area both were experts. The old man gave Sean some interesting insights into the London book trade, both past and present, which he found fascinating. Sean, in returned, told his host about the trials and tribulations of being a book scout in Boston, and how frugal the rewards had been for him lately.

"Being that you're American," Anthony began squirming in his chair, "What manner of business has brought you to London?"

"Funny you should ask," he said smiling, "I'm still not quite sure myself, but it seems that I'm being hired to locate a book for a collector, a guy I haven't even met yet, it's all a bit strange."

The old man arched his brow, "Must be a pretty rare book if it can't be found in this city," he probed further, "Tell me, what sort of book is it? Perhaps I can point you on a proper course of direction."

Sean sat up straight, resting the tea cup on a small table, "Again, I know how stupid it sounds but I don't know the details just yet. I've only been in London six hours, and being that my host was running late for our meeting, I decided to pass the time on my favorite street in the world."

"Do you customarily jump on airplanes, heading to foreign countries, to seek work from people you've never met Sean?"

"Look, You don't have to point out how utterly ridiculous all of this is, believe me, I know," he was shaking his head, "Money is extremely tight, and the offer made was substantial, so I felt I had nothing to lose."

The old man sat back, crossing his legs, his curiosity noticeably peeked. "Any chance you can divulge the name of the individual in whose care you are being employed?"

Sean jumped at the chance. "Yes, actually it might help if you knew anything about him, being that he is a rare book collector, and your paths may have crossed," he paused taking another sip of the tea, "His name is Sir Nicholas DeBury."

The old man dropped the cup of tea in his lap, Sean seemingly startled, as he watched it then shatter hitting the floor. You would have thought he had mentioned the devil.

"Sir Nicholas DeBury! A scoundrel of a man!" he stood limping off, cursing under his breath, while looking to find a towel to wipe himself off. This was getting better and better. Sean felt a queasiness deep within his stomach. He was now sure there was cause to regret coming to London, but at this point, what could he do?

The old man returned moments later to find his guest pacing in front of the book shelves. The two men stared at each other a moment, the elder man agitated, the younger man somewhat worried. Mr. Taylor spoke first, urging Sean to retake his seat. He then sat, and removing his sweater, sat as well, stirring a new cup of tea. It seemed that he had regained some of the composure he had lost moments before, and began apologizing for his earlier outburst.

"Forgive me, young man. That man's name brings about the worst in me," he calmed himself.

"As I said previously, I'm in a bit of a financial jam right now, and he offered me a large amount of money, to simply come over and hear his offer. I really didn't see any harm."

"Son the devil is often times tempt us with offer's which at the time may seem good, only to reveal something altogether different, much later, with the passing of time."

"You 're certainly not suggesting that he's the-"

"Devil? No. But he may as well be, at least as far as anyone choosing to have business dealings with the man."

If the old man wanted Sean's attention, he certainly had it. "Tell me what you can, Anthony, I know nothing of the man, except of course that he has the finest private library I have ever seen."

"You've see his library?" the old man sat astonished at the thought.

"Of course, earlier this morning."

The old man stood, setting his cup down, "Wait here a moment," he pleaded. Sean watched as he walked down the rooms center corridor, towards the front entrance of the store, flipping the sign on the. door. The sign now read 'closed'. He then turned and wobbled back to his seat, edging closer to the book scout. Leaning in, he began speaking just above a whisper.

"Sean, have you ever heard of a book called The Philobiblion?"

"Of course," he paused, "In fact there is a copy of one in DeBury's library, behind a glass case." Then it hit him. Before the old man could say another word he was dumb struck, "Holy shit."

"It's author is one Richard de Bury, no?" the old man allowed for the flood of thought to finish racing through Sean's mind, "Sir Nicholas DeBury is a direct family descendent of the very same Richard de Bury who authored The Philobiblion in 1345."

Sean sat with a blank look on his face. Everyone who has ever known or studied anything about famous book collectors, knows that no one will ever apex the collecting fervor of the first notable English book collector, medieval bibliophile, Richard de Bury. Born in Suffolk, 1287, the man's obsession for amassing books rivaled no man before or since. His was a literary awakening that took him to every comer of Europe, hunting his leather-bound treasures. He ravaged the bookstalls of Paris, Rome, Venice, and Flanders, procuring cvery volumc somconc was willing to part with. History had made record of a meeting between de Bury and Petrarch, in which Petrarch damned the foolishness of his countrymen for parting with such valuable antiquities as books at the time were. His emplacement as one of King Edward the III' s most trusted advisors, and the position of local Bishop, made the use of power and prestige a tool that served him well when funding what would become the largest private library of the time. It was in the last, reflective year of his life, that the old bishop wrote the first surviving text on the joy and peril of book collecting, The Philobiblion, one of the most famous, and as far as history was concerned, the first book of its kind on the subject.

Sean broke the daydream, "That explains how he had a copy in the glass case I saw, I had up to this point believed there to have only been three copies in the world, hell that thing could actually be the original manuscript, if what you say is true."

The old man chimed in, "The story of course is that Richard de Bury gave his collection away, just before his death, in an effort to start a university library, and not just any library, but Oxford University Library," he let out a cough then began again, "But a few years ago it was discovered that the bishop was notorious for buying not one, but two copies of every book he acquired. Now it's of course true, that because a method for printing had yet to be developed, the books are not exactly the same, but most of the works are copied in general content, and were supposedly passed down the centuries, from generation to generation."

Sean took in the fascinating information with a hint of skepticism. "One thing doesn't make any sense though, Richard de Bury was a bishop. How the hell did he have a family tree to pass anything down? Every biography I've read on the man has never suggested descendants."

"None you ever read will," he said. "The Catholic Church was quite secretive in keeping silent the bishop's liaison with French bookseller Jean Deumont, a woman of considerable means he had fallen in love with, long after committing himself to the Church. In an effort to retain his high social positioning, the affair was kept secret. Jean Deumont gave birth to a son in the same year de Bury died, which was given the father's namesake, the small changes in the spelling occurring over time. A deal was struck with the Church Hierarchy to keep the affair from being made public so long as de Bury' s inheritance fell on the child. What books had not been promised for starting a university, it is assumed, form the basis of the collection you have seen."

"How did you come by this information?"

"As with many medieval people who were educated, Jean Deumont kept a diary," he continued, "Her diary had somehow wound up in a convent, somewhere in the south of France, where it stayed for the next six hundred years, until the convent was abandoned, it's contents going to auction in Paris about eight years ago. Few people have come to realize the connection between Sir Nicholas DeBury, and his ancestor Richard de Bury. The family has done remarkably well at keeping everything secret," he was now changing the subject, "No one living has ever laid eyes on the collection of books de Bury amassed, tell me Sean, what was it like?"

"The condition of the books is beyond imagining," he said.

"Then the proof of their relation must be certain, by that fact alone," he thought for a moment, "If each generation has added to the collection, great works from all historical periods, as I think should at this point be assumed, then the library you saw may be the longest continual collection of printed material that has ever been assembled by man or museum."

"It really is, from what I could tell, more stunning than the collection of books I saw in the Pierpont Library, in New York City," Sean said.

The old man had become lively, "Consider this Sean, if the collection began before Johan Gutenberg invented movable type, and if the books in the collection were purchased as they appeared for sale on the market..........."

"Oh my God," Sean burst out

"Indeed my friend. Sir Nicholas DeBury might have a nicer collection of books than God Himself!" the two men laughed at the thought.

After a few moments passed, the old book man straightened out his face, his tone more serious, "If the two DeBury's share a common interest in their love of books, I would imagine the similarities end there."

"What do you mean?" Sean asked.

"Sir Nicholas DeBury has been pretty ruthless in his manner of acquisitioning certain books that pique his interest," he continued, "A few years back, I can't remember the exact date, Sotheby' s Auction house offered for sale a rare collection of manuscripts, dating back to the latter fifteenth century, from a Grecian monastery that had been destroyed by fire. There were, I believe, forty manuscripts for sale in total, the largest I can remember collectively going for sale at the same instance in my lifetime. One of the conditions of the sale was that no one individual could purchase them all, owing to the fact that the seller, who remained anonymous, wanted to give learning institutions the option to acquire some of the works. The seller of course knew that if an individual with enough money showed up at the auction, the public might never have the opportunity to see them, and peculiar as it may have seemed, the seller also felt as though no one person should spend such an outrageous amount of money on the manuscripts while ignoring the plight of his fellow man."

Sean broke in, "I think I remember reading something about that sale in the New York Times. Something about London attracting the most elite book collectors in the world, back in 1992, I think."

"Sounds like the very one m'boy," the old man said clearing his throat, "The facts are this; DeBury bought one third of the manuscripts for an undisclosed sum of money with the other two thirds going to a German book seller, Klaus Mainz; a French bibliophile, Martin Depardieu; and ironically, the rare book department at Oxford University."

"I'm with you," Sean urged for more.

"In 1998, Klaus Mainz met with a most unfortunate accident while skiing in Bischofshofen, Austria, while on holiday. The ski patrol found his body at the base of a cliff, broken and pummeled from what appeared to be a horrible fall. Last year, Martin Depardieu's body was fished from the river Seine, in Paris, when a pleasure craft happened upon his bloated figure floating upon its surface."

Sean was unimpressed. "Both instances could logically be explained. I would hardly suggest foul play."

The old man interrupted, "I would wholly agree with you my boy, except for a few startling revelations that accompanied both news reports. Klaus Mainz didn't ski, nor ever had in his life. What would have compelled him to venture onto one of Austria's most treacherous slopes?"

"And Depardieu?"

"Oh, he won the national swimming competition in Nice, fifteen years earlier."

Sean was a bit unsettled, not wanting to believe that there was any real cause to fear DeBury, but his conscience wasn't allowing much room for hope otherwise. "Still Anthony, there is still an awful lot of room for coincidence."

"Yes I suppose that's what the authorities handling both of the cases surmised as well, but I should at the very least point out, that DeBury showed up at both estate auctions, purchasing each of the deceased's library holdings," he said finishing the last bit of tea, "Sir Nicholas Debury is a man who is accustom to getting whatever he wants, Sean, and heaven help you if you've agreed to do business with that man."

"So far I haven't agreed to anything more than a meeting," he sipped the remaining portion of his tea, "Do you have any idea where he gets his money?"

"Who knows for sure," he eyed the front door watching as a curious passerby was peering a questioning expression through the front glass, "One would have to believe much of his operating wealth comes from the large publishing house he owns, DeBury Publishing. I know that the company probably owns about a quarter of all magazines published in the U.K., and at least a third of the latest hardback titles, all bear his insignia on their spines."

"Is there any reason to believe he may have criminal ties, the mob maybe, or perhaps... "

"I'm sorry Sean, I know very little about Sir Nicholas's business dealings, what I do know is what is whispered within the community of booksellers here in London," he looked away for a moment, uncrossing his legs, "Excuse me for a moment," The old man stood walking towards what appeared to be the bathroom. Sean stood as well, brushing some lint off his pants, and readying himself to leave, he would have to rendezvous with the limo shortly.

After a few more moments had passed, the old bookseller returned, a fourth cup of tea in his hands. Sean laughed.

"You better go light on that stuff old timer; I hear drinking too much tea can ruin your sex life."

"Hell m'boy," he retorted, "Takes five cups just to get the bloody thing up," they both laughed.

Sean put his hand on Anthony Taylor's shoulder as the two men walked towards the store's entrance. "I've really enjoyed my time here, your shop is filled with a great selection of books, and the company has made for a wonderful afternoon, but I'm afraid I have to get going."

"Please feel free to stop by anytime Sean, it has been my pleasure having you for tea," he stopped, grabbing Sean by the arm, "I've known many a man who would sell his soul for the right book. Men will do anything to fulfill a passion, believe that if you believe nothing else I've said. And watch yourself with DeBury, nothing is worth your life, or your soul."

Sean smiled, unsteadily, "Thanks for the tea and thanks for the advice," he paused for the last time as a question appeared in his mind, "One more thing. Have you ever met Sir Nicholas DeBury personally?"

The old man nodded, "Once about four years ago," he looked away, "There was an auction at Sotheby's which included some rare material on witchcraft, A 1492 and 1530 edition of The Malleus Maleficarum by Jacobus Sprenger and Heinrich Kramer, Martin Del Rio's Disquisitionum

Magicarum 1599, Jean Bodin's De la Demonomanie des Sorciers, 1580, and Nicholas Remy's Demonolatreiae, 1595. At the time I had positioned myself there, representing a Swedish collector who had wanted to remain anonymous, with the idea of purchasing the books at any price. DeBury was among the participants, bidding on that particular lot of books. A few minutes into the bidding, I can't tell you exactly how long, there were only two parties holding any chance of purchasing the books, myself and De Bury. As the bidding became feverish, I having resigned to having them at any cost, I felt a nudge from behind by an individual I had not noticed earlier in the room. I was warned, in no uncertain terms, to back off the volumes, as the books were to be DeBury's at any cost, which would, if necessary, include my life. I immediately got up and stormed from the room as I could hear from a distance the hammer fall and DeBury announced as the new owner of the aforementioned volumes. At my age what was I to do? He obtained the books he was after, while destroying my reputation at the same time."

"I'm sorry."

"Just be careful Sean, whatever he wants with you, you must be on your guard every minute. He plays with low scruples, and you could easily get left in the wake of his purposes, whatever they are."

Sean thanked the man again, assuring him that he was more than capable of taking care of himself, and waved good-by, heading north up Charring Cross Road, to meet his driver, William Dodd.

He thought how strange, something as simple as a book could bridge two people from opposite worlds, nationalities, and age, allowing a simple afternoon of tea to become so enjoyable. His curiosity was more than peeked, it was now apprehensive, the better part of his inner character telling him to get back on the next plane home.

But to what?

Sean was certain whatever small contents had been left in the apartment, were now gone, along with his deserved eviction. Perhaps it was time for a bit more dangerous risk, one in which the reward might seem a bit greater. God knew his luck needed the change.

Ten thousand dollars. He picked up his pace, sprinting towards his rendezvous with destiny.

> "An apology for the devil: it must be remembered that we have only heard one side of the case. God has written all the books."
>
> Samuel Butler

Paradise Lost

"Let us denounce hostility," the uninvited guest announced. "You may call me 'Lucifer.' I have many names, in many languages: Astoroth, Beelzebub, Scratch, Legba, Satan, Auld Nick, and so on," his hands were rolling with his words. "My real name you could not possibly pronounce. Nor, could you know the meaning of the term 'Lucifer' implies 'Bringer of light.' It pleases me to be referred to in that manner, even if the name does not seem to be synonymous with your term 'Devil.'"

Father Koutrakos did not seem well; his eyes fixated on the being sitting opposite him. His heart and mind were disheveled. The being he had come to know from scripture resembled nothing of the man that sat before him now. Yet, an inner voice assured him that this was indeed the profligate beast who chastised all penitent men, leading them into his nest of sin.

"I can, of course, see how much difficulty you're having with all of this, Father; but you needn't worry about the validity of our meeting. I am indeed real, and I am indeed the one you call 'Devil.'"

The old monk took a deep breath and found some confidence, participating in the dialog.

"It is beyond my understanding why you would choose such a one as I to bear the burden of your words; I am very simple and obviously terrified by your presence. Won't you spare me the candid nature of your diabolical testimony?"

The trespasser smiled, "I know you fear me. I can sense it, and I can smell it." He moved his face forward, mocking an inhaling sniff, "This is, of course, warranted. I am also pleased that we are now overcoming your unwillingness to accept what is fact. I could, by no means possible, express my true feelings to one who did not truly believe; faith is a tool that works for me, as well as for my Creator. And you, my pious monk, seem to have it in spades."

The old man squirmed, realizing there would be no comfortable position in which to rest his body, as long as Lucifer was in sight. "Then, I am to act as biographer?"

"By your choosing, free will being what it is," he smirked as he arched a narrow eyebrow, "the decision to record my words onto vellum parchment will be a choice you can make for yourself after I have finished extolling the most livid confession any human priest or counselor will ever hear. I have never been one to socialize with the likes of you pitiful creatures, despite any belief you have otherwise surmised. God and I are on a course of permanent separation; that is my hell, one I could not have realized a millennia ago. If I can find within the nature of one human being a cause to be forgiven, then it may be possible for me to right things between the One who created me and myself. I want to go home- a return to heaven if you will. And, as much as I abhor the very thought of bowing before one of you wretched human beasts, it is, I feel, necessary. So, I am before you, in the physical manifestation of appearance that I was in heaven."

The abbot was stupefied by the brashness of the interloper's request. His insults were deplorable, especially for one who sought not only forgiveness, but also the compassion that would be necessary if such a request were even possible. In addition, this had angered the monk and satiated his willingness to fear the fallen angel. "It is not difficult for me to believe what you say, Devil; it is impossible! If you seek sympathy, my heart is void of the necessary compassion to bestow it."

"Yes, Father, I believe you think this to be so. But within your piety, there is room for more compassion than even what you are aware. I see; I know." The devil crossed his legs, revealing hooves where bare feet should have been. This was purely for effect, and Lucifer knew it. He would keep the monk aware of his own fear, reminding him in subtle little ways, that the man sitting across from him was indeed the fallen one. "You must understand, that it has never been my nature to ask forgiveness or sympathy. I have become extremely comfortable with my role in the vastness of the universe we share. I have long believed that we angels were void of a soul, a gift you humans take for granted. Now I am unsure; and I am willing to repent if the truth I seek exists." His words then fell silent.

"How is it that you have convinced yourself that you are not beyond salvation? In what way can you believe that God owes forgiveness to one so vile as you?" the monk said.

"You are a spirited old man, Father, and I have done well to single you out; but you are ignorant to SO much. YOU know only what you have read; that is all. And what you have read has never been edited by my hand. Now, I charge you with an honored task. I shall shortly dictate events which have, until now, been lying dormant in the memory of an angel who was wronged by his Creator."

"And, should I refuse?" he questioned.

The devil laughed aloud, "Father, no one ever refuses me." He paused, "Sooner or later I prevail; it is unavoidable. I have laid waste entire empires who thought differently. I am maintaining my civility with you out of respect for the absurd nature of my request and for my newly found guilt of past deeds. You are a human; I am angelic. Things are known to me, which would take a thousand lifetimes for you to discover and then another thousand for you to comprehend. I know your weakest link and your most desired sin. You are only human, after all." He was smiling again. The demon's tone had been beratingly sharp.

"My faith lies in my power to defeat your advances; I am stronger than you believe," the abbot enduringly rebutted.

"Yes, truly I am mistaken. Why, you have removed yourself from society, walling yourself in this earthly prison, doing nothing more than following a strict code that by its very nature separates you from any real temptation. I find you weak in that respect; but then, who am I to judge you Father?"

"You insult me Lucifer," he said while hating the way the demon's name rolled from his lips. "Why seek my help? I am, after all, only human."

"You monks are a different sort, and I have yet to understand you," he seemed puzzled. "I have never claimed an understanding of salvation. But, if salvation is, in fact, what I seek, it must be obtained by the willingness of a human to forgive my past indiscretions."

"It would seem I am to have my sanity removed by your words," the monk was distressed.

"You, who have caused so much pain to so many, come hither to this holy place. You wish to bear the weight of your forgiveness on my shoulders, and I am powerless to deafen my ears to your voice and its horrible utterances."

"Free will dictates your right to forgive, Father Koutrakos. I ask only that you listen, sparing me your biased judgments until I have concluded my offering," Lucifer said in a calm, respectable manner. "I promise not to take much of your time, and your eyes will be opened to so much more knowledge than your race deserves."

There was nothing between the two individuals for some time, save the radiant flicker of a lone candle sitting on the table that separated them. The cold stare of the devil was met with the angered expression on the abbot's face. How could Father Koutrakos fancy this fallen angel's request while, at the same time, having his humanity berated in such a repulsive manner? Lucifer realized this, as well, and refused to take the evil smirk from his face. Father Koutrakos was too far engaged to deny the demon's requests, now. How many a mortal man would be willing to trade places with Father Koutrakos just to have so many mysteries of Biblical proportion answered? The old monk looked into the beast opposite himself and found cause to speak.

"You say you have come to me for help, but your aberrance of the human race is all consuming. Where am I to find the sympathy needed to aid you in your quest to be forgiven? Your very nature imparts the impossibility of such a request. Why, if you possess such intelligence, do you not see this?"

Lucifer shook his head, "I do not require your sympathy, Monk. I am the most powerful being besides my Creator in the limited scope of your understanding," he pointed, shaking a finger. "I existed before the word sympathy came into being, and I will surely be here long after it is no longer a term of description."

"But the scriptures call for your damnation," he suggested.

"I do not believe in your humanist theories of predestination. From the time I was cast from heaven, I have labored a path of my own choosing. Could you honestly worship a being who pre-ordained man's future; it would be pointless. What makes you human is that you have been given the right to choose. Many do not believe in otherworldly beings; that does not make us any less real. If you doubt this, I shall allow you the opportunity to place a pitcher of water in hell. All believe sooner or later," he said as he chuckled. The abbot obviously was disturbed by the correlative image. "My Creator has a compassion to forgive in such limitless scope that even you could not possibly fathom. My goal is to probe His limitations. You should be honored."

The old man became reflective. It was his duty to lead souls along the path of forgiveness, but who could be prepared for insanity of such magnitude? Moreover, did Satan have a soul at all? God must be testing the old man. How could this event be explained in any other way. Would the participation of Father Koutrakos lead him towards the path of righteousness, or would it lead to eternal damnation? "Why not ask God for forgiveness in person, Demon?"

"Father," the fallen angel said turning away, "God and I........ we have not spoken in a very long time," he was looking at an effigy of Christ, resting on one of the bookshelves. Lucifer seemed sad, regretful in a tragic way. It was easy to forget who he was, what he was.

"Why now?" the monk urged, "After so much time, so many years?"

"We all become comfortable with our roles, and I am no exception," he turned back affixing his stare in the direction of the old man. "You will not believe me father, but there is more innate hatred in you humans than all the beasts in the land and the sea combined. And as man's ability to hate has grown with the passing of time, so has my contempt for your species."

"You are a beast of lies," the monk said. "So you say."

"I speak from the scriptures and I speak from my heart."

"You pass judgment, and I have been allowed no council. You refuse me and I have revealed nothing to you. You think the light mentioning of my name in the Bible gives you some insight into my character? Perhaps you are not as wise as I had previously thought. I am not without fault, and I can now see I have made a mistake in coming here. However, I have charged you with the burden of illuminating my being with whatever light exists in your soul, and you dismiss me as if you wish me to resume a role of terrorizing man, tempting him to my vile wishes. I have come to you in an effort to find absolution. You refuse me as if my true self is already known to you. So be it. I felt this to be a mistake," he began to stand, acting as though he might leave.

"Wait!"

Father Koutrakos was now realizing the weight of this confession. Would he be in some way capable of ridding man of Lucifer's devilment if he could find within the fallen one, some degree of discernible salvation? How many souls might be spared damnation? This might seem impossible to believe, but at what price would he be willing to ignore the devil's request? Yes. He would place himself upon the altar, sacrificing his sanity if need be. Something deep within his heart told him this would be the last confession he would ever hear, but that it was necessary. He would battle for souls yet to be born. Could he exalt himself to believing he could restore Satan to a heavenly edification? It no longer mattered. He would do what he must, disregarding the consequence. By his presence alone, the devil had seen to that.

"I will hear your confession, Evil One, though I am doubtless I can fulfill your desire."

"Now that is simply the wrong attitude to take," he mocked. "But I shall proceed at once. Where would you like us to begin?"

The abbot thought for a moment, digesting his reluctance to proceed. He would have to be very careful, and reserve the eagerness to believe anything his unwelcome guest had to say. He was the prince of lies, and this was a fact that could not be forgotten. "Let us begin wherever your guilt advises us to go," he was taking a controlling tone. If this was to be given a chance, he would have to maintain a degree of superiority over this being that he feared. This would not be easy. “Tell me of heaven and of your rebellious brethren before you fell.”

Lucifer meandered a bit at the question, taking leave of his seat, and walking over to the small window. He began to stare out toward the ocean, his mind altogether someplace else. He hesitated an immediate answer as if to somehow probe the recesses of his mind for long forgotten memories, ones that he would rather have dismissed altogether. “I remember little of my creation,” he started slowly, his back to the abbot. “I only remember an extraordinary existence among thousands of beings like myself; I believe you call them angels. For our kind, there was no birth nor death; we simply came into being by the simple wish of our Creator - a means of provisional accompaniment, I would presume.”

“If there were so many of your kind, how then did you come to be favored?”

“I would assume because I was first among the angels,” he remarked,” Yes.... I was his favorite...... one tends to forget...I know how hard that concept must be for you to grasp, Lucifer, exalted angel of God, roaming the streets of Heaven.... but of course, that was very long ago and as you can plainly see, times have changed.” The demon turned from the open window, an incoming wind tussling his tightly fastened pony tail, and spoke directly at the monk, “Before the birth of man, before God turned from me, my existence in the realm called heaven was one of indescribable bliss.” His eyes looked glassy, reflecting a sullen gaze. “Imagine if you can father, Lucifer arm in arm with the angel Michael, arm in arm with the angel Gabriel, singing praises to the Creator from the top of our lungs.”

“It is unimaginable.”

“Yet, it was so! Just as I tell it, every word true,” he paused. “For an unfathomable amount of time, we lived in a most harmonious state, that is, until the birth of man.”

At the core of Lucifer’s being was the simple fact that he seemed to be no more than a being of jealous rage. Rage, that had gotten horribly out of control. “If the scriptures are in factual order, your expulsion from heaven precedes the birth of Adam. Was it not your own desire for power, a lusting for greed, that brought about your departure from heaven?”

“Man understands so little. Let me tell you a story, old man, one that

I hope will shed some light on what you have come to believe from Moses and his books," Lucifer ran his long weedy fingers across the various manuscripts lining the library shelves, eyeing them as if the information he was about to share was hidden somewhere in the historical annals of their illuminated pages, "I.... We angels, I mean, all knew of the plan for creation long before it was to be carried out. For me, as well as many of my brothers, it was beyond tolerable limits to accept you beings. Was our existence not enough? Why did the Creator need to create a race of mortal beings?!" He had become excited; his body fevered by his escalating emotions. "I begged for Him to release this foul idea. No good could possibly come from this infernal design. But you know Father, He was already in love with you humans before the first breath of life left His lungs and entered yours," he motioned with his hands. "Vile creatures, I said, they will find every means to betray You, for Yours is a love they can never understand, let alone comprehend. And yet He saw fit to create you still."

"You were jealous then and wished revenge?"

"Mortal, your tiny brain cannot possibly imagine the emotion of hate, the way it would enter your world through me," he was shaking his head. "When my obvious pleading had failed to illicit my desired response and when the reality formed before me the actuality that we angels, the first of his children, would no longer satisfy His needs, I made my request of Him."

There was a deadened silence as the monk tried to visualize the events. "You directly challenged God?" The monk was noticeably shocked at the thought.

"Don't seem so amazed at this imagining Father; you have come to believe God is perfect, whence all the while He was the only tool by which perfection has ever been measured." He spat upon the floor beginning once more, "Yes. I challenged Him. What of it? He was wrong in what He was about to do, and I would not be privy to such folly."

The abbot tried to contain his contempt for the devil's blasphemous tone, suppressing the desire to wrestle him to the ground and physically cause him harm. This was certainly not characteristic of the holy man but Lucifer was no ordinary sinner. This was Sin itself seated before the monk.

The abbot noticed too, that every time Lucifer became hostile, his physical characteristics would shift, changing into the horrid beast he had seen before, and causing the monk extreme discomfort... When the devil calmed himself, he looked beautiful once more.

"I know this is difficult for you to hear, Father," Lucifer interjected. "But, imagine how it must have been for me," he put his hand on his chest. "At no time before had I desired leave from my Master's side, but His decision making had become callous, and I would have no more. I refused to play second favorite to the lesser beings He was about to create."

"You acted as though you were a spoiled child," the monk began. "If it were possible for Him to make a mistake, it existed not in the creation of man, but in exalting you to such high status."

"I have often wondered whether he regrets that decision myself, and it stands to further prove my point about his imperfections," he cleared his throat, "Could a God that created me, the devil, be without flaws?" His appearance shifted for a moment to the horned creature he had terrified the monk with earlier, and then back into his more pleasing form once more. The old man sat, unimpressed.

"Do not blame him, for the cause of you. Clearly free will existed for you as well."

"It would seem."

"So you challenged Him?"

"I did not seek to overpower Him if that is where you are going," he leaned against one of the bookshelves. "I approached Him, yes, even though He knew of my desire before my eyes met His; I would be heard. I kneeled before Him, because I loved Him," a tear welled, as his face was becoming red with anger. "I asked of Him for the power to create my own heaven, my own earth, my own beings of servitude. I wished to leave Him to his mortal creations and seek solace elsewhere, away from His merciless betrayal. I wanted my own place to reign, with beings who would love me and adore me. It was not enough for me, Lucifer, to exist in His realm, powerless to stop the madness that was about to commence. If He should desire companionship beyond that which I had so willingly given for so very long, then I shall come to need Him no more as well!" He turned from the monk, shielding his face, and its sorrowful expression.

Father Koutrakos was unsure of exactly what to say. His hands were sweating, and he tried to formulate a question; but he hadn't the words. The room had become too quiet. Was he to somehow feel sorrow for this pitiful creature? Surely not. This was a beast, the beast; he would distance his heart from any sympathy it was prone to feel. Yet, both the monk and the angel were products of the same being; and the more the old man pondered his own rationale, the more he became ambiguous as to where his duty to the sorrowful creature lay.

"Lucifer," he still could not believe this conversation was happening as the words leapt from his throat, "did you not weigh the cost of your actions, considering what price you might pay with your insolence?"

"What I am willing to admit, Father, is that I was blinded somewhat by my rage, but not of wanton desire! I, in no such fashion, wished these events to come to pass. All was beyond my control," he took a seat in the chair once more. "I have often sat perched alone atop the highest of mountains, reflecting, wondering that if my Creator had given me organs such as you humans have, would my heart stop cold, beating naught at the thought of what was to happen next."

The old man interrupted, "If you had known, would it have changed anything?"

"It is hard to say, but it is not in my nature to imagine that I would have proceeded any differently," his expression changed, becoming a bit more relaxed. "I have no regrets for my actions. Please understand that I just wish to be forgiven for them."

"Forgiveness will be manifested only in your acceptance of wrong doing, fallen one," the abbot was leaning across the table. "You bore such contempt for the creation of man that you blinded yourself to the imagery that there might have been room in God's heart to love us both in equal measure."

"You really have no understanding for how much He loves you worthless beings. There was no room left for Him to love me!"

"I think you are wrong demon and that is why you have come to this place. You must realize that this line of thinking has been your error all along. What you need to understand is that forgiveness cannot be obtained from a monk like myself who has no sympathy in your imagining man to be so vile a being."

"Why, old man, is what I say so hard to believe?" he was making room for an elaborate description. "Wars commence across the whole of this planet, even as we speak. Men kill other men for money, for land, for power, and for the color of their skin. You even go so far as to enslave one another, as if you have that right! Religious leaders fornicate with those that trust them, and further bum their fellow man in the heretical fires of this horrid age, staking their bodies to fry, as if it is their right to give and take life. You who would sit so piously on your throne of wood, blaming me for the sins of the world. When next you pass a pool of rainwater, look at the reflection while you peer into its placid shape. The image staring back is in whose heart you will find the horror and sin of this world."

The old man sat speechless for a moment. The old devil was right. "There is some truth in what you say. But even so, your vanity has led you to hell; it is, in no way, my intention to follow," the old monk coughed. Then, he cleared his throat, "I have found solace and peace having my faith in a Being I have never seen. Yet you have stared at His very face, and managed to ignore His majesty. And, for one so cunning, your actions upon this earth seem to have been unwise."

"You hasten to judge me, vilifying my actions, when you yourself know the words I speak are true," he was laughing. "Look at yourself. How long has it been- forty years- since you turned your back on the world? My little monk- so wise, so stupid. You have walled yourself in this ready- made prison, because it has become the only means with which you deal with humanity.

Why do you think I chose you? You monks are the only people who understand the place from which I have come. Face your own reality, Father, you know the only means of living a sinless existence is to remove yourself from the area most concentrated with the sin of man. In case you're confused, that would be the whole fucking world!" He was standing again, flailing about, while the old man sat staring, unable to fully understand his use of language. "Remember this, Father, that man is given free will and angels are not. I chose to take free will," his elongated fingers now clinched tightly into a fist, "It is because I have laid eyes on the Creator that I can reasonably ignore what you assume to be fair judgment. Sometimes, my pious little man, God makes mistakes."

"You will never find the forgiveness that you seek if that is what you truly believe."

Lucifer gave no immediate response, turning and scratching his chin. He thought about what had happened: his fall from grace. It had been so long ago; yet, he still was unable to persuade himself to see that the reckoning with his Creator, was a fault of his own doing. He squared his eyes with those of the humble abbot, "Am I to simply disregard what I know of my experiences, shelving my memory as you would a homeless manuscript? Forgive me. I feel that if I can impart upon you some nature of my plight, that you may be able to understand what you readily will yourself to refuse."

"You have come to believe yourself to speak of truths; your words are steeped in a bed of self-righteous indignation that has, over the passing of time, become impenetrable," the monk was cautious with his words, but direct. "I have resigned myself to helping you if that is truly what you want" (the monk not believing that it was), "but until you find within yourself the plausibility that it was, undeniably you who overstepped your bounds, I am afraid that I can be of little assistance if repentance is what you seek."

The monk trembled to himself as the tone of the fallen angel was changing in harshness, turning more sinister as each word came forth. Liquid seeped from his wrinkled brow. No turning back now, he thought. "You began your fruitless ascent to challenge God?"

"I would still question the fruitlessness of my actions, Father. I was going to win regardless. My Creator would see the erroneous decision in dismissing me, as I was now setting out to convince others like myself to rise up and rebel, striking for an independence that was so richly deserved by us all." Lucifer had a degree of pomposity about him now, but looked the part of a child more than that of a mighty angel.

Father Koutrakos started in again, "Had you come to believe God knew nothing of the approaching event?"

"What should I care? It would have changed nothing," he cleared his throat. "Once in motion, my desire took a life of its own: the first sin, I suppose. And the Creator would be powerless to stop it. I, Lucifer, had convinced many angels like myself to rise up against this wrong, forming a legion of hosts prepared to back my advances. The Creator would have to yield."

"And what of those you could not convince?"

"They were of no matter to me. The Archangel Michael had long known of my plans, since it was he who I first approached to join in our fight; but his loyalty to our Creator was greater than my ability to convince him otherwise. And incidentally, I can be rather persuasive. He listened openly to my plan for succession, but was unwavering in his decision. And so I labored myself to the task of convincing each and every angel to see things from my perspective. Why should we be slaves to a God who needed beings of another kind to satiate His unsatisfied appetites? I was doing this for the benefit of all angels, who were just as dejected as I."

The devil was tiring of this quid pro quo session with his elderly counterpart. He could never make the old monk understand his point without carrying him back to the moment in which his rebellion took shape. "Allow a digression, Monk," he began. "God chose to denounce me- me- His greatest creation," his voice escalating again. "He warned me to think no more on the matter unless I wished to bear the call of His wrath, and I was dismissed without furthering a single demand."

"So it was after this confrontation that you assailed to challenged God?" the abbot's eyes now wild.

"Not exactly," there was a sly smile turning upwards on the right side of his face. "At that point there was to be no avenue of reasoning with my Creator, so I would commence an activity of an altogether different sort, putting into motion the most vile and unimaginable of plans."

"Continue," the monk urged.

"First, clear your diminutive little brain of its preconceived notion of heaven," the devil paused as if convinced that the old man was doing just that. "Now understand this: heaven is everywhere and nowhere. You can't see it, but it is all around you, just in a different state of consciousness. It is, in this sense, beyond description. The architecture, the streets, the buildings, the libraries, they all surpass many times over the greatest offerings of your world. The colors are such as to not be described in a spectral chart your eyes could see. Beings roam freely, enveloped in love and harmony that is stronger than the relationship of a parent to a child.

There is no pain, only joy," he was beginning to smile with such fondness, as if he were standing right there. "This was where I would plant the seeds of succession, my cause to disrupt such order and balance. If I was to suffer the creation of man, then Heaven would suffer the wrath of an angel scorned."

"Can you not see that you went too far, Lucifer?"

"Not nearly so far as I would have liked, Father."

"And God allowed this thing to happen?"

"The Creator paid little attention to me, since he was busy creating a new world, and everything in it," he paused. "My importance to Him was of little concern; of that I am sure."

"From those angels who chose not to follow you, was there any intervention or any means of preventing this war?"

"Not to the point where it would have done any good. What was set in motion was what would be, the path to segregation unbroken. The only variable that concerned any of us, was the time and place of our stand."

"Then there was to be war in Heaven."

"As no war, Father, you could possibly imagine," the demon's face turned away as he moved toward the window which was still open from before. The winter wind was growing colder, as the ocean had begun to stir. A storm was readying itself to return for a second night, as the sky darkened and the clouds turned a frightening gray. Father Koutrakos watched the figure bow his head before the opening; his hands were clinched tightly behind his back. Then Lucifer turned; his soulless eyes connecting with those of the old man. It was time to talk of war. It was time to turn the confession so the demon could tell of his expulsion from the realm of heaven.

The abbot steadied his eyes upon the beast, bracing himself for the dialog Lucifer seemed more than willing to offer. With the wind howling outside the monastic dwelling, Lucifer again started to speak.........

> "The library of the average middle-class person is in ninety-nine cases out of a hundred the cruelest possible commentary on his intelligence, and, as a matter of fact, if it contains a couple of volumes worthy of the name of books, their presence is more often than not an accidental one."
>
> William Roberts

Alea Iacta Est

Sean had returned to the estate of Sir Nicholas DeBury at about six o'clock that evening.

The sleek limousine came to a stop at the front gate of the posh, London residence, Its passenger was nervously anticipating the coming meeting with DeBury. Sean's mind was heightened to a new sense of awareness, and he was approaching the introductions with a wary degree of skepticism, to say the least. There was discomfort and excitement, at the same time.

William Dodd was the first face he would see. As the little driver appeared through the tinted window, he clicked the latch and opened the door for Sean to exit.

The air was cool and crisp. Sean nodded approvingly to the driver, thanking him for the short excursion. He then began the ascent up the stone path toward the front door. Images raced through his head, concerns of what Mr. Taylor had said back at the bookstore. DeBury was dangerous and ruthless; be on guard.

There was no one standing outside the front door to greet him this time, and he was able to see something engraved into the wooden framework that hadn't caught his attention when he first arrived. It was an image maybe, no, a seal. He had seen it somewhere before, possibly in a book. Its outer image was oblong, shaped like a melon, with fine detailed engravings inset into its boundaries. In the center was the image of a bishop, holding in his left hand a scepter of some sort; his right hand was raised, making a sign with two fingers and a thumb. Behind the figure was what appeared to be a three-tiered cathedral with Christian symbols inset, the likeness he was unable to positively identify. There was gothic lettering in Latin outlining each side of the seal. The words read; DIM. ELMENSIS. EPI. S. RICHARDI. DEI. GRA. He recognized the image immediately; it was the seal of Richard de Bury. The bookseller had been right, the two DeBury's were definitely related. The plot was now beginning to thicken. Sean raised his hand to deliver a knock; but before his fist could connect with the heavy oak, the door opened to reveal Finneas Frakes awaiting him on the other side.

"I trust your outing has been an enjoyable one, Sir," he said with a classical bit of pomposity that befit his butleresque image.

"The day's been fine, Finneas. Thanks," Sean said slipping by the man in one swift hurried motion. He didn't like the way the butler's eyes moved up and down his frame every time they were in proximity to one another. He was watching for something, but Sean wasn't sure what it could be.

"Splendid Sir," the butler was now alongside of Sean. "Sir Nicholas returned home half an hour ago and said that he would meet you in the library shortly. If you would be so kind as to follow me this way. He is very anxious to meet you."

"Yeah," Sean said, "That makes two of us." The two men walked with Finneas slightly in front, down the corridor. Sean did what he could to commit to memory every item in the home as they passed. He needed to be more comfortable in his surroundings. The extravagant furniture, the original oils, the marbled busts - it was all so fascinating.

Finneas stopped just shy of the glassentine entranceway of the library, and he watched Sean's eyes light up as the Bostonian viewed the contents from the bottom floor. The library seemed to have grown from earlier that morning. The butler shifted to his left, unlocking and opening both doors, from the center. Sean made a hesitant motion, then entered the volumous chamber. The books with their century old pages seemed to call out to him from the shelves, and he wished himself to be locked inside the room forever. He knew that no matter how long he lived, he would never see a collection of such princely assemblage again. He debated on whether or not he should murder the inhabitants of the house, steal the books for himself, and live happily ever after. He then rationed that a person would never get away with such a thing, so he perished the thought immediately.

His steps were slow as his body moved across the wooden flooring towards the center of the room. A roaring fire illuminated the fireplace as Sean sidestepped the leather couches surrounding it. Something caught his attention. He had been so infused in the books earlier that he failed to notice the striking painting above the fireplace. It was both immense and fantastic; the vibrance of the oil was leaping from the canvas. The imagery was unmistakable. It was the scene of a wilderness, with two prominent figures in physical contortion, each displaying a suggestive body positioning. One was Christ, the other, Satan. He stared at the painting; it's beauty reminding him of a similar work, The Temptation, by Jacapo Tintoretto, circa the sixteenth century. It was, no doubt, an original; but it looked five - maybe six hundred years old. Impossible. If it was that old, it had to have been painted by a master; and surely its image would have shown up in a book of Italian art, somewhere.

"Exquisite, is it not?"

Sean was embarrassingly startled; his body was jumping nervously at the voice sounding behind him. He hadn't realized how entranced he had become by the painting's image. When he turned towards the direction of the voice, his eyes fell upon the person who could be none other than Sir Nicholas DeBury.

The man was noticeably younger than Sean had expected - maybe late forties, early fifties -much younger, in fact, than he had seemed on the phone. DeBury stood probably six feet tall and was encased in a tailored suit, that Sean felt certain had been delivered by Hugo Boss that very morning. His facial features were tight, his cheekbones were high, and his eyes were a dark hazel. Of hair he had very little on his head, and Sean bemused himself with the thought that DeBury's conscience had probably caused it all to fall out. His build was very slim, and his overall demeanor seemed pleasant and charming. He held his hand out like a game show host as he presented himself to Sean. The book scout was reluctant to take the man's hand. Still, he did not want to seem rude, so he embraced it with his own hand, the two men exchanging civilities. DeBury smiled, revealing to his guest years of well perfected dental work, his teeth gleaming as he spoke.

"It pleases me so that you have decided to visit our little corner of the world," DeBury said letting go of Sean's hand, "I am Nicholas DeBury."

"Please to meet you. Sean Wilde," he offered little information.

DeBury walked toward Sean, joining him in front of the fire, where both could admire the painting. He brought a hand to Sean's shoulder, making the American uncomfortable. "Truly amazing, wouldn't you agree?".

"I would be lying if l said I wasn't speechless. It's magnificent."

"Do you know the shame of it all, Sean?" he paused, but the book scout remained silent, "You and l are the only people other than my immediate family who have ever laid eyes on it."

"Why is that?"

"Do you have any idea what lengths certain ambitious individuals, if not institutions, would go in order to acquire that painting?"

"I can only imagine," he didn't know what else to say.

"That painting was done by the Sienese master, Duccio di Buoninsegna, in the twelfth century. It is as prized as any treasure in this room, which is why the world, for seven hundred years, has been blind to its existence."

"You'll have to forgive me, Sir Nicholas, but everything in this room is hard to believe," he was noticeably shocked, "If that painting is genuine, it must be worth more money than most fortune five hundred companies."

DeBury smiled approvingly. "Sean," he began, "I could pay your country's national debt with that painting," both men nodded." But tell me, what is money when compared to such priceless treasures as those in whose company we are now surrounded, "he was holding his arms outstretched, his body turning from the painting and facing Sean as he made the analogy.

Already Sean was hating himself for having so much in common with his host. Financially, of course, they were as far apart as heaven and hell; but both men knew where the real value of wealth lay, and it wasn't in some well-kept shares of stock on Wall Street. It was here, in the glorious splendor of the library that surrounded them. Floor to ceiling, the treasures represented a millennia of human existence and experience. The greatest minds left their marks on pages that stood upright, only a gesture away from the inquisitive mind. DeBury motioned for Sean to take a seat on one of the crushed leather couches. Sean obliged.

"May I pour you a drink, a glass of Scotch whiskey perhaps?" DeBury had obviously familiarized himself with his guest's preference.

"That would be great, thanks," Sean said, while watching his host move toward a silver tray which held a variety of liquors. DeBury poured the clear liquid over four cubes of ice. The Englishman then held out the drink. Sean accepted it and then positioned himself across from his guest while sinking into the other couch. "I have a rather preferential taste for Napoleon Brandy myself, but to each his own," he held the glass in the air, as if to give a mock toast, and pressed it to his lips, never taking his eyes off Sean.

"Look, Sir Nicholas, I don't mean to be rude," it wasn't as if Sean really cared. "But how about discussing why I'm here and what talent it is that you think I have that can be helpful to you?"

"Ah, blunt and to the point, very good," DeBury said. "First things first, I'm afraid," he stood and walked back to the silver tray as Sean sat wondering what was to happen next. His host reached between a bottle of Hine cognac and Chopin vodka, lifting up a sealed envelope and tossing it toward Sean. It took no amount of effort to realize what it was. Breaking the seal, Sean was greeted by the face of Benjamin Franklin many times over.

"The ten thousand dollars' cash I promised you for coming," DeBury said, "a gesture of my sincerity, and my word. If we are to partner together on this little venture, I feel that an element of trust needs to be established between us from the onset."

"Whoa!" Sean was unnerved. "Don't think this means I agree to anything; I came only to hear what it is you had to say, collect my money, and go home - I promised nothing more." He was trying to bait Sean, no doubt. But Sean Wilde trusted no one, least of all, a rich foreigner he had never met before. When he lost his father, he too lost trust in other people. This wasn't necessarily an opportune way to live; but it was the way he felt safest, owing no one anything, expecting nothing in return.

"Forgive me; I meant to imply nothing," DeBury was smiling a condescending smile. "I think when you have heard what it is I have to say, the necessity of your involvement will become compulsory."

Sean wasn't buying the sales pitch. He knew, even if half of what the old bookseller had told him was true, the most logical step was to take the money and run. Still, he had to hear out his host for the transaction to be fair; so thumbing through the pristine, neatly packed bills, he waited for the man sitting across from him to begin again.

"Sean, tell me," he looked at his feet, then stared up at Sean, his demeanor altering slightly, "Have you ever heard of a book called the Manuscripta Diabolica?"

The book scout thought for a moment and then found a faint recollection, "I've always heard of its legendary existence, but I've never seen any pictures of it or really heard it mentioned trading hands."

"Do you know of its contents?"

"Supposed to be kind of a 'Hope Diamond' of books isn't it?" Sean was remembering an article he had read in some un-recountable scientific journal, "written by Satan himself, I think, if you believe in that sort of stuff." Sean said dismayingly. "You aren't about to tell me that the service you want me to perform involves that book, are you?"

"That 'book,' as you so eloquently put it, is so much more than you could possibly imagine my friend," he poured another glass of brandy and began again. "The legend surrounding it is, of course, a mystery; but its relative value is beyond calculable figures."

"What do you know of it?" Sean asked.

"Its contents were compiled by a monk, Saint Andreas Koutrakos, who occupied the Docheiariou Monastery, on Mount Athos, Greece, in the late fifteenth century. It is taken on Orthodox authority, that he played a role of biographer to the Devil, compiling the musings of the fallen angel in a folio volume of illuminated pictures and words," he paused. "The monk scripted the words in gothic lettering, each chapter in a different language. I would assume the old man did this to make the work difficult to translate, which he succeeded in doing quite well, since there exists no full translation of the work anywhere. If any one person has deciphered the book, no one is saying what is contained on its pages. Legends vary; but it is believed that the manuscript contains predictions of future events and a history of Biblical musings that may rival the Bible itself." DeBury was allowing a moment for Sean to digest the information, and he seemed to be a little perturbed that Sean wasn't paying attention with more excitement. "What is known about the Manuscripta, is that it was guarded by the monks as if it were the Holy Grail itself, or maybe "unholy," whatever the case may be. We also know that at some point during the turn of the fifteenth century, it was smuggled off Athos. At that time, the monastery of Docheiariou was attacked and pillaged by Barbary pirates who stole many of their most sacred relics and treasures. The marauders left the commune in complete ruin and most of its inhabitants butchered. However, the details on what happened after the pirates left are what baffle historians. The pirate vessel involved in the attack washed ashore in Salonica, Turkey, some months later. Her entire crew was present, but all were dead - their remnants nothing more than skeletal entities. They bore no sign of decay, and the entire collection of artifacts that they had stolen was littered about the deck. The Manuscripta was in plain view."

"Sounds like a nice ghost story, but a little far-fetched for reality, don't you think?" "Not in the least," DeBury was not amused with Sean's quick dismissal.

"Well, you must agree that there are numerous events that could have led to the pirate vessel being in such a state. God knows the plague was ravaging Europe at the time, and hygiene aboard a vessel of that sort was prone to diseases of the worst kind." Sean noticed DeBury's agitation. And, not wanting to disrespect the man, Sean changed his outward skepticism, for the time being. "Assuming the story's got some truth behind it, what happened to it then?"

"The contents of the vessel, now in the hands of the Turkish government, were sold at an auction. The Manuscripta Diabolica found its way to an Italian book collector, Camillio Domencio, about a month later."

Sean interjected, "I don't recall ever hearing of a Camillio Domencio."

"He was a collector of some fame, from Florence I believe, and managed to procure the volume at great expense from the Turkish government. There is very little I know of Domencio, but what I can tell you of interest is that, within a short time of acquiring the book, he fell ill with a virus of unknown origin and died sometime shortly thereafter. His library had been willed to the Vatican in Rome; but due to extensive book buying debts, his remaining family had to auction off part of his collection before emissaries from the Vatican could assess the contents."

"Had there been any reason to suspect the book had been 'cursed' at that point?" Sean asked.

"It would be impossible to know for certain; but from what little I have been able to gather, I believe that the Vatican and the Greek government sought to obtain the manuscript from Domencio's holdings. Someone knew of that book's relevance, Sean; that I believe, is certain."

Sean sat more attentive now, processing the information. He still found it difficult to accept what DeBury had already taken for fact, but admitted to himself that this all was making for a hell of a story.

"It was at the auction of Domencio's library holdings that the Manuscripta Diabolica would come into my family's possession."

Sean sat with false amazement as Sir Nicholas began explaining his family relationship to Richard de Bury, and the long history of how the book collection had come to be, not realizing that Sean had heard the entire story earlier that same day. When he had finished, Sean remarked, "But Richard de Bury had been long dead by the time that book showed up in the market."

"True, of course," the Englishman replied, "but almost every generation of DeBury has continuously added to our family's prized library holdings, and it was Sir Thomas DeBury who, in fact acquired the manuscript."

"Go on," Sean persisted.

"After Sir Thomas DeBury obtained possession of the book, it was taken back to our family's estate in Paris, France, where it was carefully placed within a glass curio that housed some of our family's most prized volumes. It would remain there, safe, for the next two hundred years."

"In that amount of time," Sean started, "did anyone in the family ever try to get the book translated?"

"All the family records that I have read indicate failed attempts at a complete translation; but technology being what it is now, I believe an accurate interpretation could easily be achieved. But even without the book's translation, an interesting bit of ephemera relating to the Manuscripta has come into my family's possession within the last century. Here, I think you will find this very interesting," DeBury stood and pulled a tattered book from one of the nearby shelves and held it out for Sean. He took it, staring at its ragged condition. The book smelled of mildew and was laced with the remnants of extensive bookworm trailing. He opened it carefully, recognizing the Arabic lettering within.

"My father bought that volume you are holding from an estate sale fifty years ago. Sir Gosse Philipe, the most complete collector on material related to Piracy, sold his collection at auction," he smiled, proud of his father's acquisition. "What you have there, is a log from the vessel Tunis, the same pirate vessel that washed ashore in Salonica. The Barbary pirates were notorious, unlike other pirates, for keeping a detailed log book of their raids and expeditions. About two years ago, I was able to have the Arabic translated; and this, my friend, is the English translation of the log's last notes." Debury thrust a paper in Sean's lap, "Please, read its contents for yourself."

Sean felt at first as if the men were getting a little off base; but he had been paid well for his time, so he held the paper next to the book and began reading;

The year is 1560
Log entry, day forty

We continue daily to find the skeletal remains of our fellow crew members in various holds within our vessel. The remaining men have become mutinous. Madness abounds. Our crimes are catching up to us in ways we could have never predicted. Soon, we shall all die. It is inevitable. Allah has abandoned us. Since our last attack, our slaughter of the monks on Athos, every hour, on the hour, there is a horrifying shriek from some corner of the ship; and we scurry to find only the skeletal remains awaiting us of what had once been a member of our crew. There is no blood. There is no warning. Who shall be next? It matters not. Whatever god or demon these monks prayed to will soon have his vengeance enacted fully, as he hunts us down, one by one. Two of our crew members hurled themselves into the sea, and the sharks that have followed our vessel for days, now wait in anticipation of more meals. We have started to gather together at night, aboard the deck, awaiting the angel of death to strike. We have long since lost our course, as our instrumentation has stopped working. Hell has us; we wait for its embrace. No more. The screaming continues. Was that another? How much longer? Our suffrage is exhaustive. The remaining men tear at their own flesh, as if we have some disease or pox that can be removed by self-mutilation. Another scream! We have released a beast that is devouring us one by one. Darkness envelopes our soul. We, the floating damned.

"That is the last entry in the log," DeBury interrupted. "Something happened aboard that ship that was not of this world; and I believe, at the very least, it shows some degree of Maleficia surrounding the book."

"Look Sir Nicholas, I don't want to seem rude; but if all this rhetoric is supposed to heighten my interest, you've got the wrong guy. I deal in things I can see, not a bunch of supernatural mumbo-jumbo."

"Believe me, Sean," he was reassuring his own sanity, "I have never been one to put stock in such things as well; but you must admit, it is all rather puzzling, is it not?"

"Yeah, on that we are agreed." Sean thought for a moment then questioned, "You say your family was in possession of the book for some two hundred years. Did they ever have a problem with ownership of it?"

"None that have been recorded in any family records, it was if the book had come home, a place it had always meant to be," he looked away." If only it had lasted."

"Why, what do you mean? What happened to it?" Sean inquired.

"The fucking French Revolution, that's what," DeBury noted with disgust, standing and walking toward the silver serving cart, pouring himself another drink.

"How could a revolution in France affect your ownership of the Manuscripta?"

DeBury pulled the fat, stocky glass from his lips, and grinned, "What you must first understand, Sean, is that my family's complete collection of books is not kept in a central location. We have, for obvious reasons like war, natural disasters, fire, theft, and so on, been very protective of our varied acquisitions. We have lessened the risk of compromising harm that could possibly befall all the volumes, by purchasing homes in various locales around Europe, and stocking parts of the collection in each. Even now, what you see in this room only represents a quarter of our holdings."

Sean was astonished at the thought, but it made perfect sense.

"Even if something happens in one area where the books are housed, it leaves the family, notably me, with the task of replacing only the volumes lost or damaged, not every book, which would be impossible," DeBury stated.

"So the Manuscripta Diabolica was being housed in France at the time of the Revolution?"

"Paris, to be more precise, but yes, it was," DeBury sat his glass on the coffee table between them. "There had been no time for my family to properly react to the peasant uprising, so my ancestor James DeBury fled, narrowly escaping Madame de Guillotine. About a thousand rare books became the property of one Napoleon Bonaparte, as our family's estate fell to the new monarchy."

"And the Manuscripta was among them," Sean finished.

"Indeed," he coughed, "but there is still much more. "He cleared his throat and began:

"Shortly after Emperor Napoleon acquired my family's library, the book mysteriously disappeared from the monarch's possession, by what circumstances I've no idea; but the book showed up at a very famous auction in England, the great Roxburghe Sale, in the summer of 1812. The individual who placed the book for sale was able to obtain complete anonymity, so I have no idea who sold it or why it was being sold. The bidding for the volume became feverish as the 2nd Earl Spencer, the Marquess of Blandford, and my ancestor, James DeBury, all vied for a chance at ownership. You have to understand that at this time in history, all English noblemen were amassing great libraries due to the fashionable importance being placed on the individual amassment of rare works. Prices for rare books had never reached such phenomenal heights, and the amount obtained for each book coming to auction was astronomical indeed."

"So, did James DeBury get the Manuscripta back?" Sean asked, his interest peeked.

"After intensive bidding, he ousted the two nobleman, and brought the book back here, to London, where it would stay for seventy more years."

"Where did it go then?"

"Every so often, a select quantity of truly priceless books gets moved to whatever house the present living DeBury is occupying, and in the spring of 1882, the Manuscripta Diabolica was carried to a small estate in the West German town of Mainz."

Sean spoke up, "Of course, the city Gutenberg pressed the first printed Bible."

"Exactly," DeBury acknowledged, and then continued. "It resided there with little problem until Adolph Hitler came to power in the late 1930's. As I'm sure you are aware, there were massive book burnings all over Germany as Hitler tried to turn his nation's people into zombified constituents. And, as you may already be guessing, the Nazi party seized my family's assets, books included."

"This is just too incredible to believe," Sean interjected.

"Just wait," DeBury was hinting at more. "As my Grandfather watched in horror, the Nazis burned his most prized possessions, books of incalculable value today; and when he foolishly tried to protect them, he was shot and killed. My grandmother hastily fled the country with my father in tow, and the Manuscript a was thought to have perished in the pyre of burning paper. Oddly enough, the volume survived and was found among Adolph Hitler's possessions only a few yards from his dead body, when U.S. troops stormed his bunker towards the end of World War II. A legend is told in the town of Mainz, that a local butcher watched as repeated attempts were made by the SS soldiers to burn the book. They consistently endeavored to place it in the bond fire which rendered no damage whatsoever to the book, or its pages."

"Now that's getting out there a bit, don't you think Sir Nicholas?" Sean scoffed. "Of course, it was only legend, as I say," he motioned a hand toward the burl inlaid humidor sitting on the coffee table between them. He pulled out a Bolivar double corona, and offered Sean a cigar as well. Accepting the stick of divine Cuban craftsmanship, the two men cut and lit their cigars, enjoying the feeling of brotherhood that the shared experience was creating between them. They were incredibly different people, but if their fortunes and opportunities were separated, their shared passions would not be at all that uncommon.

"So what became of the book after the army's confiscation?" Sean took a long draw from the tobacco releasing circling smoke about his head.

"The Manuscripta Diabolica was brought back to your country and placed in the Smithsonian Institution, where it resides at this very moment," DeBury eyed Sean between the columns of smoke. The room was much quieter as night had come to London, and the two men sat reclined in their leather upholstery, snug in conversation before the fire.

Something was still puzzling Sean, and pulling the cigar from his mouth, he questioned DeBury further, "Do you know if anyone has ever made a full translation of the book's contents?"

"That again, is the great mystery surrounding it," DeBury stated. "No surviving copy of its contents survives in public domain, that I am aware of. And because so much of that book's history is steeped in legend and lore, only the current owner would know of its language for sure."

"Your family never made an attempt at transcribing the work either of times it was in your family's possession?"

"I believe there probably were attempts made, Sean, but anything of relevance has disappeared with that book."

"Enter, Sean Wilde. Let me guess, you mean to have it back," Sean joked half heartily.

"At any price, Mr. Wilde, at any price," DeBury's facial composure had changed, growing harder now. Before, his demeanor had been reserved, maybe even relaxed. He was now noticeably uneasy, commanding an air of immediate seriousness and resolve. Sean was catching a glimpse of where the man's fierce reputation had come from.

"My God, you're serious!" Sean said becoming increasingly uncomfortable.

"Oh, I am deadly serious Sean," he responded directly.

"Just what the hell is your intent?"

"I mean to steal it back!"

"What?!" Sean stammered to his feet. "You plan to break into the Smithsonian Institution? Are you out of your fucking mind?!"

"Let me assure you, my American friend, that I am quite sane. I have, over the last few years, made numerous attempts to show both my family's original records of purchase for the volume, and proof of its theft, both during the French Revolution and the rise of Nazi Germany. But neither your government nor representatives from the Smithsonian will give me the time of day," he was sweating. "That book belongs in my family's library, since we have paid for it twice. And, I will have it back."

"This is just ludicrous," Sean began, "You are whacked in the head if you think I'm, in any way going to be involved in some 'Brink's Job' on the fucking Smithsonian Institution. What the hell are you thinking?"

"Everything has been well planned, let me assure you; and your safety is guaranteed."

"Excuse me?"

"I would have no need of you, except for the fact that neither my family nor I can, in anyway, be linked to this venturous undertaking; and I have taken great precautions to ensure that things stay that way. Secondly, I have in place all the necessary people needed to make this venture work. You, my friend, are the last piece of the puzzle."

"Listen, I've got no experience stealing milk from a grocery store, much less some priceless antiquity from one of the most heavily guarded museums in the world." he paused. "So thank you for the ten grand; be seein' you on the evening news." Sean started to walk away from the sitting area when DeBury called back.

"Please sit down, Mr. Wilde," he said noticeably irritated by Sean's over all lack of enthusiasm. "At no point is it in my design for you to steal anything. I have in place already a team of expert thieves who do this sort of thing and who are awaiting my signal to proceed."

"Well, you can call and tell them to get started, 'cause they'll be doing it with one less book scout. Besides, if you don't need my help stealing the book, what possible benefit could I add to this insane idea of yours?"

"Please calm yourself," DeBury insisted, "These extreme measures were not decided upon yesterday, I can assure you. Like many priceless relics contained within the museum, exact replicas of the book have been created to thwart any criminal element that might be willing to take a risk in stealing the book."

"Like you," Sean cut in.

DeBury ignored the rudeness of his guest. "Copies of the Manuscripta Diabolica have been re-created with the most extreme detailing, such that the original copy may or may not be on display at any given time. The manuscript itself is switched daily. What I need is your skill at identification, something I believe book scouts possess in greater need that book sellers. I have a team of experts, as I said, that will get you in, I need you to identify correct volume from the other fake editions."

"Let's put aside all rational thought for a moment and assume I would be willing to identify the manuscript. Why couldn't I perform the task after the book is stolen?"

"Inventory is done daily," DeBury began, "The fake manuscripts must be left on site, in order to buy the appropriate time necessary to fool the institution and distance myself from any wandering eyes that might look my way. I have commissioned one of London's leading bookbinder's to create a facsimile of the Manuscripta, so that it may be switched for the real volume, keeping the book count the same when we lift the original. By the time the Smithsonian realizes the true manuscript is missing - and be rest assured they will - the book will have long been in my possession, a continent away; and they will be unable to prove anything."

"You seem remarkably sure of yourself," Sean added.

"I have not patterned a life immersed in failure of any sort, Sean; and I will set the plan in motion for my family to take possession of the book once more."

"I've no doubt that you will, Sir Nicholas; but for me at least - well, as I said before - I'll be watching the evening news. Hope your successful." Sean was refusing while trying to joke at the same time. This man would have that book at any price, it was certain; and, that it might cost Sean his life or well-being seemed of little concern. As Sean sought to dismiss him completely, DeBury spoke once more.

"The job pays two million dollars. I will give you one million up front, in the bank of your choosing. Then one million upon completion, when the

Manuscripta Diabolica is in my hands. All I want you to do is be my eyes, and validate the authenticity of the real book. It is that simple."

Sean returned a fevered response, trying not to allow himself the time to imagine how much money he was being offered. "There isn't a damn thing simple about any of this! Think of what it is you want me to do. Granted, Sir Nicholas, I don't have a lot of material assets to feel.

"First, I disdain murder; it is unnecessary. Secondly, at such time as the mission is completed, your involvement and your new-found wealth should keep you quiet because, at that time, you will have much to lose, I don't see the need for fear or repercussion on your part."

"I've got no real choice, then?"

"In life, Mr. Wilde, everyone has a choice," he stepped back, walking toward the other side of the room. "More whiskey?"

"Go to hell."

DeBury chose not to respond, and Sean stood there in the library, dumbfounded as to how to get away from the mess he had so reasoned himself into. He was a dead man either way he looked at it. He knew DeBury had no intention of keeping him alive beyond the use of his talents. His life was marked; it was just a matter of time and circumstance. Why the hell did I ever get on the plane? But the answer was always the same: money. It made people do stupid things and Sean could now go to the head of the class. The game had begun, whether he liked it or not. The only remaining question was how well a street - smart book scout could handle himself at the poker table with the high stakes gamblers. He would soon have his answer.

"1 know this is pointless to ask now, but 'why me, of all people?' "

"I need someone who is as desperate for cash as I am for regaining the Manuscripta Diabolica. I also need someone who can fade in and out of the public eye without drawing much attention to himself; you fit my needs," DeBury began to pace about the library. "I have learned through many book dealers, both on this coast and your coast, that you are one of the most knowledgeable outsiders at identifying dated material, even though you have failed miserably at putting that skill to any real beneficiary use. So this is where we are now. I will make your financial woes disappear forever; just lay your hands on that book."

At this point, it was pointless for Sean to be resistant; all he could do was play along. DeBury could have been bluffing, but then he held all the cards. Sean would have to play on a level he wasn't wholly prepared to venture into. What he had to believe was that there was a dangerous assassin who would surely take his life as soon as the mission was complete. It was time to press for more details.

"Where do we go from here?"

"Glad you asked," DeBury pulled out a file lying haphazardly on the couch where he had been sitting and thrust its contents toward Sean. "The picture you see just inside the file there was taken ten years ago of the Italian thief, Vincent Conducci, known to Interpol and the F.B.I. as 'the ghost', or Il Fantasma. He got the title because he has never been seen or caught by any law enforcement agency that has tried to apprehend him. The picture you are holding represents the only known photograph of the man, as he is supposed to be the greatest living thief. Il Fantasma has managed to steal priceless works of art from the most impenetrable galleries, and he has stolen many famous jewels from kings and statesmen alike. He is the best at what he does, bar none; and his services have cost me a small fortune."

"If he's so secretive, how did you meet him?"

"Oh, I haven't met or seen the man; he doesn't conduct business that way," DeBury quipped. "Vincent Conducci has a liaison, an individual who handles all arrangements concerning his business affairs. This liaison happens to be non-other than his sister, Cecilia Conducci, who runs an art lover's book shop in Venice, Italy.

"How convenient," Sean snapped.

"Indeed."

"So what happens next?" Sean inquired.

"Tomorrow morning, I have made arrangements for you to board a plane bound for Venice, arriving at the airport Treviso, around noon. Mr. Dodd will see you off, preparing you with the necessary hotel information and a map of the city. There will be specific instructions detailing the whereabouts of Cecilia's bookstore and the way in which she should be approached. I would imagine there will be some measure of security through which you would pass before meeting with Il Fantasma. I am sorry, but I have no idea what to expect beyond that. Whatever details surround the procurement of my book lie in the hands of Vincent Conducci and his team of thieves."

"What about this nut case who'll be following me?"

"Please put Mr. Carbuoni out of your mind; he is there to help you should a crisis occur, nothing more." DeBury failed at his attempt for reassurance. "Focus on the job you are there to. perform, that need be your only concern. And let me say again, when the manuscript is in my hands, your money issues and our relationship will be absolved."

Sean hated the way DeBury was insinuating his demise, but best to play along. "As you've left me little choice, I guess the game begins tomorrow."

"Tomorrow then," DeBury paused as the two men stood, both eyeing each other with a defying stare. "My Chef has prepared a wonderful dinner of southern French cuisine, Daube de boeuf along with some delicious pastries; won't you join me for dinner, and we can put this business behind us for the evening and talk of books and men. I'm sure you have many more questions to ask."

Sean thought rationally for a moment, keeping his anger, if not his tongue, in check, "I'm famished more than I'm hating you at the moment, so dinner it is."

"Splendid," DeBury said while ushering Sean from the library, "I'll tell Francois to set the table for two this evening. Feel free to wash up or mull around the library for a bit; we'll dine within the hour."

The two men parted company; Sean returned to his room upstairs and lay on the soft surface of the bed. A small television was airing the local news, as he could hear a broadcaster for the B.B.C. reporting the day's events from the small mechanical box near his bed. He stared at the ceiling, the same way he had done just a day ago in Boston, thinking then how bad things were, realizing now how worse they'd gotten. There was nothing to do but wait and see what would happen when he got to Venice. There, the game would take shape. He felt so unprepared, so uneasy. But like it or not, the bastard down stairs had cast the first die. It would be up to Sean to call the marker. If he failed, he was a dead man. Dinner would be soon.

Sean Wilde pulled his weary frame from the bed's surface and started for the shower, cursing his stupidity under his breath. He would throw on a change of clothing and dine with a man he found fascinating and deplorable at the same time. Tomorrow, it would begin. His clothes hit the floor as he stepped into the stall. Tomorrow.

As the warm water within the shower struck Sean's body, his ears were deafened to the news report coming through on the bedroom television.

Apparently, there had been a burglary or break in, in one of the rare book stores at 83 Charring Cross Road. The victim, one elderly man in his late sixties, an Anthony Taylor, had been found stabbed repeatedly in the back room of his small business. No witnesses were coming forth at this time, more to come in a moment....

"Don't go lookin' for snakes you might find them
Don't set your eyes to the sun you might blind them
Haven't I seen you here before, no there aint no heroes here."

Metallica

A New Dawn

"Before my arcane fellowship of angels I radiated confidence, now dauntless towards the task ahead. I, Lucifer, strongest of those assembled around me, now stood proud. We who had been afflicted with the offense of being cast aside," the unnamable said, his arms outstretched. "Objects of neglect and malcontent now epitomized resolve, strength, and fortitude. Our legion had grown incomprehensibly deep. We who were once servants would be subjected to rule no longer! I would bring forth new order to the realm you call Heaven, and I would do so by whatever means necessary," Lucifer said shuffling away from the leaded window. "I centered myself within the angelic amassment and bid council with my Creator, challenging Him and any who chose to stand by His side." The fallen angel was now looking at the monk intently, such that the old man could see his own mirrored reflection in the demon's soulless eyes. He had never heard one speak so boldly and without concern for the words being said.

For the elder monk, time had come to a relative standstill. Each moment that followed became lost to a haze of disbelief, bewilderment, and the simplistic challenge to maintain a semblance of sanity. Time spent with the monster, this aberration of Heaven and of nature itself, had seen fit to lay waste another day. Darkness in the accompaniment of night filled the image framed within the library's window.

Would the other monks residing within the monastic domicile be concerned with his absence from their communal routine? It was doubtful. Often enough, he, as well as his fellow brothers, could spend days within their cells fasting and praying. This was the life for a man on Athos. This was the life of a man beholden to God. The monk's presence was unlikely to be missed for some time.

But what of that time? Could he convince or even convey a meeting such as he was a part of presently, to his fellow monks? Was his credibility of such stature that a meeting of this magnitude, this abhorrence, should be believed? Thoughts such as these, the old man decided, had little relevance now. He was in the company of a being he now trusted to be Satan himself. He was in attendance of evil incarnate.

The abbot, returning a stare as direct as the one Lucifer was meeting him with, delivered a questioning response, "You in some way believed there to be a chance you might succeed?" There was not a moment's pause, for the fiend answered at once.

"Of course not," Lucifer stated matter-of-factly, shocking the monk with the response.

"I do not under-"

"Allow me cause for explanation, old man," the demon interrupted, turning his back to the monk and cupping his pale, weedy fingers behind his back, "Regardless of the intellect you humans assume me to possess, my standing - my wile - as it shall now be stated, in no way lies within a reckless need for wanton destruction. I always serve the greater plan, yes, some greater purpose. I have fastened temptation to an art form. I achieve my desired result by laying a path that causes the greatest amount of destruction. My methods, like that of a sharpened blade, cut in many different ways, dear Father - so many in fact, that to dance with me one will feel a sting in varying degrees on so many different levels. And so it was, that for challenging my Creator, I would craft dissension in the words I spoke to my brethren." The devil turned as a small, sharpened protrusion appeared at each temporal lobe.

"Ah, demon," the monk began, "You speak in tones unfamiliar. You ramble on with riddles. I understand nothing of what you say."

"You will," Lucifer implied, continuing. "I, so enraged with a hate unfathomable to one like yourself, never lost sight while lying within the reality of my situation. Embittered? Yes. But even with contemptible thoughts presiding over the genesis of my future scheme, never, not for even a moment, would I lose sight of one fact: there could be no hope of winning a direct challenge with our Creator. I was angered with empirical rage, but I was no fool. A damning pity that those who stood by me did not realize this."

"Then how should you find cause to challenge God at all?"

Lucifer began a solemn walk about the room. A clapping resounded quietly from where his hooves met with the floor. The old man froze, watching as the devil cast his profiled image, a shadowed figure complete with horns, onto the stone wall just beyond the flickering candle. "My overwhelming desire was to distance myself from Him who was my Creator. As an angel of light, this was not within my power to grant. I wanted freedom, but I did not wish to be alone either, a difficult position to be sure. I felt if I should stay the course I had interred myself then it might be in my personal interest to take as many beings with me as possible. This is an insight to my character that still presides within my daily war against all mankind. So there it was. I would make my stand, I would invariably lose, and in the worst event, I would be destroyed. But," Lucifer smiled holding up a pale, elongated digit, "I might also be banished, along with a host of my angelic brethren, enabling me to hurt Him in equal measure."

"You are a damnable being," Father Koutrakos muttered, turning his eyes from the beast and casting them to the floor.

"Scorned, I find to be the better of the two words," he said, taking personal comfort in the monk's unease and relative discomfort. Lucifer smiled as the old man looked up, staring at his demonic form. "It had not been an easy task, let me assure you. For all my pressured urging, I was amazed at the number of angels who resisted my call to arms."

"It is a difficult picture you paint. How shall I imagine the father of all life allowing you the freedom that would necessitate a rebellion such as the one you now speak of?" The monk grappled to his feet, and his robe rolled down to his waist, exposing his aged frame, "One only has to believe there to have been some divine cause necessitating your departure from heaven, yes, let us believe it more His will than your wile, demon, that would set out such a damnable course."

Lucifer arched his back, flipping a hand in the air as if to swat an imaginary fly, "I have spent little effort or time rationing the reasons for any act the Creator commits. You humans, your soon - to - be existence, that was enough to validate my actions. My Creator was without the ability to reason. Such obviousness abiding, what was I to do? I was the most powerful angel in Heaven! I was not some whipping boy! Some being to be looked upon lightly!

How was I to tolerate an existence of mediocrity and shame, always playing the part of servant to the better- loved human? Tell me, Father, should a wife cook supper for her husband and his mistress? I think not. At the time of this reckoning, there simply did not exist the quantitative room for us both. One would have to go."

"And that was to be you."

"Or, Father, the human."

Father Koutrakos' eyes moved from the angel, his gaze falling upon the pictured iconography hanging from the library walls. There were so many varying images. Everyone depicting some biblical scene from the imagination of its creator. He looked to find a painting of Heaven, or perchance an illustration of those beings which lived within the realm. The old monk wanted help. He needed an image for his mind to embrace. Such imaginings were hard. The literal digestion of Lucifer's words painted a blurred picture of what the civil war in Heaven must have looked like. He mused for a space of time, but his thoughts and the images they produced, gave him no comfort.

"Father," the demon whispered, his tone calming now and reassuring, "Allow me to expunge your obvious confusion." Lucifer caught the old man in his stare and motioned with a new and excited fervor, "On a day of little matter, in a time and age I have long since forgotten, in a realm I no longer occupy, myself, and a legion of beings like myself, stormed to the throne of our Creator. We were armed with weapons and we were armed with our tongues. I spoke for our legion, demanding that the Creator banish all thoughts and ideas pertaining to the creation of man, or we, who numbered many, would incite upon the kingdom a Holy War as a means to preserve the old ways. Our ways."

"You were to make God submit to you?"

"It was, of course, the design of my plan. But as I have confessed to you, I was more than aware of its doomed origin before the first call to arms was uttered."

"Then war commenced?"

"As I told you earlier, I was branded a fool and offered forgiveness if l yielded my desires and accepted my place within the realm of my fellow angelic hosts. This, however, was now an absurdity in my eyes, and it was nearing time for action." He moved forward taking a seat in front of the abbot once more. "I called out, denouncing my Creator, responding with words alluding to the fact that I would spend a thousand lifetimes of existence if only to see the downfall of his new creation and the final demise of man's existence. But alas, Father, words are quickly vanquished by one's actions, and my action was to evoke war."

The old man allowed his mind the creative freedom to wander. He still found though images of God, of the devil, and of war in heaven, difficult to surmise. "My mind is without the ability to imagine... "

"A state of ignorance you should well embrace, my penitent one." Lucifer stated, crossing his legs with an air of haughtiness. "I will admit to you now, even as the words leapt from my throat I was unaware of what to expect. I, at the point of which I speak, can say I had never seen my Creator riled to anger. There had never been cause to even lift a hand or bear arms against a fellow being, and if honesty should lace the very words that spring from my lips presently, there was a further unknown: What should we expect from battle? There existed no death. No pain. Not any that had been made known to us, anyway. There was not a single being present that was not in some way confused by what outcome should befall us. None of course, but our Creator."

The monk engaged his mind in a mental schematic of two angelic masses facing one another, but with little understanding of what conclusions to draw. His mind drifted to a past he had resigned himself to forget. Constantinople. This figurativeness enlivened his thoughts with blood - soaked battle cries, and the horrid imagery of men slaying men. Was this what transpired in Heaven? "The impression you paint is void of personalities, merely an outline of shapes and images. I hasten to imagine the thoughts impressed in the minds of those angels who were assembled for war."

Lucifer stood from his seated position, spreading his arms wide, and becoming visually descriptive with his story. "There was no defining moment in which our battle commenced," he grumbled, "The Creator continued to ignore me. Me! In the flickering of an instant," the devil said, snapping his fingers, "an amassing horde of angelic beings took flight, their assemblage frightening to behold. Then at once, another convocation of angels took to the air! Before a word could come forth, the two armies embroiled in the most hideous display of aggression to be imagined. Bodies were strewn upon bodies. The skies of heaven became dark and thunderous as angels engaged in a loathsome thrashing of one another. I was taken aback at the scene before me - who could imagine angels, beings whose only purpose was to love and honor their Creator, evoking such frightening devilment upon one another? It was extraordinary to behold. With such a commitment to destroy one another, we had all forgotten to ruminate on how the Creator might respond."

"Why do you believe God allowed this thing to ensue? Why did he not stop you?"

"How should I know the answer to such a question? Oh, in some way I've no doubt my little war may have been part of some larger plan, but I am afraid I am without the liberty to say." He was now looking away from the old man, "And no matter what you are inclined to believe, and no matter how well prepared I was for knowing that some terrible judgment was soon to befall us all, it is still awe - inspiring to see the Creator riled to the point of real anger. You think I can be scary," he smiled, teasing the old man with his monstrous appearance.

"So the battle commenced... and then?"

"Shaking the entire realm, yes. Angels flowed in what seemed to be a never-ending pattern from all visible stations, clashing in unmerciful aggression. Each clawing, scratching, hitting, and trying in some way to bring about defeat of the other. It seemed as if 'Lucifer' had created a new emotion, that of hate, and brought it to the realm of Heaven."

"You speak with fondness of deeds past," the monk interrupted, "yet you profess to have sought council with me seeking penance. Help me understand." The abbot's eyebrows were arched, his forehead wrinkled.

"It is believed by your kind that I failed in my holy war. That in some way I lost the battle and was banished. This is not so." the devil began shaking his grotesque finger, "I could never have left Heaven without causing some revolt or some magnanimous upheaval. My Creator would have never allowed it. Pride had nothing to do with the war. Hate for the species to come, the human being, caused the upheaval," the fallen angel remarked. "So to be free of Him, to be free of you, I proceeded forth with my personal revolution. I did what was necessary, even though I would gladly have relinquished the task if only the idea of you beings was abandoned." The demon paused, dropping his hand to his side. He was quick to begin speaking, not allowing the old man the opportunity to interject a single thought. "The battle continued for some time, the length of which it is hard to recollect. I do remember that the tumultuous cacophony of wailing and crying did not continue long before the Creator became involved." He watched with intentful stare as the monk held on to every word that he said. "A burst of light and a thunderous explosion, the like to which you could never imagine, ended the sound of battle. The hoard of angels descended rapidly from the sky. They were trembling, each and every one on both sides, as the fighting came at once to an end. I had been locked into battle with the angel you call Michael, always having wished to test my superiority over him. Blows were thrust as we showed one another no quarter of mercy, rolling about, ripping at our angelic flesh, unknowing what to expect. Could I kill him? Could he kill me? What would exist in our consciousness if one could render the other motionless? We would find out soon, I surmised. I pinned the angel under my body raising my fist in the air, focusing all my energy into such a calculated blow that Michael, who had refused to side with me, should have found himself erased from the heavens and all memory by my hand. But as I said, the Creator appeared," he said, shaking his head.

The monk tried to hide the smile that had already started to appear.

There was to be some justice in the devil's story yet. It wasn't the lurid tale of battle the old monk wanted an account of, it was the reckoning that was soon to follow. Before he could ask a question, Lucifer entered the throws of more articulated conversation.

"Even I trembled as He approached, Father," he stated. "This thing that I had birthed, this rebellion, was about to come to an abrupt ending." He left his seat, spreading his wings, which now appeared to leap from his back. The demon seemed more hideous now than ever before. He could see that he was unnerving the monk, and that fact elated him greatly. He turned, eyes glowing red, and gave in animated detail a flowing tale of what event transpired next. "''Ah, my Creator was enraged! He and I could now relate as He could now have some understanding of how I had felt! Betrayed was I! Cast aside! Was the human worth such a trial as we were all now experiencing? I began to speak, turning my attention from Michael, who lay beneath me shielding his eyes. But, I found I could do nothing of the sort. A cloud of fog was enveloping me, the wind from the direction of my Creator causing my body to shake uncontrollably. I was unaware, in that moment, of anyone but Him."

"You were not afraid?"

"I was petrified," the demon responded. "His eyes were like the glowing fires that beset your vanquished city of Constantinople. They carved holes in my heart, piercing my very being. I loved Him. I hated Him. It is often one being sees need to hurt another, regardless of love or loyalty. So I cried, 'Is this what you would drive a son of Heaven to? The human cannot be worthy of such!' I had begun pleading my case for what would be the last time."

The monk was feeling a flood of emotions. He was shivering from fear, yet was racked with desire to know more, and he was consumed by the image of the beast before him. Sweat fell from his head. He was cold for a moment, then at once, hot. He wished his heart to slow to a more normal level but it showed no sign of regulating a pattern that brought him any comfort. He was embracing all manner of discomfort as the demon shortened the distance between them, drawing close to the monk. The stench was unbearable, the sight unfathomable. Then, Lucifer moved his lips.

"My body, through no will that I had commanded, arched forward and lifted off the floor of Heaven. I was now suspended in the air, encircled by a cloud of smoke. My limbs were frozen. I was void of power and void of will. I could see below, Michael trembling to his feet and quickly taking leave of the place I was now bound. Even my mouth fell silent. I could no longer speak, no longer reason. I was at the mercy of the being I had dared to defy. I was slave, He my master. My oppressor then set about quelling the business which I had so decidedly began. Those angels who defended His honor were allowed their leave, but those who had followed me, even though they tried to flee as well, were rendered motionless. Then, when at the point He was satisfied all was calm, He turned to me, addressing my former questions. 'You are not a son of Heaven!' He said to me with a cold stare that soured every vessel that led to my angelic heart. I braced myself for the worst, but was shocked as He turned from me and faced the frightened legion of angels gathered motionless by His suppression. They too, were awaiting judgment."

"Did you feel remorse for what you must have suspected would happen to your brethren?" the monk stated as if to seek a hint of forgiveness in the fallen angel's tome.

Lucifer drew back from his trembling counterpart. "What care I for them? They were a means to an end. I had shown them their right to choose, the gift of free will. The fate of the angels that followed me into battle, whatever it was to be, was the product of a decision each had chosen to make. This is true even now with the human existence. The secret to my power runs an equal course to the decision-making ability of humankind, never mistake that. How dare you should imply that their fate was in any way my fault. I was responsible for my actions, but that was all."

"You are most cruel, Lucifer."

"So it has been said."

"You not only cursed yourself, but damned an unwitting legion of your brethren as well."

"That is certainly one way of viewing it, Father," he chuckled. "But I see the undertaking as a form of liberation, of freedom." He held is arms upward, his demented form grotesquely in full view. "You should have seen the sheer terror on each of their faces as they awaited judgment." Lucifer further deepened his degree of animation, looking down again.

"Picture, Father, my heavenly form, frozen and poised above the chaos and calamity below, watching as the Creator motioned with His arms as the heavens parted," he paused, enacting the role of God. The monk noticed that in the display, Lucifer was levitating three feet above the stone floor. The abbot saw an alarming beauty in the muscular grotesqueness radiating from the demon's form. "My angelic brethren trembled as the floor of heaven seemed to open, the putrid stench of sulfuric decay and smoke rising from beneath them. Those who had defended the Creator could be seen nowhere, and this was to their advantage. For who would willingly bear witness to the horror awaiting the rebel forces? Oh, the lamentations of those who were left were many and sonorous. Each angel tried to resist, to flee, to find any means of shelter from the wrath that was soon to befall them. But they were not allowed the right of departure. And then, realizing that something horrid was to take place, I did find a moment's feeling of sorrow for them. They had no idea what to expect. But I did. Or at the very least had some imagining. I wished at once to shield my eyes, but found that the Creator would not allow me the pleasure. He wished me to see the fate that was upon their heads."

Lucifer dropped to the floor of the room, acting out the expressions of the fallen legion as he further delved into the tale. "The one whom you call 'God' towered above those beings who crouched in fear before Him. Their terror was apexed only by the fury of my Creator's voice. There was no room for forgiveness or mercy, though all cried and begged for it. It was as if they had forgotten what they had been fighting for. And rightly so, for none of it mattered now. Then came a thunderous sounding, more akin to a roar than to actual speech. The words resounded on every plateau in His realm. 'Those who were once my glorious children,' He began, 'Turned from me now, from Him who loved you most, who breathed thy very existence into being, stand in my presence no longer! Forever take with you thy memories of what each had and what each shall have no longer. I renounce thy very being. Just as thy mind was led so easily away, just as you renounced me with such foolish endeavors, I shall be suffered naught to look upon you further. What were once angels, be ye no more!' Then, the being who authored their very existence called forth the legion of angels who had dissipated earlier, and demanded they attend His sentencing. Oh, and to be sure, it was a wretched sight! Those who had sought to defend our attack now gathered around those who crouched, shaking, and scared. Judgment was soon to pass." He paused to make sure the monk was of full attention, then redirected himself.

"Next, the floor of Heaven opened and all were aghast as those angels who had defied their Creator clamored foolishly to one another, just as a suckling babe to its mother. Then, they began to fall from view, one by one, into the gaping pit of horrors below. 'Look not upon thy brethren with pity, 'the Creator commanded, 'For they are your brethren no more. What were once angels of light, now before you, exist hither only demons of darkness. What home they once called Heaven, forever now make thy new home Hell. Remember this day, yet remember these beings nevermore. 'When the speech ended I watched each angel try with futility to cling to anything within the only realm each had ever known. But all hope for them was truly lost. I watched as they tumbled from sight, their incessant screaming and wailing revealing to me the expectant horrors I was certain awaited each below." Lucifer looked away as if the memory were now reality. "I remember the last angel I saw, whose name in your tongue would be 'Astormecht,' as he looked at me with the most sorrowful expression I have ever seen. He looked worse than even a begging child who has not had food in weeks. A tear, which to that point I had never seen, rolled from his eye as his immortal fingers dug about the floor of Heaven, his torso now being swallowed in the cavernous maw of hell below. He saw in my eyes a glimmer of sorrow, yet realized I was without remorse. Then, he too was no more, sliding from my gaze." The devil stood, shoulders hunched, seemingly exhausted from the narration.

The monk sat cupping his hands and fidgeting. He too, was exhausted by the tale. How horrible were the images described, how loathsome the tale. The temptation to believe what had been told to him was filling the monk with dread. He must remember that everything he was being told could easily be a lie. If this was the devil, yes, if this was indeed Lucifer, he could in no way allow himself to lose grasp of this fact. It was to be remembered that Hell was littered with souls who had thought differently.

The old man, his brow heavy with discontent, raised his head to meet the eyes of the demon once more, but found his intruder to be looking away, his thoughts obviously distant. This would make it easier for him to express himself. "What then for you, devil," he began, "What of your fate?"

Lucifer recomposed himself, seeming to snap out of the temporary haze he had allowed himself to wander into. "It happened," he said, giving the abbot a cold and calculated stare, "that my Creator turned to me, releasing both my tongue and my imaginary bondage. My body collapsed upon the floor of Heaven, as I ached from both the mental and physical anguish that I had just experienced."

"You felt pain?"

"For the first time, yes. I was exhausted, but I still managed to pull myself up, realizing that I was now in control of my body once more." The demon took a pause then continued, "He who you call 'God' said nothing. Neither myself, nor my Creator could find words to express our feelings. I was unable to say anything that might defend my actions. This was, after all, what I had wanted all along. But I tell you with patent sincerity that, at the very moment of which I speak, I became unsure. Had I been too quick to judge the designer who breathed my existence into being? I at once sought council with feelings I had buried, hoping to somehow diminish. I was now void of the confidence that had risen about me earlier. I knew it was well past the time to think such thoughts. Regret being what it is, I could do nothing but wait. My rationing had indeed been premature, but what was to be would be. I readied myself for judgment."

"You were then cast from Heaven?"

"That was just it," Lucifer shrugged, "nothing happened." The demon had now taken a seat and redirected his thoughts, crossing his legs, "My Creator chose to say nothing, turning from me in a cold manner, much the way you did when I first entered this monastery. Oh, I was aghast, expecting in some way to be obliterated, cast out, or destroyed. But nothing was happening. The time in which the silence lasted, I cannot remember. I do, however, remember motioning my battered body forward toward Him who created me. I was unaware of what to say, what He might say. But I was content to reach for Him and ensue some degree of dialog that might free me from my surmounting guilt. Had I been wrong to cause such an uproar with one whom I loved? No. I would continue to reason with Him further. He had to understand."

The monk shook his head at the old angel, "You were such a fool."

"Who among us is not?"

"Then you concede your misgiving?"

Lucifer ignored the man, choosing to once again finish his story. "His back was turned from me as I reached out to touch Him. But before my hand touched His Shoulder He turned His face toward me, and I noticed a single tear slide from His eye. I have never felt more shock and despair in the whole of my existence than I did at that very moment. My heart, if such organs I did possess, sank to the pit of my bowels. I was as a lamb on the altar of sacrifice."

"How is it that you were surprised? Had you no realization of what you had done?"

"It mattered not," Lucifer responded, not allowing himself to become agitated by the contempt the monk was displaying. "As I pulled away, my surroundings began to distort. The landscape of Heaven was changing, my Creator starting to vanish before me."

The demon bowed his head before father Koutrakos with a solemnity the monk had yet to see. He seemed to desire to pull the remnants of his memory from the stones below his feet. This recollection had taken some degree of toll on the old angel. His form now returned to a pleasing shape. His sorrow was obvious to the old abbot. The monk followed Lucifer as the devil placed his hands on his knees, turning his gaze upwards once more. "Beneath my feet," he started, "what had once been the very street of Heaven now was replaced by fertile grass, newly created. I looked around at once, noticing that the realm around me was no longer that of Heaven, but now replaced by what you humans would call a jungle. Roots, plants, trees, animal life, they were all around me. Nothing yielded in recognition or familiarity. So much went through my mind, so many questions. The only point of certainty was that I was in some new abode, some new realm. I was alone. Absent from anyone or anything. The realm I was now imparted was this very one. The realm you call Earth."

"You were not damned with the host of angels sent forth from Heaven?"

"Oh, I was damned to be sure. Just not in the way I had immediately realized," the devil paused looking away, "Those who were my brethren. Those who were cast from Heaven were far more forgiven than I. What awaited me was a punishment beyond imagining. My hell was to be far worse than I could have ever imagined. Shall I tell you of it, Father?"

"Continue at will, Lucifer," the old monk returned, eyes wide. "This is how my Creator met with His vengeance..."

“Nothing-not photographs or movies, memories, or paintings, nor all the words of Henry James is a match for Venice in person.”

Paula Weideger

VENICE

Sean’s first thought when he entered the main gate of the Treviso Airport was how different the surroundings of this airport seemed when compared to those of London. The quantity of people moving about the infrastructure was the same, but each individual that passed. him seemed much more relaxed, in no particular hurry. And while still busy, gone was the fevered scurrying of people who needed to be somewhere yesterday. Was this the way of the Italians?

He stopped for a moment, looking down at his ticket and shuffling through his bags for the passport he had misplaced. Then satisfying himself that it was in fact in his bag, he looked up again trying to find some sign of directions in English among all the foreign Italian words.

Sean was as out of place as he had ever been. He could hear the conversations going on around him, deciding how odd it was hearing so much speech and comprehending so little of what was being said. The Italian language was beautiful, one could even say passionate. But it was foreign, nonetheless. He would have to muddle through conversation as best as he could and hope that the people were as kind and understanding as they looked. He slid his fingers through his dirty blond hair. For now, it was just him and his little Penguin phrase book.

After passing through security and adding another stamp to his passport, Sean settled himself to find the first ride into the city that presented itself. He had done more traveling in the last five days than he had done in his whole life, and the thought of his new self-appointed title of 'world traveler' made him laugh to himself. What quickly stripped the smile from his face was the very real fact that this wasn't a pleasure trip. Hell, it wasn't even business. It was life or death. His, to be more to the point.

There was a comfort to Italy though. Maybe it was because DeBury wasn't here. Or perhaps it was the country's beauty he could see beyond the airport's windows. There was so much that kept him in constant confusion. He knew he wasn't safe. Every few seconds he would scan the crowd as if the assassin DeBury had placed over him was going to suddenly reveal himself with a sign around his neck that read 'Mr. Assassin.' Sean shrugged off the last thought and stepped through the sliding glass doors as they opened with his approach, throwing his hand in the air to hail the first cab he saw. He didn't expect the speed at which the nearest car approached. Nor its condition.

The first taxi that responded to the signaling came in the form of a classic Fiat 500. Quite possibly, Sean thought to himself, the smallest car he had ever seen. He was quickly trying to decide what he might have to tell the driver to avoid getting in the thing. He didn't want to be rude, but the poor car looked to be about half the size of a VW Beetle, and probably weighed less than he did. As the little yellow machine pulled alongside, Sean bent down to see if a real person was driving, or if somehow the Italians had invented automatically powered cars.

"Buona pomeriggio, signore. Posso Aiuto?" a tiny, well-tanned man called out after he manually rolled down the passenger side window. Sean was taken aback. He shook his head knowing full well his first attempt at communication was headed for immediate disaster. He smiled at the driver, while his hand slid into his back pocket feeling for his small Italian dictionary. He felt so embarrassed and truthfully hoped the man might see his plight and offer him some assistance, but the little man just sat there smiling, awaiting Sean's response. Then, as if the gods of foreign language smiled, the small guide book opened to the page he needed.

In a voice the taxi driver must have thought sounded like Sean was trying to speak underwater, the words brokenly poured forth.

"P... Parlo.... I'm sorry...... Parla Inglese?" Sean garbled.

The driver snickered. "Si, si. You get in my cab, I speak all de English you want to hear, no?" He started laughing again as he watched Sean's face exhibit immediate signs of relief. It was funny seeing an American's face go from pale white back to its original state of light pink. Now, however, it was time for Sean to return a little sarcasm.

"You sure there's room for both of us in here?" he said, half joking-half serious, peering his head inside the tiny vehicle.

"You get inside," the driver began, "Maybe we discuss my car's shortcomings on the way to the city."

Here was a smart ass who could speak English well. Sean thought they would get along perfectly. He nodded his head in agreement, and opened the car door as gingerly as he could. He didn't want to cause the vehicle any serious harm, it seemed to have been through enough already. As he entered the vehicle, bending over as far as he could, his head still came in contact with the top door frame. He cursed under his breath for the bruise that was sure to appear tomorrow. If that wasn't enough, his body slid on the vinyl seat, smashing his knees against the dash board and pushing them into his chest. The Italian was laughing hysterically.

"You done smashing up my car?" he began. "An entry that smooth need to be on some Olympics or something"'

Sean returned the man's joke with an aggressive stare. He couldn't hold it for long though. The two men looked at the various scrapes and dents that surrounded them, and both started laughing.

"Sean Wilde," the American said, holding out his hand introducing himself, "Russian ballerina."

"I am Jaco Fernetti. Piacere di conoscerla. Taxi driver and all- around renaissance man. Pleasure to make your acquaintance, Sean," he said, muffling the laughter and placing his hand in Sean's. "You okay?"

"I'll live."

"You got no bags with you? No luggage?" the man said, looking over Sean's shoulder.

Sean patted the duffel bag and a new, smaller leather shoulder bag now resting in his lap. The new bag contained a subtle reminder of why Sean was here. Housed within was a flawless facsimile of the real book he was after, The Manuscripta Diabolica. He looked back up at the man, his smile having faded with the remembrance of the extra weight." 'Fraid I travel pretty light, Jaco. Can you take me to the inner city? Venice, I mean?"

"Jaco can do anything you ask," he started, "but get you out of trouble," he said smiling. "You need any place in particular?"

"Actually," Sean said, thumbing through his duffel bag for a crumpled map of the city, "I'm looking for a shop. A book shop to be more specific." He paused. "Lemmesee...... ah, here it is. La Biblioteca de Amare Arte. Ever heard of it?"

"Si," Jaco said shaking his head, "It is in the district of San Polo, a part of the city that houses the Rialto Markets. Very famous pescivendolo. Excellent fish. Molto Bueno!" The little Italian was kissing his fingertips, or maybe licking them - Sean was unsure. "We go there right away," Jaco said assuringly. Then his eyebrows lifted. "But first," he said, "you show Jaco some lire, no?"

Sean looked at him with a quizzical stare for a moment, then realization hit. "Oh yeah, money. Hold on a minute," he said, reaching in his front jeans pocket, extracting a wad of crumpled Italian bills that choked his driver's throat. Jaco pushed the money back at his passenger.

"You get yourself killed pulling money like that out!" he said, eyes wide.

"You crazy Americans," he said shaking his head at Sean. "You lucky Jaco's an honest man. I only take this one," Sean noticed his driver was extracting the two largest bills from the wad of cash in his hands, "And this one." The two men looked at each other, each smiling before Jaco started again. He was looking at Sean's rather haggard Jean and T-shirt combination. "You need to first go buy some new clothes. Maybe get some luggage, buy some sense if you can find some for sale anywhere. Then sit yourself down to a nice Italian meal. Yes, my friend, I take you to this book store of yours," he stated with all the confidence that came with the comfort of having been paid up front, "But first you need to take care of you."

"I'm fine, Jaco."

"You no look fine."

"You think we might get on with the trip?"

"Of course, my friend," Jaco said, shifting the vehicle into gear. "But you no look fine," he stated, mumbling to himself as the tiny yellow car sped from the terminal gate.

Sean sat back as far as he could. The seat was uncomfortable and he was feeling a bit jet-lagged. As if this wasn't enough, he could feel the rumble of the small car's engine as if it was in his lap, and his body jumped as the car sputtered and bounced at every bump the road presented. Any effort to sleep, any moment of respite, was continually thwarted by the insistent willingness of his driver to pull conversation from whatever facet of space he could.

"So. How long you stay in Italia?"

Sean opened one eye, perturbed. "I wish I knew, Jaco. I'm here on some business."

"You no look like you the type for business."

"Do you always ask so many questions?"

"Si," he shrugged with confidence.

Sean was becoming mildly irritated. If he was honest with his feelings though, any diversion from the reality he was now a part of was nice. "It isn't the type of business I'm at much liberty to discuss," he said in a way that didn't come across rude.

"You in that kind of business," Jaco said, winking as if to denote some understanding of some sinister business illegality. "My lips are sealed," he said, making a twisting motion with his fingers to his face.

"Whatever you think, Jaco," Sean quickly interjected. "I promise it's nothing you might imagine." He paused, looking away, "It's really difficult to explain. But the answer lies somewhere between Venice and America. I've just got to find out what that answer is."

"Many people come to Italy with secrets, my friend. This country- it is full of them. Everywhere you look, everywhere you go," he looked away from the road and directly at Sean, "Even Jaco. He full of secrets too."

The car made a sharp turn as Jaco, too busy talking to Sean instead of keeping his eyes on the road, jerked it back into the correct lane. Sean was getting way more conversation than he preferred. The little Italian was begging for idle chatter, so reluctantly, Sean obliged.

"And what kind of secrets do you have, Jaco?" Sean asked half-heartily.

What a mistake.

Twenty minutes had passed since the two men had left the Airport Treviso. The tiny car was now cruising bumpily down the N11 causeway, crossing the Laguna Veneta, and making its way toward the downtown waterways of Venice.

Sean sat crunched between the back of his seat and the front dashboard, now convinced that he knew Jaco Fernetti better than anyone else in the entire country of Italy. He had gotten an earful of Jaco's birth, family history, and even his personal vendetta against the entire country of France. Apparently, the taxi driver had lost his wife when she ran off with a Frenchman a year earlier. He stated his necessity for a Holy war against the country of France for having produced a lover of such extraordinary abilities. Surely, Sean thought, it could have nothing to do with lack of conversation they must have had. Sean was half listening to Jaco's ranting, trying his best to be polite, but believing all the while that when the car finally reached the city, it was Jaco who should pay him.

It was easy to forget why he was here. It wasn't easy to forget that he was presumably being followed. Marked, as it were. And all this because of a book. A fucking bundle of pages bound in an encasement of leather. It was just too preposterous. Yet for him, all too accurate. How odd it was that the very thing that fueled the passion in his life was in some way going to bring about the end of his life. The sum of all his life experiences had not seen to prepare him for the stakes that had now been raised. There was a sense of justifiable inadequacy, and all that lay before him now was the element of fate and chance. He reached into his new bag, caressing the faux manuscript.

Before leaving London, Sean had made a phone call to the English bank, Barclays, in Paris, France. His arrangement with DeBury, or more correctly put, DeBury's arrangement with Sean denoted that there would be the sum of one million dollars deposited in an account of the book scout's choosing by the time he boarded his flight for Venice. To Sean's amazement, the money was there. If, by some miracle, he made it out of this fiasco alive, that's where he would go. He would stay as long as his visa allowed. He didn't feel comfortable having his money in a bank in England. DeBury was in England, and that was enough. Sean had stopped briefly before leaving the Airport Treviso and called Barclays again, questioning the balance once more. Sure enough, one million dollars. He couldn't believe it. He was the richest dead man he knew. Funny, he thought to himself, money had changed nothing.

Jaco was still ranting when Sean refocused on the man's words.

"So if n I ever get my hands on that son of a bitch, I gonna ring his neck like a chicken, I swear ta God," Jaco ranted, his hands waving madly and, as Sean noted, unattached to the steering wheel. The little man had once again freed Sean's mind of momentary worry. He then turned towards Jaco, smiling.

"Surely the whole country of France isn't bad just because your wife ran away with a Frenchman, now is it?" Sean was goading the little man.

"You side with a France," Jaco jumped back, "You can get out of the car now, funny American!" Jaco had himself in a mock rage that was making Sean laugh apologetically. Then, looking at one another in silence for a moment - Jaco with a look of seriousness, Sean about to burst any moment with laughter - they both started laughing. Jaco was the first to speak. "I tell you, Sean, don't ever get yourself a married. Women, they foul creatures. They gonna break your heart, then they gonna spit in your eye. Every time, I tell you."

"Spoken with the voice of well - hampered reason," Sean said making every effort to agree. "Not that I have anything to worry about, but I'll take the advice, my friend," Sean returned, bewildered that he was calling this man 'friend'.

There was a moment of silence that passed between the two men. From the window, Sean could see the beauty of the fantastic city now coming into view. He gasped, not realizing he had done so aloud. The view, at least what he could see, quite literally took his breath away. The Italian recognized his passenger's reaction immediately.

"Y'know, Sean," Jaco began talking again, "this city, Venice, it survives against all the odds. It is the gateway to paradise, my friend. Powerful, mysterious, grand - like no other city in the world. Whatever you want, Venice give it to you. You fancy the arts? Venice has the greatest paintings in the world by the greatest artists. You like a food, a little wine perhaps? Venice got the best in the whole world. And women? Venice produce the best you will ever find. I should have known better than to marry a girl from Genoa!" Sean could see the pride his new acquaintance had for his home, and he admitted to himself that it was making the whole allure of the city more enticing as he looked from the rickety vehicle. "Even the sea," Jaco continued, "She try to swallow us whole many times. But we say, 'Fuck you ocean'." He was waving his middle finger in the air, not realizing that other cars were passing and honking their horns, having taken offense to a gesture that wasn't really directed towards them. "We survive. You take the attitude of the Venetian, Sean, you can survive against any odds too, my friend. Remember what Jaco say. He no tell lies."

"I believe you, Jaco. I believe you," Sean was turning away from the man, entranced by the beauty that seemed to jump now from every facet of the city. He could see people conversing and laughing with one another in the street. Old men could be seen playing cards and sharing a bottle of wine on a small table as the Fiat passed by. The canals were in view as well, and Sean was having difficulty digesting the watery streets, their beauty adding so much to a city that was already doing just fine on its own. The city could not be summed up in mere words, sentences, or even paragraphs. It would take encyclopedic volumes to describe this beauty that had somehow come to be outstretched before him. Venice was the perfect blend of modem convenience married with old world charm that had somehow given birth to both the richness of art and the empowerment of grandiose architecture. It was a charm that beguiled the visitor viewing it for the first time. Jaco was smiling, allowing his customer the full brevity of the moment. He had seen this reaction before, and knew it wouldn't be long before he would see it again.

Stone buildings rose, climbing from the water's edge. Chrysanthemums decorated wrought iron porches above each building's doorway. Sean decided then and there the city must have looked this way two hundred years ago, minus the technological element, of course. Little did he know the city had looked this way five hundred years ago. That was the charm. That was Venice.

"Here we are, my friend," Jaco said, pressing the brake and pulling the car to a rather abrupt stop. "I now gonna do you a big favor," he said, turning from Sean, who was a bit surprised at their sudden stop, and exiting the vehicle. "Wait here."

As Jaco walked away from the car, Sean, wiping some sweat from his forehead, could see that the vehicle had not just stopped anywhere. It had been situated next to a stunning bridge, the Ponte degli Scalzi, near the Fondamenta Santa Lucia, on one of Venice's most coveted sites, the Grand Canal.

The Grand Canal is often described, to those fortunate to have seen it, as the most beautiful street in the world. That it was made entirely of water probably has a lot to do with that remark. It winds in a state of profound liquidity through the very heart of the city, shuffling locals and tourists alike, from destination to destination. The architecture was causing Sean difficulty in breathing. From the car, he could see every type of boat gliding across its rustling waters. Some looked of recent build, some of medieval construction. The lack of view caused him to abandon the car in an effort to get a better look.

He had hardly gotten the opportunity to grasp his two bags before Jaco had returned, motioning his passenger forward with his hands.

"You come with Jaco, my friend. I arrange a trip for you down the canal."

"Jaco," Sean started, "I really appreciate the offer, but I really need to get going."

Sean's act of hesitation was immediately ignored. "No. No. You get there by water. I promise it will be just as fast and it is the only way to experience the-city first hand," he said, urging Sean to follow him to the canal's bank. "You will like this much better. Jaco has arranged everything." He finished the sentence with authority.

Grabbing his duffel bag and a pair of sunglasses he had laid at his feet,

Sean followed the little man to the edge of the canal. There a gondola, a sleek, black boat resembling the boats seen in so many renaissance paintings, seemed to be awaiting him. From one end of the craft he was met with a smile, less a few teeth, by a tall, elder ferryman. Jaco was smiling from behind Sean while presenting the two.

"This here is Luca Pesaro, the finest boatman in all of Venice!" Jaco said as the boatman accompanied the introduction with a nod. "He will ferry you down the canal, my friend, to the Rialto Bridge, where he will let you out. That's the more commercialized district, where your art shop is."

"Book shop," Sean returned, now convinced the two tradesmen had some unspoken racket going for gullible travelers.

"Of course. Book shop. Yes," Jaco said, the boatman nodding approvingly in the distance. "One thing though," Jaco said, watching Sean's eyes roll, "Luca does not speaka English too well, so my advice is to enjoy the ride but try not to talk his ear off like you did mine on our way from the airport. Luca can nod yes or no in just about any language, but you 're in trouble if you a' lookin' for deep conversation. All he does is just nod his head." Jaco said, presenting the man again, who was in fact nodding with approval void of any idea as to what was being said.

"Of course," Sean returned, wearily shaking his head and lighting a cigarette. He then tossed his bags in the slender vessel. He had barely taken a drag from the slender fag when two fingers appeared at the edge of his lips, extracting the lighted stick of nicotine.

"Luca," Jaco said as Sean, shocked at the audacity of his new acquaintance, watched the cigarette fade from view and fizzle in the canal's watery embrace, "he no a like people smoking in his boat." Sean looked to the boatman who was in fact nodding with a smile that hadn't left his face since Jaco had given him some of Sean's money. Sean would have responded, but once again, Jaco was quicker with his tongue.

"This is a number where you can reach me should you need anything while you are in my city," Jaco stated in a way that suggested he owned Venice rather than merely resided here. "And remember," he stated with just enough of a pause to allow Sean the opportunity of filling in the gap.

"Jaco get you anything you want," Sean said, now laughing and finishing the man's sentence. "But he no get you out of trouble," they could both be heard stating in unison.

Sean scanned the waterway, then the surroundings on shore behind him. He was looking for someone - anyone - that might stand out in the crowd. The person DeBury had hired to 'shadow' him. But this was useless. Before him was an ocean of strangers. It saddened him also that when the thought came to mind, the two closest friends he had in this part of the world was an elder book man, Anthony Taylor in London, whom he had no idea was dead, and a Venetian taxi driver he had now known for almost an hour. He would have to brush up on his 'people' skills when he got back to America.

The two men shook hands and parted company. Shortly, Sean sunk into the floor of the small gondola which was now drifting from its mooring, joining the other boats gliding through the large Venetian waterway. He turned once more and watched as the taxi drove off, then glanced down at the small card the driver had given him.

> Jaco Fernetti
> Taxi service/Gondola service/Wine importer/Tour guide/
> Ghost walk phone-041-520-03-87 fax-041-520-12-42-04

No wonder a Frenchman stole this guy's wife, Sean thought, how could he have possibly had time for a woman! He put the card in his back pocket, then shot a curious glance in the direction of the elder figure oaring the slim vessel behind him. The man smiled back at Sean, saying nothing while tending to the boat's direction. Luca's passenger was welcoming the lack of conversation. Relaxed now for a moment, Sean sunk back in the craft, taking in the brevity of what sites lay before him as the two strangers floated down the Grand Canal of Venice.

Water slapped at the sides of the slender boat, as the magnificence of Venice's architecture surrounded Sean on each side of the canal. Remnants of both Gothic and Baroque style littered the banks of the waterway, entrancing the visiting book man. One thousand years of history seemed to be present in each and every nook and cranny. To his left was the Palazzo Labia, where Cleopatra's life was artistically rendered on the Palace's walls.

A bit further down the canal was the San Marcuola Church. To the right, a seventeenth century Turkish warehouse -the Fondaco dei Turchi.

Every aspect of the city humbled her new guest.

Water buses, or vaporettos, whizzed by causing the gondola to rock along in its wake. Motor boats, none of any grand size, slid happily along as well.

Venice was nothing like what Sean had expected, yet it was so much more.

Being fascinated by the wonder of a city which literally rested on the water, he tried to commit each and every sight to memory. In fact, he was so overcome by the scenery that he was disappointedly shocked when the craft came to an abrupt stop.

They were now at one of the most fantastically beautiful bridges in the world, the Rialto. They had reached the heart of the city.

Luca Pesaro nodded, trying his best to avoid speaking if at all possible, and offered his aid in helping Sean from the boat. Sean turned, throwing each of the two bags across his shoulders, paid the fare thanking Luca, and exited the boat in the direction of the markets.

Sean headed northwest down the Ruga Degli Orefici, in the direction Jaco had said he would find the bookstore. He had no more than a ten-minute walk, and he felt wholly immersed between the stone buildings as he shuffled along the street. There was the unmistakable smell of fresh pasta being made, fish being cooked, and yes, the sweet grape scent of newly opened wine permeating the air around him. The day had been kind. There was not a cloud in the sky and the warmth of the sun was a perfect seventy-two degrees. The soft, faint whisper of the Ocean breeze followed him everywhere. Italy, Sean decided, was at her finest.

As he puffed on a cigarette, he could see in the distance a sign above a doorway that seemed familiar. He had just turned right, walking east on C. Beccarie, when the wording came into view. The signage was clear now. It read: Biblioteca Arte. He had found the shop.

Approaching slowly, remembering suddenly why he was here, he peered inside as if to catch a glance of the woman he had been sent to meet. His eyes were greeted not. with a recognizable face, but a heightened air of activity. People were mingling, coffee cups firmly in hand. Sean counted at least twelve faces at first, and the store reminded him more of a cafe than a bookstore.

He could see books arranged on shelves running down the side walls, and there seemed to be an amassment of books piled on the coffee tables in plain view. His eyes once again scanned the room for the woman, Cecelia. There would be no way of picking her out in the crowd though, so he opened the glass door, flicked his cigarette to the ground, and ushered himself inside.

No one stopped to look in his direction when he entered the store. The Italian dialect being spoken from person to person reminded Sean very quickly just how much of an outsider he was. This wasn't America and he wasn't in Kansas. There was an immediate degree of discomfort. He had no choice but to maintain some distance from the other people. He would try not to seem 'too' American, as he began doing what nature intended he do - peruse the bookshelves.

One had to look no further than this place for a good book on art. It housed volumes on every famous painter imaginable. Sean followed the alphabet toward the ending shelf, looking for a book that might display a painting or two by his favorite artist. He bent down, reaching towards the bottom shelf, and slid a thin volume out. Squatting now, he placed the book between his knees and started flipping the pages. He was so engrossed by the paintings rendered on the pages that he didn't hear the approach of the woman now standing above him.

The scent of her perfume startled him as he looked upwards, catching her staring down at him, and embarrassingly slipping off his feet onto the floor. The woman then held out a hand and began to speak.

> "I know well what I am fleeing from but not what I am in search of."
>
> Michel de Montaigne

Brave New World

"I found there to be no need in the bothersome worry of pondering a fate I had so willingly brought upon myself," Lucifer rolled the words from his tongue, their weight falling heavy on the intended ear of father Koutrakos. "It was now time that I sought to explore my new dwelling. My new home, as it were."

It was father Koutrakos who now took to his feet in a slow and steady motioning. He pulled the robe that had been sagging from his body tightly towards his shoulders, allowing the garment to envelop him completely. He had chosen not to interrupt the demon from his tale, not wishing to seem rude. This was the odd trait about the old man. Even the prince of darkness was shown a degree of respect. And, mused the monk, maybe this was why he had been chosen to hear the demon's confession all along.

There was a cold air about the entire domicile. He had also noticed the candles (and there had only been four burning in the whole room) were now reduced to a point in which they would soon extinguish themselves altogether. This would have to be rectified with an air of immediacy, for there could be only one fate worse than being alone with the devil in a lighted room, and that was being alone with the devil in a darkened room!

Lucifer did however, cut short his confession, allowing the monk to go forward with his duties. He ran his fingers through the mass of twining hair that seemed radiantly displayed about his head. He was comfortable here, in the dwelling of this particular human. Not for an instant did he see a need for man's existence, but he seemed to meet this particular human with an air of equal respect. He had been an intruder, and should have been met with only contempt and malice. There was also the fact that had he allowed himself to appear to any human less pious, well, that individual would have suffered death by sheer fright, no doubt. Yes. This was one human almost worthy to be met with compassion. And, if compassion could be found for himself, then maybe forgiveness as well. Lucifer sat pleased with himself, alone interred within a degree of vanity only he could know.

As the elderly monk withdrew from a shelf four new candles he had made by hand only a week before, the devil, crossing his sinewy arms to the front of his well - pronounced chest, started his tale once more. "Before me," he began, watching as the monk returned to the small desk between them with the candles and a small knife with which to cut the wicks, "there seemed an endless expanse of new and notable terrain to explore." Father Koutrakos had now placed the candles upright, positioning them upon iron bases, and, as he set the crude little knife down beside the waxed structures, drew back suddenly, surprising himself at the shock of seeing flames leap from their tips unaided.

Lucifer sat smiling.

"I beg of you," the old man said shaking, his hands clasping the robe about his chest, "Please dispense with such displays of your obvious power. I am quite frightened enough as it is and we should both muse upon your tale rather than your fanciful trickery."

"Indeed," Lucifer said with a snicker. "Forgive me."

Not likely, the monk thought to himself. Not ever.

"There is no need to be frightened," he assured the old man. "I told you no harm shall befall you."

"Let us dispense with your reassurances, evil one," the old man scoffed. "If you are the devil, believe that you can reassure me of nothing."

"Very well," Lucifer said coldly. "May I continue?"

"Please."

Father Koutrakos took his seat once more and allowed the demon to speak. "As I believe I stated," he began, "I was confused by the surroundings of my new domain. Had I been granted my wish? It seemed at first to be so, yet I was without the benefit of a much - needed explanation of this new habitation. So many questions, you see. Then, while I explored the beautiful new terrain, I came across a pool of liquid. What you beings might call a river or pond. I bent over to feel the substance, and a most horrid realization presented itself," he said motioning with his body, contorting, and changing to his devilish state.

"I saw myself for the first time as you see me now. I had become a hideous mockery of my former, beautiful self. I was a haggard devil, as ugly and repulsive as I had once been beautiful. Where once my wings were feathered plume, now in place were these," he was looking over his shoulder, "wings like that of a flying rodent." He paused. "And from each temporal point a horn curled forth, grotesque and horrid. The sight of myself caused me to fall back upon your earth, sobbing uncontrollably and uncomforted. I was cursed. Damned by my Creator."

The monk interrupted. "Did you not believe there would be a price for your sin?"

"For defending the honor of my race? For trying to prevent the birth of the human?" Lucifer took to his feet.

"For defying God," the monk returned solemnly.

"He brought this war on Himself."

"You are wrong."

"Hear me out, Father Koutrakos."

"It seems I have no choice."

"Everyone has a choice, dear man."

"That is exactly my point, demon. And when you accept that there existed flaws in the decisions you made, perhaps you shall find the forgiveness you profess to seek. I can do nothing to help you, if it is even possible that you can be helped."

Lucifer stood puzzled, crossing his arms and rubbing the cleft in his chin. The old man was getting bold, and he was already becoming uncomfortable with the feeling that his position of superiority might be threatened. Had he really been in search of salvation or was he in need of a human's sympathy? He would allow himself to continue his tale and see what happened.

"After you saw what you were," the old man said, wishing to return to the fallen angel's tale in an effort to avoid a philosophical dispute, "What course of action did you take?"

"I took to the air," he began, "wishing to survey the land in which I was imprisoned. I was surprised by the relative ease in which my body lifted from the ground, and it was only a few moments before I was among the clouds, viewing the fertile expanse below. I then returned to the land where I set about wandering the terrain. My Creator had made many wondrous things on which to look upon. The plant life, the landscape, the beasts. It was very different from my former realm, but just as interesting. I tried at once to communicate with the beasts, but each turned from me. I am certain they were created with a natural hatred for me, internally placed by my Creator."

"Even the lower forms of life embraced a scorn and housed an aura of contempt for you," the monk imparted.

"I did not see them as lower life forms," the demon said raising his brow, "but yes, it was as you say. For the first time, I was alone. Flowers would wilt as I passed, re-growing in my departure. I was feared by the lowest of life forms, unable to exact a means of communication from anything or anyone. I was alone with my memories. Alone with my hate. In truth, I had hoped to find some of my brethren who were cast out before me. But they were nowhere to be found, and I knew not of their exact fate. I was alone in my own miserly way. A hell of sorts."

"And tell me, devil, do you not agree that this was a justifiable fate?"

"Who are we to know that which is just and that which is not?" Lucifer said. "I have never condemned any man, angel, or beast. I am without that right. I calculate my actions as no more than a result of what wrong had been done to me. How is it that, given all I have revealed, you can see this any other way?"

"You foolish, foolish angel," Father Koutrakos began, "Man has clearly feared your intelligence far more than should be deserved. Perhaps you just lack sense, being somewhat unintelligent on the whole. We whom you call human have come to build you as some powerful deity. Yet you are less than we, for the ability to even contemplate the manner in which you derive your skill of decision making - well, it is absurd! You, fallen one, are void of a sensible compass."

Lucifer thought to conjure some hideous offering that would put the old man in his place. The audacity of any human to berate him so openly should have riled the demon to action. But, he reminded himself, No one is more patient than I. There was much to discuss, and he wasn't about to let anyone stand in the way of his moment.

The truth was, he was quite amused at the willful disgust the old man had for him. But it might be harder to gain sympathy than he thought. The old man was quite opinionated, and he was quite forthcoming. He would remain objective and hope at some point the monk would do as well.

The monk, his robe partially loosened by the sweat of its owner, began pacing about the room, his eyes never leaving the fixated point of the quietly seated angel. He began rationing Lucifer's request in his mind, that of absolution. He could find no means to achieve this. The fallen one showed little if any remorse. His crime had agreeably been of such an unspeakable nature; how should he really be expected to continue such a hopeless offering?

Still, the conversation, the confession, had been candid, forthcoming, and if it could in anyway be believed, incredibly interesting. Lucifer showed no hesitation to answer whatever question that was presented. And for himself, one who had studied the scriptures as long as he had, hearing what Lucifer had to say proved to be interesting to the point of obsessively compelling. Father Koutrakos could probe questions that haunted him. Possibly explore events which might come to pass. He must forward himself with the utmost of caution, for there was sure to be adversarial meandering in every word the demon spoke. It should never be underestimated that this was the Devil. A being who had seen the very face of God. Who had ever had the chance to partake in a conversation of such magnitude with a being who had witnessed more than any other. The hour was of little matter. The day was of less concern.

He would hold tight to his sanity and probe the beast further. He would take the necessary precautions, and engross himself upon the faceted learning of diabolical activity and the roguish uprising of his demonic counterpoint. Then, having learned all he could, he would put the offering in a voluminous manuscript with the hope that future generations could, having learned more about evil from one who spawned the very word, thwart the devil's advances. It would be a testament to his life of devotional study, and a fitting epitaph. He veered from these thoughts suddenly, and began speaking to the complacent being opposite himself.

"How much time passed before the birth of man?" he began. "How long did you roam about the earth?"

Lucifer cleared his throat, smiling. "As I stated before," he said, leaning forward, his words riding on a breath of air both soft and solemn, "time means nothing to me. I had, up to that point, simply no concept of it. I had wandered alone, for quite a considerable period of time before the horrible nature of my reality was to commence."

Father Koutrakos looked at the angel with a confused expression.

"Don't seem so surprised, old man," Lucifer directed him. "You see, what I had envisioned of hell was my current situation. I was quite unaware that my Creator had a different plan altogether. The totality of my punishment had hardly begun."

"Forgive me," the monk said, bewildered still, "I do not follow."

"You will," Lucifer stated, somewhat agitated by the monk's over-enthusiasm to know of the demon's punishment. "Walking about, I came upon a sight which would vex me to the end of my reason. In the distance of a most lush and vibrant forest, in the floor of the earth, was a footprint. Then, at once, my reality hit me with all the realization of an atheist who enters Hell."

"And that was...?"

"Don't you see? My Creator had not banished me to some otherworldly realm. He had cursed me to be imprisoned in the same realm with the beings I hated most! The footprint was that of a man!" Lucifer said, enraged and shaking his fist. "It was the irony to end all ironies. Oh, horrid realization! Oh, cursed Lucifer! Here was I, the one being who had instigated the whole war in Heaven. One who preferred banishment to coexistence with the likes of the human I was now stuck with for all eternity. It was too much for me to bear. At once I set out to eradicate my own self."

"You sought to kill yourself?"

"I had no idea if it could be done, no concept of death. Anything would be better than the coming hell. I tried to drown myself in the newly created ocean. When that failed, I flew to the highest mountains, hurling my body from their peaks and allowing my angelic form to crash upon the ground below. It did no good. I could not even destroy myself. Would that I had been banished to the hell that interred my brethren than to exist in a curse such as this. My Creator was laughing at me, oh to be sure! My blood became as fire. As it boiled, I screamed obscenities towards the heavens such as would deafen the most heartless sinner. I was willing to accept any wrath just to be pardoned this one. What could be done? Something must be done!"

The demon sat exhausted from the verbalization of his sufferings. Father Koutrakos took advantage of the moment.

"Then you were not a prisoner of Hell?"

"We shall discuss Hell soon enough, father. You humans have it all wrong, at least, in part," he snapped, bothered by the interruption. "I flew skyward demanding council with my Maker. None was granted. Having searched for the one who would be called 'man' and being unable to find it, I began trying to destroy my Creator's other earthly inhabitants."

"You sought to exact cruelty, regardless of the victim."

"Yes," Lucifer said, abruptly putting an end to any further opinion the monk might wish to bestow. "I would kill that which you call 'bird' only to watch it spring forth with life anew. I would trample plants just to watch them spring forth renewed by the earth. My rage grew unrequited, leaping out of control. I was powerless to exact even the slightest reprisal. My vengeance could not satiate its appetite. It seemed I could do no more than exist, horrified by my state and exhausted at the inner workings of my turmoil. But something happened. I had managed to tire my being to a point in which never in the whole of my existence had I felt. Then, I did something I had never before done. I laid upon the earth, and I slept."

Father Koutrakos found it odd hearing Lucifer talk in such a manner. Human compacts such as sleep were strange to hear described by a being who had known an eternity of existence, but had lived without the everyday human experience. The tale began to lend a certain credibility to the demon's admission of who he was. He beckoned the beast further, "And you had never experienced sleep before?"

"It is easy to forget the· differences between the angelic realm and that of the human," he answered. "Our similarity in bodily make-up is all that we share." He was now rolling his eyes. "Let me dispel some myths you may have. There is no reason for a being of heaven to eat, sleep, fuck, shit, or hate. I was now the exception." Lucifer paused, knowing that he was confusing the old man. He would start over, trying to explain with more patience. "Yes I slept. I had no realization that my expulsion from heaven left me imbued with certain characteristics that likened me to both the human and my new realm. I sleep even now, but I do so very little. Once or twice a century. Sleep wastes both time and opportunity."

"You wish to dispense your energies tempting man."

"For me, there exists nothing more necessary."

"You are such a sorrowful waste of God's talents."

"You just blasphemed my Creator."

"I..."

"Don't be so sure there exists any more necessity for you than there exists a need for me. Who can say I am not a tool, much like that of death? A harvester of sorrows. How is it you can know what true purpose I really serve? I could not be, if not willed so by my Creator. That I am still here in this world, should reveal to you there is much you fail to see." He paused, redirecting his words. "Shall I continue father?"

"Forgive my interruption."

"Forgive my existence."

"Please," the old monk said, ignoring the devil, "continue."

"Know that while I slept, my Creator brought forth the first human soul. A man," Lucifer said as he spit the word from his lips. "Sleep had been a trick. Part of the Creator's necessitated plan, one would presume. On my new home, in my new realm, the one you call 'God' brought forth the first human. As you may fathom, this brought a new level of rage and deceit between us. I was consoled only by the fact that what was His for the creating would be mine for the destroying. I was still the most powerful being besides my Creator that existed! I would kill this thing called 'man', sending him back to his Maker. The new world was not to support us both, of that to be sure!"

Lucifer got up, clenching his fists tightly, noticeably enraged. Father Koutrakos made no attempt to take his eyes from wildly animated demon. Things were beginning, ever so slightly, to make sense. What if God had been testing Lucifer? Perhaps the demon had been disposed on the earth as a means of purging these thoughts of hatred, rather than embracing them. Perchance God still loved him and wished him to embrace the creation called 'man'. God had given Lucifer free will.

The abbot directed his words to the brazen entity across the room. "Lucifer," the monk was smiling with a stance of superiority, "perhaps you were too blinded by hate to realize that God had given you a second chance. Could it not be that you were put on, earth less for punishment and more as a means of redeeming yourself through the acceptance of the human? You had been given free will."

"I took free will!" the demon interrupted, "I was given nothing!"

"It was still your choice."

"Nonsense," the devil returned, his facial expression distorted and repulsive, "I was Heaven's outcast. The human my sworn enemy. All that lay before us was to be death and destruction. Believe this, Father. It is the only truth you should accept."

"You are blind."

"And you, old man, are impossible."

The monk was smirking. It was not a smile of victory, or even that of self-satisfaction. It was a knowing that he had implanted an idea within the mind of Lucifer that uneased the fallen angel. The devil could now ponder an eternity, wondering if there was any truth in what the old man said.

Lucifer returned to his seat, his mind transfixed firmly in the memories past. Regret was foolish emotion, he thought. A human emotion. There was what was fact, and nothing more. History was all that mattered. His-story. And his story had somehow gotten sidetracked. Taking a deep breath, he began expelling his take on the matter once more.

"I suppose it is easy for a being like yourself to sit and propose what my existence may or may not have involved. For me though, I am what I am. I regret nothing, yet I harbor sorrows. Tell me, how can this be?

Perhaps I am too complex for human understanding. Perhaps I am far too simplistic. It seems you will make of me what you will." He was now trying once again to change subjects directly relating to any misgivings on his part. "You know, Father," he stated as his lips parted, displaying a set of teeth containing sharpened incisors, "I did set out to kill the new creation - 'man' - once I happened upon him in the realm of earthly delights."

"What stayed your hand?"

Lucifer sat back, crossed his arms, and began once again.

"The only thing that could..."

"The head never rules the heart, but just becomes its partner in crime."

Mignon McLaughlin

A Chance Meeting

"Benvenuti, signori! Desiderano?"

Looking up from the floor, Sean's eyes addressed the shapely figure of a woman now smiling down at him Her hand was outstretched toward him 'offering assistance. He felt like an idiot, clumsily lying on the floor.

Accepting her hand, he pulled himself to his feet. He was momentarily transfixed by her features, all decidedly beautiful. Her jet-black hair was styled in a wildly modern fashion, cut short, and indicative of the styles worn by many of the more fashionable women he had seen in the airport earlier. Her hand had been soft to the touch, and her complexion seemed as though it were as smooth as porcelain. On his feet now, he could determine her height, which appeared to be about five-six, perhaps five-seven. A blue sun dress, mapped in multicolored butterflies rested off spaghetti-like straps fastened to her shoulders. The material creased at every curve her body made, and draped down to her ankles. She exuded a degree of raw sensuality that made Sean uncomfortable. He then preceded to embarrass himself further by stammering for words. In Italian, no less.

"Non capisco, I'm sorry.... l don't...," the words stumbled out.

"It's quite all right," the Italian woman said reassuringly, "I speak pretty good English." She was smiling. Her English was flawless, almost without an Italian accent behind it at all. "What's that you've got there?" she said, cocking her head so her hair tussled a bit. She was pointing to the book Sean had pulled from the shelf earlier, the one that was resting on the floor now.

Sean caught himself staring at her face rather than hearing the words coming from her mouth. "It's a book on... -" he had to look at the cover to remember what volume he had picked up - "........ Tintoretto. Jacapo Tintoretto. He's one of my favorite authors.... I'm sorry," he was shaking his head, stumbling over his words, "Artists. I meant to say 'artists'. Sorry." He was noticeably embarrassed by his lack of social grace. Fortunately for both his ego and his disposition, the woman seemed to pay no mind.

"You are familiar with Tintoretto?"

Sean, seemingly surprised she would ask, responded, "Oh. Jacapo Tintoretto has got to be my favorite artist of the sixteenth century. His work is incredible." Sean was relieved that the woman was carrying the conversation. It allowed him to feel more comfortable in her presence, and truthfully, provided a commonality between them.

"I to feel the same," she reached down to the floor, picking up the book and brushing his jeans. "Did you know most of his work can be found in this city?"

"I... really had no idea...I..."

"Oh yes. Tintoretto is linked to a large history of Venice's art culture," she said smiling and presenting a hand of well- manicured fingers. "My friends call me Angel. My real name is Angelina da Fabriano," she offered, arching her back forward, "I'm part of the local scenery I'm afraid. And you would be...?"

"Sean," he spat, gathering his thoughts, "Sean Wilde. It's nice to meet you as well."

There was a certain twinge of excitement as he felt the soft flesh of her warm palm. The mysteriousness of her eyes and the way they seemed to look right through him, held his mind captive. He could do nothing but stare. That is, until a realization hit him that with the passing moments she probably wanted her hand back.

"Excuse me," he said with embarrassment as he released her hand, letting it fall. So much for a suave approach, he thought.

"There's nothing to apologize for, Sean," she said, shifting her stance and smiling. "Let me buy you a cup of coffee. I would love to hear how things are in America these days. I have not been to your country in quite some time."

Sean looked around the room. He felt he should be more forthcoming and tell the girl he was here to meet someone else and truthfully, didn't have time for civilities. But there was a certain reality making itself very clear to him - Here, he wasn't some down and out book scout. No one knew who he was, and he had a pocket full of money. God, just once could he play the role of prince instead of his usual role of pauper? In America, his chance of being approached by someone as beautiful as this was unfathomable, unless perhaps she was a prostitute. Here in Venice, he could be anyone he wanted. He willfully decided an hour's worth of conversation couldn't hurt. So, he proceeded to gracefully accept her offer and the two began their conversation at a small table around the bookstore's cafe.

About two hours had passed before Sean thought to look at his· watch. He knew he needed to end the conversation and find the liaison he was here to meet. There were many women in the bookstore and any of them could be his contact person, but he couldn't pursue any action until he dispensed with the present one. He looked back up at the woman.

"Listen," he was trying to befit some clever prose that might assure him of some future opportunity with her, "talking with you.... I mean... Well..." He couldn't look her in the eyes, "I would love to meet you for dinner later, but I'm afraid I need to take care of some things at the moment, and, well, I... "

"What kind of things?" she inquired.

"I haven't been totally honest," Sean began. "My business here actually concerns a woman I'm supposed to meet. Actually, it's the woman who I've been told owns this bookstore."

"Cecilia?"

"You know her?"

"Everyone in the market knows her," Angel began, "But if you were thinking of meeting with her today I'm afraid you are out of luck," she said, before taking a sip off her latte.

"Why? How do you know?"

"Every Tuesday she goes to the stands of the Erberia to buy fresh fruits and vegetables." She paused, looking Sean squarely in the eye, "I know this because she and I usually shop there together. I live right next to her, just down the street. I did my shopping earlier this morning so I ended up coming here instead of going shopping with her."

"But I was told... ah, never mind," he said, "It's important that I see her at once. Do you think there's any..."

Angel cut him off.

"You should spend the remaining day with me instead," she began, offering an alternative that needed no real persuasion. "Cecelia will be in tomorrow and there are very little hours left in the day anyway. What would be the problem meeting with her tomorrow?"

"I have a rather eager client that needs me to attend to some business at once, and my time really isn't my own at the moment, so-"

"Nonsense!" the woman said, ending Sean's excuse mid-sentence. "There is too much to see in Venice for a person to ignore on their first day." She continued, even though he was rolling his eyes, "Cecilia can wait until tomorrow. Please. There is one sight you simply must see today. You will have all day tomorrow to conduct your business affairs. Besides, Sean, you would probably waste the remaining day just trying to find Cecilia."

"You don't understand. I would love to spend the day with you, but..."

"Please, Sean," she wasn't letting up, continually batting her dark brown eyes. "Just today. What could it hurt?"

"I-"

"Then it is settled, no? You are coming with me. I have a surprise to show you. Something you will love." She wasted no time grabbing his arm and tugging him from his seat, urging him to the door. Apparently, the Italian people didn't take 'no' for an answer.

Venice, for Sean at least, was becoming a series of diversions. The city offered far too many things to alter one's mind from its intended course. One minute it was the landscape. The next a beautiful girl. Would it really matter that he took his first day to explore his new surroundings? Probably not. He was sure to have the most beautiful guide imaginable, and there had been no sign of the woman he was intending to meet anyway. What the hell, he thought. He would more than likely be dead soon anyway, so what did it matter if his mission started tomorrow?

"Okay, okay... I'm coming," he said, giving way to the urge and following her to the entrance of the shop. Today he would purge Sir Nicholas DeBury from his mind. And Il Fantasma as well. Today he would take a vacation from the worry that so cluttered his life. Today he would share his time with a beautiful woman from Venice. Today was for him.

When Sean hit the street with his new guide leading the way, the smell of Italy, which had been lost amidst the coffee flowing in the bookstore, put his senses in overdrive. Angel could see the expression of wonderment on Sean's face and smiled, realizing to herself that it was great to have someone so void of worldly experience in a city like Venice. A city which was so utterly imbibed with all the Italian culture had to offer. The art, architecture, bakeries, cafes, and the pasta! All waiting patiently to be discovered. Experiences of unimaginable bliss the two of them could share together.

The late afternoon began with a stroll along the district of San Polo. Angel showed her new acquaintance every sight worth seeing. She first pointed out the general architecture of the city, watching Sean's facial expressions as he marveled at the stone work, the carvings, and every minute detail of artistry that had been crafted throughout the centuries. Everywhere he looked in between was water.

His guide explained the entire history of the area. How the whole city floated on the Adriatic Sea, and how, quite literally, every street was made of water, not earth. It had been this way since the city was founded atop mud banks in the 10th century. For Sean, the churches and the overall panorama escaped the power of words. He thought how fortunate it must be to live in a place like this. Yes, how wonderful indeed.

Before he rationed how much time had passed, Sean noticed the sun's glow fading subtly on the horizon. This put him in a state of unsureness. He didn't want to lose what obvious degree of romance might exist between he and his guide, but he in no way wished to entertain thoughts of false hope either.

He decided a halfhearted separation, at this point, might help to provide the answer he was looking for.

"Look," he began, "today has really been wonderful, really," he was laying it on thick, "but shouldn't I get you a cab or something? It's kinda getting late."

"Non Affatto!" she replied. "Don't be so foolish! You shall let me cook for you," she was responding the way Sean had hoped. "My apartment is small, but it is comfortable. And besides, the vegetables I have were bought fresh this morning, and I am not in a habit of accepting 'no' for an answer." Her face was stern, her stance serious, and her arms crossed determinedly. Sean decided he would feign reluctance, but all the while, inside, he was dancing on the ceiling. "First," she changed the subject before Sean could utter a refusal he clearly had no intention of, "there is that special thing I wanted to show you."

Sean's imagination was running a gamut of imaginings, as he was unsure he was ready for her revelations. Angel then, taking his hand in hers, led him down a narrow street, the Rio Terra.

The couple had not walked very far before they crossed the waterway Rio dei Frari, and continued along until they came to a sight that took Sean's breath away. Before the Bostonian book scout stood the Scuola di San Rocco, one of the most beautiful buildings in all of Venice. The building's outer facade paled itself in comparison to the treasures that lay inside its walls. She knew this, her date did not.

The Italian woman placed her hands over Sean's eyes and clumsily led him inside. He could see nothing, but could smell an old-world mustiness, not to mention a change in the temperature. It was colder now. A draft was prevalent in the room, and the texture of the floor was smooth, unlike the street. Then, when she was satisfied with their respective positioning in the building, she slowly withdrew her hands, softly whispering the word 'open' in his left ear.

As the images slowly came into focus, his mind allowed itself to grasp the very reality of what he was seeing.

Images first appeared of The Virgin Mary, painted in various stages of her life on the ground floor walls. Instantly he knew who had painted these tapestries. They were the brilliantly rendered offerings of Jacapo

Tintoretto, and these very paintings had been lavishly depicted in the volume of artwork he had been looking at earlier when he arrived at the book store. His eyes and his mouth were both wide in disbelief, the beauty of the paintings rendering him speechless. He at once decided that the book had been unable to do the artwork justice, and it was hard to grasp the fact that he was standing before images that had been painted some four hundred years earlier. He swore to himself that he could still smell the paint used in their creation. He turned, shaking his head, and went to find where his guide had disappeared.

Before he could begin any real search however, Angel called from the second floor, pleading with Sean to come up. Filled with a sense of both wonderment and awe, he quickly obliged, climbing the staircase to meet the woman and whatever treasure waited above.

As he joined her, his feet clapping the floor in a fevered burst of excitement, his eyes met with huge wall paintings completely surrounding him on all sides. They displayed imagery from New Testament themes, all painted by Tintoretto as well. One painting caused him to pause for a particularly long stare. It was the last painting on his left, and he froze in its presence. It was a rendering of Christ being tempted by Satan in the wilderness. In many ways, it reminded him of the painting that had been on DeBury's library wall, just above the fireplace. An image of a beautiful Satan, offering upright two loaves of bread to a hungered Christ, who sat refusing the sustenance. He was unaware how great of an impact this painting was starting to have on his consciousness. All he could do was stare at the piece, himself caught once again in the very reality of why he was here in Venice.

Sean snapped at once from his dreamlike haze, when Angel grabbed his waist from behind, startling him for a moment.

"Beautiful, is it not?" she said.

"Utterly amazing," he began, not knowing what words could really do the artwork justice, "I just.... I don't know what to say. I'm truly speechless," he said, the words trailing from his lips as he began once again to get lost in the painting.

"What is it about this particular painting that fascinates you so?" the woman inquired.

"I really don't know," he stated. "It reminds me of a painting I saw somewhere, not too long ago. There's so much language being offered in just the position of their bodies on the canvas. It..... just speaks to me, that's all. I can't really explain it." Sean then turned towards the woman, not wanting to ignore her. He was coming once again to grip the reality of why it was he was here. DeBury was his Satan. In one hand, he held the promise of riches untold and in the other, death. Temptation came in many forms and many guises. His willingness to accept his circumstance weighed heavy on his heart.

Angel interrupted the thought.

"Shall we go now so I can make dinner for us?" she said, smiling. "My home is only a short distance from here and the Scuola is beginning to close. If you are sweet, I shall bring you back tomorrow."

Reluctantly, Sean pulled himself away from the painting and began following her down the stairwell.

As the two left the building, Sean reached in his pocket and slid out a cigarette, putting it to his mouth, then lighting it. As he felt a soothing rush of nicotine he looked at the building once more, and decided at least for the remainder of the night, he would purge all thoughts of DeBury. Tomorrow, he knew, would be a different story altogether.

Only a small tip of the sun was present on the horizon. The day had come and gone. As the street vendors began closing down their stands, Sean and C.C. made their way down the narrow streets of Venice and became immersed within the flowing hordes of people heading towards their homes for the evening.

Night had found Venice in much the same way it does the rest of the world.

Sean now found himself entering the home of this new and mysteriously alluring woman. There was an instant comfort about the quaint little home as he eyed the decor and watched as she excused herself shuffling to the kitchen to get the two of them drinks.

The room was furnished with a rustic flair, indicative of the city that surrounded it. The flooring was a terra-cotta colored tile, and the walls had been nicely painted with pastel colors over the natural stone finish. Wrought iron sconces hung from the walls. Iron candle holders stood from the floor, cupping vanilla - scented candles. For the furniture, there consisted a small couch and two red cloth covered chairs.

The whole apartment couldn't have been more than twelve hundred square feet, if that. But it was incredibly warm and inviting. Sean immediately found himself before the pictures hanging from the wall, black and white cityscapes mirroring the city he was in presently. There didn't seem to be any pictures of family or friends, which to him seemed a bit odd. Still, there was an authenticity to this place, a feeling of quaintness that settled nicely on his consciousness.

"For you," Angel said, holding out a small glass of Tuscan wine. "A rare vintage, for an even rarer chance meeting;"

"Thank you," Sean said, accepting the glass, and swirling it slightly before taking a sip. He was watching her closely. Her eyes were clearly locked on his, and as time slowly passed, he became even more raptured in the moment.

"I know you probably think me to have been a bit forward, but please assure yourself this is a bit out of character for me. I'm not the type to bring strange men home, is all I am trying to say," she said, firmly directing conversation.

"That can only be by reason of choice," he retorted, proud to have thought of something original to say in the moment. She had in fact blushed at the remark, a confirmation that he had responded appropriately.

"So," she said pushing a little, easing any discomfort he might have been feeling, "Tell me why you are here again? In Venice, I mean."

"Whoa. Not so fast," he smirked. "I didn't say I was going to tell you why I was here." Sean had his light defenses up, teasing the woman. "Let's talk more about you."

Time to lie. "Of course. I do pretty well for myself, actually." Sean felt, as the words poured out, like the little wooded doll, Pinocchio. At least the only thing growing was the organ between his legs and not the one on his face.

There again. The unsettling feeling in his stomach had returned. Odd. Alcohol had never affected him this way before.

Angel wasted no time resting her glass on a nearby table, offering him assistance as he staggered slightly. "Maybe we should go back inside," she suggested, and he agreed. She then proceeded to lead him back into the den and positioning him so he could rest on the soft, pastel patterned couch. He thanked her for the help, and watched as she walked towards the small, marble fireplace, making the dress she wore look as exquisite as the designer could have ever intended it to look.

Then, in his stupor, a weighted realization came to mind. He tried moving his right arm, but it wouldn't follow the command. His stomach sickened. His blood began boiling. Next, his leg fell asleep. How unbelievably stupid could he have been?

And there was something else.

On the table in front of him were some scattered pieces of mail. Mail that was addressed to a person by the name of Cecilia. Cecilia Conducci.

He would have cursed himself if it had been possible - but his lips wouldn't move. The woman standing before him had played him for a fool. The Delilah to his Samson. Her name, what was it again? Angel? Demon?

Cecilia Conducci. The woman he was supposed to meet was standing right in front of him. Could he really have been so blinded by her beauty that he had lost all ration of common sense? Apparently, he could have.

He could hear her voice now, growing faint and deeper in tone. "Sean? Sean? Are you okay?"

He wanted to speak. To yell. To call her a fucking little bitch! Of course, he wasn't okay. His body was shutting down. Poison. The wine had been laced with some type of poison. God, he was so out of his league. What the hell did some book scout know about the mind of such criminals as he had been accompanied by these last two days? Not enough it seemed. His mind was swirling, but foremost in his thoughts was not his health. It was his ignorance. His stupidity. He would try to fight the numbness.

"Rest, Sean," Cecilia pleaded. "Fighting will only make things worse." The woman standing over him was now offering comfort he neither wanted nor truthfully needed.

Saliva was dripping from the corner of his mouth, but he was powerless to place a hand to his face and wipe it off. His throat dried quickly. His vision blurred. Dumbassdumbassdumbass.

The room was spinning now. His last thought, the only thought a man would have at such a time, was that he was going to die and he hadn't even gotten himself laid. There seemed to be no room in the world for the ignorant. A smile in his mind's eye formed when the realization hit that soon he would join his father on the other side.

With all the power he could muster, he bent each of his fingers toward his, palm, all that is, except the long, middle one. Then, for Sean Wilde, the world went incredibly black...

And the Lord replied to Satan,
"You may do anything you like with his wealth,
but do not harm him physically"

Job 1:12

The Ordinance of Temptation

Winter was permeating every facet of the library as the dark of night encased the two beings seated within the chamber. The soft hum of the ocean could be heard just outside. The storm had finally ceased its ranting, and all was quiet once again. That is, except the voice of Lucifer; the devil of old, speaking coldly in the darkness.

It could be said that if nothing else, the confession had been an enjoyable diversion for the ancient being. He had never really spent much time in the company of a man. Oh, he had observed them many times, but his general association had been one of causing harm, or some gift of discomfort. Never had he allowed himself the exchange of thoughts and ideas. embraced. You govern, judge, and execute such horrid temptations within man's ear. You give suffering its very definition. Yet before me, you radiate a lacking in wisdom, courage and that of compassion. You are without a self," the monk said, staring coldly at the fallen angel. "I do not claim to understand you. If I am the inferior being you claim me to be, what more can I offer than just those musings of an old man, whose time 1 fear will soon expire just as the leaves on the trees that grow here on Athos."

Lucifer sat bewildered, with a look of questioning on his face. He raised an eyebrow, watching the monk as he stared back, transfixed in both honesty and fear.

"All I have revealed to you, and in my words, you can find no sympathy?"

Father Koutrakos wasted no time with his response. "Sympathy need be extended far beyond the likes of you, oh fallible angel. Find sympathy for man, who has had to endure the hardships of your nefarious nature. Countless souls who will suffer an eternity for your lack of complacency and your never-ending quest for revenge. I find many words to describe you, ancient one. Sympathetic is not one of them."

The devil leapt to his feet. He was angered that this confession was getting him nowhere. His breathing was heavier now, but he managed to withhold the shape- shifting that occurred every time he became rattled. That is, everything but two small bone-like horns. He would have liked to pick the little monk from his seat and rattle him about the room, but this was not why he was here. Was the monk just incapable of understanding circumstances on his level, or was his own propensity to feel justified in his war with mankind just too great? Was he really without a conscience? No. He was without justice. Now was the time to press further and separate the monk from his lowly opinion.

"Make a note of this, Father, somewhere in the recesses of your mind," Lucifer urged as he paced noisily about the room. "After the 'fall', when by all recollection a time of settling had occurred, I found myself alone brooding about on the peak of some nondescript mountain upon this earthly realm. I had been alone so long that my mind had given way to contemplate my singularly existence far from my former home. Time had caused me to feel somehow devastated by the distance placed between myself and the Being who created me. I had the whole expanse of earth below my feet. Above me lay an endless sky, which with the mere notion, in could ride upon with my wings. Yet I was void of companionship. Eternally alone. Was this really what I had wanted?"

"It seems you are never satisfied," the monk interrupted, "But a fitting price to pay for losing the battle against your Creator."

"Have you heard nothing I have said?" the demon charged back. "I won the battle. I succeeded in distancing myself from both the Creator and my brethren who were unable to understand my unbridled contempt for your species. If I could not thwart the creation of the human, this had been my alternative. How was I to understand that my love for Him who created me was without the ability to die? Eternity is a cruel existence without the complete control of one's emotions. This is where I had erred in my judgment."

"If I am to understand that your 'fall' as it were, was of your choosing, why did you feel you had the right to be upset with such an alternative existence?"

"My hate for what the human had brought me to do had no direction in which to manifest. I had the kingdom of earth to rule. I was my own king as well. King Nothing."

Father Koutrakos watched as the devil reached towards one of the bookshelves and withdrew a book of hours, hurling the manuscripted volume at the old man. He pulled back, jerking to one side, thinking the object would smack him in the face, but was astonished to see it land safely on the table he was sitting at. Then, as if some diabolical force was turning the pages, the book opened to an illuminous page which in Latin read: 'Genesis.' The monk then looked to Lucifer who stood smiling back at him.

"But everything," the demon smirked, "was about to change."

Staring at the vellum pages now opened before him, the abbot struggled with both fear and apprehension with a topic he knew was soon to be discussed. Lucifer had left little to the imagination when he had told of his fall from Heaven. He knew there would be little held back when the demon discussed the fall of another species. Man.

"What I had come to realize with the passing of time and my interment on earth, was that it had never been my Creator who necessitated the reception of my hate. Why had I not waited until man had been brought forth and simply shown Him why my hate was justified? Perchance, I thought, I could gain favoritism with the Creator again. I would seek out the human, and give him cause to perform evil. The human would, of course, fail my test, thus showing inferiority in the species. Let them all suffer damnation as well, I thought. Then, when the Creator saw it had been I who was right all along, He would free my brethren trapped in the foul region they had been sent!"

The old man stared, unbelieving, at the position in which Lucifer took on such matters as those being discussed at present. His viewpoint was warped to extremes. Hate had consumed him to such a degree that the old man felt there was nothing more he could do but wait out the demon's confession. The old man throughout the course of his life had seen the power of confession. Many had come to him purging a lifetime of ill pains and regrettable actions, only to leave renewed in both body and mind. But Lucifer was different. It hadn't been God who had caused the misshapen shape of the demon's features, but eons of hate which refused to yield to anything or anyone. Father Koutrakos, for the first time in forty years, felt the dread of hopelessness. He bowed his head, speaking to the floor rather than the devil.

"So you set forth to tempt man," he said.

"Please, old man," Lucifer responded, "Do not give me credit where it is not due. Your species was ripe for sin, that is all," he continued, giving a metaphorical jab, "The Creator just made you humans stupid, allowing you a brain with no real thought on how to use it. You were unallowed to question, then told to obey. In fact, if one muses on the topic, there was really no difference between the human being and the beast you call 'dog'. Why your species didn't thank me for the knowledge I bestowed, still is a mystery in itself."

"Thank you?!" the monk scowled.

"You are welcome," Lucifer said infuriating the little man.

"You are brash, and without a soul," the abbot began directing his words in a much more forthcoming tone, "It is one thing to imagine you, and another altogether to be held captive in your presence," he was now standing as well, his hands clenched tightly, "You are despair realized, and embodied by hopelessness."

"Am I?" Lucifer interrupted the harshness being directed towards him, "I think not. We are all entitled to some right of opinion I suppose," the demon shrugged, "I have come to you to confess all. Have you no patience with me? I think it is you father, who is without compassion."

The monk was enraged, but knew the hopelessness of challenging

Lucifer to a linguistic battle. In terms of finding some mental fortitude, the old man would have to accept the fact that wisdom and intelligence were not necessarily the same thing. The demon before him was very intelligent. How could he be any other way? Wisdom however, had made no home within the beast, and this was to his advantage. He would need all the wisdom he had to survive the night.

"I see this is going nowhere," Lucifer stated, "Shall I leave?"

The monk looked down again, "No."

"Then shall I continue?"

"Do as you so choose."

"Very well," the devil said casually returning to his seat. He knew, regardless of how mad the monk became with his tale, he had no choice but to listen. He had given a life to what was being validated by every word the demon said. Like it or not, he like so many before him, were pevertedly fascinated by Lucifer. For he appealed to so many humans, on so many different levels.

The monk, in turn, shifted his body to a more erect position. He was obviously waiting patiently for Lucifer to speak. His brain was cataloging each word the demon spoke into separated chapters, much like that of a book. And his intent of what was to become of the information was still unknown to even himself. Lucifer wasted no time obliging him with more meanderings of a demon scorned.

"As I stated earlier," he began, "I sat alone on the top of my mountain, unaware I was soon to become face to face with my Creator for the first time since my expulsion from the realm you call Heaven. His appearance frightened me for up to that point, I thought I would never see Him again. How long had it been since the war? A year, a century, a millennium? It mattered very little. Time it seemed had caused his anger to subside, and of course with the realization I, too, had been wrong to take so much aggression towards him, my anger had subsided as well. "I wished at once to embrace Him," the demon said, looking away. "I can see by your reaction, that you cannot fathom this, but love, if ever it is true, never dies."

"How did He react to your wanton display of affection?"

Lucifer laughed. "He would not allow me so much as the opportunity to look upon His face. A light radiated so brightly from Him, that I was forced to speak looking away from Him. I cowered. I was infuriated, but powerless to impose my affection upon Him. Little time passed before He called out to me in a tone that caused me to shake nervously."

"You were fearful then?"

"All tremble in the presence of He who is the Creator!" Lucifer snapped. He had not wanted the old man to see any weakness in him, but the fact that the manuscripts across the room were shaking rather violently of their own accord, had been proof enough.

"When I responded, acknowledging His presence, I readied myself for some abuse or punishment at His hand. Perhaps· it had taken Him all this time to devise some sort of torturous end for me that would be exacted at this very moment. I had been allowed to roam this purgatorial realm for such a grand space of time, it only made sense that my time for final judgment had come. But this was not to be the case."

The monk wanted to imagine the scene. A dialogue of giants. Personalities of good and evil. "What did God say to you?" he inquired.

"At first, nothing," Lucifer said, "He was tormenting me with His silence, and He must have stared at me for a long while before coming to terms with what He had to say. I had falsely expected some show of kindness, forgiveness, even mercy. But words are sometimes lost in the presence of a being who can read one's thoughts, and He knew my contempt for your species had only grown worse with the passing of time," the demon said as he took to his feet, animating the role of his creator, 'You, who were once first among my angels, beloved, and adored above all, now embrace within you cause to do harm to the human which I have created and now brought forth?'. I do, I spoke in a broken tongue, shaking. With all my power of deception, I am without the ability to deceive Him who knows all. Then again, He came at me, saying, 'Thou wouldst do well to abstain such thoughts from thy mind, lest I pass upon you the judgment now suffered by thy brethren.' This angered me, and I turned, forgetting to shield my eyes. The pain of looking in His direction was intense, bringing me to my knees," he said, falling before the old monk, "and causing me to flounder upon the earth's floor. Blinded, I called out, demanding to know of my brethren's fate and what had become of those who had rebelled against His tyranny."

"You are brave to a fault, demon," the monk interjected. "Are you never with the ability to humble yourself."

"I am being humble now, allowing you council with me."

"By whose request? Mine or yours?"

"I shall leave if you wish."

"That will not be necessary. Please excuse my interruption and continue," the monk stated, sarcastically apologizing.

Lucifer returned immediately to the tale. "Without warning, and in my blinded stupor, the ground beneath me began shaking. It convulsed, rumbling until it opened, cracking below my feet. I grasped clumsily about for anything that I might hold onto. A root, some branch from a tree, anything. Each crumbled at my touch. Then, I tried to lift from the ground, beating my wings in avoidance of slipping into the gaping earth. But, my Creator had rendered me motionless as well as blind. I could do nothing but give way to whatever horror lied in wait for me. So, relaxing the futility of my struggle, I ceased all act of resistance," he said in a solemn tone, "I was allowed only a moment to see the infernal realm below. Hell, as it were. The screaming and wailing caused a sickening in my body, as my eyes, still blurred from the light of my Creator, struggled to comprehend what they were seeing. The sight was hideously indescribable."

There was a longer pause than usual as the two beings looked at each other in the darkness. Father Koutrakos looked upon the demon with scorn and fascination, wondering how powerful were the emotions of love and hate. This devil had a personality that was sad and regrettable, only because he could control neither emotion. Though he had embraced free will, he seemed to be robbed at the same time of the one thing father Koutrakos possessed -humanity.

"Why do you believe you were spared their fate?" the monk, now in a quandary, spoke first.

"I have often pondered that very question, but I am afraid I have no answer. I have never understood the reasoning behind any decision my Creator has ever made. Never. So I choose not to brood about them for long periods of time. My advice is to ask Him when you see Him," Lucifer stated, returning to his story. "But as I said before, having digested the torment of my brethren, the ground closed immediately as if it had never opened. And so I laid at the feet of the Being before me, wishing to beg forgiveness. But something happened. My hate took hold and I doubled the contempt I had for your species, now more concerned with vengeance than with salvation. At once I started to devise how cunningly I would individualize each and every single torturous act, brandishing upon your species the most serious of offenses. I would treat you no better than you might treat an ant. You certainly deserved to be crushed beneath my feet. But again, my thoughts had run away, and I had conceived them too close to my Creator, who heard every word as if I had stated them aloud."

"And I am to guess He was not pleased."

"He called forth immediately, willing my body into the air as I froze, awaiting whatever conception I had of death," the demon remarked, "Then His light ceased, and I was allowed what would be my last view of his face. We were eye to eye. Then He spoke, saying; 'Craft what devices you may, fallen angel, but naught with thy hand cause harm. A tongue causeth thy banishment from the realm above, so here shall it be thy only weapon as well. Thou shalt not render a hand to cause death nor pain to that which is called 'Man'. For such proclivitive action, I shall suffer you to a punishment far worse than the beings you have seen presently. Heed this warning, angel who stood once by my side, for should a human die directly by thy hand, you shall suffer in ways thou canst conceive. 'Then, as if He thought me void of opinion, without the decency of a response, He was gone. Leaving me once again to my punishment on your realm."

Everything was starting to make sense to the old monk. He had always wondered why for man, Lucifer chose a manner of temptation. Why had he not just simply struck out, killing the humans he hated? Without God's prevention, no human would have ever been allowed to walk the earth. The demon would have killed everyone. His thoughts went askew, and he fell from his seat, surprised by the demon whose mood had changed, beginning a display of hostility.

The old devil leapt to his feet as his body distorted, morphing into his evil guise. He then kicked the chair in which he had been seated, shattering it as if it was no more than a piece of glass. His rage, and the display of aggression, caused the old man to feel a sharp pain, like that of a knife, deep in his heart. And he sat about the floor, clutching at his chest, his beard whiter than before.

"What more could He do to me?!" Lucifer screamed, and thrusting a clenched fist toward his abdomen. "Cursed was I to share the realm of the human, and I could do nothing to rid myself of the accursed beings! Was there no end to the nightmare? I was the most powerful angel ever created, and I could do nothing to appease myself nor rid the world of so foul a creature as you beings were to become. I believed that my contention was so great that all hope for me was lost."

Then, without warning the demon stopped his wild display of posturing, and calming himself, held up his index finger, "Now it was time to turn my anger into something useful - Mischief," he said, eyes ablaze with the fire of impassioned hate. "I would sharpen my tongue as once, in Heaven, I had done before. I was now to do the human in. And I would do this in such a way as to show your race's vast inferiority to mine. I would damn you with my words. My Creator was to give you a conscience, then it was through this that I would see you damned. I would ease its values, imparting self-serving ideas. You would turn from one another, caring only for yourselves. You would come to hate one another for the simplest of reasons, a mockery to the one who created you. Worthless pawns, deserving tribulations untold. And at the center of it all, you would be granted the choice of free will. And still you would serve only the idea of self. Tell me, Father, how have I done?"

"Be damned, Lucifer," the monk returned.

"Do not hate me for this, Father, what else was I to do? See this from my viewpoint, I beg you. What could be easier, without the consequence of punishment for me, yet decisively better than killing you," he said with a horrible gleam in his eyes. "Surely my Creator would damn His new creation just as easily as He had damned the old. And what better service could I provide than to give my tormented brethren the good company of you beings?"

Father Koutrakos was agitated, and wished to change the subject. But there was a last question that needed answering.

"Lucifer?"

"Yes, Father?"

"Why are you allowed reprieve from Hell?"

"Ha, you humans have always had it wrong. I have never been confined to Hell. I am a being married to the earth and sky, the human realm," he stated. "The only occupants in Hell are those who are damned to it. I am many things, Father, but I have yet to be damned."

"Even now, you occupy the earth?"

"Under varying guises, but yes."

"Then what hope does a human have against thwarting your advances?" "You who have spent a lifetime walled inside this reverent prison have no idea?"

"One can sin anywhere, demon. Even here."

"Then the answer should be simple."

"That answer being what?"

"None."

"We seek him here, we seek him there, That demmed, elusive Pimpernel."

Baroness Orczy

IL FANTASMA

Black.

That's how Sean's world seemed when he opened his eyes. His breathing was slow and unsteady. There was something over his head, inhibiting both sight and comfort. A bag maybe. The material felt like burlap. It was suffocating him. He could taste the remnants of last night's wine on his breath, as it had no means of escaping the enclosure that surrounded his head. The one realization he had, however remote the comfort given his present state, was that he was, in fact, alive. At least for the moment.

What a dumb ass, he thought to himself as he revisited the night before in his mind. If he only hadn't been so blinded by his own yearning. He was foolish to imagine a woman as beautiful as Cecilia would have found him that attractive, and if he had used even a fraction of common sense, he wouldn't be in this mess.

His wrists burned. Something was holding them tightly behind his back. A rope perhaps. Shit! He had to get past his self- contempt, as it was not going to aid him in getting out of the mess he was in. Still, an obvious fact remained. Sean was no match for these people. Thieves, mobsters, killers. He was a book scout, for God's sake! No training he had ever undergone was of any use presently. His wits were the only means of freeing himself, and even those were now being called into question.

With the exception of the marching band that was playing in his head, his body felt okay. The only thing of any real immediate concern was how long he could avoid asphyxiation with this bag over his head. He couldn't understand how a guy could go from being on the verge of homelessness one day to being the main character in some Ian Flemming novel the next day. All roads seemed to lead back to one word. Dumbass!

Sean stopped fighting the natural urge to free himself. With every tug, the ropes tightened, cutting deeper into his flesh. He would need to wait things out. Let his captors make the first move. He then stopped wriggling, listening closely for any sound that might lend some clue as to where he might be being held. He felt sure he knew whose captive he was. All rational pointed to Il Fantasma. But why the need to have him bound? They were supposed to be partners, regardless of how reluctant Sean had been. But then another thought occurred. What if unbeknownst to him, DeBury had double crossed this 'Ghost'? Was there a chance Sean was being held captive for a ransom he was sure no one would pay?

When a man is held against his will, his mind, should he allow it to ponder too much, can become his worst enemy. Sean was finding this out the hard way. His heart rate had increased considerably, and with an increasing rapidity of breathing, the limited amount of air he had around him was dissipating. If he kept this up, he would soon pass out. If he passed out, he could die.

Off in the distance, he heard something. The clapping of shoes against a floor, maybe. It was so hard to focus.

Sean could hear multiple voices now, all exchanging dialogue in Italian. This could in no way be of any help. He couldn't comprehend a single thing being said. Would that he could awaken from this nightmare.

Suddenly, he caught a familiar scent. It's funny what the senses, under duress, pick out. It was perfume. No doubt. The bitch Cecilia was close by. And someone else was with her. Possibly more than one person. He hated being at the mercy of another person, but the weak always fall prey to the stronger, more cunning adversary, as any fly who has been trapped by a spider will surely testify.

Someone was reaching towards his face. Oh, God.

"I am really sorry for having done this to you, Sean," the lovely Venetian woman said, removing the bag from Sean's head. "I was really having fun with you yesterday."

Cecilia stood over Sean, looking down at the bewildered look on his face. A brown burlap bag was crumpled in her left hand. He winced as his eyes were being blinded by a bright light shining from overhead. His eyes, blurred with uncontrolled tearing, tried to focus. There seemed to be the figure of a man seated behind a desk off in the distance. Perhaps it wasn't. a desk, but a table of some kind. It was hard to tell. He looked up to the woman who had taken a step back as if she expected him to strike out like that of a wild animal just set free. But he was far from free. And, if the truth be known, he would love to wring her pretty little neck.

He shook his matted head of hair, wishing he was anywhere else. His head hurt. His ego was crushed. And he was pissed with no means of purging the aggression. Why was there a need for him to be duped? Sean wrestled vainly with his bonds. Unless someone willingly freed him, he was going nowhere.

Cecilia then walked back, bending over and kissing his cheek. She was outfitted in a sleek black body suit that pronounced her figurative assets. When she withdrew, noticing how upset her display of affection had made her captive, she spoke out.

"Please. Do not be upset with me, Sean," she noted with condescension, "this was all for your own good. You have no idea the measure one must take to ensure that their identity is kept secret. We take no chances with anyone when it comes to protecting this secret. Do not take what has happened to you personally."

"I know this much," Sean came back in a furious, raspy voice, "you had better take these fucking ropes off my hands before I do something both of us may regret!"

The room burst into laughter. Cecilia too, was unable to repose her humorous outpouring. These people were a long way from fearing Sean, and he felt like an idiot sitting there, bound as if some lamb for slaughter. He had just sounded like a clichéd movie actor. And as for some hero complex he may have held, well, he was on his own. These people could do whatever they wanted with him. He was at their mercy. He dropped his head, awaiting the verbal bashing that was soon to follow.

"By all means, lover," Cecilia said, extracting a sharp blade from behind her back. She then began walking towards him. Sean went totally silent, expecting the worst. The woman bent down, compressing her chest into Sean's face, and reaching around his back. He felt the cold edge of steel as the blade came in contact with his wrist, and he could feel instant relief as it sliced through the rope that had held his hands together. The woman then withdrew herself, preparing herself for whatever reaction Sean might take. She had a firm, manlike grasp of the weapon. Sean was not going to further his embarrassment by challenging her.

The book scout rubbed his wrists as the soreness of prevalent discomfort set in. He gazed about the room once more. Flanked on either side of the man seated behind the desk were two other figures, obscured in the shadows surrounding them. With the exception of the light shining just above the table, the room was dark to the point where Sean could make out little else in the room. There could possibly be a couch to his right. And in the corner, there looked to be the outline of some overturned crates. Cecilia had resigned herself to join the other three figures around the table.

Sean tried to stand. But the sudden rush of blood to his head caused him to stumble and he collapsed back to the floor. He was rubbing his neck as his head throbbed. Whatever Cecilia used in his wine had left him in unrelenting discomfort. He could feel a little strength returning, but only very slowly. He looked at the foursome with contempt. He still couldn't make out the other three faces. Sean wanted to speak but could think of nothing clever to say. Then, while rubbing his eyes, he heard from the far-left comer of the room, someone throw a switch.

The room suddenly filled with light. And too much of it. Sean pulled his hands to his face, trying to adjust.

"That better, Sean?" the woman said sarcastically.

"Go to hell," he aptly responded.

"Soon enough, for all, I'm sure," another, new voice spoke.

Sean had regained both his strength and his sight, now standing in full view of his captors. He started to speak but Cecilia beat him to it.

"Sean, I would like you to meet my brother, Vincent Conducci," she said, presenting the man seated behind the table. "Otherwise known to the world as Il Fantasma."

Sean looked past Cecilia, ignoring her and what appeared to be two goons as well. The man that had been seated stood calmly and made his way around the table, moving closer towards Sean. He looked to be a bit shorter than Sean. He wore a simple T-shirt, un-tucked from a pair of baggy jeans, and looked extremely relaxed in the sandals he wore. His hair, which was as black as night, was long and slicked back and pulled into a tight ponytail behind his head. His facial features. were strong, and his skin well-tanned. Vincent was not quite what Sean had expected. Perhaps he had expected someone a bit more professional looking. But then, he had seen too many movies.

Vincent didn't offer a hand as he stopped several feet from his captive. He was surveying Sean, sizing him up. Decidedly, there wasn't much of a conclusion to draw. His dark eyes stared directly into Sean's.

It was Sean who spoke first.

"I'd like to say it's nice to meet you," he began, "but we both know all this has been a load of bullshit, and I'd be satisfied if we could just dispense with civilities, and get to the point of why I'm here and what you intend to do with me."

"I wholly agree, my friend," Vincent said, speaking with a heavy Italian accent, "but first, allow me to echo the sentiment my sister spoke of earlier. I am truly sorry that we have to take such extreme measures when dealing with my identity, but such precautions are necessary when dealing in my line of work. The authorities would love nothing more than to discover my whereabouts."

Sean stared back coldly, not wishing for an insincere apology.

"You are in a safe place, let me assure you," Vincent urged, "And there is no one among us that desires to do you harm."

"Please listen to him, Sean," Cecilia urged from behind him. "We must all work together if we are to pull off this task, and we need a mutual trust among us."

"My sister's right Sean. There is a lot that can go wrong with a theft of this kind, and everyone must equal themselves before our task. Let me say again," he redirected conversation, "I am the most wanted thief in the world. My secrecy is of paramount importance. If I were to be captured - and be assured there are people right now spending their whole law enforcement careers trying - I would be bound to prison for life. Such a prospect has warranted such extreme measures as you have had the unfortunate luck of experiencing. For this I am sorry."

There was a sincerity in his words, but Sean offered no sign of understanding. The truth was that he was the odd man out. The one person who had no business here. He was, in truth, letting his guard down a little, but he knew he was in a den of thieves, playing cards with a band of vipers. Worst of all, he was without the protection of anything or anyone. No ace up his sleeve, as it were. He could trust no one. These people played by an entirely different set of rules. And for him at least, there were no directions for playing the game.

"I'd like to know what you've got planned," Sean said as plainly as he could.

"Of course," Vincent returned, ''but first let me introduce you to the people you will be working with. If we are to work together we must acquaint ourselves with each other, no?"

"Fine by me."

"Good," the thief began, "As my sister stated, I am Vincent Conducci," he said, now holding out his hand. Sean hesitatingly obliged him. "The one who the papers call Il Fantasma. I have made a name for myself because I have never been caught, and I am rarely ever seen. In order to keep things this way, I ask that you refer to me only as 'Vincent' from this point on. My secrecy protects my clients, and has, depending from whose viewpoint we choose to see it, become more important than even my own life. It is not something that will, at any point of our mission, be compromised."

Vincent then motioned for the two men standing behind him to move forward, which each did responding immediately as they were instructed. Sean moved a few steps closer as well, but remained at a distance. He then looked over to Cecilia, who was standing as if she were modeling some clothing with her arms crossed and her hip cocked to one side. She would not stop smiling at him. Vincent suddenly spoke up, bringing Sean back into focus.

A large man appeared to the thief's right side. "This is Luigi Basso,"

Vincent said. "He is my - how do you say- 'muscle,' if you will. He is in charge of my general protection, and of those that are involved in my endeavors, as well. I trust him with my life, as you must do also. He is an expert in all manners of tactical weaponry, and will insure our safety throughout the present task. He has served as a mercenary, and in two instances I am aware, an assassin. In all your life you will find no better means of protection than signor Basso."

Sean looked at the man who had not offered his hand. He was a big Italian no doubt. His gaze met Sean at eye level. The quality of his dress was impeccable, the suit well-tailored and sharp. Sean noticed the faint remnants of a scar running from his right eyebrow down through his lower cheek. His hair was greased back in typical Hollywood mobster fashion, and Sean thought to himself, if there was a poster boy for la Costra Nostra, this guy was it, hands down.

"Wait a minute," Sean said, interrupting the introduction, "we've got a little problem." He was noticeably uneased.

"What do you mean, Sean? What problem?"

"Before I left London," he began, while trying to convey an air of serious concern, "DeBury revealed to me his insurance plan for assuring himself my involvement. He has hired some nut case Mafia assassin to 'shadow' me until the job's complete. I can't remember the guy's name, though. It was something like.... um..."

"Lorenzo Carbuoni?" Vincent said, finishing Sean's sentence.

"That's it!" the book scout affirmed. "Have you heard of the guy? Is there anything we can do to shake him out?"

The room burst into laughter. Even Luigi Basso broke a smile. Sean was befuddled at what he had said that was so funny now.

"Lorenzo Carbuoni," Vincent was saying, "is Cecilia's hair stylist in Venice," he closed, barely able to break the news to Sean through the laughter.

Sean shook his head, his brain on fire at having been played for a fool. He was to be duped to the end, it seemed. These people had him pegged, and there was no getting around his awkwardness.

"Take it easy, Sean," Cecilia spoke up noticing that the American was taking no humor in being made fun of. "There had to be some insurance that you would come to Venice quickly so we could get on with things. If you had simply agreed from the start, Sir Nicholas would have had no need to lie to you. I.... we.... are sorry. Forgive us."

"Fuck you people!" Sean said, as if he was going to exit the room. He had no sooner turned than Luigi motioned to block his pathway, saying nothing but making his intent very clear. Sean stopped mid-stride, and turned back towards Vincent who was now leaning with his back to the desk.

"Ease up, Sean," he said while lighting a dark colored cigarette. "While there is certainly no need to fear Lorenzo Carbuoni or his deadly cutting shears," the room burst into laughter once more, "there is ample reason to fear signor Basso," he said with his eyes glancing in the direction of the large Italian blocking Sean's path. "Nothing is going to jeopardize our task, *capire*? So just relax, my friend, there is no need for violence."

Sean was noticeably pissed, with no real means of venting his rage. He would in all reality be in such a position as this for some time.

Vincent then spoke up, breaking the silence between the two.

"If we could, let me continue the introductions."

"Please. By all means," Sean said, seething to himself.

"Very well," the thief said, "The individual to my right is Simone Pisano."

Pisano held out his hand immediately, and Sean returned the gesture with noticeable reluctance. This new acquaintance was a rather small man, somewhat like Vincent, but a bit more petite, and feminine looking. His hair was black and rather unkempt given his well- attired outfit. His most outstanding feature was a rather large hooked nose in the center of his face. Sean thought he looked like a bird somewhat. His smile was pleasant enough, and his demeanor seemed, on the whole, reserved. As Vincent started to speak the man humbly resigned himself, stepping back and nodding on approval of what was being said.

"Signor Pisano is among the finest computer and electronic masterminds I have ever had the pleasure of coming across. He has been with me for twelve years, and he has been able to override every technological obstacle that has ever presented itself to be a problem," Vincent said. "He will be our means of communication when we begin our business venture shortly."

Sean watched as now Cecilia stepped forward, her curvaceous frame holding him captive for a brief moment before more aggressive feelings took hold. She had hurt his ego more than anything else, and that part of him was the most delicate to repair.

"This is-"

"I know the bitch, Vincent," Sean said, wearing his contempt for her on his sleeve. "We met some time ago, although I can't remember just where at the moment, hold on...lemme see...."

"There is no need to be ill- mannered Sean," Vincent retorted.

"No need for.... ?" Sean said, aghast. "You people are nuts! I've been lied to by everyone, knocked unconscious, tied up, threatened, and will at some point, no doubt, face death or at the least long- term imprisonment, all because one morning I answered a phone and entertained a conversation with a book collector! No need for rudeness? Fuck you people! I don't want a part of any of this!"

Vincent let Sean rant for some time. In truth, he understood perfectly the way his guest felt, but it seemed of little matter to him. He needed to get beyond this point and on to more pressing matters. The four of them had been readying themselves for months, preparing for the heist and sorting through the details. He was not about to let Sean screw any of that up. After allowing the book scout a reasonable time in which to voice his temper, Vincent broke in. It was time to continue.

"I understand your reluctance, Sean, and I know you want no part in this," he began, "I want you to have no part in this either. But, as none of us here are expert enough to identify the object we are after, and DeBury's assurance is solidly against going forward without you, you will just be forced to accept the fact that you, my friend, are fucked. Accept this. Help us. And I assure you, there will be money for all at the end." He paused, taking a long drag from his cigarette and locking eyes with his captive audience of one. "I can get you through this, but you will have to trust me. Can you do that my friend?"

Sean would have rather made love to a rattlesnake. Which, he thought to himself, might be very similar in feeling. These people threw around the word 'trust' as if it were an item in a shopping cart. If he heard one more person even mention the word, he felt he would explode into fit of unbridled rage. These people had not the faintest idea of what the word even meant. So he chose, rather than to answer the question directly, to redirect the conversation.

"So what's your role in all of this, Vincent?"

"I was just about to get to that my friend," he began while Sean agitated his facial features at the sounding of the word 'friend.' "My work will be coincided with that of my sister. The two of us are responsible for obtaining this item, this book, that DeBury wants so badly."

"She...?" Sean questioned.

"Is a thief as well," Vincent said, finishing the sentence. "Most every job I have been involved with or performed has been carried out with the aid of my sister. Cecilia is always at my side. She is the only person I completely trust."

"Then..."

"Il Fantasma is not one, but two people," the thief stated, moving conversation along. "Through my guidance and protection, my sister and I have perfected our art to such a degree that we can perform any task of thievery, provided our conditions and, of course, our price, is met."

"So what do you know about Nicholas DeBury, the man you're working for?" Sean asked.

"I know very little, and that is how I like it," Vincent stated. "I never concern myself with the character of any client, this being most unnecessary. What concerns me is their specific request, and the size of their purse. Should both meet my requirements, we proceed to the point where you and I are at presently."

"And where exactly are we, presently?" Sean inquired.

"The plan," Vincent responded. He then instructed Cecilia to fetch all documentation concerning the area they would be working in. "My sister and I have been gathering documents, floor plans, and supplies for quite some time, and I have sent her to obtain them so that we can discuss what is to happen in great detail. We will be leaving for Washington D.C. this evening."

"Tonight!" Sean exclaimed in disbelief.

"Yes, Sean. There is no need to waste even another minute," Vincent urged. "While I know this is moving very fast for you, the four of us have been planning this for many months. Our need now is only to bring you up to speed. Your role is a simple one, and you only need to know of the small procedural tasks in which you will be involved. I need to know if you have the fake manuscript."

"It's in a leather bag, wherever you've taken it."

"Good, then I'm sure my sister has it," he said, redirecting himself. "Are there any more questions before we get started, then?"

"None that would make a bit of difference at this point," Sean said coldly.

"Excellent," Vincent said, turning toward Cecilia who was now coming into the room carrying a bundle of documents in her arms. "Ah yes, here we are," he said, taking the rolled papers from his sister and laying them on the table. He then motioned for everyone in the room to gather around the table as he undid the rubber bands holding the items together.

"Sean?"

"Yeah?"

"What do you know about the Smithsonian Institution?" Vincent said, smiling as he looked up from the documents laying on the table. Sean stepped in closer, but still maintained a small distance from the other four.

Spread before him were what appeared to be various blueprints and some obvious maps, all showing different aspects of industrial design and floor plans. Sean was about to have all of his questions answered...

"The only way to get rid of temptation is to yield to it ...... I can resist everything but temptation."

Oscar Wilde

Testaments

"Now it came to pass, as time drifted by, I sought to test my wile on that of the human," Lucifer continued, smiling, his features now radiating beauty where a few moments past there had only been grotesqueness. "It was time to undo the platitude on which you beings stood. So, I called out to the realm above! Let us see how the human will resist the twisting of my tongue! Allow me just one object on the whole realm of earth that the being 'man' could not have rule. One item was all I asked for. Though the Creator did not direct an immediate answer, as often is the case with Him, it was eventually made clear to me. He chose a simple, harmless, wonderful little tree. It was enough, I said."

Father Koutrakos had taken up a quill and begun jotting small notes to himself on a slender piece of parchment. His demonic guest had become quite detailed in his descriptions of otherworldly events. And he had not wanted to forget any details, should later he choose to make a record of them. If he had imagined all of what was being said to be a dream, some imagining vision, he had now convinced himself otherwise. Through some foul rationing, the old man was able to find a degree of validation in what the demon had said. In truth, more than he cared to admit of what had been said made sense. These revelations were causing him a high level of emotional distress. He wiped his sweated brow with a small piece of his cloak. Had he overstepped his bounds by allowing the conversation to continue? Moreover, could he stop listening now even if he wanted to?

He questioned himself no further on the matter, and looked at the angel quietly seated across from him. The fallen one simply stared back as the old abbot sat marveling at his features. He wondered, if this was the demon's true form, how such a being of immense beauty could have gone so far from the path of righteousness. The monk had always believed that nothing happens unless it was willed by God. In the realm of imagining, was it possible that God wished Lucifer's expulsion all along? Perhaps it had been a plan only He could understand. Had, in fact, Lucifer been part of necessity's plan? How could such evil have grown within a being in a place where suffering is supposed to be nonexistent? He struggled with the very ideas that presented themselves and, with these musings, began to make himself ill.

"You do not look well, Father," Lucifer said. He showed no real concern, only making an observation of fact.

"I shall be fine," the monk returned, wiping his forehead again. He was now running a fever. The cold winter air, coupled with the appearance of his uninvited guest, had indeed made him sick. But pressing past any illness, he persisted in his endeavor to know more.

"Please continue," he said, coughing.

"Very well," the old devil mused, seemingly bothered that he had been interrupted at all. "It had been my desire to approach this new being, man, from the very moment I saw him. I was fascinated by the way your species looked. In form, we looked much the same, but there was something altogether different about you. Your species had an organ toward the lower part of your torso that was confusing to me. And there was a difference even so between these additions on the species of both 'man' and 'woman'. While this in no way changed my opinion of you beings, it puzzled me at first. But I pondered very little on such matters, and feigning the patience I have become known for, I waited and I watched. I was at first unsure of how to make an approach or what action I would take. My plan needed ingenuity. A crafty, proseful, verbal piece of manipulation. So, I watched as these new creations moved about their new home, my new home. And I plotted their demise."

"Were you not fearful God would exact His vengeance towards you should you move against man?" the monk inquired.

"Not in the least," Lucifer said, speaking with an air of haughtiness that was rivaled only by his sense of self-righteous indignation. "Man was to be my testing ground. I would prove to my Creator once and for all, the extreme fallibility of His latest genesis. I felt He would then be able to see things from my perspective," he said, pausing briefly. "But I still remained unsure of exactly what to do. Then a realization came to mind! The problem that I was having rested not in my hands. What if I could suggest one being tempt the other," he said, motioning with his elongated fingers. "Yes! One could suggestively damn both, and I would obtain two souls for the price of one alone! The woman was the key to everything. I did not believe my plan would have worked the other way around."

"Why did you believe this?"

"You would not believe me if I told you."

"Given everything I have witnessed tonight, you should try me."

"Very well monk," the devil said, "at the brain's very root, a woman is a smarter species of human than a man. I doubt if the man could have been as persuasive as was the woman. And regardless of whether that musing is true or false, we know that I was at least half right."

"What made you think this to be true?"

"I have had a thousand lifetimes in which to do no more than observe your species. In that time, I have seen the intuition of a woman move mountains, and save the most hapless infant from mortal death. You have come to believe the pain of childbirth a woman's curse, and the pain is. But if a child were entrusted to the care of a man, well, your species would have never survived. The Creator likewise endowed the female with assets man could not live without, but the reversal is not true at all. Whole governments, wars, and societies have collapsed over man's need to possess but a single female. Yet the Creator played a cruel trick by not giving woman the power of physical strength over man. If it were any different, man would be no more than slave to that which you call 'woman'. But then again Father, I am Lucifer, what do I know?"

The monk mused on this for no more than a minute before willfully moving from the subject. Lucifer appearance was as that of a male, but Father Koutrakos knew he was neither man nor woman.

"So you skillfully began the first act of temptation?"

"Indeed, monk," Lucifer returned with confidence. "The combined shame they would soon feel for having disobeyed their Creator was to be beauteous indeed. Oh, but if you could have witnessed their groveling, their incessant pleading, the woeful tears cascading like waterfalls from their eyes - it was magnificent. I had triumphed after all, and I had done so with my first attempt. What sprang from my throat were mere words. Syllables dancing deceivingly from my lips: You beings had not been half as hard to deceive as I had hastened to believe. I, Lucifer, had single handedly damned your entire race. I waited acknowledgment from the Creator."

"All was not lost for man, demon," the abbot said.

"Yes. As you say, this was true." Lucifer shook his head while smirking as a means of conveying not humor but disgust. "Imagine for moment, if you will, the rage which I felt when He forgave you worthless, hapless degenerates," the demon spit the word with contempt, his face frowning, his eyebrows twisted. "Where was forgiveness for my brethren damned in Hell?! Where was a pardon for the angel Lucifer?!"

"Perhaps man offered a sincerity that you beings did not."

"Man," the devil growled, "the bane of all creation," he stated as if there was to be no disputing the matter. "What my Creator had done," he said, continuing his story, "would pale by comparison to what would befall me next."

"And that would be...?" the monk stuttered as he felt the words leap from his mouth.

There was a few moment's pause as the demon stared back, as if the monk should already have some idea at what he was alluding to. The fallen angel stroked at his chin. The emptiness prevalent in his eyes was_ numbing. No real time passed before he began speaking again. "When, before the 'fall', I had approached my Creator in Heaven, I had asked for the ability to create my own race, my own legion of beings to follow me. To serve. I was harshly reprimanded for such a request," the demon said as his features began distorting and his voice climbing. "Imagine, monk, how I must have felt upon realizing that the very Being who had denied me this right in which I speak, embedded within your species the cursed gift of reproduction!!"

The table began shaking where the monk had been seated, listening. Manuscripts fluttered, their pages bending and turning at will. Objects lying about the room, lifted from their stations and started floating on the stagnant air. The leaded window began to open and close, bringing a colder chill to the room as it allowed the outer wind inside.

And upon the stone floor now sat Father Koutrakos, cowering and afraid. Something was happening within his body. Something strange. His bones seemed to ache, as if they were weakening somehow. The pain was strangely inconsistent. It would appear for a moment, then disappear altogether. There was little time to concentrate on himself before the demon spoke again.

"My Creator," he said clenching his fists and posturing in an aggravated manner, "had granted you beings, so less a species than I, the gift to make more of your own species! You were given the power to create, and Lucifer was not! And, to further the point, He had done so in a way that brought a perverse satisfaction to the transaction as well!" The demon fell to his knees and drew his hands to his face, covering it. "Oh, I had been damned far worse than my brethren! And how was I to imagine such an ingeniously clever outpouring from the Creator?! He let his hands fall, staring at the monk who in turn, was cradled about the floor. "Now, here is Lucifer," the demon spoke, holding his hands outstretched, "a being confined to the earth, alone with the very species I deplored more than you could possibly fathom, forced to bear witness daily, hourly, the continual creation of more humans by your very own hands. Yet I could not raise my hand against you," the angel said, bowing his head. "Imagine the ingeniousness of it. What finer torture could there have been for Lucifer?" he said looking up at the monk again. "An act of brilliance. An act of horror. My Creator had caused for me, an act of permanent suffering. It is true, Father. Vengeance is mine, sayeth the Lord."

The monk willed himself to speak, even though he was frightened and shivering. "In all.... your ranting... demon, how... could you see.... the weight of your actions... giving cause to a lesser degree of punishment?"

The demon, at such a speed as to impress upon the monk an air of otherworldly strength, moved speedily across the stone floor - appearing inches from the old mans face. The monk could feel Lucifer's hot breath all around him as the demon began to speak. "Test me not, Confessor," he said, heightening the abbot's fear, "there are a multitude of insidious devices I can conjure forth, without killing you. Careful with that tongue, I am having a sensitive moment, eh?"

The old monk said nothing. Shivering in a pool of his own sweat, he simply watched as Lucifer drew back, and returned to the other side of the room. The calamity had stopped. Everything that had been displaced by the demon's aggressive outpouring had returned to its rightful place. The room was quiet once again.

"Forgive me, monk," the angel said, "I can lose myself at times. I have never shared these thoughts with another soul, let alone a human one. For me, it was as if every wish I had asked of my Mak.er had been granted - just not to me, but to the one being I deplored. He had used my own hate against me. How much suffering was one being to take?" he stated, looking back at the monk now pulling himself from the floor. "How was I to exact vengeance now?"

"Perhaps," Father Koutrakos said, "You should have simply withdrawn all further malice and contempt."

Lucifer laughed aloud.

"We all are endowed with what has become our 'nature.' Our character, if you will," the demon said. "Mine was not to lie down and accept my punishment lightly. I thought there could still be some justice for Lucifer yet." He winked. "I regressed for a while. It is not easy to contemplate such foul stratagems at once. I could not kill you beings. But," Lucifer said, holding his finger up proudly, "What if l were to impress upon one of your kind, the same musing? The Creator had not said, you couldn't kill one another. It had not been very difficult to tempt your species before. Perhaps I could do so again? There could be no way He would forgive such a blasphemous act. This would surely damn the human."

"Lucifer,"

"Yes monk?"

"Why do you not see, that no matter what you do, the action will be somehow offset by God?"

"Why? Because I will it so, Father," the devil said, taking a swallow. "I have satisfied myself to this measure. It is, as I stated before, in my nature. It is what I am."

"If you believe this, there can be no forgiveness," the monk said as he shook his head with disgust.

"Forgiveness. Yes. Well, I should hope that when you have weighed the remaining tale, you will see things far differently. Shall I continue?"

"I could save your time," the abbot said. "I can surmise that you were the voice that caused Cain to slay his brother Abel."

Lucifer began cackling, the tone of which was horrible to the ear. The monk had never heard a laugh so full of despicable delight. "And was I not so delightfully appeased? If I could tempt a human to kill another human, there was no limit to the horrors I could suggestively bring forth. A brother. Flesh of likened flesh. Destroyed at the hand of the other brother. His own parents' offspring. He might as well have killed himself!"

"And you bathed in this delight?" the monk said.

"To be certain." Lucifer returned, "I had not only tempted one brother to slay the other, I had also caused more lamentation in the home of those who were first upon the earth, and I had caused a stirring in Heaven. Two souls had been freed. One dead, one damned. My tongue," the demon stated as he paraded about the library, "is the very definition of 'art.' This act had been deserved in my eyes. And I was satisfied once again."

"So long as everyone else was in misery."

"It is as you say. It is all I have. Idle time, eh?"

"You then set out to cause more suffering."

"Not so!" Lucifer said, as if somehow offended.

"What do you mean?" the monk, now confused, started to ask. "When, after the time of history's first murder," Lucifer began, "I completely withdrew myself from the affairs of the human. I watched. I observed. But I never interfered. My act, 'sin,' I believe you call it, had now taken on a life of its own. It had become almost a being in itself. My first child. Ha! I was not without the ability to create something, was I?"

"I am afraid I do not under-"

"No longer was it a necessity for me to tempt man on an individual basis. No. Man would now destroy himself. Even I was amazed at the lack of complication that needed to occur. I needn't do a thing. The evil wondering of man usurped even my scope of fathoming. You beings would hasten to destroy yourselves, you didn't even need me further."

"What eventually called you to action?"

"Nothing."

"You are saying you never again tempted man?"

"Not until after the flood."

"What?" the old man was stunned, his medieval mind had come to believe that all negative events that happened in the world were a result of Lucifer and his angels. Lucifer was essentially denying this.

"Oh come now, Father. Your species was going to bring about its own destruction. This was forthcoming. How long did the human believe he could continue such an inflammatory mockery of his Creator. Even now, as I recall the day, I can remember walking along a much-traveled path only to look down and find my feet wet. Father, I was many miles from the nearest body of water. Instinctively, I knew. Man was to be no more," he said, smiling. "Finally, the Creator had realized all I had said was true. All was to be well for Lucifer."

It wasn't long before the old man spoke. "Yes, Lucifer. It would seem as if you had proven man's inferiority. But God must have found some salvability in our species. Did He not save Noah, giving humanity hope?"

"Yes, Father. He did," the demon said with contempt. "The one whom you call 'God' visited me as I sat atop a huge rock, watching the waters of this planet rise. All around us were the clamoring of human bodies. Useless beings of humanity suffering the impetuousness of their sin. He came to me, trodding the water's surface, and walking through the vastness of human life grasping for mercy beneath His feet. I caressed the sight with my heart, and waited for my apology."

"I am to guess God had other plans."

"Is this not always the case?" the demon mocked him. "He revealed to me the one you called 'Noah' would survive the destruction. I was saddened by this, but not inconsolable. What pushed me beyond my station was that through this man 'Noah', he would allow man to continue existence upon the Earth. Yet my brethren still lamented in Hell. I refused to be in His presence as He had gone completely mad. At that very moment, I resigned myself to find Hell, and spend the remainder of eternity chained there, if need be. I had given up. He would never see you beings for the disgraceful entities you were. I was damned and, wishing to part from His company, soon left to find Hell."

"You sought Hell as a refuge?"

"You imagine it to be worse than the punishment I was currently suffering?"

"Anything must be better than Hell."

"You are very wrong, monk. Nothing could be worse than earth. Earth was hell. At least for me."

Both beings watched as the last flickering candle extinguished itself, and darkness enveloped them both. The monk was so afraid he could barely move. His body quivered, shaking with some spasmic will, void of his command. Blackness lay just beyond his vision. He would have to reach the other candles laying just across the floor, on the shelf with the manuscripts. He took one step. Then another.

Suddenly, right before his face, flames leapt from the ends of two candles held firmly within both hands of the demon. They couldn't have been inches from his face. The old devil stared back from just behind them, smiling at the monk.

"Looking for these?" he asked in a way that reminded the old man just who and what he had been dealing with all along.

"If you are intent on sending me to my grave," the monk said, grasping his chest, "then do so now and be damned. I have no heart for such tricks."

"Forgive me."

"There can be no forgiving one so full of deception and contempt."
"Your 'God' can forgive anyone, monk."

"I am beginning to doubt it," he said, referring to Lucifer.

"As I monk, as I."

The discussion trailed as the demon placed the two candles where the former ones had been and resided himself to sit on the table now, between them. The monk walked to the window in an effort to assure himself the window was indeed closed, and that the winter air was safely barred from the room. His body temperature had dropped and his chill was causing him a great discomfort. Returning to his seat, the little man bundled himself tightly, clinching his outer garment, waiting for Lucifer to speak. This didn't take long.

"So it came to pass," he began, "that I found the very gates of Hell. But try though I might, I was not allowed entry."

"Were you not a prince of Hell?"

"No. Hell was being guarded by the fallen ones. An angelic host which fell from Heaven instructed to not allow my passage. I could not enter Hell, though in my own way, I had given rise to its existence."

"This seems unfathomable." "Yet true."

"What, demon, did you do?"

"I returned to Earth, and began roaming once more."

"What did you find?"

"Everything to be as it was. There was no trace of human remains. No relics that would show you beings had ever existed at all. But 'Noah' and his ilk would set repopulating my realm once more."

"And you would begin some new amusement?"

"No. My plan had changed. I was to avoid direct confrontation, believing that the sin I had brought forth in the past incarnation of Earth was still embedded in the humans now allowed a momentary reprisal. Incidentally, Father, it had."

"How," the monk began to inquire, "was sin to manifest without your hand?"

"You humans believe me to be more important than I am. At least as I pertain to sin. Sin began growing in a place it can't be weeded out- in the heart and mind. Sin is alive. In no way was there a necessity to tempt the human. You beings already welcomed sin, just as though a newborn babe. I have, essentially, become unnecessary. It is true, I will tempt an individual soul if it befits some larger purpose, but this act is largely a wasted outpouring."

"Why?"

"Humans invent new ways to blaspheme and torment one another. Your species bends the Law of your Creator to whatever befits your purposes. You justify the morose and befriend scorn. Let me also share this with you," the demon leaned closer as he spoke, "Hell's growth rate triples that of Heaven and it is truthfully a wonder there is any room left at all!"

"Man came into this world void of sin. It is you who imparted this disease upon our heads."

"I brought forth nothing you humans did not willingly embrace or desire. But of course, you would seek to blame me, thus validating everything I have said. Still, I accept this of you humans. I am as necessary to you as air and water. You need me. I am your lover and I am your piteous excuse for your suffering."

"You are a beast, and you are an abomination. You are a disease and you are nothing more."

"I am these as well, to be sure, but I am so very much more."

"Where can we go from here, demon? You and I. We see nothing in the same light."

"Let us go to Hell."

"I……I am sorry… ?!"

"There, the light burns such that we may find a commonality between us."

"I…I…am not-"

"Listen, Father. Lucifer has a story to tell. 'Tis of hope abandoned. 'Tis a tale of Hell…."

"There is no genius free from some tincture of madness."

Seneca

To Coin a Stratagem

Cecilia glided across the floor, aware all the while of Sean's intentful stare. He could see she was carrying documents of some kind just under her arm, but he was oblivious to what information they might contain. In truth, he was paying more attention to the blueprint of her walk more than those she was carrying. As she passed, she seemed to purposefully brush his shirt, the smell of her perfume now teasing his senses. He acted as if it meant nothing, but Cecilia knew differently. She knew his pride had been hurt and that he wished, no matter how mad he had become, to consummate their relationship on a much more intimate level. He was, after all, just a man. She smiled as she contemplated the unspoken request to herself.

Cecilia then came to lay the documents on the table, as everyone in the room now congregated around them. Vincent wasted no time shuffling the papers and unraveling the large sheet on top. His small hands jostled the papers until he had the largest of the diagrams in full view.

"I want everyone to pay close attention to what I am about to show you," he said, turning to assure himself each person was paying attention. "What you see before you is an aerial map of the various buildings and streets that make up the grounds of the Smithsonian Institution. As you can see, this is quite a large area. There are twelve main buildings that can be seen on this map, all of which house relics of both historical and cultural value to the Americans. Thankfully, we need only concern ourselves with one of these buildings. This one here," he said, pointing to a large oblong building towards the top left area of the diagram. He watched as each person nodded with approval at what he was saying. "This is the National Museum of American History," he stated. "This is where the prize we are after is kept, and it is here that we shall concentrate our efforts," he said taking a breath, and allowing everyone to get a firm grasp on the diagram's layout. He then made eye contact with Sean, who seemed to be hanging on every word Vincent was saying. "Most of the institution's rare books are housed in this building here," he said, as he pulled out a map of the National Museum of American History from underneath the pile. It showed three levels, and Vincent was pointed to the first floor while continuing. "This area you see here is known as the Dibner Library."

"This all seems very convenient," Sean interrupted. He had not realized his thoughts had been expressed aloud.

"Let me assure you, my friend, it is hardly that," Vincent returned. "You will all notice the location of our target," he stated, pointing again to the map, "its position is at the comer of 14th Street and Constitution A venue. The problems with internal security I suspect will pale in comparison to those we are likely to face once we are outside, especially if an alarm is triggered." He had now moved his finger towards the right of the building, pausing at the sight he intended all to notice. "This structure over here is the Capitol Building. Each of you can see how close it is in proximity to our target. With the recent terrorist attacks in the U.S., security in and around this area should be extremely tight. Each of us will need to prepare ourselves for anything, and be constantly on guard."

"What will we do should we draw attention to ourselves?" Sean asked, noticing he was the only person who seemed to be concerned or have any questions.

"I shall get to that," Vincent snapped, "but allow me first the opportunity to explain the specifics of our internal operation. Getting into the museum will not be the problem. We will gain access during regular operating hours, thus alleviating ourselves the trouble of breaking in after hours. Our actions from that point on will be what determines the fate of our mission."

Sean backed slowly from the table, as a queasiness had come to his stomach. He was becoming dizzy, the images of lines and graphics starting to blur. The four people around him were professional thieves. He was a simple book man. He found himself sweating, unable to control his relative discomfort. He overheard someone tell Cecilia to fetch some water, just as he went weak at the knees, collapsing on a nearby couch.

When he opened his eyes, it was to a woman shoving a glass of cold water at his lips.

"Sean," Vincent said standing just behind Cecilia. "'are you going to be all right?"

"Yeah, yeah," he said, sitting up and rubbing his eyes, "Your concern is touching," he commented sarcastically, "but I'll live."

"As soon as you regain some sense of composure we shall begin again," the thief commented.

Sean stood up and walked back toward the table, noticeably embarrassed. No one said a thing to him though. In truth, they all understood how he had felt. But what concerned Vincent the most was how much of a liability Sean might become if things got as hectic as he imagined they might. Time would tell. For now, there was still much to be discussed.

Vincent made eye contact with each person in the room before starting again. He was pointing to the oblong building he had referenced earlier.

"The American History Museum, henceforth know to us as the AMHM, is divided into three distinct levels, with a lower level on the western side of the premises, here," he said, pointing to the boxed diagrams floating on the page. "Now, as I stated before, our concentration will begin here, on the first floor." Vincent coughed and looked up at Sean as if to assure himself that the sickly book scout was indeed paying attention. He could do little else.

"The Dibner Library is located towards the back of the building," Il Fantasma began again. "Slightly offset to the right of the museum's main entranceway. As it is off - limits to all visitors, I have made arrangements for both Sean and Cecilia to enter under the guise of research personnel," he said, looking at the two of them. "Before we get into the specific way our theft is to be performed, let me tell you of our known variables," he paused long enough to clear his throat. "The Manuscripta Diabolica is encased in a viewing wall behind a thick acrylic pane, on the third floor, here," he said, pointing to the top of the blueprint. "It is located in the museum section entitled 'Printing and Graphic Arts.' This is where our first difficulty lies."

"The fact that the volumes are separated by three floors," Sean blurted.

"Exactly," Vincent said, as he motioned his finger down the printed diagram. "I think we are all aware that several copies of this manuscript exist which have undergone extensive fabrication. Each volume looks and feels like the original, and all volumes - save the one on display- are housed on the first floor, within the vault of the Dibner Library." He watched the puzzled looks forming on the face's gathered around him. "Our problem, first and foremost, is getting all the volumes together in one place so Sean here," he said, pointing at the book man, "Can attempt a correct identification. Secondly, a forgery, preferably the one Sean has in his bag, will need to be returned to the display case on the third floor, while the other books are returned to the vault. We all wish to leave things as we found them so that our presence will remain undetected until we are well out of the country. Once this has been done and the real volume is secure, we can proceed to a yet- to- be- discussed point of rendezvous."

"This is so fucking whacked!" Sean exclaimed while throwing his hands in the air. "Nothing is worth this. You people can't find any way else to make a living?"

"I always wished to make my living as a book scout," Cecilia said sarcastically.

"Fuck you, you conniving little bitch," Sean said, unaware of the speed with which Luigi Basso's fist met with his kidney. Sean collapsed to the floor immediately. Vincent would stand for no one cursing at his sister. With a simple wink from his boss, the large Italian had promptly put Sean in his place.

"I suggest," Vincent said, looking down at Sean who was still reeling from the shot to his back, "You first mind your tongue. Maintain civility with us. No one here has shown you any disrespect. Remember, you are not involved in this mission for the pleasure of stealing a book, nor really to make money. You are here to get through this because you will be killed if you don't, caprisce?"

"You people can rot in Hell," Sean said coughing up his words.

"At some point, my friend, but not today."

Everyone seemed to be equally agitated. Sean, wishing to be anywhere but where he was, would have to make peace with his situation. His continued efforts to cause problems were getting him nowhere. He was going to play a role in the theft, like it or die.

The pox-faced Simone offered a hand, and Sean accepted it, pulling himself up from the floor. The pain was still prominent and he eyed Luigi Basso with contempt. But the Italian made no show of remorse.

"Sean?" Vincent spoke up.

"What?"

"May I proceed with our objective?"

"By all means," he said, coming closer.

"Very well," Vincent said, making eye contact with the others. "Here is how we shall enter the building and carry out our plan," he said, as he shuffled through the blueprints once more. "The museum closes at five-thirty. Cecilia, you and Sean will enter the building at noon together. You will go directly to the Dibner Library where you will spend the day faking research and familiarizing yourself with the layout of the Library. When the announcements come over the intercom that the library is closing, at about five-fifteen, you will both excuse yourselves to the rest room facilities, and stay there until the building has been closed up. It takes about an hour for the museum staff to leave the building, so make yourselves comfortable. When the hour has passed, Cecilia, you exit the rest room first, then, when you are sure all is clear, go and get Sean." He turned his attention to the book scout, "Sean, you will be alone for quite some time, a thought that does not sit well with me at all. Should you decide to exit the building, or feign some plan of escape, I shall have Luigi here take you out. Can I be more direct?"

"Now why would I do something like that?" Sean said with a smirk.

"Because it is exactly what I would do if I were in your position."

The two men locked eyes with one another intently. Each were throwing imaginary bolts of fire at the other. Vincent wasted no time beginning the directive once again.

"We are fortunate that there is no high- tech anti-theft system within the library itself, only security cameras which will have been taken care of by the time you both emerge. Towards the back of the library there is a small, steel-caged room. This is where the older, rarer material is kept."

"How will we get in?" Sean asked.

"I'm getting to that," he said, bothered by the interruption, "The door to this area can be opened with a key, which means it will be nothing for Cecilia to break in. Once you are inside the room, you will notice in the far-left comer a five-foot tall safe. Inside are the books we are after. The safe has a combination lock, which Cecilia will also be able to penetrate quite easily, so waste no time assembling the books together."

"Where will you be?"

"It will be my job to obtain the volume on display," Vincent said. "I will enter the library at two o'clock dressed as maintenance personnel, thus having access to areas I normally wouldn't. Behind every walled exhibit is a narrow hallway that allows a curator access to each display from behind. I will, by the time you have obtained the other books for comparison, have already procured the volume on display, and will begin making my way back to the Dibner Library via a series of air ducts overhead. Once I have made my way back, Sean can compare the books and we can take leave of the building."

Sean spoke up. "Once we've determined which book is real, then what?"

"I will return a fake copy to the display upstairs. You and Cecilia will have eight minutes to place everything back as it was and exit the library. We shall meet up at the elevator opposite the Lemelson Center, just beyond the library's entrance. Then, we shall simply take the elevator down to the lower level and exit the building," Vincent stated, taking a moment to clear his throat. "Mr. Basso will be awaiting us in a black Mercedes sedan, and we will meet up with Simone at a yet- to- be- determined area."

"How will we deal with security, though?" Sean asked with a look of worry.

"Mr. Basso will have already handled those issues by gaining control of the main security office located on the lower level. This is his specialty and we shall leave him to whatever device he deems necessary to acquire control." He paused, smiling at the large Italian, who already had a plan of his own. "There are a limited number of guards on duty after six p.m. and at precisely ten after six, Mr. Basso will commence his duties, and free our worry of any personnel which could monitor our movements. Simone here," he said, reintroducing the little man with the beak-like nose, "will be in a van across from the building, on Constitution Avenue. He will be controlling the cameras and our electrical issues when Mr. Basso usurps the security office. Simone will maintain communication with each of us via these small earphones," he said pulling out the tiny device he was describing. "He will be the center for all communication. We will not be able to communicate with each other, but we will have him as a means of central communication and he can relay any messages necessary. Simone here is our all- seeing eye."

"And what if something goes wrong?" Sean asked, sure that all of this sounded too simple.

"We improvise," Vincent returned.

"That's the best answer you've got?"

"It is the only answer you need. Cecilia and I have been in difficult situations before. No doubt we will be in them again. But we have not gotten this far because we fail in our intended tasks. The four of us," he said, purposely dis-including Sean, "know exactly what needs to be done. You, Sean, need to stay close to my sister and you will be fine. This will all be over in the next forty-eight hours."

"So I would take it we're leaving for America soon, then?"

"Sooner than you think," Vincent remarked.

Suddenly, Sean felt a sharp pain near his collar bone. It happened swiftly and without warning. The book scout had been unaware of Luigi Basso's approach from behind. He had been too focused on Vincent Conducci to realize what was about to happen.

The Italian had placed two fingers near a pressure point of Sean's body, causing him to collapse unconscious to the floor. He was then lifted up and taken to a car awaiting him outside the building. Vincent was not going to give the stranger any free time to wander about this facility. His nature of secrecy had been paramount, and no outsider he was being forced to work with was going to jeopardize that.

Il Fantasma' considered what lay before him. Sean would awaken in America, with the plan well under way. The American would adapt because he had no choice but for Vincent this was just another theft, no different than many of the ones he had performed in the past. He pulled out a cigarette and looked over at his sister, who returned a smile. Tomorrow, America and the Smithsonian. For the five of them, it would all be over soon.

"Through me one enters the sorrowful city;
through me one enters into eternal pain;
through me one enters into the lost race....
Abandon all hope, ye who enter here."

Dante Alighieri

The Gates of Hell

Bless me, Father, for I am Sin," Lucifer said, as he snickered at the old man seated opposite himself. "Should it please you, I should like to now speak of the realm known as Hell."

It was at once obvious to the elderly monk that the most interesting insight the demon could possibly offer was to be on the subject they were now to discuss. No one had ever crossed to the realm of Heaven or the pit of Hell and returned to give a graphic depiction of either dwelling. During the fall of his former city, Constantinople, he had come to believe he might have some idea of what Hell must be like. Anarchy. Rape. Murder. In this age, Hell could be seen everywhere.

Father Koutrakos had purposely avoided asking questions that dealt directly with who or what God was, as well as any biblical correlation. Hell, and the scope of the damned, was another matter altogether. It was a topic to be avoided, and yet it held a fascination that the old man found engagingly tempting. If the old demon seated his opposite knew anything, it had to be the geography of Hell. He allowed his fingers to pull at his beard, which had whitened considerably since the devil's appearance. He was thinking to himself what question he would ask first, but the fallen one spoke first.

"We have addressed many things, you and I, old man," Lucifer spoke up as he sat upon the cold floor, his legs crossed like that of an Indian chanting beside a campfire, "but what I am about to offer you, may violate all you have come to understand of mortality and the future interment of your very soul," he said. "For the dwelling you humans call Hell is all too real, and its jaws are like that of a lion, willing to accept any meal, any offering, any prey."

"And what of it, devil? What can you offer me that will aid my imagining?" the monk requested, somewhat goading the angel.

Lucifer smiled. There was as much suggestiveness when the demon did this as there was in any word he would speak. "Let us travel back for a moment, if we may," he said, "to the instance when those of my legion were obliterated from the realm of Heaven." There was a moment's pause as the demon cleared his throat, and Father Koutrakos had come to view this action from the demon as all too human. "I had come to believe the angels who fell from the realm of light as beings who had been destroyed or vanquished as if they never existed. I was, of course, wrong in this thinking. My Creator had gone to great lengths to ensure they received a maximum bit of suffering."

There was a long pause as an air of sympathy seemed to encapsulate the devil's aura.

"If I had been omnipotent," he began again, "if I could have had the slightest insight to the insurmountable suffering that would have befallen my brothers, I would have banished any notion of involving them in my plot. I thought at worst, they would have been destroyed. This I could have accepted. They would have been better off."

"You would have avoided no such thing, Lucifer," the monk said, unnerved by the fact that he had addressed the demon by his name, "do not expect me to believe such nonsense! You are a creature of habit and a beast of lies, I..."

The demon, whose head had been bowed as the monk spoke, lifted it now, the sight of which brought the abbot's speech to an end. A tear, small, simple and singular, slid from the empty, lifeless eye below the fallen angel's right brow. He was not riled to anger with the old man's words as he had been many times before. He was accepting the abuse, almost welcoming the chastisement.

Then, before the monk could return to his former sentence, the demon stood and moved toward the window as his form resigned to its pleasing shape. The leaded glass opened without assistance, presumably with no more than a thought from Lucifer's mind. The winter wind wasted no time in its effort to embrace the fallen angel. And from behind him, the monk could see rain falling once more. There was an eerie silence. All that could be heard was the whistling of the wind, the falling rain beyond the window, and the soft, flickering flame crackling on the wick of the candle next to him. Lucifer was deep in thought, musing to himself as to where he should take the confession.

The monk in turn sat with his eyes wide, dilated, his ears perked with a willingness to accept whatever the angel might say. This might have bothered him had he not been so taken by a willingness to know what only the demon could reveal. He could await a question no longer.

"Man has come to believe you rule Hell, and the demons that preside within," he said. "Are you suggesting this to be untrue?"

"At times," Lucifer began, "I believe you humans invent whatever befits the purpose of a given age, deriving what beliefs you will, interpreting what necessitates your needs." He turned from the window, which closed on its own, as he faced the monk. "I govern naught but the being you see before you," he said, posturing his body before the abbot. "I am no more the king of Hell than I am the king of Spain. My Creator has left me with nothing save what you see before you now. I have fashioned a resolve to fill the realm of Hell, yes, but this is all."

The demon then moved across the floor, in more of a gliding motion than a walk.

He had come to one of the many book shelves, and lifted a manuscript, perusing the pages.

The monk sat bewildered, wondering to himself where this action was leading. He continued the musing for only a moment before the demon stopped, and clutching the manuscript in his obtrusively elongated fingers, walked towards the monk and placed the volume gingerly on the desk in front of the old man. The abbot perused the opened page. The first letter of the first word was illustrated with a hideous illumination - a monstrosity devouring figures which seemed to grope in agony. The monk remembered the image, as he had been the individual who painted it. It formed the first letter of the first word that began the book of Revelation.

"This is how you imagine Hell, is it not?" Lucifer said, addressing the image.

"It is what I have come to believe from the scriptures," the abbot returned.

"Hell, my pious one, is this true, but it is much, much more."

Father Koutrakos forgot himself as he yearned to hear the description. He hated his desire for this knowledge so vile and repulsive, "Tell me of it, I beg you!"

"Very well," Lucifer said. "Where am I to begin?" His finger tapped the side of his head. "Let us set aside the basic truths. There is indeed a lake of fire, a molten pit of suffering, but it is on reservation for only certain souls, of which I am sure to be one. But Father, Hell is ever changing, ever shifting. It forms itself around each individual interred within. It customizes itself to each being and the act of sin perpetrated in life. Believe me or no, Hell is a living, breathing entity. Its expanse is vast, like the depths of the ocean and its arms are always open, begging for more souls to devour. But these, dear man, are but words. Why not allow a more personal take on the matter?"

"Demon," the monk asked, "What do you mean?"

Lucifer stared at the monk, locking him firmly in his gaze. "It is possible, old man, for me to take you as far as its entrance, but I can take you no further as even I am not allowed inside. No one that enters the gates of Hell may be released. Not even me."

"You are offering me a glimpse of Hell?"

"If you've the mental compass, yes. It is the least I can do for one who would share his time with me."

The old man sat speechless. How should one respond to such an offer? He was unsure whether he should follow his heart, which would never have resigned itself to such a consideration, or his head, which would welcome the knowledge gained. The abbot could not fasten a decision. This night had been long beyond imagining. Even now, he was still having to convince himself Lucifer was no dream, but a bit of some horrid reality that could be attributed to no other being but the devil. And still, there was another question: could he embark on a journey to a place such as the one being discussed and return with his sanity still firmly attached? He could not visit a decision before Lucifer interrupted his thoughts.

"Then it is decided," the demon said, not allowing the monk to further a choice on the matter. "You shall be my Dante, and I your Virgil," he said referencing a work unfamiliar to the monk as it had been written, but not yet printed. "Shall I show you sights the Italian Poet could only dream? His was a meandering of sheer fabrication. Yes, Father! I shall impart our bodies to the very pit of everlasting torment. You can then judge for yourself, having a new bit of knowledge gained," he said, winking at the monk who was wrought with the pain of accepting the decision. "What say you, Confessor? Shall we proceed to Hell?"

There was no response. The monk was rendered speechless. Then, as he began to speak, he was duly interrupted by the demon.

"Your silence speaks loud enough," he said as his voice resounded throughout the library walls, "Hell awaits you and I!"

Before Father Koutrakos could offer the abstinence of refusal, or even motion toward disdain at the offer, the room around which the two were seated began shifting, distorting itself, and changing shape. The monk looked down at his hands, and then felt about his face. All on his person seemed normal, yet his surrounding was changing.

Then, a sudden burst of light! His eyes blurred with the intense illumination, but when his hands dropped from shielding them, all was dark. So dark, in fact, that he could not even see the demon he believed to be before him in the distance. His heart began the aching that would soon be followed with its rapid increase. There was momentary panic.

Had he forgotten himself altogether? Had he become so enthralled with the revelations of a fallen angel that he had come to lose all sense of who he was? He would never make it back, he would be damned for even entertaining this request. Hell. The very idea had wrecked his senses. The old man collapsed to the floor, feeling for the reassurance of its cobblestone structure. But what had formerly been stone, was now nothing more than grains of dirt.

The monk, upon his knees, lifted the sand basin, watching it sift through his aged fingers. Lucifer stood above him with his right hand outstretched.

Father Koutrakos looked at the elongated digits, declining their acceptance. He wished to stand, but there was an unruly weight to his new surroundings. Slowly, he willed himself to rise, pulling at his robe, and coming to his feet in a slightly hunched position. He tried to focus again, but found that only the darkness remained. There was an unusual smell, emanating from where he had no idea. It was the smell of cinder, ash, and fetid decay. Then, there was the pungent odor of what seemed to be rotting flesh slowly drifting on the stillness of the air.

From the blackness, Lucifer emerged. There seemed to be just enough light to illuminate his figure. And the monk could see on the face of the demon a certain prideful gleam, as if the beast were elated to be hosting their misadventure. Had he tricked the monk somehow? So many questions plagued the abbot. He had been a fool to accept such an offer as this.

And then there was the issue of his physical condition. His muscles ached as if pulled and tested upon the Rack. As he stood there, alone in the darkness with his demonic guide, he felt no internal comfort of any spiritual offering, only the feeling of dread and despair. Then he addressed Lucifer, who was standing only a few feet in the distance.

"Have you tricked me, demon? Have I accompanied you to Hell then?"

"Not even close," the demon responded with deliberate elocution.

"Then where, pray tell, are we?"

"We are presently on the outskirts of Hell," Lucifer said as he paused looking outwardly into the unknown distance. "This is where my Creator took me when He came to visit me in the garden, not long after my expulsion. If you look to my left, out in the distance," the demon motioned, pointing a finger, "you will notice, Father, a small glowing light."

The abbot strained the muscles in his eyes, but could see no such light. Then, as if a veil had been lifted, the image became clear. There was indeed a light emanating off in the far away darkness.

"Do you see it, monk?"

"Indeed," the old man responded, "I see it now."

"Good. For that is the direction we will head ourselves presently."

"If you were going to use magic and cause the library to change," the monk said, "why not take us directly into Hell? Why this place?"

"Ah, old man," the demon said, shaking his head," 'Tis no trick I performed, no 'magic.' I simply lifted the veil of your consciousness. We are still very much in the library of Docheiariou, Father. Man lives here, in this sea of darkness, throughout a lifetime. The human mind stays focused on issues of little importance to its soul," he stated, holding out an arm. "In the distance to my left, Hell awaits. But to my right, possibly Heaven? One has but to decide, spending a lifetime living for one or the other. I have performed no trick, Father, I have only lifted that which keeps you blind."

If the old man had had a difficult time grasping the concept of Lucifer's appearance before him, it would be twice as difficult to comprehend this current imagining. He was to believe he was still in the library, yet not? There was little time to ponder the thought further, for his guide spoke up immediately.

"You have come to worship a being you believe merciful and kind," the old devil said. "What I am about to show you will beg a new question, Father: could a being worthy to be worshipped create such a place of fiendish torment, so perfected in horrors, imbibed with a nature full of such vile, disgusting habitation? In the scope of what you humans define to be nature's definition of both reason and sanity, believe that henceforth they will both be tested. No mortal being has ever viewed, with their soul intact, what you will be shown momentarily."

"Then why bring me here at all?" Father Koutrakos questioned.

"For but one reason," the demon remarked, "I wish you to find sympathy in my right to question Him which you believe perfect. I wish you to find the same empathy for His directives, that you seem to have misunderstanding mine. What you shall bear witness came into being by His hand, not mine."

"Lead on, demon," the old monk said as he gathered himself, "my patience wearies with your offerings of blasphemy and the lacking repose you welcome for an act that was necessary, given your betrayal."

"Priest," Lucifer chuckled, dismissing the comment, "Follow me."

The elder monk followed the fallen angel as the two unlikely companions began trodding upon the road too often traveled.

The old man could feel the ground becoming hard, its coarseness increasing the further the two walked towards the, light. Stones were becoming more pronounced. Rocks jutted from the sand below like the fangs of a serpent. Still, the darkness never lifted its veil encompassing every move they made. The air thickened with every step. His heart too, felt some unexplainable weight as well. The surrounding aura radiated some sort of dread, more pressurous than any burden the monk had ever carried within him before. Occasionally, the old man would look up to find Lucifer only looking forward.

Without warning, Lucifer stopped. They had come to the edge of a cliff, as the monk made note of the ground's end. The demon's body barred the monk from what image lay on the other side. Then, as a look of curiosity fell about the monk's face, the demon locked eyes with his counterpart.

"Why did we stop?" the abbot questioned.

Lucifer said nothing, but resigned his arms to open and reveal what lay in the valley below. He motioned his body to the side allowing the ignorant man to view what lay just beyond his sight. At first there seemed to be only darkness, but then, the blackened haze gave way to what lay in the distance.

At the sight before him, Father Koutrakos collapsed to the ground, slightly cutting his flesh on the many rocks jutting from the earth. He could not restrain himself as he foolishly fought back the coming tears, which paid him no attention. He was transfixed on the abject horror below. Never had he felt so devoid of hope, so longing for comfort.

Lucifer had not lied. This incarnation was beyond imagining.

The old man peered over the cliff into the wide chasm below. There appeared to be some likeness of a river, or perhaps a stream, that served to divide the base of the cliff they were on and the land opposite. The old monk marveled at the river below, which shifted its directional flow constantly.

"What do you see?" the demon called out from behind the abbot.

"Below is a river," he said, "And beyond this, a territory surrounded by a wall."

The demon addressed the man once more. “That is no river, monk,” he quipped. “Look again,” he said, pausing, “What do you see?”

The old man stared again, straining his eyes to focus. The devil was right, at least in part. What looked at first glance to be a flowing stream gave way to a more sorrowful sight.

It was void of water, yet filled with a mass of human flesh. Bodies upon bodies writhed in constant motion and gave an almost liquid appearance as they slithered through one another as would worms below the soil. Their naked flesh cavorted in such agony as to render the monk silent. A body would rise, clamoring for something to grasp, then it would disappear below the figure of another, the process continuing again and again. The monk withdrew himself, tightening his cowl as he saw the pale, bloated faces below.

“What of their crime?” he addressed the demon.

“They committed no crime,” the angel responded. “Those are souls who believed in nothing. The atheists, I think you call them. Many were fine, upstanding human beings causing less harm to their fellow man than many of those allowed to pass into the realm of Heaven.”

“Then.... why...?”

“They did not believe,” Lucifer said. “It is as simple as that.” He shrugged his shoulders, “They are, of course, my favorite souls, for their damnation required so little effort. Watch. See how they clamor to the surface, seeking relief that is granted but for a passing moment, much like their mortality on earth. Then, in an instant, they are carried below, drowning in a belief they so willingly chose to ignore when they but lived.”

“Why do they not suffer a torment of fire?”

“I am disconnected with this age,” the demon said angrily. “Is your world only lit by fire?”

“I...do not understand... “

“You will,” he said, cutting the old man off. “Might we continue, or have you seen enough?”

The monk wanted to say anything but his mind was entangled with too many thoughts and far too many emotions. He could no more fathom this moment than he could fashion a response.

“I cannot believe...... my eyes,” he said as a tear rolled down his cheek.

"What you have seen is not meant for you to accept as a mortal, Father. Still, it is my gift to you," the demon said. "You have allowed me your council, and so I allow you this moment. Let this image scar your brain."

"Why would you allow me to see this? What could it further your cause?"

"My cause?" The evil one looked surprised. "You have me all wrong. I am done with man. What is your soul to me? What have I to gain that I have not purged already a thousand-fold. My war with you beings ends tonight! When my confession is finished, when I have offered you all that I know, perhaps I shall find forgiveness. Catalogue these moments, so that man may be swayed from damnation. This is my gift to your race. It will have little effect to be sure, but, you never know."

"Then take me further," the monk said with much reluctance, "let us proceed to Hell."

Even as he spoke the words, there was a certain twinge of uneasiness in his gut. If he rationed out the dialogue, he had just asked Lucifer, the Devil himself, to take him into the realm of Hell. However this night had begun, it had since altered itself tremendously. His emotions were fettered, as was his soul. He had a horrible feeling his quest for knowledge was to somehow undo him completely. Time would tell.

"Very well, then," Lucifer directed, reaching out his hand only to watch the monk cower backwards. "You will have to allow me to transport you across the ravine if you truly wish to see anymore, old man," the demon urged, pushing himself forward, noticeably frustrated that he had seemingly gained no ground with the abbot of Docheiariou.

The monk turned around, not wishing to respond, nor to face the demon. He did, however, allow Lucifer to approach his back and to grasp him from underneath his arms, in a manner that would allow him to view the territory below, yet keep his face from close proximity to this devil.

As he looked down at the hands now clasped around him tightly, he saw they had changed, reverting to elongated talons, having no semblance or aspect of humanity. Even through his robe he could feel a certain coldness that accompanied their touch. There was an intense pressure of force that came as they locked around him as well. Dread. Malcontent.

Loneliness. All were feelings that seemed to pass from demon to human as the old man readied himself for the journey that lay ahead.

At the cliff's edge, Lucifer, holding the monk tightly, spread his wings and began to beat them furiously. On either side, the abbot could see their tips as they furled to his right and to his left. Then, within minutes, the two beings were upon the air, as Father Koutrakos could now see distance between his feet and the ground. His eyes closed immediately. He had come to both shock and disbelief. Though he tried, he could not will himself to keep them closed much longer. Suddenly, he felt them dive to the ravine below.

When the monk opened his eyes, he was only a few yards from the writhing mass of bodies twisting and whining about, imitating what had earlier appeared to be a river. They were grotesque, foul, and bloated, reaching upwards as if to grasp his feet as they glided past. Their nakedness was horrid, their longing for release unbearable to look upon. One soul managed to touch the old man's bare feet. He at once turned away, not realizing he was burying his head into the chest of the demon. He felt sick. How had he allowed himself the permission of this viewing? He had always fastened himself a wise man. Nothing, he thought, could now seem further from the truth.

The two beings, one mortal, one an old, spiteful angel, came to position themselves on an expanse of land below, near the edge of the soulful river. They were on the ground for mere moments before a hand reached from the river just behind the monk, clasping firmly to the old man's heel. The old man screamed. As the abbot fell, another arm wrenched his leg slightly higher, and he felt himself being pulled into the sea of damned souls.

He reached for the demon, willing his help, but unable to ask.

Lucifer's response was decisive and quick. He motioned with his eyes and the figure pulling the old man became luminous with flames, freeing the man, screaming in pain, and rejoining the writhing mass of flesh in which he had been interred. The fallen angel then helped the old monk to his feet, knowing he might faint at any moment.

"The soul suffers as if still encased in the flesh of life," the demon remarked, watching his guest struggling to breathe. "You would do well to watch where you step, and stay very close to me," he said smiling. "If I lose you here, there will be nothing I can do to get you back." There was a momentary pause as the monk nodded his head, assuring the demon he knew well what was being said. "Now let us move on." Lucifer turned, assured the monk would stay close behind him.

With every step, the monk assured himself that he should have never accepted such an offer as this. He would welcome any dwelling save the one he was now in occupancy of. He had seen enough. If there was a greater repugnance awaiting him, he shuddered at its imagining.

The old man, following the devil, began to survey the dwelling. He could see, far in the distance, what appeared to be a wall, but could not make it out completely. The ground's surface was sharp and more jagged than ever it had seemed before. But he was on a pathway now, and free from the possible harm it could cause his feet.

As he looked more closely at the area his feet progressed, he saw what had the appearance of names carved in some foreign language, on each and every stone paver. Lucifer turned to check on the old man, only to notice him slowing to look more closely at the path.

"Upon each stone, Father," the demon said solemnly, "are carved the names of each angel cast from Heaven. They are spelled in the language of my past realm, which is why you should find little hope of pronunciation. If you put an ear to the stones, you can hear each name pleading with the Creator for some merciless release from their hell. Each stone exists as a reminder to all who pass this way, that up ahead lies despair eternal. This road we walk, Father, leads to the very mouth of Hell." ·.

The monk fell to his knees.

"I can go no further," he said with a hand outstretched. "No more, I beg you."

"Very well, old man," the demon said, "we will leave, as you wish. I thought you too weak for such a journey." Lucifer was baiting the monk. "And you are quite right. What lies ahead would separate your mind from your body, ah, to be certain."

"What lies ahead?"

"Things more indescribable than what you have seen presently," he said, "But let us be off."

"No," the monk said, damning the very words he spoke as he said them, "we shall press on." He wished to resolve himself to the task of completing this journey. Perhaps, he thought to himself, the knowledge he would gain would be worth the momentary torment of what he would come to view.

"Are you certain, old man?"

"No. But I will follow, regardless."

"Now that's what I like to hear."

Lucifer turned from the man and began walking again. The two beings were upon a road that was to take them to the very mouth of Hell. An angel from Heaven, and an old monk from Athos. The darkness encapsulated the two as they pressed on. Hell was ready for Father Koutrakos, but was the old abbot ready for Hell?

> "How did I get here? Somebody pushed me. Somebody must have set me off in this direction and clusters of other hands must have touched themselves to the controls at various times, for I would not have picked this way for the world."
>
> Joseph Heller

WASHINGTON D.C.

10:32 a.m.

Sean Wilde was awake. His head was swimming as his mind played host to blurred memories, reminiscing the events of the past week, and how he had come to be here, but he was awake.

But where the hell was here?

He sat upright, his eyes scanning the view before him. He was in a room. A bed. He rubbed his eyes. There was a familiarity in the air and something told him he wasn't in Italy anymore. His mouth tasted funny. As the grogginess began to pass, he could clearly see he was in a hotel, and a nice one at that. The bed he was in felt extremely soft, the linen of silk perhaps. There was a writing desk to his left, a small couch to his right, and behind it, what gave the appearance of a very large bathroom facility. A finely pressed suit was hanging from a hook on the back of his bedroom door.

Had he awaken from a bibliophilic nightmare? The thought made him laugh.

As he chuckled, a sharp pain in the back of his neck reminded him of a reality all too factual. This was no dream, he was in Hell.

Sean rolled himself out of the bed, and waltzed naked across the room in search of some cigarettes that seemed to be calling him from a desk nearby. Pulling one to his mouth and lighting it with a match, he read the label on the matchbox. The Ritz Carlton. Shit!

Sean then walked toward the door to explore the rest of his new dwelling. He ignored the suit hanging off the back door, and turned the gold colored knob, swinging it open.

On the other side, he was met with four people, three men and of course, the woman. Their eyes were wide, staring back at his nakedness there in the door way. He froze, embarrassed by the thoughtlessness of his act. He slammed the door back quickly, realizing they all knew him now on a much too intimate level, and cursed himself under his breath. He could hear a voice from the other room. It was Vincent Conducci.

"'We can see you are fully awake, my friend," he said, his words muffled by the separation of the door, "and I would say thank you on behalf of my sister, but as it is, we have all seen quite enough of you already." Sean could hear laughter. "If it would be all right with you," Vincent began again, "for posterity's sake, could we possibly see you in that suit hanging from the back of your door? You might seem a bit too conspicuous entering the Smithsonian dressed as you are presently."

The book scout rapped his head against the back of the bedroom door. Idiot, he thought to himself. He couldn't seem to do anything that feigned a sense of intelligence around these people. He paused, taking a long drag from the cigarette. First, he would take a shower. Then, perhaps he would climb out the window while he left the water running, and make his escape, ending this bullshit. He carried himself to the heavily draped window, pulling the curtains apart, and peering to the street below. Five stories below. Could nothing work to his favor?

Entering the tile- floored bathroom, he opened the clear door to the oversized shower stall and turned the water on, making the necessary adjustments to render a perfect water temperature. He stepped inside, wondering to himself how all this was going to play itself out. He picked up the customized hotel shampoo, placing a small portion in his hand and rubbing it through his head. He tried to think of any way out of this, but he could think of nothing. He had no business in association with these people. He had played many roles in his life. He just had never thought 'thief would have been one of them. Yet here he was, in one of the nicest hotels in the world, about to engage himself in an insane attempt to relieve the Smithsonian Institution of a prized relic, The Manuscripta Diabolica. As the water crashed against his willowy frame, he welcomed the invigoration, and drifted for a moment to his imaginary place. The city of Paris, and his million-dollar bank account.

11:19 a.m.

When Sean emerged from the bedroom this time, he was clothed in a well-tailored Italian suit, designed by none other than Georgia Armani. He looked good, and he knew it. He felt odd, having never experienced dress of this kind, but his appearance seemed to impress the people in the room. He could see Vincent and Simone having a discussion over what appeared to be some blueprints near the kitchen. Cecilia seemed to be packing a bag of some sort, and Luigi Basso was watching CNN on television.

Cecilia was the first to address Sean. She moved toward him wearing a black, pinstriped blouse, which seemed, in many ways, to compliment his suit. Large gold hoops dangled from her ears. She was gorgeous, though Sean tried to only allow himself to feel contempt towards her. His anger had waned considerably, as he had resigned himself to follow through with his forced task, but allowing himself to fall for this woman would be taking things too far. Trouble was, the mind and the heart don't exactly converse with one another on matters such as this.

"You look ravishing, lover," she said. "Perhaps when this all over we could-"

Vincent cut his sister off mid- sentence. "Sean," he said giving Cecilia a stem look, "I trust the suit, it fits you well?"

"Yeah, but this ain't my style," Sean returned, "I'd much rather have my jeans back on."

"Don't worry, my friend, your mode of dress and style is not far from reach. Both your jeans and shirt have been folded and put away in your bag. I apologize for any inconvenience that you may be caused, but I must have you maintain the similarity of a research person."

"Yeah, well, I feel like a fucking penguin."

"Must you preempt everything you say with foul language?"

"Not all the fucking time," he said, sensing a degree of victory. "Just say the word, I'll be out of your hair."

"Soon enough, my friend," Vincent said, "For now we must tolerate one another. Shall we review the plans, or are you comfortable with your role?"

"I think you can be sure I'm not comfortable with any of this, but I'll be much happier when all this is over. Let me know what I'm supposed to do."

"Good," Vincent nodded, then picking up the television's remote, he clicked the CNN broadcast off. "Luigi," he commanded, "go get the car if you would, it's time to put our plan in motion." He then rambled off a lengthy dialect in Italian that separated Sean from the conversation.

He hated when they did this. It wasn't so much the seclusion from conversation that bothered Sean as much as it was the aspect of not knowing whether he was the subject of conversation. These people were perfectly comfortable in their role, and he was not. The plan, as he saw it was insane. Four days ago he was in Boston, worried about getting kicked out of his apartment. Today he was readying himself to break into the Smithsonian Institution and steal a priceless antiquity from the past. He had gone from not even having two nickels to scrape together to now having a million dollars in a bank in France. He couldn't help feeling as if his next step was to move from the land of the living to the land of the dead. None of this really mattered, though. This shit was about to go down. He just hoped he wouldn't be going down with it.

Vincent turned now, ending his conversation with the others. Simone approached Sean holding something in his hands.

"Sean," the small Italian said, "This is a small earphone I need you to place in your ear. It will allow me to keep communication with you from the van stationed across the street. This," Simone said, withdrawing a similar device from his bag, "is a microphone which will allow you speak freely with me. It is of the utmost importance we maintain contact with one another. Should anyone get separated or in trouble, this will be the only means in which aid might be provided. Wear them at all times."

Sean took both gadgets from Simone, amazed at the technology that must have gone into their creation. James Bond would have been impressed, he thought.

Simone stepped back, allowing Vincent to step forward.

"If you're ready, Sean, we must be going," he said, "Mr. Basso should be around with the car any moment. Is there anything I can get you? A drink perhaps, to calm your nerves before we get started?"

"Only if I fix it myself," Sean said half smiling, half in disgust.

"As you wish, my friend," Vincent said stepping aside and allowing Sean passage to a serving tray holding the alcohol.

Sean walked over and grabbed a bottle of Glen Morgan scotch. He then poured himself a rather large drink. Everyone else in the room gathered their belongings preparing themselves to leave. Sean let the effects of the alcohol burn his throat and soothe his nervousness. He couldn't believe this was actually going to happen. He was no thief, but it seemed he was about to learn from one of the world's best. He looked across the room and caught Cecilia giving him the eye. She winked as he set his glass on the tray dismissing her flirtation.

"Sean," Cecilia said, trying to get his attention, "I put your two bags over there," she said, pointing to an area of floor beside the couch. "You might get them together, we're about to Leave."

Her captive said nothing, but walked towards the bags, checking the contents. If the fake copy of the Manuscript had been misplaced, they wouldn't get too far in making a switch when the theft went down. He opened the duffel, eyeing the contents. A pair of jeans, a T-shirt, flannel socks, a pair of well- worn Timberland Eurohikers, two packs of cigarettes, a lighter, passport, wallet, a serious quantity of Italian bills, and the remnants of about eight thousand American dollars (the remainder of the ten thousand DeBury had given him) were all there. He then opened the other bag and viewed its only content, the facsimile edition of the

Manuscripta Diabolica. Everything was accounted for and just as Sean had left them.

"Are you ready, Sean?" Vincent said looking down at his nervous counterpart.

"Truthfully?" Sean said.

"No," Simone said, snickering before Vincent could answer.

"Then yeah," Sean returned, "Let's get this shit over with."

"Very well," Vincent said, stepping aside as they all came together in front of their hotel room door. "Let us begin."

Cecilia was the first to open the door and exit the room. She was then followed by Simone, Sean, and closing the door behind him, Vincent Conducci.

It began at that moment. Even as the four awaited the elevator that would take them to the lobby, Sean revisited the plan of theft over and over in his mind. He reminded himself these were professionals, the very best thieves in the world. He was as safe doing this sort of thing as he could hope to be, which. in truth, assured him of absolutely nothing. Still, the whiskey had been of some comfort.

As the elevator door opened with the light buzzing sound of a bell, Sean looked at the three persons grouped about him. They seemed as calm as if they were lying in a hammock on a Sunday afternoon. They seemed to have no concern of any consequences that might come from this action should it fail somehow. Where did people like this come from, he thought. Where they born without a conscience or where they made this way by some poor parental attempt at child rearing? He guessed it didn't much matter. Nothing really mattered much now, save getting out of this alive and without a lengthy jail sentence. He ran his fingers through his hair.

The elevator opened on the ground floor, and they stepped into the luxurious hotel lobby. These people definitely knew how to live, he thought, looking around in wonderment.

Vincent motioned their group towards the clear glass hotel entranceway, purposefully not checking out with the hotel's registration desk. Sean felt a heightened sense of general awareness, as if a sixth sense had somehow gone off. His heart began racing as they stepped from the hotel's entrance and toward a large Italian who stood holding open the back door of a black Mercedes sedan.

The cool wind lifted his hair as he took a deep breath. Sean then watched as Simone bade Vincent farewell, turning from their little group, and departed to acquire the van that was waiting in the hotel's parking lot. Cecilia then climbed in the back seat, followed by Sean. Vincent made some small talk with Luigi before walking around and seating himself in the front passenger side.

As Luigi Basso closed the door behind him and put the idling car in gear, Vincent turned to address his frightened passenger in the back seat.

"This is where we begin, my friend," he said. "Remember to stay calm, stick closely to Cecilia, and all will be well. We've done this type of thing before."

"Y'know you could still let me out," Sean stated in jest. "No one has to know a thing."

"Relax, my friend," Vincent said, turning back around away from Sean, "By this time tomorrow you will be a very rich man, and all of this will be behind you."

"That's what I'm afraid of," Sean said, reclining in the back-seat's leather upholstery. He watched out the window as they passed the scenery laced with all types of governmental architecture. This time tomorrow he could indeed be rich, and yes, all this would surely be over. But, he thought, would he be alive to experience any sort of reward?

He then closed his eyes as the car sped along, heading toward Constitution avenue, towards the Behring Center, towards the Smithsonian Institution...

"O, dread and dire word. Eternity! What kind of man can understand it?" "To bear even the sting of an insect for all eternity would be a dreadful torment. What must it be, then, to bear the manifold tortures of Hell forever?"

James Joyce

A Glimpse of Judgment Eternal

Father Koutrakos could not take his eyes from the stones beneath his feet. The names listed on each one seemed to lead on forever in the distance. Seeing their permanence scarred deep within the pavers, filled him with a dread he wished to distance himself from. They were the names of those cast from Heaven. Each with a name, a separate being, a fellow creature, damned.

He allowed a tear for them. He knew from experience how difficult it was to resist the urging from the beast that walked in front of him now. He imagined these fallen angels, how they must have felt with their realization of a deed gone terribly wrong. What words had the old demon used to get them interred in such a place as they walked toward presently?

As a stream of liquid fell from his cheek, the old man watched as it burst on a block upon which was carved a name of one of the unfortunates. He heard at once a scream, horrid to his ears, as it sizzled on the paver below. Looking up, he saw his guide had stopped, and focused his attention on the old monk.

"Your tears will not ease their suffering, old man," Lucifer said. "They are well beyond your sorrow."

"I shall pray for them regardless, demon, for what have they to lose?"

"Do as you please father, just keep up the pace," the devil said, "We still have a way to go, you and I."

Whether he meant that statement to imply the aspect of confession or actual distance, the monk was uncertain. All around him, save the path, was black. In the far distance, he could see, over the demon's back, a light - faint, but ahead nonetheless. The old man was tired. He wished to himself that this night and the presence of the demon had never come to pass.

As they kept walking, something occurred to the old man. With each step the surrounding area became not warmer, as the abbot had feared, but colder. The temperature was falling- and fast. Where, he thought, was the heat of Hell?

Suddenly, a sound!

He couldn't make out the specifics of the noise, but he was sure he could hear a distinct sound. Before he could address a question to the demon, he saw a shape approaching from the comer of his eye. Turning to his left, he saw the darkness give way to an illuminated horror. His mouth gaped wide, as did his eyes. He could not believe the vexation of the image.

Before him there appeared two humanesque figures, naked and being harassed at the hands of what seemed to be skeletal tormentors. Flesh dripped from these inquisitors and themselves being of such a repulsive nature, of such disgust, the mere sight caused the old man to tum away.

The being that seemed to be of female origin was being prodded with a staff of some sort. One skeleton had her body spread open as the other shoved ridged devices into her opened orifices. The horrible screaming combined with a sinister cajoling laughter sickened the old man. He turned from the woman but found no release in what he saw happening to the man. The male figure was being fastened to a metal grate while a host of skeletal harbingers shoved hot coals under his writhing form, watching him languish uncontrollably as he battled with an escape that was futile and a never-ending torture. The sight of this small showing left the monk unable to speak at all.

"I would suppose you to wish some explanation of their crime?" the demon said. Father Koutrakos nodded. "Well, I am without a proper answer," he began, surprising the abbot with his response. "Hell is different for everyone. Its tortures and its visions conform to the mindscape of each soul differently. What you are witnessing may seem to you a vision of two souls being harassed by skeletal minions. What the souls themselves see may be far different."

"What do you mean?" the monk asked.

"Perhaps what to you is a skeleton appears to them as some love one they wronged in their former existence. Perhaps it is a past friend. It could likewise be some imaginary beast they have conjured in their minds, which unfortunately have now been opened to the universe's secrets. Hell changes father. Hell adapts. Hell customizes itself for each and every soul that it embraces. It tortures each being by taking what fears they harbor, combines this with their sin, and multiplies these emotions to such an explicable level that their soul is shredded, utterly destroyed, and what is left defies all mortal comprehension. Hell is a nightmare realized and justice, blind no longer."

"Oh, the pain these unfortunates must bear...," the old man muttered softly commenting to himself under his breath.

"Pain?" the unnamable said, addressing the comment. "What is pain of the flesh, when compared to the mental anguish and loss of hope endured by one's very soul? Physical pain exists, of course, but it is only a precursor to what awaits the damned," he said, shaking his head as if the old man had little chance of grasping a word he was saying, "And Father," the demon's eyes were wild now, "it is forever!"

"From what I have beheld, how can the mental anguish outweigh what is obviously such abominable physical torment?"

"The human compass is only capable of utilizing a menial degree of its actual capacity to understand. This being said, we must turn toward the mortal release of death," the demon said, pausing. "Once a soul emerges from the body which holds it captive, the power of the mind expands, and those secrets of the universe which have been unknown are at once made clear and simplified. That is why there exists no sin in the realm you call Heaven. With such knowledge gained, sin cannot be reasoned, therefore it cannot exist at all. Even in Hell, there is no sin. There exists in this place we explore only the remnants of actions perpetrated in another time, in some other place. Hell is but another word for justice. These souls," Lucifer said, pointing to the two individuals being persecuted, "have not only been made aware of their sin, but they suffer two distinct, yet separate consequences."

"And those would be?"

"The soul languishes in the contrition of not being able to put right their former wrong, and they see their own perverseness laid out clearly now before them. Wretched, is it not?"

"I... I have... not the words... I..."

"Hard to believe the Being that created you is likewise capable of something so repulsive as this, no?"

"I do not question His will, demon."

"Of course not, Father," Lucifer quipped, "of course not."

The two intruders allowed the conversation to lapse and trudged forward down the path. Father Koutrakos could not help but turn around and look back at those persecuted. The images had vanished though, making the old man question whether they had truly existed at all. The demon, not so much as turning his head, addressed the monk.

"Hell is playing tricks with you, Father," he said pressing onward, "It is trying to deter you from the path. It knows you do not belong here, and seeks to frighten you away."

"Are you telling me that the images I saw were not real?"

"Oh they were real, but they were of some activity taking place within its walls," the demon said, "not in this outside plane. As I told you before, there is nothing sinister in this outer realm but the souls you saw clamoring for mercy a short time ago."

"How can Hell know of me?"

"I told you, old man, Hell is alive," he said. "It may not have always been this way, but it has become a being in itself. It craves the perniciousness of mankind, and perhaps finds no real malevolence in you. You must understand, it seldom sees one of such pious stature this far south of Heaven."

The old man made no comment, as there was nothing for him to say. He was as a stranger in a strange land, a guest both unwelcome and uninvited. He also felt a light sense of self-permissiveness. He wanted to go on. To see what lay ahead. This was an aspect of his humanity he had wished to forgo, but his curiousness prevented him to do otherwise. Were he able to find humor in his world, he might laugh aloud at the fact that he was following Lucifer, willingly, into Hell. The absurdity of what was happening went beyond his mental grasp. How much longer, he mused, before Hell was visible before him.

When the abbot looked up from the stones that had so kept his attention, he stopped cold as if frozen like a block of ice. Lucifer continued for a few steps further before stopping himself.

They were only a few yards from the very gate of Hell. What barred the monk from entry was a sight as vexing as any he could have created with his own mind.

The monk collapsed to his knees, for what else could a sight such as this one render a man to do? On first inspection, the gate appeared as if it had been carved by the finest Italian artisans that had ever laid pick to marble. In truth, it resembled more a Grecian wall relief than anything else. But then his eyes focused tighter to the image, and he realized that this was no carving, and the images displayed were unmercifully real. They were not made at the hands of a man.

The entire wall, spanning as far as he could see both vertically and horizontally, contained no mortar, brick, or stone. This wall was an amassment of human torsos. Figures whose bodies writhed in continuous motion - wailing in such perverted agony as to make their close proximity insufferable to hear. The image was well beyond the old man's worst imagining.

Limbs protruded from the human wall, grasping and clawing for the old man. As Lucifer approached, passing each, they would recoil, cursing and spitting profanity as the demon looked their way. The facial expressions were an exhibition of loathing and repression. Their mouths were open, their screams deafening. The horror behind their eyes spoke volumes about what lay in their mind's comprehension.

And the smell.

The stench of the walled damned was fetid, putrid, and disgusting. The odor of excrement and decay permeated the air, making it heavy and unbearable. The old man became overcome with dread and fear, as this was a sight he thought to cause a man to embrace madness.

The air about the two was freezing now as well. Father Koutrakos pulled his robe as tightly as he could and wished for it to be twice as thick. Lucifer noticed his physical discomfort.

"I wish I could ease your suffering, little man, but as it is," he said, "I cannot."

"Why... Why is it so cold?"

"You were expecting fire and brimstone?"

"Yes."

The demon laughed. "As one nears Hell," he began, "there is an emptiness that exists, such as to separate one's humanity from one's spirituality. This causes an internal frigidity that is far harsher than normal cold, for what emptiness can be rivaled when one's soul is torn apart? I myself, feel nothing. Perhaps I cannot at all, or perhaps I never could. The fires of Hell serve as no more a vessel of heat than they do cold. What keeps your body warm as you walk upon the earth is your life-force. There is nothing that resembles that life here."

The demon stepped back and, turning from the monk, walked closer towards the wall. As he did this, the old man called out.

"What of their crime!" the abbot said, addressing the wall of figured suffering.

"Who?" Lucifer said, "Do you mean these souls here?" Just as he spoke the words, he reached out towards the wall and plucked a body from the mass by its outstretched arm. The figure, which resembled a man, was thrust to the ground writhing, spitting and kicking. "Observe," Lucifer urged the old man.

Father Koutrakos watched as the body tried to stand, its sorrowful legs unable to bring it upright. It reached for the old man, slithering as if a worm upon a hook. The old man noticed the being to be void of eyes, its mouth void of teeth. Yet it began to speak at the old man.

"Fasssssser," it said, as if more snake than man, "You mussst help me." It reached forward, "Sssso long here ssssso very long here. I would do anysssing, anysssing, for only a momentssss releasssse. Take me wisss you fassser," the creature begged.

"I.... can do nothing for you, my son," the monk addressed the damned one, "Oh, but I am so very sorry. What have you done, that I may pray for you when I am to the earth returned?"

"I....," the being could barely speak, "I ssstood in the market plassse and chanted for ssse releassse of Barrabasss. I wasss amongsss those persssonss who condemned your Chrissst to deasss."

The old man looked up from the sorrowful creature, remnants of what had once been a man, and at Lucifer who was standing with his arms crossed.

"Why do this?"

"Do what?"

"Torture me with a soul I cannot help."

"Simply touch him with your hand, Father."

The monk reached out, without the simplest notion to question the exercise, or what might happen as a result. As he touched the being's forehead it changed, reverting back to some semblance of the human he had been when he was alive. A relief perhaps for the abominable soul. The monk, however was not privy to this transformation.

He found himself not before Lucifer, and not before the pitiless soul whom his hand had touched, but in some new place, in some earlier time.

Oh God in Heaven, he thought as he looked up from this sandy street comer. He knew instantly where he was. He moved closer now. He could smell a camel. Who were these people? He was part of a large crowd, all gathered for some reason in front of a large building.

Two figures, no wait, three, appeared before the crowd.

One was unquestionably Roman. The other was........ dear God in Heaven!

The old monk fell to his knees, tears flowing with control abandoned. The figure to the right of what seemed to be a man of some power, was holding his head down. Blood, which even as far away as the old man was he could see, trailed from a macabre tiara about the man's head.

And those gathered around him, all chanting, all screaming. "Free Barabbas! Free Barabbas!"

There was no mistaking where he was. There was even less imagining to whom he was looking at. The old man was now part of the memory of the man he had touched, reliving the damned soul's sin for himself. He clutched his chest. This was too much.

Just then, as if somehow signaled out from the crowd, the crowned man looked up, locking eyes on the old monk, who in turn put his eyes to his face, sobbing with wild abandon. He had not wished to be seen. Not by Him.

Somehow, in that very moment, he was overcome with such injustification for any sin he himself had ever committed as to cause a paramounting shame that he thought was to stop his heart.

When he pulled his hands from his face, he was back in Hell. The entity before him was changing back to its damned form, and the crowd was now gone.

"Be careful whom you touch/' the demon said. "Just as I told you not to stray from this path, so you would do well to keep your hands to yourself. This place has so many ways of entrapping you. Your mind, however strong you think it to be, is unable to bear the hopelessness of these damnable wretches. Their sin will overtake you and you will become its slave. Remember, these souls are beyond your help. They may seem like humans, but they are not. They are the remnants of life no more. Detritus of an age gone. Heed my words."

As he said this, Lucifer reached down and lifted the wretched soul from the ground, hurling him back towards the wall of bodies. The soul screamed, flailing about until it joined the mass once more, its cries horrible for the old man to hear. The abbot wanted nothing but to alleviate each being's suffering, but there was truthfully nothing that he could do. His helplessness then became eclipsed only by his sadness. His worldly failure formed the very gate of Hell. And there was no questioning the fact that this place was already grasping for his soul. He felt himself weakening with every step he took.

The stone pavered pathway ended before a large door which, by conservative estimation, was approximately fifty feet tall and approximately the same in length. It seemed to be ornately carved, but in red, possibly marble in design. Toward its center, the old man saw Lucifer pounding his fist.

The doorway wasted no time in efforting a response.

As the two doors swung inward, the monk stepped back, watching as a third figure stood boldly in the doorway. This being mirrored no other personage he had seen before. In its obvious divination, it mirrored the old man's concept of what an angel should look like. It was beautiful to look upon, all robed in white, trimmed with gold lining. It was large, and like Lucifer, well defined as many of the mythological statues he had seen carved in Greece as a youth. His hair was black and curly, resting on the clef of his shoulder. Behind him were wings that resembled that of an eagle, though much, much larger. In his hand he grasped a parchment, and wasted no time in his stride toward the two interlopers.

"From these walls get thee distance, fallen one," the being said in a voice that made the abbot shrink with fear. "You have no station in this place; and this human soul - take it away at once! Flee to your earth demon, I will come for you soon enough."

"Ah, my dear Michael," the demon addressed this new being. The monk recognized at once that it must be the archangel Michael. An angel who could leave this place and touch the face of God. The abbot stood, watching the two beings exchange aggressive remarks. "Thou would do well to consider with whom you are speaking, brother," Lucifer jibed.

"Call me not thy brother, and name me not with any such affinity that wouldst describe a caring for you on my part. Demon of the earth, go ye from here immediately."

"I have found a soul worthy of witnessing what lay here interred, and it is my wish to make him aware of things he is not presently. It is my wish that he know why I exist."

"You who are an aberration to me, have no relations in these parts. Warn the soul you have brought that dreadful things happen here, the likes of which will separate his mental capacity from reason. Pray him to look about at the vile filth that thou hast made real."

"Not I, brother - our Creator."

"A millennium has passed, and still you find blame in a Being that loved you more than He loves me. Your blasphemous undertones befit your haggard shape. Find another realm, Lucifer, or allow me to bind you thus, and bring you inside."

"Time enough for that, to be sure, but as it is I shall take this soul away at your request. Perhaps you could tell me how the old man is?"

The angel Michael lunged at the demon, who, calculating his move, sidestepped the charge and shoved the glorious angel into the stone floor. The abbot jumped back, cowering and wishing not to be seen. Lucifer then pressed Michael's face into the paver, straddling atop the angel and whispering in his ear.

"Remember this one, brother?" the demon said as Michael's eye was inches from a carved name of one of his former angelic cohorts. "Malificache. I believe it was your mate before the fall, am I correct? Pity- no more than a succubus of Hell, now!"

The angel threw Lucifer from his back, and into the wall of souls. Each writhing being grasped the old devil, holding him fast. Then, angered beyond reason, Michael reached for Lucifer, who trapped by the wall of souls, could not move. He lifted the demon from his temporary interment, and thrust him on the stone path.

From each stone footing, arms, angelic in nature reached from the carved names and held Lucifer fast.

"Would that I could bind you inside forever!" Michael screamed, "But it is not yet time. Be ye warned though, I am coming for you, and I promise it will be sooner than you think!"

The hands released the demon. "Come for me, brother, I will be waiting," he said standing as Michael backed inside the doors which were now closing.

"Yes, demon who was once as a brother to me. Until I carry you inside these doors and bind thee for all time. Until then," he said as the doors slammed tight.

Lucifer turned and offered a hand to the monk, whose beard had become whiter than snow. The old man was shaking. Never in his wildest imagining could he have fashioned that he would bear witness to such things.

"Please take me from this place," he said, requesting departure. "If I am not dead. If my soul is still my own. My heart can take no more and I have seen too much this night."

"Very well Father," the demon said, "We shall leave this place at once."

Before the old man, Lucifer waved his hand in the air, and the surroundings began to change. No more were they in a pit of despair. The old man felt as if at once a weight had been lifted. They were in the library of Docheiariou once more.

The old man's stomach heaved, releasing its contents upon the floor. The faces and the experience of Hell was firmly etched in his mind, and this discomfort of seeing the damned caused his body real unease. His mind now was completely discombobulated.

The monk wiped the residue from his chin and looked for the demon who was now seated just as he had been before their trip into chaos. The devil wasted no time in resuming conversation with the old man.

"Loathsome, was it not?" the unnamable said.

"There are no words fit for description," the monk returned.

"You are quite right, my friend. But now you know," he said, "My time with you is growing shorter - there is much I have to attend in my kingdom here on earth. Perhaps we can discuss what you have seen at some later time. For now, if it pleases you, I should like to discuss other matters of my existence. Hell is going nowhere."

While the old man was a reservoir of questions, the idea of trying to momentarily put aside the things he had seen was reasonable. He was exhausted, sickly, and his mental capacity was waning. Where conversation was to go from here he knew not. But he would welcome the closing of Hell. He had seen enough this night.

"As you wish, demon," the monk said, waiting for the demon to redirect their conversation.

Lucifer sat back, crossing his legs. "Do you remember what I told you earlier?" He paused, "When I told you what the Creator warned me: Never kill a human, lest He separate Himself from me verbally, forever?"

"Yes," the monk said.

"I disobeyed him just once, but that was enough," he stated, "I wish to confess this to you now, if you will allow this."

"Please demon, purge this deed from your heart."

"Very well," Lucifer said as he took a deep breath and began to speak.

"In matters of conscience, the law of majority has no place."

M. Gandhi

Carpe Diem

Vincent was looking down at his watch. Thanks to solar power, it was now illuminated. The time for action had come as he waited inside the dark, tightly cramped supply closet.

It was five o'clock. The Smithsonian would be closing very soon. Already he could hear from just outside the door the muffling sound of some desk clerk vibrating on the overhead intercom and informing those persons still in the museum that it would be closing shortly.

He wasted no time slipping on the last article of clothing he needed - a uniform shirt from the night janitor lying at his feet.

Buttoning the article of clothing, he frowned at the dead man lying on the floor. As was often the case, certain innocents had to be sacrificed for the greater good of a given mission. And just below his feet were remnants of that cold, hard truth. He hated this part of the work. If only the old man hadn't put up a fight and ripped off his hood, exposing his face. No one could be allowed to see his identity and jeopardize his future earning potential, much less his freedom. Besides, he reasoned to himself, the money at stake was significant, and the man had been warned not to resist. Now dressed in the clothing of a janitorial worker, Vincent Conducci -Il

Fantasma - emerged from the closet, scanning the hallway for anyone that might happen by.

No one in either direction. He then turned his body clockwise, extracting a six-foot ladder from the same closet, and began walking down the first-floor hallway towards the nearest elevator. He mulled over the directive again in his mind. As long as the other participants followed through the plan as it had been discussed, this would all be over in one hour. He, of course, felt complete relaxation with his own role. Besides, this was not near as hard as stealing artwork from the Louvre, which he had successfully occasioned a time before.

In fact, of all the thefts Vincent had organized, never had anyone been willing to meet his eight-million-dollar fee for the likes of a book. It had been an absurd request. That is, until the Englishman handed his sister a deposit receipt drawn on their Swiss account for one half of his aforementioned price tag. He had wished to know more about this book, as he always did extensive research on any item he was targeting. Unfortunately, none existed on this particular book, aside from the mythological aspects DeBury had described - which he had no real interest in.

There was also his back- up plan to consider.

If he got into any trouble, he would scurry to the rooftop, where he had earlier managed to stash a backpack with some emergency items. A theft rarely needed such provisioning, but he was taking no chances.

Vincent smiled, now entering the elevator with all the confidence necessary to see this plan through. He looked briefly at his watch once more. 5: 11 p.m. The theft was now underway.

5:22p.m.
Dibner Library

Cecilia and Sean had been seated together for several hours, saying very little to one another amidst the pile of books that were strewn about the table. It had been fairly easy to fake their researching efforts, as the library had been full of books that seemed to pacify Sean for much of the day, calming his nerves.

Cecilia was unsure of what to say. There was a part of her that in some other time and some other place, wished to meet Sean all over again. His innocence was charming, even if his somewhat justifiably brutish nature had slightly offended her. And while his looks were a bit rugged, he still was undeniably handsome, and with some well-placed guidance, from her of course, he could be made to suit her just fine.

For Sean, there was no denying his true feelings. Cecilia was intelligent, rich, and beautiful. His only contempt for the woman had been due to the company she kept and the business to which she was employed. Which, he was deciding the more time spent with her, could be reasonably overlooked. She, in truth, was a threat to his masculinity. He knew he was smart, but the wealth of his knowledge had been learned from bookish activities of a very un-malicious nature. This was about as far as he could get from the crowd he was in association with now. How could he hope to overcome these problems that stood in the way of relating himself to her? Still, when this was all over with, who could say what might happen? Beauty went a long way.

Cecilia looked down at her watch. The time had come.

"Sean," she said, pulling the book down from his face, "We need to go."

The book scout took a deep breath. No matter how long they waited, he was never going to be ready. No turning back now, he thought. Placing the volume he had been reading on the table, he stood without speaking, watching Cecilia's eyebrow arch. He then slung the leather bag containing the fake copy of the Manuscripta over his shoulder.

"Go to the rest room as we planned," she whispered from across the table. "Cut out the lights and find a corner to wait in. As soon as the library closes and Simone sees that the Smithsonian is clear, he'll alert me, and I'll come for you," she said as if this was supposed to bring Sean some degree of reassurance. "I know you are worried, but if you will do as I ask, this will all be over in less than an hour."

"Then what?" he raised the whisper, somewhat bothered by her lack of interest in him personally, "I go my way, you go your way, and life just goes back to normal?"

"If by normal you mean that we will all be quite wealthier than we were when we started - yes."

"Great," he said, turning away from the table. Cecilia stood quickly, catching his arm with her well-manicured hand.

"I know this has been hard on you," she said batting her deeply intoxicating eyes, "But we have only done what has been absolutely necessary for this plan to work. It has been just as hard on us to involve you as it has been for you to work with us," she implored, "and all I am asking you is that you don't hold anything I've done against me when this is all over."

"Cecilia..."

"Please, Sean," she said, putting a finger to his lips as if that would bring him to silence, "Promise me."

Sean looked around the room to see if they had attracted a stare from some scholarly onlooker, but no one seemed to mind. In fact, only one other person was still using the library at all. Everything seemed as well as could be expected.

Then he looked back into the Italian woman's eyes. He couldn't have denied her if he had wanted to. "All right," he said, "I promise."

She smiled warmly, perhaps even affectionately, at him, and released his arm. She knew the conversation had already taken too much time. Nodding with some silent approval, she returned to her seat and allowed Sean to leave her side.

He walked away slowly and with reluctance. Cecilia, in that instance, had left his mind. This was all about the book now. The Manuscripta Diabolica. There was no turning back now. By tomorrow morning, he thought as he shoved the men's rest room door open, he would either be dead, rich, both, or none. God in Heaven, how had he come to this? As the door closed behind him, he felt a chill move down his spine. At that moment, he was no longer Sean Wilde. He was some fossil of a person who had formerly been called by that name. The Sean he knew would have never allowed this to happen. Now, all he could do, was find a stall, lock the door, and wait in the darkness.

5:45 p.m.
Constitution Avenue

The small Italian man was in his element. Simone was seated as if he were a mad scientist in front of several computers as he monitored the happenings inside the Smithsonian Institution across the street. Television cameras linked via satellite to the security cameras inside allowed him to view every internal facet of what was happening inside the building across the street. He cracked his knuckles and smiled.

He had already made contact with each of the people inside.

Cecilia and Sean seemed to be quietly tucked away in the Dibner Library's rest room facilities. Vincent was positioning himself in an area that would gain him access to the necessary air ducts. And Luigi Basso was pulling the Mercedes around, readying himself to handle their security issues.

All seemed to be going well and according to the discussed plan. The Institution's halls were clear of all but two security guards, one patrolling the second floor, and one moving in Vincent's vicinity on the third floor.

He adjusted his headset. "Vincent," he said as his voice transmitted to the thief through his tiny earphone, "You may have company in a few moments," he warned.

"Simone," he responded, cupping one hand to his ear, "How far away is he?"

"He is in front of the Vietnam Memorial, twirling some keys. He is nowhere close to you yet, but keep up your guard."

"How long before you have control over the electrical supply?"

"As soon as Luigi gains us access into the security booth, which should happen very soon."

"Good," Vincent said, "Let me know as soon as we have control of the security cameras."

"Si," Simone confirmed, his voice drifting off.

It was hard to believe he was here, in the back of a well-equipped van, monitoring four personages who were about to steal a priceless relic. He had been a computer programmer for most of his life, but the boredom of that existence had taken its toll. He longed for adventure, for some God forsaken freedom from a cubical existence. And when his sights turned first to hacking into other computers, it wasn't too long before his path crossed Vincent Conducci's.

He had been a wonderful asset to the thief, lessening Vincent's chances of being caught through computer technology. In turn, Simone had been made quite wealthy, and gotten all the adventure he had desired.

As he shifted his body forward slightly, he could see the large Italian man stepping from the car and moving towards the security booth. Things were about to get heated.

5:50 p.m.
Lower Level West/Smithsonian Institution

Luigi Basso stepped from the car, clicking the chamber of his Beretta, and shoving the gun into the front of his pants where it would be of easy access when the time came that he might need to call it to action. There was a deadpan look on his face as he made no showing of any human emotion. Buttoning up the front of his jacket, he closed the car door behind him. A calm came over him, as he turned from the car. He was all about the business at hand.

Luigi was now moving toward the main security office in a stride of confidence and poise. He had resolved himself to gain control of this facility by whatever means necessary, and that was just what he told himself was going to happen. He unbuttoned the top two buttons of his sport coat. In the distance, he could see a thin man inside the security window shuffling about. He now undid button number three.

Tom Duncan had just placed his newspaper on the table and lifted the convenient store bought cup of coffee to his lips. Looking up for a moment, he saw from the security window, a large, well- dressed man approaching. Must be a lost tourist, he thought to himself. The museum had been closed now for twenty minutes. There was one in every crowd, he mused. Setting his coffee down, he stepped from the booth to see if he could be of any assistance to the individual.

"Can I help you, sir?" Tom said confronting the man.

"You can," a voice returned, "I am in need of some assistance as my car is unable to start. Could you perhaps give me a hand?" The voice was thick in Italian undertone, the English shaky.

The security guard paused for a minute while a puzzling look came over him. "I can call a tow service, but I can't leave my station. I'm afraid I'm the only one here at the moment," he said, smiling.

Bingo.

"Well," Luigi said, "Can I come inside the booth and make a quick call?"

"No one is allowed inside the security office, sir," the guard stated, becoming slightly agitated, "I'm afraid you're gonna have to wait outside. I'm sorry."

Luigi prodded a bit more. "Please," he urged, "I just need two minutes to call my wife."

"Listen," Tom said sternly, trying to make his point without seeming rude, "I understand your problem, but you'll have to wait outside." The guard stepped back a couple of feet, then offered his help again. "Tell you what," he said holding out his hand, "Give me your wife's number and I'll give her a call."

The large man smiled back, unbuttoning the final button of his sport coat. "As you wish," he said, not wanting to waste any more time in dialogue.

There was no time for Tom Duncan to react. His eyes grew large at a sight he now could hardly believe was appearing. It was an instrument of death, and it was pointing in his direction.

Tom's heart skipped.

The bullet made no sound as it whipped through the air, burying itself deep within the security guard's chest. A flood of emotion overcame him as he thought about his bullet proof vest in the trunk of his Impala sedan. It had been too weighty, he thought. Too restrictive. Besides, what was going to happen to a night guardsman at the Smithsonian?

Before his thought was finished, he was looking up at his attacker as he lay on his back, writhing from the blow. Tom grappled with his chest, as blood oozed from the small wound. He could feel himself slipping, so he tried to focus on anything he could. He saw his coffee cup on the counter. Then, his newborn daughter at home. His hand, sticky with his own woe, reached for the gun holstered to his side. At least he had to put up a fight.

Luigi pumped another round into the guard, this time rupturing the man's spleen. All went black for Tom Duncan as the Italian stepped over his body and positioned himself at the man's upper torso. He then began to drag Tom's lifeless body into the security office.

The only eyes that could see the aggressive display were those of Simone Pisano, monitoring the action from a van across the street.

They were still keeping to the allotted time.

5:50 p.m.
Third floor/Smithsonian Institution

Thirty- nine minutes had passed since Vincent had taken the elevator to the third floor and, with the use of his ladder, gained access into the air ducts overhead.

He had a troublesome altercation with a security guard moments ago, as the man had questioned why he was replacing ceiling lights so late after normal operating hours, but Vincent had managed to sway the man, assuring the necessity of the act.

Now he was moving through the upper cavity of the Smithsonian's walls. He had entered the ceiling from the third-floor photo gallery and was making his way towards the area labeled 'Printing and Graphic Arts.' Gone was his janitorial disguise. He had shed the clothing for the sleek black spandex body suit that would allow him easy movement through the tight enclosure. About his head was a mask, causing him to find likeness with the feudal Ninja warrior of Japan.

Crouching in the air duct, he started moving with calculation, as if some jaguar hunting its prey. There was truth in this. His prey was not flesh and blood- but bound of paper and leather. Prey.

Pray.

Vincent thought of the money he would make. He thought further of the adulation he would bestow upon himself for successfully completing the mission. Pity, he thought. There needed to be awards ceremonies for acts such as this.

As his pride grew, so did his proximity to the targeted exhibit. Only a few more feet and he would be poised above the back hallway that would provide entry into the display. Now all he had to do was get the affirmation from Simone that they had taken control of security, and that Luigi had shut down the alarm system. Quietly, Il Fantasma waited above for the signal that all was clear. He waited, well positioned, and ready to strike.

6:00p.m.
The Dibner library
First Floor/Smithsonian Institution

This was bullshit, Sean thought to himself as he sat on top of the closed toilet lid, in the far comer stall of the darkened men's room. If this were some movie, there was no question as to whether it would have been labeled a comedy. There was a complete uselessness in dwelling on this, though. The situation he was in was his own, no getting out of it now.

He reached down to his leather bag and withdrew the fake copy of the Manuscripta Diabolica. He couldn't see it in the dark of course, but there was a sudden need to feel it in his hands, if only to pass the time.

In a few moments, he would have to call on every facet of his intellect to distinguish between the real volume and the fake he now caressed in his hands. He would feel the construction. Smell the pages and check the markings. If anyone in the world could distinguish between the two books, it would be Sean.

And there was another clue that might be of some aid.

DeBury had told him, the night before he had left London, that the Smithsonian staff may not have noticed a small, microscopic seal that had been branded on the last leaf of the book by an earlier relative of the DeBury namesake. Sean would need a magnifying glass to find it, or to feel for the indentation with the tip of his finger. But, Debury had said, if it had escaped the notice of whomever commissioned the faux books to be made, it might aid him to know of its existence.

But Sean knew the hard part of DeBury' s request would not be the identification of the volume, but its extraction from the library.

Then the book scout jolted, as he heard the sound of someone entering the room.

Simone had not given the go ahead via his earphone and Cecilia had not efforted contact either. He was busted. Hell, nothing had even happened and he was headed for trouble.

Just then, he heard the rattle of his stall door.

He pulled his feet from the floor, placing them on the toilet's lid as well. He thought his heart - as well as his blood pressure - would skyrocket through the roof.

His arms clamped around his knees as he tightly bunched himself into an imaginary cannonball. What would happen next was anybody's guess.

But something caught Sean's attention. A familiar scent. Perfume?

"Sean," a female voice whispered from the other side of the door.

The book scout clicked the latch open, thinking it must be time to act. As the door swung inward, he swallowed a large lump that had formed in his throat. Odd though. Simone had not transmitted any message to him that they were ready to move into action. His hand moved to the small transmitter in his ear. Perhaps it was malfunctioning, he thought. As the door swung open, he came to realize why the pensive Italian hadn't spoken to him.

Cecilia, outfitted in a black spandex body suit, stood in the doorway. Though Sean couldn't see her, he could smell her perfume, and sense a change in her behavior. Before he could question what was to happen next, she was upon him. Her body entangled with his, as his withdrawal couldn't distance him from the wet embracing of her lips to his.

Sean fell back, bruising his tailbone on the closed toilet lid. Though he was shocked, there was. no part of him that resisted her advancing passion. This is what he had wished for since the moment the two had met in the book store of Venice. Her timing, he thought, could have been better.

"We do not have much time," she said, withdrawing for a moment. Her hands reached for her neck, as she arched her body forward. Her intent was all too clear.

Straddling him from atop, she unzipped the fastening clip that ran in a straight line from her neck to her waist, parting the slick material and exposing her upper torso. Her left hand cradled the back of Sean's head and compressed his face savagely into her firm, heaving breasts. Charged by the rush of excitement, his lips teased her erect nipples, causing her body to tingle as she moaned with the anticipation of having him firmly inside her.

Sean could feel every curve and every muscle of the woman's well-proportioned frame. He jumped as he felt her right hand unzip his slacks, reaching in and taking hold of his pulsing organ. Sweat began to drip from his brow as he readied himself for the pleasure that would soon follow.

Within seconds he could feel the warmth of her body, as she placed him between her thighs with one swift, violent thrust.

Cecelia moaned as her body began to oscillate, embracing the firmness of his full erection. Her body heaved, grinding rapidly up and down. She could feel a rush of pleasure building as the heat of their bodies ignited in an aggressive display of sexual liberation.

Sean wanted nothing more than to draw the moment out for as long as he could, but his body could not restrain itself from the release of otherworldly pleasure.

In the darkness of the Dibner Library's rest room facilities, the two beings both climaxed in a torrent of feverish emotion and desirous need for one another's physical gratification.

6:03 p.m.
Lower Level West
Security Office/Smithsonian Institution

Luigi Basso was reading the sign- in sheet lying on the table before him. Only three guards were scheduled for duty tonight, the two that he could see on the security television to his right, and Tom Duncan, lying dead at his feet.

All was going perfectly to plan.

The Italian killer then went to a large control panel that seemed to be lit with all types of blinking lights as he searched for a switch that would turn the alarm system off. He smiled as his eyes fell upon two keys jutting from the panel. He then turned each to the left, positioning them on the label marked 'off.

The security system was now disengaged. The thieves had complete control of the Smithsonian Institution.

Luigi broadcast his success to Simone via the tiny transmitter on his lapel. All had gone according to plan and it was now time to alert the others.

Simone Pisano, seated across the street in the back of the van, transmitted the message, giving each of the thieves' permission to act. Their prize lay only moments away.

But something happened. Without making a sound, and unbeknownst to Luigi Basso, the body lying at his feet began to move.

"Death tugs at my ear and says; 'Live; I am coming.'"

Oliver Wendell Holmes, Sr.

A Time to Kill

"You must remember, old man, at this point I had done no human physical harm," Lucifer confessed. "I had obeyed the Creator, using only my wile to tempt you beings into sin. But something happened that changed the scope of my realm, my earthly domain. A challenge to my sovereignty, if you will. And ignore it- I could not."

The monk, still rattled from his vision of Hell, sat awaiting the demon's answer. It seemed to him the devil was likewise awaiting a response.

"What about this realm changed?" the monk asked.

"Is it not obvious?" Lucifer spat. "The Creator sent forth his Brood, and tested my resolve to its very limit of endurance."

There was but one realization, the demon was speaking of Jesus Christ.

The monk smiled. He had spent the night weighted down with the surmounting harrow that had been Hell. Now, perhaps, they would discuss a subject more inclined to his liking. Perhaps the playing field would become even once more.

"Tell me, demon," the monk sat wishing to goad his oppressor to anger. "What was it like to be faced off with a being you could not defeat in the realm that you called your own?"

"You speak as if to chastise me, monk," Lucifer returned, "but once again, you, being an ignorant human, know nothing of what you speak." He said as he cackled. "Allow a digression." The fallen angel then uncrossed his arms and took to his feet. His appearance remained pleasing, reassuring the monk that he was not riled by the old man's words. Then, the demon began circling the old man as a shark encircling a wounded fish. He wasted no time delivering that which lay deep in his memory. His pace was steady as he walked. He would confess all and hold nothing back. Lucifer had indeed murdered a human being, and the pious abbot would soon find out the unlikely event that lost the demon's uncontrolled rage.

"I have no time, nor do I have the wanton desire to revisit the events of His coming to the world and the legacy told by His infernal disciples. You have all you need for that written already. What I shall confess is my relationship to all of this."

The monk sat with an anticipation he was unaware he had. Lucifer was to talk of Christ. The New Testament was about to undergo a diabolic revision of sorts.

Lucifer brought his motion to a halt, then turned to the old man and spoke.

"What you have come to read is not without its truths, but it is likewise incomplete. What you - that is man - has come to believe is that I wished the death of your Savior, or at least His destruction. Yet nothing could have been further from the truth. There was no being alive who resisted his martyrdom more than I. The 'God' you worship willed the death of His son, and I gave him direct challenge to this. The Temptation you have read of in the wilderness had less to do with those three requests you have been told I presented. Hell, Father, I would not have expected His allegiance based on those offerings myself. I was not ignorant of whom I was dealing with. That is just the only part of my tempting He told his disciples, and since it was they who wrote what you have read......... well you can see where I am going with this."

"No Lucifer, I cannot."

"Very well, indigent," the devil barked. "Try this," he said, drawing forth a lofty breath of air and expelling his blasphemous offering. "I shall speak with directness. He knew why He was here. I knew why He was here. But, what was I to do? I reasoned the matter as simple to define yet harder to control." Lucifer could still see puzzlement on the old man's face. He was clearly agitated. "Confound you, human! Why must you seem so detached? I could not defeat a god! Yet before me, in my domain, my Creator had unfurled His last but most effective device of torture. He was sending a god in the form of a human to walk upon my earth. My home. So let me paint you this picture so your brain will not be undone by the pressure of my words: I, Lucifer, now damned to the earth, trapped with the humans I abhorred, un-allowed release, unable to procreate, now had to ready myself for the ultimate culmination of all these horrors rolled into one hated acursment -the presence of a god in the form of a human, brought forth by the womb of a human!" Lucifer fell to his knees laughing hysterically while from his eyes poured tears of defeated sorrow. If he was not mad, Father Koutrakos was unaware what to classify the demon as. "Can you sympathize with such hopelessness, Father? Can you imagine, for one instance, what this did to me!" The demon was on his feet once again, his arms outstretched in a questioning shrug. "How was I going to defeat this?"

"I should think it impossible," the old man pointed out.

"Oh, thank you for your helpful insight, my dear man," the demon snapped. The monk had not meant to be rude, he was just stating what he believed to be fact. "No, I mused. There were only two points with which to concern myself. The first was that I needed to try and sway this being to join allegiance. The second, was at all cost, if I could not succeed with the latter, at least I had to prevent His martyrdom. He could not be killed, and suffer a human death, sacrificing himself for the humans I so despised. This would not allow Him to be forgotten. He might start a movement with such a sacrifice. I decided my Creator had gone too far with this folly."

"How does all this relate to a murder?"

"Listen, for my confession has yet to begin."

"On with you, then," the monk urged, "I am listening."

The unnamable cracked his knuckles and looked skyward, as if to find something in the open space other than the oaken beams overhead. He then looked back in the direction of the old man. "Where to begin?" he said as he searched his mind for some point to start, "I had not wished any direct confrontation with the one whom you call 'Christ'. It is He who came to seek me out, at various times during his mortal interment on my earth. I had watched him from a distance since the very moment he entered the world."

"If you are not omnipotent," the abbot questioned, "how did you know of His coming or His birth?"

"As I am a demon of the air, I can sense a change in the events and happenings of this realm. I am not without my gifts, and when that particular Man entered this world, it was as if my senses were scrambled in one frightful instance. I could not think nor could I focus on anything but His presence. Now upon the earth, there was one like myself. Something that had never happened before.

You see, l was not made verbally aware of His coming, even though I was now having conversation with my Creator every hundred years or so." The demon paused as the monk shot him a look of confusion. "Oh, I see. I have caught you off guard," he casually commented as he began to pace about once more. "I talked to 'God' more frequently than you might think. The circumstances of our relationship are not such that should allow for mortal comprehension. But just so you know, I could not have taken you to the realm of Hell earlier, had He not allowed it. Everything happens by His will, or lack thereof, l should say. But we shall talk of this later. Allow me the return of my confession."

Father Koutrakos had heard such beguiling things these past two nights. Lucifer had challenged every belief the old man had ever held about who and what the demon was. A life spent studying the scriptures had been important, yes, but if anything this beast was saying held a degree of truth, the scope of life for a human being it seemed, was opening far wider and with much new understanding.

"I was there, Father. I too pilgrimaged to that tiny trough in the town called Bethlehem. I had to see what had caused me such troublesome worry, which I could not account a reason for." He paused, taking in a deep breath. "So I followed the environmental change until I came before him, disguised as if I were some loathsome shepherd.

"There, lying helpless, rested my doom! In a feed stall, no less!" he said laughing hysterically. "Imagine it! I could have willed the death of this tiny babe, He was so helpless. It certainly would have saved myself some future misery, one could suppose. Yet, I could do it not."

"Why? If He was so helpless, why could you just not have killed the Christ? Were you concerned what God would do?"

"I have never been able to explain to myself what it was about this child that stayed my anger. Even now, I cannot relate this to you. Feelings of hate, even for myself, became distant in His presence. I had to remind myself who He was, and who I was to maintain any sense of anger. What I did know was that the world had changed, and that I now had a powerful new adversary. I would watch Him all the days of His life, and think of some way to rid myself of Him on my own terms. But know this, Father, I fashioned that if I could sway this being to my side, in this I could upstage my Creator and turn His vengeance back upon Him. This was my rationing. This became my pursuit."

"I am sorry. This is so difficult to comprehend," the monk expressed.

"It is I who am sorry, old man," the angel remarked, "Perhaps I am moving a bit too fast."

"No, no," he returned, "I pray you, demon, please continue."

"Very well," he said. "At once I sought to seek answers from my Creator. I wished explanation for this being's presence in my realm. But no such conversation was to be granted."

"If you were on speaking terms as you say, what was the cause God would not have council with you?"

"I am without an answer," he said, shrugging his shoulders. "Who can understand the rationale of 'God,' Father?"

"Indeed, Lucifer, on that we can agree."

"It truth, I suspect He would not council with me because He realized nothing I could say or do was to make any impact on His will. Throughout the term of life you humans call 'history,' I have many times changed His decisions on various matters, which should again beg the question: how could a being who claims perfection, be so, if one such as I could sway even His mind?"

"After spending two nights with you, I think you have many times answered this," the abbot stated. "You yourself have spoken of an incomprehension with understanding why He does some of the things He does. I believe even when His mind is brought to change, it was because of His preordained will to do so. Perhaps He is just wiser than you are, Lucifer. One should believe this, I think."

"Ah, monk. You are wise, and yet you are human. I have lived an eternity and have not seen the marriage of these two things in such personage as I see them now," Lucifer said, smiling at the old man. "Let us move from pondering the will of my Creator, we have not the eternity for it." There in the darkness of the small library, the two beings joined in a moment of unified laughter. But the fallen angel wasted no time returning to his point.

"So here, there was now some very real adversary upon my earth, and I had thirty winters to prepare for a way in which I would somehow cajole Him to my side. Your scriptures leave no record of the many conversations we had, this 'Jesus' and myself. That is, of course, because they were compiled by men such as you, not gods, such as were we. Man is fallible and a lowly product of his time. I have been amazed at the willingness for a human to worship my Creator based on these measly chronicles of parchment written by the hands of men, and yet, it is so." He paused. "But forgive my proclivities," he stated, moving back to his former observations, "It was difficult to ever present myself before the one you call 'Christ' and hold anger, as I stated earlier. But come I would, always appearing in the form of some animal when He was a child. We would talk of anything you might imagine, and for hours. He wielded the most complete power in the universe, yet He remained so simple, and threatened me not in the slightest."

"Do you think Christ was aware of who you were? What you were?"

"I believe this to be true," Lucifer said, "But I cannot say for sure. He never referred to me by name, even when He was a child, but as nothing escapes Him, even then I am sure He knew with whom He was talking." The demon looked around the room, momentarily reflecting on the past. He seemed fond of the memory he recollected. "We would talk of all manner of things. I would pose some question, He would parable some response. So simple was He. Though I knew this was the son of my Creator - born of a human no less - He appealed to me. One could not be in His presence and not be utterly fascinated by the things He would say.

There was little resemblance between my Author and His son. I found myself having to purposefully keep my distance, for He captivated me to no end. If you wish to know the truth, Father," the demon said, looking deep into the abbot's eyes, "I was slowly falling in love with Him."

The monk was about to fall from his chair. "I am not ready for this, devil."

"Nor was I!" he responded loudly, "So I did the only thing I could do."

"And that was?"

"I left Him at once. At around the twelfth year of His life, I returned to Him no more. I could not allow myself to be taken by Him. But I did him the favor of augury. I warned Him that as He grew, man would surely come to hate Him for the simplicity of His rationing and His offering of peace. The human could not understand peace, I said - better to ration these musings to a tree. I told Him He would endanger Himself and someone might attempt His life should He talk to man, the way He had occasioned Himself with me. Humans liken themselves to kill what they do not understand. At least that seems to be the way of it. And do you know what He said to this father?"

"I...I... cannot imagine...!...."

"He looked me, Lucifer, in the eye, and as a tear rolled down His cheek, He said 'I know'.

"I know." The demon said again, bowing his head shaking it from side to side. "Can you believe this father? I have spent an eternity just trying to analyze that offering. That tear. Was it of hope, fear, knowing, hopelessness, mercy, sorrow? It has baffled me to this moment."

"You speak as if you bore a kinship with the Son of man."

"Did I not? Who can say. We understood each other, He and I. Never did He withdraw from my offering of conversation. If you wish to call that friendship then what, pray tell, are you and I?"

"I......."

"No need to answer, - Father, just know you this: at the time of His birth, I did not know He was here to die. This fact only became obvious when He opened His mouth as an adult. He spoke to man as simply as one would speak to a child, yet few were of compass to understand the simplicity of His infinite wisdom. That His own disciples were blind to

His coming martyrdom, well, that in and of itself shows how ignorant the human can be. This man, if you could call Him such, was to pick a fight with human nature. Any fool could see He was going to lose. But I, Lucifer, would try my hand at preventing this, for if there was one being on earth crafty enough to thwart His coming doom, well, it would have to have been me, would it not?"

The abbot shook his head in shock and disbelief. Was he to believe that the very Devil himself was setting out to prevent the death of Christ? The depths to which their conversation had gone seemed to challenge him in such a way that he could scarcely digest the language. Lucifer was not changing the history of the Bible, nor at any point had he refuted its offerings. He was adding a new twist, and revealing gaps in what the old man had come to understand of the written word. This is where it became so difficult not to believe every word the devil said.

"How did you intend to prevent this?"

"The way I purpose everything I do," the demon said. "By waiting and by watching. Much can be learned of human activity this way. I would follow Him as He walked the earth, and as he found Himself in trouble, I would seek some way to intervene. It was not to be long. The regime of Rome was not going to stand by and allow some son of a cabinet maker to become Caesar. No, no. But even for all my wisdom, I could have never guessed where the real problem was going to come in trying to keep Him alive."

"What was the other problem?"

"Fool!" he screamed. "His own people!" Lucifer exclaimed. "His own race was going to try and kill Him! Who but Himself could have seen this coming? Not I, that to be sure. Something had to be done. So, I begged Him to the wilderness, away from those buffoons that followed Him like slaves. I needed to reason with Him. He needed to be aware of what these people, were going to do to Him. He needed to embrace me. I did not wish Him to die, Father, and I knew one thing to be certain," Lucifer said, pausing to allow the monk a word.

"And that was?"

"He did not wish to die either."

There was a longer pause this time. Both souls sat contemplating this meeting infernal. The old monk looked at his wrists which seem to have aged quite a bit since the conversation had begun. He could see his veins pulsing and his body was just as battered as the fray of his mind. He was as uncomfortable as he had ever been in his life, but not because he was alone with Lucifer, as had been the case earlier. Now the old man grappled with the words of one who had seen all. He was liken to believe none of the demon's words, and yet there existed truth and sense in all the beast said.

Lucifer sat passive. Not once had he changed his form or given any real show of rage. Yes, he had at times become excited, but this in no way gave him cause to frighten the aged man. Lucifer enjoyed this time with the monk. At no point had he resigned himself to pressure the man's soul, even though he was human and deserved no act of mercy on part of the demon. There was a willingness on part of the abbot to hear the demon speak, and for Lucifer, that was enough - for now.

"When He came into the wilderness, I was waiting," the demon began, "I asked the three questions of Him that you have come to know from scripture," he said gesturing with his fingers, "as an effort to make sure He was in fact who I thought. You must realize - His Father, my Father, could have been tricking me, sending some angel in disguise of His son. I was not so foolish as to believe the Son of man could be coaxed into such simple temptation as so described by His authors. I assure you, most of what is written about me has been filtered through a very narrow view of who and what I am. I am not the fool you may believe. But pardon this digression," he said, moving further into details, "We spoke, He and I, for a long time. He did not welcome my presence, but He did not ask me to leave either. I presented my case - His case - and begged Him to reconsider his position. He said what was to be, was to be, and that I should leave well enough alone. He told me I was married to my role, just as He was destined to His. I told Him He was a fool. He told me I was damnable wretch. I told Him He was beyond the comprehension of man. He told me that I was, too. I begged Him to give up this ridiculous quest of saving mankind. He begged me to give up my quest of damning mankind. I told Him I could have loved Him. Then, that man-god spoke back, ripping my heart apart forever."

"What did he say?" the monk questioned.

The demon put his hands to his face and began crying. The monk was confounded. Lucifer parted his fingers and explained himself.

"He said...... He understood... and that it did not really matter. He had long since loved me, even so," the old devil said, returning to his sorrowful tears.

Drool escaped the old man's gaping maw, as he sat with his tongue tied and his mind blank. He had never felt the need to comfort the demon until this very moment. Was a man such as he able to believe Christ to love even the devil himself? It seemed so. Yet even still, the monk was not so far gone of mind as to reach forth physically and place his hand on the beast, even though he wanted to do nothing other than that very deed. The demon before him had touched him to the quick, and no words would come forth. If, he supposed to himself, Christ could find love for Lucifer, then could Lucifer not be forgiven? The question now became paramount in his mind.

"Then," the old originator of evil began, "He turned the conversation back upon me and tried to save me. He was all about saving people, you know."

"Yes," the monk said, "I know."

"But I was younger than I am now and I was still angered by our Father who art in Heaven, so I would have none of it. In fact, I remember cursing Him, urging Him to go away from me and find Himself in the company of His Roman friends. Perhaps I said they could better convince Him of what I could not. Then I took flight. I left Him to His fate. My efforts to tempt Him into self- preservation had failed. And I have never handled failure well. As I departed, He held up a weakened arm, for He had refused food for a long period of time. And there, in the palm of His hand I saw a trickle of blood which, at the time, meant to me very little."

"So you abandoned the plan to save Him?"

"Not exactly, but it was a long time before I would see Him again."

"What do you mean by 'not exactly'?"

The demon took a seat. "After His people had turned Him over to the Romans, I tried to position the murderer Barabbas in such a light as to convince one Pontius Pilate to free the captive Prophet, pardoning him and allowing me more time to plan of some means of saving your 'Christ'. I would have never imagined, if my Maker had told me from His own mouth, that the people would have chosen to allow a murderer go free over a disciple of their own. Fools, thy name is man!!"

"What did you do?"

"I flew to the heavens on behalf of Him who awaited death, and demanded council with my Author. The angels would not allow me to pass through the gates so I gave them this warning; I said the man who decrees the death of my brother would pay for this insolence with his life! A soul for a soul. My Creator could chew on that. And Father, having heard those very words resound through Heaven's realm, my Creator did not hasten to appear.

"Did He speak to you?"

"Indeed," the demon nodded, "But it was not of care for my offering. He told me to stay my hand lest I call His wrath. I said 'I have fallen victim by thy wrath already' and that I was prepared to deal with whatever He would do to me. Even now, there was nothing worse the Architect could do to Lucifer that I had not already suffered in some way. He then reminded me that if I touched any mortal creation, He would never council with me again. I returned by saying, 'what would I have to converse upon with one who would slaughter His own child?'"

"What of His response?" The old man had become elevated with Lucifer's tale.

"I did not remain to hear. I returned to earth, but found that I had tarried too long in Heaven. I found His son hanging naked and bloodied from a wooden cross beam."

"The prophecy had been fulfilled then. God gave His son for the offering," the monk sat stating.

"Father, have you ever seen a man crucified?" Lucifer asked.

"I have seen many, many horrible things, demon."

"The first spike penetrates the flesh in such a way as to cause an insurmountable degree of suffrage. It separates nerves and muscle tissue, sending tiny pieces of metal into the blood stream. This causes intense pain yet preserves death. Especially if it is in some way rusted, as were those used on Him," he said, tossing a twelve- inch spike on the desk before the monk. As it came to rest, the old man reached for it, touching the object. At that moment, the old man could hear for himself the cries of his Christ as the nail penetrated His flesh so many years ago. The moment had been made real, if only for a second. The monk then collapsed to the floor weeping as though he were a child. He was beyond consolation, as Lucifer stood over his writhing frame. The demon then bent down, whispering.

"But enough of this. I shall tell you what happened next." His voice trailed as the monk fought to sit up and regain his composure.

Lucifer gave the old man his needed moments. He walked the floor of the library, shuffling through the various manuscripts for a time as the monk wrestled with his own demons. The old devil did not offer consolation to the monk, but when he heard the sobbing muffle, he turned from the shelves and began to alter his form, his hoofed feet clapping the floor as he walked toward the crouching monk. Then, putting his taloned digits atop the monks brow, he bent down and smiled with a sharpened, incisory glare.

"Fear not, monk," he said with a smile, "Our revenge was sweet. Shall I tell you of it?"

"S..... speak... what...you will...," he said between the now easing sobs.

"Even though there were many to blame, I sought an example to make clear my point to all. History is deaf to what I am to tell you, as is your 'Bible,' so pay attention," the demon said.

The abbot could not distance himself from the grotesqueness of Lucifer's protruding horns. "I waited an entire year, letting the disciples disperse so that my plan would not be blamed on them, thus not allowing the Romans to martyr them as well for my otherworldly deed. Then, creeping like some jackal in the night, I came to the bed of the fifth procurator of Judea, Pontius Pilate, and bade him wake. He sprang from his bed as if I were a ghost or some false Roman deity, crawling over the whore that lay beside him, and calling for his guards. They would not come, I told him, as I willed his door to lock itself and embraced his fear which was surmounting with each passing moment. He reached for his sword and thrust it through my gut, but I laughed and altered myself to the state I am in presently. He recoiled in such terror! Oh, the pleasure of it! Then, in the deep night, I began peeling the flesh from his body in small strips, consuming each in my mouth. Pilate watched in horror, unable to defend himself, as I consumed his outer tissue. Then, though barely alive,

I withdrew four spikes, such as those used on Him who is called Christ, and I nailed him squirming, upside down onto his bedroom wall. Then, stepping from his throbbing muscular component of tissue and veins, I bid him well, telling Him to send my brethren a message from earth: their leader would see them in Hell soon enough. I left the room to a screaming female, her mind utterly destroyed by what she had witnessed, and I took to the night sky. I had done it. I had killed a human being. It had been enjoyable such as no human could possibly imagine. I gloated to the heavens, and I laughed at the remnants of my task. Take that, Father, I called out! But no answer returned save the emptiness of sky. I was now truly alone, as I am before you now." Lucifer left the monk's side, reverting to his more pleasing form.

The old man then brought himself to his feet, and returned to his chair. His mind was ajar, his soul fired beyond all reason and capacity for understanding. He was not the same man he had been before the devil's visit. He was moved to a different station of consciousness. The scope of all reasoning had been usurped by the demon's words and his iniquitous acts.

The monk then noticed, from the comer of his eye, a small web, woven by the tiny arachnid which was tending it. It was in no way particularly different from the many spider webs that could be seen all about the monastery. But some aspect of it caught and held his attention. He noticed a small motion coming from one particular spot. The bulbous little beast noticed the motioning too, as his limbs quickly rode the silken strands and captured his struggling prey item, weaving it into a silken ball and storing the intruder until such time as it deemed necessary to extract the captive's blood.

The monk shuddered to himself, then turned toward Lucifer and spoke to him, wishing to visit yet another question which puzzled him.

> "We're all born brave, trusting and greedy, and most of us remain greedy."
>
> Mignon McLaughlin

The Manuscript

Il Fantasma was on the floor in an instant. The call from Simone Pisano, assuring him all was clear, prompted the thief to take immediate action. He had quietly descended from the ceiling's air duct and was now stealthily making his way down the museum's back corridor.

Vincent hadn't gone far when he found himself at the rear entrance to the display which contained his coveted prize. He looked around to make sure no one was coming down either side of the hallway. Assuring himself all was well, he turned around and noticed that the back frame of the display was held fast by a combination lock. Upon seeing it, the thief drew a smile beneath his hooded mask. Placing his ear just above the lock he began turning the dial. This was far too easy, he thought to himself. Rotating it first clockwise then again in the opposite direction, he heard a click. Then repeating a similar motion, he heard two subsequent clicking noises. In a moment, the faux wall gave way, and his hands were now positioned only inches from the book.

As his black gloves grasped the relic, he heard a noise from behind.

6:05 p.m.
The Dibner Library
First Floor/Smithsonian Institution

Cecilia was the first to exit the rest room, checking the area to make sure all was clear. Her heart was still beating from the exhaustive lovemaking that had just taken place, and her adrenaline - while satiated in one way, was still geared for overdrive in a completely different way. She caught a security camera facing directly at her position, and froze.

Simone came over her ear phone, assuring her he was the only one behind it, and that she needed to move - and fast!

Sean emerged shortly after her and followed the thief as she led him towards the back of the library. They were both now headed for the caged room which held the library's rarer books. Upon arrival, Cecilia began at once to pick the mechanical lock which was under a keyed entry while Sean stood behind her whipping his head back and forth, looking for anything or anyone that might cause them trouble. He was not only exhausted, but racked with a flood of varying emotions. He seemed to be more concerned with the female in front of him than he did the matter at hand. Sean needed to focus. Attention himself away from the girl.

Within sixty seconds, the door's lock gave way. Cecilia had done it!

As the steel chain link door swung inward, the two shuffled themselves hurriedly inside. The only unknown variable was where the curators kept the truly rare manuscripts. One thing was of fact, the room appeared well organized, much to their thankful reckoning.

Books were lined on a series of ten shelving devices, all in alphabetical order. Cecilia began searching immediately, thumbing through the volumes in a much-hurried fashion. Sean was looking as well, but refused to lift a hand to the shelves. In his mind, he was still no part of this act of thievery, though what he had opinioned really didn't matter at this point. As his eyes scanned the volumes, he heard some commotion from Cecilia's direction and looked around the aisle to find the woman withdrawing a stack of books from their place on the shelf.

He watched as she then sat the four folio- sized volumes on the room's viewing table and motioned for Sean to come over.

As he moved towards the books lying on the table, he hesitated for an instant, withdrawing the volume in his leather shoulder bag, and placing it beside the books displayed. They all seemed magnificent lying there beside one another. Oh, they were tattered in appearance, and an ignorant passerby might easily pass them by for some tattered work of a child, as the bindings were not of a brilliant nature, but contemporary of the time in which they were made. But they were exquisite as they lay, and Sean withdrew a magnifying glass from his satchel and at once began to peruse the front board of each book, comparing the inner workings. He was searching now for any dissimilarities that might separate them from one another.

He had not gotten very far when Cecilia tapped him on the shoulder, in an effort to remind him that they were still waiting on one book. The volume Vincent had yet to return with.

6:10 p.m.
Third Floor

One thing was certain. Vincent Conducci was more than just a little surprised when, book in hand, he turned his head to meet the eyes of a trembling security guard standing a few feet in front of him. The timid man had both his gun drawn and a flashlight shining in the thief's face.

Under Vincent's hood, and unbeknownst to the security guard, that smile appeared again. Vincent had been in similar situations before, and he relaxed himself. He would wait for the inexperienced guard to make the first move.

"P.... Put the b... book down, mister," a shaky voice directed itself at the thief. Vincent could not believe his luck. A rookie. Probably never even been in an altercation before now.

"Easy, my friend," Vincent's Italian accent muffled the English words through his mask, "I am going to do as you say." Vincent then sat the book slowly back into the opened display. The guard, more confident than ever, edged himself a few steps closer.

"Now.... p... put your hands out where I can see them," he commanded.

II Fantasma slid his left hand toward the direction of the guard first. Then, as he brought his right hand in view, the security guard noticed something small appear in the hand of the thief for a moment. Instantly it erupted with a flash.

6:17 p.m.
The Dibner Library

Cecilia was pissed. Sean noticed her pacing, and he was sure her brother's appearance was unusually behind schedule. He went back to looking at the books because watching her nervousness was doing nothing but making him more and more upset.

Suddenly, Cecilia stopped pacing.

"Sean," she began, "Simone just transmitted that Vincent had been in an altercation of sorts upstairs, but that he is now on his way."

"What happened?"

"He's breaking up..." she said, referring to some static mincing with Simone's transmission. "Something about a security guard...... doesn't really matter, he should be here any-"

Her speech was cut short as a grate fell to the library floor, and from the ceiling a small Italian emerged. A book was in his right hand.

He rushed the cage, placing the book on the table next to the others.

"What happened to you?" Sean asked.

"No time for talk now," he said, breathing heavily and dispensing with his hood. "Compare the books so we can get the hell out of here!"

At once Sean quickened himself to the task. He opened all volumes and began the aggressive perusal of their pages. As he viewed each page, he thought of all the adventures that had befallen the volume. From the places it had been, to the things it had seen. It took on almost a human imagining in the book scout's eyes. It was so priceless in so many ways. The calligraphic elements so neatly written upon each page, beautified every leaf of the book. The language was foreign to Sean, but the illuminated miniatures spoke volumes about what the writing meant. Each chapter seemed to be written in a different language. Odd.

Sean still could find no means to separate the books from one another. He then turned to the final leaf, opening each book from its back cover. He was now looking for DeBury's seal, microscopically pressed somewhere on the real volume.

No such seal appeared anywhere.

Sean's mind went into information overload. Had the Smithsonian staff somehow taken the measure of eradicating the seal from the last page of the book? Or, God forbid, was there another book hidden somewhere else?

Cecilia noticed something was wrong. "Sean," she said, "What's going on?"

He took a deep breath. "All of these books," he said, withdrawing from the table and turning to his conspirators, "are fakes."

"Impossible!" Vincent barked.

Sean looked frustrated. "I'm telling you, it's true," he said. "The paper is age toned, but no way is this parchment from the fourteenth century. And there's the binding," he held one of the books forward, showing it as an example. "While vellum, if you look closely, has been sewn to the pages in the last two centuries for sure. There's no way any of these volumes were assembled by Grecian monks five hundred years ago. No way in hell." While this fact had sickened Sean, it made Vincent boil with anger.

"Then where the fuck is the original?!" he said, throwing the volume Sean had placed in his hand across the room.

Cecilia, who had distanced herself from the table where the two men were arguing, noticed a small solid cabinet no more than four feet in height sitting in the comer of the room.

It was some type of vault. A safe!

The Italian woman turned toward her baffled constituents, and pointed towards the free-standing encasement.

"I think we should attempt to pry that open," she said. Her brother wasted no time and was upon the project as if his very life depended on it. The lock gave way to a series of well-placed turns, and entry was gained.

There were three books lying in interment when the safe's door opened.

Vincent withdrew the volume most resembling the ones Sean had been looking at. The book man quickly took the book from Vincent and placed it on the table.

The manuscript was similar in many ways, but somehow very different.

The book felt oily to his touch, as if the curators had shellacked the volume with some protective coating, prolonging its untimely decay. The binding was of a material very similar to pigskin, but slightly different in some way. Hell, he thought, after five hundred years, it could have been pigskin. Sean then opened the book from the back and pulling his magnifying glass over the final leaf, he sighed relief. The seal was there. He had in his hands the original copy of the Manuscripta Diabolica.

The three trespassers wasted no time dispersing as Vincent grabbed a fake volume from the table and scurried out the room and back to the display on floor number three.

Sean stuffed the priceless book in his bag but in his haste forgot to withdraw the fake copy and set it back in the vault.

He and Cecilia then set about restoring the office to its former station. They both were unaware that on Sean's person were two copies of the exact same book. One fake, the other, all too real.

6:20p.m.
Lower Level West
Security Office I Smithsonian Institution

Luigi Basso was monitoring the security cameras as he watched the only guard left in the building take the elevator from the second floor to the third floor. Everything else -seemed to be going smoothly. He had not been approached by any outside reinforcements, but kept a vigilant eye on the lookout.

His finger tapped the handle of the gun protruding from his pants pocket. He was not about to let anything happen now. If everything kept to Vincent's plan, within ten minutes the three thieves in the building would emerge from the elevator to his right, where he would be waiting in the Mercedes. They would meet up with Simone, who was in the van on Constitution A venue, and be on a plane bound for London within the three hours. Then, they would split the better part of eight million dollars.

Without warning, a loud, almost deafening noise, began screaming overhead.

An alarm! Luigi Basso looked down in disbelief as he saw below him one Thomas Duncan, barely breathing, withdrawing his hand from a small red button that had been located on the floor. It was an emergency alarm placed strategically to be set off by a guard's foot, should such an emergency necessitate the action.

The large Italian reacted in both a panic and a rage.

He pulled out the Berretta, and fired two rounds into the back of Tom Duncan's head, then fled from the security office in a mad dash for the Mercedes. How stupid could he have been to allow something like this to have happened. He shoved another clip in the handle of his gun and, arriving at the car, practically ripped the door off its hinges, then shoved his key in the ignition, revving the engine and pulling the car around to position the vehicle in front of the elevator door. He would wait for his friends here.

With the screeching alarm resounding all over the building, Luigi clicked the head stock of his gun and sat ready in the car, preparing for the worst.

6:25p.m.
Third Floor

Vincent had no more than placed the counterfeit book ever so carefully in the display when he heard the screaming of the overhead alarms. He was grossly unprepared as to what he would do, but knew he hadn't the pleasure of wasting time on a lengthy decision.

One thing was for certain, there was no time to scurry through the maze of air ducts again, he needed a more direct outing. Simone came over his earphone alerting him to the danger surrounding him. There was a security guard, stepping from the elevator, on the very floor he was on. He needed to be on guard.

Vincent knew he had about six minutes before reinforcements arrived at the Smithsonian. That wasn't much time to clear three floors and reach the rendezvous point on the lower level, he thought to himself.

"Simone," he called into his transmission device, "Do you read me?"

"Si," a voice came in static over Vincent's ear device.

"Tell Cecilia I am going to the roof," he began frantically, "And make sure she and Sean get the hell out of the library- and fast! Tell Luigi to move the car from the lower level and wait with it idling on the opposite side of 14th Street. As law enforcement arrives, the lower level will be their point of entry. Let Cecilia know of this change in plans," he said as he placed the back panel of the book's display back as it had been before. With everything returned to its rightful place, Vincent Conducci resigned himself to find a way out of this mess.

He could hear from behind him the footsteps of someone else headed his way.

6:25p.m.
First Floor

Sean and Cecilia had wasted no time fleeing the Dibner Library when they heard the alarm. And now in a frenzied panic, they were dashing towards the elevator up ahead, which was awaiting them just around the corner from the Lemelson Center.

As the two thieves rounded the corner, Cecilia saw a sign across the hall, denoting a stairwell to their right. She urged Sean that they would have a better chance on the stairs rather than to risk being trapped in an elevator. Sean wholly agreed.

The doorway to the stairwell burst open as the two rushed down the steps, their legs moving at a record pace, their knees exchanging motion as if they were on a bicycle.

To say Sean was scared would have been to state the most obvious fact of the moment. That he was about to shit himself would be far more accurate. He felt at any point one of them was going to be caught. It had to happen. There were just too many irons in the fire. If he didn't get shot by some trigger - happy cop, Sean Wilde knew he was going to spend the rest of his life in jail. All for a book. There was something ridiculous about the whole musing, yet at the same time it seemed to be a coming piece of reality. Somewhere in the furthest quadrant of his mind was the voice of some religious poet crafting the words: Live by the book, die by the book. Preposterous, yes, but not without its truths.

Cecilia was upset, but not altogether worried. She had been in situations like this before. All part of the learning curves that came with being a thief. What bothered her the most was the actual un-professionalism of this situation, and that this at all being allowed to happen. Someone had to have made a mistake, a miscalculation in judgment. They had been over every inch of the Smithsonian's operating procedures when they had discussed all that could possibly go wrong. What was the purpose of having Simone across the street monitoring the three floors if something like this was to happen, she thought? Her brother could take care of himself, of that there was no need for worry. Sean, on the other hand, might feign a heart attack at any moment. Not much longer though. They had almost reached the bottom of the stairs.

When the door swung open, Cecilia took Sean by the hand and turning towards her right, made a sprint for the point on 14th Street where she knew Luigi would be waiting in the idling car.

Sean, though nearly out of breath, was relieved to be in the open air. They were far from safe, but they were no longer enclosed by the building or its security features. In a worst case, they could separate if need be. The cops might get him, he thought- but it would be because they would've placed a well- aimed bullet in his back.

Behind them now were the approaching sirens of three police units, whining down Madison Drive and turning into the lower level, just outside the security office.

Cecilia said a prayer to the god of thieves, for there was still no sign of Vincent. He needed to hurry she thought, they couldn't afford to linger here for very long. The Italian woman turned to scan the area. Then, ahead in the distance, she and Sean could see the black Mercedes barreling towards them as if it were some provisional chariot of the gods.

6:27 p.m.
Third Floor

Vincent was moving down the hallway at record pace when he was stopped by a sudden pain from his left shoulder.

He glanced down, seeing that his body suit had been ripped, and that a small trickle of blood was oozing from the point where the pain was coming. The realization was beyond imagining. He had been shot.

Suddenly, from overhead, another bullet flew by, grazing the wall up ahead. Too much was happening. Simone was screaming in his ear, warning him of the obvious, while behind him a trigger - happy security guard was unloading his service revolver in Vincent's direction. If that wasn't enough, three city police cars had just pulled into the bottom floor garage, and it would be only minutes before they were making their way to his point.

What to do?

Breathing heavily, Vincent screamed for Simone to leave his position and take the van to the agreed point in which they would meet up. Now that the cops were onto them, they might monitor the transmission feed, so contact needed to be cut off. Vincent then ripped the communication device from his ear and tossed it aside while he tried to dodge the bullets being unloaded in his direction. He had been lucky. The wound to his arm was no more than a graze, even though it hurt like hell. But what to do about his pursuer?

The emergency stairwell was just up ahead in the distance.

Vincent Conducci burst through the door like a madman, his only intention now to get to the roof top, where earlier he had stashed a bag of small emergency equipment just in case this sort of thing happened. His mind was flooding with the various options of what to do. It became hard for the thief to focus, but he had already accomplished the most delicate task- he had the Manuscripta Diabolica. All he needed now was to escape.

The security guard was only one flight of stairs behind him when II Fantasma burst open the door in front of him, stepping onto the building's rooftop.

Vincent reached for the bag lying in a corner of an air conditioning unit. As he unzipped the satchel, he felt a presence behind him. He had not been as far ahead of the security guard as he had thought.

"Make one more move and I'll blow your fucking head off," a voice said in unmistakably clear English.

Vincent turned slowly, raising his hands, to meet his oppressor. He knew it would only be a few moments more before the man standing before him was joined by a host of his comrades. If Vincent was going to make a move, it needed to be now.

"Just what do you think you're doing?" the guard questioned, both hands raising the gun to Vincent's face.

The thief returned a response in Italian, confusing the guard and revealing nothing.

"You some Mafia boy, huh?" the man began insulting him. "Well, I got something for you, Mafia boy. That security guard you shot back there, that was my brother- in- law. You think I'm gonna tell my sister that the father of her two sons was murdered by some guinny wop, and I did nothing!?"

Oh shit. He was referring to the guard that surprised him when he first withdrew the fake manuscript earlier.

"Tell you what, boy," he began again. "Tum around so you don't have ta see this comin'. We'll play it like you was runnin' from me, resistin' arrest and all that. But one thing's for sure, boy," he said, clearly upset that his relative was lying in a heap at the base of the display case, "You won't be stealin' nothin' else."

Vincent couldn't react fast enough. As he turned his body away from the uniformed guard, he heard the man throughout one more insult.

"Time ta die, shit- ass," the cop said.

Vincent's heart jumped as he heard the gun discharge.

> "There are a thousand hacking at the branches of evil to one who is striking at its root."
>
> Henry David Thoureau

Welcomed Ignorance

"Man is a humorous beast, Father," the fallen angel remarked as he smiled at the elder monk. "Would that you beings can complicate the simplest of matters, bringing Hell from its very depths and surrounding yourselves willingly with it, every day of your pathetic lives."

"I know not what you mean, demon," the monk returned.

Lucifer, who had seemed reserved through the last few conversations, now seemed embittered with disgust. There was something strange in the way his mannerism shifted. Father Koutrakos would reserve himself to keep guard of his own emotions. The beast, perhaps, was now to show his true colors.

"Oh come now, Father," Lucifer said, "Tell me one thing, anything, man has yet to taint."

The monk sat thinking for a moment. This night had been the longest he could remember. The question was, would it ever come to an end at all? This devil before him was now posing a new question on which the monk had no immediate answer. He turned, looking toward the direction of the little spider resting motionless on his silken web, unwilling to lend aid or offer the old man any wisdom or guidance.

Man was a sinful creature. Of those commandments written in the scriptures, his species had broken every one. Depravity availed itself in every species though, and man had fallen victim to his reasonable share. But human beings were not void of some adulation. The beast before him had surely sought to place far too much blame on man without including himself in the scope of the matter. Where was Lucifer's responsibility for man's fallibility?

The demon would argue the disposition of free will on part of man. Yet there were some things that set the two of these beings apart. Had the human not forwarded the word of God? Even now, the fires of this age burned bright with the consolation of souls being swayed to the further good of glory and righteousness. Yes, devil, he thought, man had, if nothing else, attempted to spread forth the word of God. That, at least, was some place to start this infernal conversation.

"What of the advancement of religion?" the monk asked.

"It would seem as good of a question to ask as any," the demon responded. "Shall I give you my station on this matter?"

"By all means," the abbot requested.

"Prepare thyself," the evil imp said with a brazen smile. It was if the monk had asked the very question the demon had wished to address all along. "Man," he began, "reasons by a will which even I cannot explain. One might believe him to use his feet rather than his brain for contemplative thought," he said, pausing for a moment. He then lifted his nose while the abbot watched, sniffing the air. "Can you not sense it, Father?"

"What are you saying?"

"It is all around us. In the air." The monk looked confused. "Division is growing. I can feel it. I can smell it. One can do no greater harm than to separate his species by the tide of religious misgivings."

"You trouble me with talk which has no meaning," the monk offered as insight.

Lucifer heaved his well- defined chest. He needed some way of entering the conversation in such a manner that the monk might understand. He tapped his temple with a forefinger.

"The world is full of many races, all with varied opinions. Herein lies the problem." He began once more. "The simplicity of my Creator's commandments is what so confounds you humans. Perhaps I am too simple a beast to understand the human mind. Perhaps I am too complicated. I know not. Every day, as in this century and all those that proceeded it, man takes what has been said - written in scripture, I mean - and interprets it to whatever necessitates the conventional wisdom of the time. You beings have di stoned my Author's words to such extremes as to use them to confute, kill, maim, overthrow, and conquer. But now, something else brews and stirs the climate of this age."

"You still offer naught but confusion," the old man said. "What is it you are trying to say?" The monk sat understandably confused.

"I am speaking of man's welcomed ignorance of my greatest triumph against your species. It is why I am to confess all before you this night. I am through tempting you oppressed beings. I mastered a final plan long ago, and I have no need of this realm, nor thy company any more. Now forgiveness is all I wish to seek. Your species is done. This, for me, ends tonight!"

The monk chose not to respond. Lucifer had gone well beyond his understanding. He seemed as though a beast that could do no more than rant. Perhaps the subject of Christ, discussed previously, had offset the demon somehow. Father Koutrakos would give the demon time to settle down. Alleviate his obvious discontent with whatever seemed to be troubling him.

"With the culmination of scripture in the form of what was to become the book you call 'Bible', I now could work some proclivity of magic." There was a gleam in the empty hole of the demon's eyes as he fixated his stare upon the old man. Something wicked lay behind the look. Here, a moment to see Lucifer and his genius unfold. "Man's brain, being so prone to complicate simple things, now had a tool which could render him salvation, yet I had a tool which could lend him damnation."

"Explain yourself, evil one."

"Father, what item upon this earth is more important than all others?" The monk sat quiet. He was without a readied answer. Was this to be some riddle? Then, the old man rationed that he was doing just as Lucifer had said, allowing his brain to complicate a simple question. "I know not," he said, awaiting the demon's twisted response.

"I shall tell you then," he stated, readying the response. "There is nothing more important by its very nature, than a book," he said as if there was no refuting the point. He then postured as if he had just revealed some grand secret of the universe. "Why do you not think I chose a library with which to hold this conversation? A book is the only means by which a man may reach eternal salvation, or bum forever in damnation. What, monk, is ultimately more important to a human than that? What is life on earth compared to the incomprehensibility of one's soul across the vast openness of eternity? A book is its author's soul transcribed. A book is the only thing which may imbibe the mind's faculties with some greater hope of understanding that it would not know otherwise. And what should exist of more importance upon your earth than my Author's words transcribed by some human underlings? Why He would use a human to express Himself is confounding, given your fallacies, but this act could serve some benefit to me as well, I rationed."

"How so?"

"The scriptures are simple. 'Do this, and I'll do this.' 'Don't do this and I will surely do this.' Do you follow me, Father?"

"Not easily."

"The Creator has stated His rules. Man has but to follow. This should be easy, especially considering those poor bastards who lived before this manual was even written. I mean, Jesus Christ, Father, man is so pathetic your species caused my Creator to write you your own guide for living your lives, since your attention span obviously could not get what the words 'Thou shalt not' meant when He said them aloud. Are you to believe angels have some book by which to maintain their status? One altercation was all we ever had. Just one. You humans cannot go three minutes!"

If the angel had wished to hurt the old man, he had done so. There was a defeat of soulless proportions on the man's face. He tugged at his robe. He fidgeted with his hands. Then, the demon addressed him.

"I am sorry if I have offended you, Father," he began, "this was not my intent at all. I merely wish to point out things that man tends to overlook. I have survived an eternity being hated by both men and gods. Imagine how that should feel. At least you have a soul to cling, I cannot be sure to have even that. What I have is wisdom gained from an eternity watching man and his actions. But this wisdom is of an infernal nature, as it has no conscience. And I have spent a thousand lifetimes coiled within its welcoming embrace. We are who we are, your 'Christ' said to me. Who are you, Father?"

"I am a man," he responded, directing himself at the demon, "A being of flesh and blood, emboldened with little more than a conscience of which you seem to be without. Yet we sit, you and I, discussing much that is relevant, and that which is not. I have lost one life only to gain another. I yearned for knowledge in my youth. I yearned for the love of a woman. All was lost to me. Perhaps it was the will of my Creator. Perchance it was a stroke of bad luck. I know what I believe, and yet you confound my very understanding of it."

"As does man, for me," the demon said.

"Perhaps a human being's only chance at thwarting your advance is to have some better understanding of who it is you really are."

"There is nothing of me to understand," the evil one said, "And after tonight, I will no longer be man's problem anyway."

The monk changed the demon's direction of speech, moving back towards a subject he had approached earlier.

"What is this way in which you hope the Bible to benefit your cause?"

"It isn't the actual book itself that is going to help me, dear man. It will be human understanding of it which will beset my purposes."

"Explain, demon."

"With pleasure," he said, bowing. "The damnation of man lies within the salvation of man. By its name, it is called Religion," he said, confounding the monk. "Answer me this, confessor, how can so many souls see such differences in something as simply written as your manual has been? Have you ever considered why the Bible has been written by lay men, not doctors, lawyers, philosophers, and statesmen? It is this way so the most simplest being of your entire race could understand it. Yet what has the human already begun to do?"

"What?"

"You have begun to divide yourselves into groups who would choose to interpret it as each sees fit. And it is in this division that I will see my greatest triumph over man. I have never had time to wallow with the likes of those who would do or perpetrate evil. Women burn across the whole of Europe even now, said to worship me. Man calls them 'witches', I think - as if your species can find no better use for a woman than this foolishness. And do you know who exacts their punishment? Religious men. I confess to you, Father, my time is spent on the shoulder of the most pious, not the most depraved. What have I to gain by what is already mine? Biblical division. Religious division. This will ultimately destroy man."

"It has yet to do so."

"It is a slow sin. It takes time to grow. But as sin divides the soul, so will man seek to divide the Church. When this incalculable division completes itself, I will have won. Even now I -can smell the stirrings in Wittenberg, Germany. Trouble is afoot."

"I do not follow."

"What will happen is this: A group of my Creator's followers will amass, congregating to worship Him, much as you monks have assembled together here on the island of Athos. But some will disagree with one another, finding or wishing to worship differently from others - so they will form a separate group. This group will ultimately divide into a smaller group, which over time will separate into yet a smaller group, and so on and so on, as the centuries pass by. Mark this well - at some point, the 'Bible' will have given birth to more separate houses of 'God' than you can possibly imagine. As the divisions grow, so then will it divide men amongst each other, then it will see to divide the family- man's strongest weapon against me - until the whole idea of the Creator is weakened to the point where no one will rationally believe Him to have ever really existed at all. 'God' will seem as if a figment of a lesser age. A memory given to a time where men were of a lesser intelligence. All the while," he said, snickering, "man will be no smarter than he was the day he was born. Then, as if this wasn't enough, those same divisional bodies will send forth men to 'save' other men. These people will actually be trying to undo what has already been done, further dividing the body of a given religion and causing confusion even within the worship of the same Being. How's that, Father?"

"You are not omnipotent."

"No, but I am also not a fool when it comes to the nature of man. My insight is based on what I have witnessed to this point. I am no genius. But

I can see things that are plain enough before me." Lucifer was basking in the little man's disturbed look. "We must like ration my Creator's take on all of this, as well."

"Please, I have heard enough of this," the monk said. "You confound me to the quick and I am weakening even now with these images. Should anything you say be of even a slight truth, man has no hope of usurping your woeful intentions."

"But you seek to find blame in me, as if the words I speak are somehow my fault! Father, it is man that is to blame. My ideas only come from a reaction to the aloofness you beings purport," he said, shaking his hands toward the monk. "But you are right in one aspect. Man, as a whole, has little hope. Individually, you will be fine. I cannot reach you all. I only promise to do what I can to make a hell for those of you who will not see things my way. But even now I need to do little more. As I said last night, the race of man has already done more to harm itself than I could have ever devised if l had but a thousand more years to prepare."

"I cannot accept this," the old man said.

"What care I for your acceptance?" he said, chuckling at the statement. "I do not exist for your pleasure. In all actuality, we must believe that my only reason for existing at all is for the pleasure of my Creator. He could simply wish me into nonexistence if He so chose. Yes, we could ponder these and many other questions if I had but the time. It is often a very lonely existence when you cannot even find friendship with the likes of a shark. But this is not the things upon which I dwell."

The old man stood up, wiping his forehead with the sleeve of his heavy cloak. His body seemed to be going through an exhaustive metamorphosis. He felt that he might die right at that very moment. The night had been so long.

When he glanced over in the direction of his demon, there appeared nothing. No one was there. Then, as he turned back around, Lucifer was only inches from his face.

The old man jumped back, stumbling on the bottom of his robe and falling to the floor. There was a crunch as one of his legs gave way to the stone flooring he was now upon. His leg was broken at the knee.

As he grasped the broken limb, gritting his teeth in agony, Lucifer began his calculated approach.

"I am sorry if I scared you, Father," he said as he knelt at the side of the old man, "I shall alleviate your suffering if I can."

The old man wanted nothing to do with Lucifer. He felt as though he was some horrid little pawn set for some larger, more sinister purpose. One that had little to do with the demon's wishes of forgiveness. Still, age and strength prevented him from physically challenging the demon's approach. He withdrew in horror as the fallen angel placed his hands upon the monk's leg. As angelic flesh touched his human flesh, Father Koutrakos collapsed his upper torso to the stone flooring of the monastery floor. His mind flooded with all the past images of his entire life. He saw his birth, his life, and his beloved Helena. Then, as if he was dead, he felt himself floating above his own body, looking down as the devil himself worked upon his broken leg. When the demon withdrew his hands, the monk felt himself drawn back into his body and he sat erect, void of his former pain. He had been healed by Lucifer.

"What just happened?" the monk asked.

"I touched you."

"Of course, but why... how did...?"

"When an angel, damned or from Heaven above, touches a mortal, that being becomes as us. Our power, our minds, open yours- expanding your ability to understand and allowing you to see with more than your eyes. But we usually only appear at the time of your death. Angels serve as the soul's reaper. Good or bad, it is we who come for you when you die."

The monk had not wished to visit this subject with his demonic counterpart. Death was a fear for all men, and though wise and pious, he feared it as well as any other. Furthermore, he knew he was quickly drawing nearer towards its eternal embrace, as his years of living were soon to pass. He was about to solicit another subject, but Lucifer beat him to the punch.

"Father," he said in a questioning tone, resembling the inquisitiveness of a child, "Why is it that man fears death so?"

"I...... suppose... I.."

"I will not make you answer," he said, "I know why you fear death."

"What is your reckoning of it, demon?"

Lucifer stretched his frame, standing from the old man's side. While his body remained pleasing, his back bore the bat-like wings the old monk had come to fear. It was as if his shape sought to portray both of his faces at the same time. He was his own self-contradiction.

"Father," he said, pulling his wings inward, "Man fears what is unknown. Man likewise fears what he is unable to control and make peace with. I believe, just as a human cannot grasp the simple reality of eternity, likewise what the human really fails to understand is the offering of life."

The old man looked up from the floor, puzzled. "Once again, demon, you have me at a loss."

"Do I really, old man? I have never had a life, so pardon any misgivings I might usher forth, but I do believe I have some take on the matter. Will you allow me my arrogant supposition?"

"Speak what you will.'"

Lucifer assumed a position, hopping on the monk's table, and resting as though he was an Indian around a campfire. He then peered back at the monk seated on the floor.

"Most human beings miss the very gift of their existence. At least, I believe this to be so," he said looking down at the old man. "I have watched the pendulum swing and a millennium pass, and I have seen all that one could possibly imagine. Yet for all that is, I see so few humans embrace the reality that is theirs every day they live. I've even done some interesting calculations on the matter."

"What do you mean?"

"Would it impress upon you to know that only one out of every three thousand one hundred and fifty-six people stop to smell a daisy growing in a field? Do you know what it takes to make a daisy exist at all? It takes your 'God's' will. Yet the average human will live an existence not stopping for even a cursory glance at this marvel that in a thousand life times could not be re-created by human hands. Would that we had a lifetime for me to throw numbers at you, old man. You would find misery in every figure. Artists get it. Poets get it. That's why no one gets them!" he said laughing, "A man will work, he will acquire, he will seek the recognition of his peers, he will amass riches, and he will ignore his entire purpose for ever having been. And do you know why, Father?"

"Why?"

"No, Father.... that was a question," the demon looked on, his face void of expression, "I do not know why."

"Not all men are as you say."

"No," he said, "There is a young Italian named Da Vinci who might just change the world, if your generation does not burn him, too............ but I digress. Life is but part of a soul's existence. It is a stage that serves to feel out Heaven's unwanted, I think. Rather than create new angels to populate His realm, I believe my Creator offers angels a new stage of development - human existence. At least this is my take on the matter. I believe life is the test period for God to weed out angels like me. Those who use life to appreciate others, appreciate His creations, they are who He offers the gift of eternity. The unmentionables get cast to Hell, and as of this moment, I think He might have come upon a pretty good plan. There has not been war in Heaven since I left."

The monk sat dumbfounded.

"Also, Father, there is this," Lucifer said, quite pleased with his take on things, "Everything... all life can really come back to one simple request my Creator made."

"What request is that, demon?"

"Love one another."

"Love one another?"

"Love one another," he said. "One would think the request so simple, yet for the human, a thing of impossibility. If each human could embrace the simple kindness of such a request as this, I would be powerless. Yet I feed from the very effort it takes to be resisted. What amazes me to no end is that a slight difference of appearance is the only thing it takes to call such feelings to surface. Your human life is nothing when compared to the future that lies in wait, yet you cling to life as if there is more meaning to it than should be imagined. And here again, for the human, simplicity gives way to confusion - even madness."

"Demon," the old man said, "You have refuted everything I have ever believed to be true."

"No, I do not believe I have," the demon returned, "I have said nothing that contradicts the teachings of the Bible or the beings that wrote it. All I have done is presented my take on what I believe you humans to have misinterpreted." Lucifer then jumped from his seat on the table and threw his arms in the air as if to show some acceptance of defeat. "Must Lucifer always be to blame, Father?" he called to the empty air. "Must man always blame me?" he screamed, smashing his hands to his chest.

"I find no blame with you," the monk said, "I accept responsibility for who I am and what I have become."

"Yes, old man," the demon stated turning towards the monk, who had now resigned to pull himself from the floor, "That is why I chose you. For who else would understand an old beast such as I?"

"Let us not go beyond ourselves, demon," the monk retorted, "I am far from understanding any part of you. I am really just coming to terms with who lam."

"I understand, Father, and you have been most patient with me," Lucifer said as he toned down his offering apologetically. "Before I leave, is there anything you wish to know that I might answer?"

The old man thought for a moment. The lengthy escapade into the theoretical boundaries of death and what lay beyond had left him with more questions than he could possibly have imagined before Lucifer first entered the library. If this were an ordinary angel, or even some ghost of pastimes, he would have been on his knees begging for the being to stay. He would question everything that could be imagined.

But this could actually be Lucifer. The Devil himself. He was forced to stay with questions that would not cross their unspoken line. He could not allow himself to imagine God any other way than what he had come to know from scripture. So he proposed a final question.

"Demon?"

"Monk?"

"I do have a final question."

"Old man, you have but to ask it."

"Very well. What is the nature of sin?"

"I am sorry.........?"

"Why is sin necessary?"

The demon's lips parted as the entire library filled with the cacophonous tone of exacerbated laughter.

> "When you see a snake, never mind where he came from."
>
> W.G. Benham

Escape

Click.

Vincent, in the breath of a moment, was given his life back. The gun had misfired.

No one was more surprised than the man that stood dumbfounded, shaking the weapon, but Vincent was not about to let him ponder the misfortune for long. From within his right sleeve, and fastened to his wrist, he extracted a small, silver blade. It was no more than four inches in length, but it was sharp and made to throw with great precision through the air.

Il Fantasma whirled around, flicking the instrument at a wide- eyed security guard before he could fire the gun a second time. The knife flipped end over end, until it found its mark deep within the jaw line of its victim. The guard doubled back, as blood spurted from the wound. He clamored for the knife, tripping and cursing the thief as he fell upon the tarmac of the roof; While he struggled to extract the object now killing him, Vincent charged his duffel bag once more and began extracting the first contents he saw.

Reinforcements would be here soon and there was no time to

concentrate on anything else. Behind him he could hear the gurgling sound of blood ebbing from the throat of the dying security guard.

The Italian fumbled through the bag, then peered over the side of the roof, praying that there would be some sign of Luigi or the black sedan.

Cecilia was the first to enter the car shouting voracious obscenities at Luigi Basso, who was becoming more and more aware by the minute just how bad he had fucked up.

Sean entered the back door, covered in sweat and bathing in fear. He was clutching the leather bag as though it was his very lifeline.

Simone interrupted Cecilia's tirade, much to the relief of large Italian seated behind the steering wheel. He was now coming through loud and clear over her earphone.

"Vincent's stuck on the roof and-"

Cecilia redirected her anger toward the man several blocks away in the van, "How the hell did he get on the roof!"

"There's no time to explain," Simone yelled back, "Just shut up and listen!" He waited for her to stop speaking. "Hold your position," he said in Italian. "He will be coming from the roof shortly, and he will be looking for the Mercedes. No one has seen the car. You should be safe simply waiting where you are," he paused to take a breath, "Tell Basso to drive the four of you towards 9th Street, and make a left. Drive two more blocks until you come to H street and make a right in front of the Smithsonian American Art Museum, which is dimly lit because it is closed for construction. We will dump the Mercedes there, and the five of us will take the van to the airport, and board our flight for London."

"Simone," Cecilia said getting ready, by her tone, to put up a defensive stance.

"Cecilia we don't have time to argue specifics!" he screamed, "Follow the plan!"

Cecilia, pissed that things had not gone to her professional standards, ripped the tiny transmission device from her ear, and threw it into the back seat, narrowly missing Sean's head. She then proceeded to rap Luigi on the head once more, calling him an *idiota*.

Sean said nothing. His mind was filled with visions of lengthy prison terms and a tattooed guy name 'Spike' calling him 'honey.' He needed anything possible to provide his brain with just a momentary offering of separation from the moment at hand. Hell, he could read a book, he laughed to himself.

The book scout looked down inside the duffel and noticed his personal fuck-up.

He had forgotten to put one of the fake volumes back on the shelf. By tomorrow morning, the Smithsonian would know why they had been there. They would know one of their books was missing.

Sean sat looking at the two books. Jesus, he thought, there might be some way to use this as an advantage when he confronted DeBury. Nab. He shook his head, reminding himself just how far out of league he was with these people. Besides, this mess he had been dragged into was far from over. He would be happy just to get far enough away to see DeBury.

He returned his eyes to the front seat, noticing how distant Cecilia had become. He then sunk down in the seat, awaiting their next move.

Simone pulled up to the darkened street, and parked the van in front of the closed exhibit. There was nothing for him to do but wait.

The little Italian man clicked the engine off and, allowing his mind to wonder, began to spend money he had not yet made. He thought of heading for the coast of Sardinia when they got back to Italy. He would purchase a small house in Porto Cervo and end this bullshit. He had experienced enough adventure to last him a lifetime.

After this heist was over and the thieves split their money, he would walk away with enough cash to ensure his grandchildren would never have to work again. He had been foolish with his past earnings. Whores, cars that didn't last, vacations to exotic locales, hiring Pavarotti to sing at his step- daughter's wedding - he had spent the past earnings as fast as he had made them. Now it seemed, if they could get back home, he would end the business of crime, and lose himself on the island of Sardinia. Settle down permanently. It was a plan.

With the grappling hook firmly in place, Vincent began to scurry down the side of the three-story building. The night air was cold, or maybe Il Fantasma was shivering for another reason entirely.

He was no more than a story down the building's exterior when he heard the roof door open and the clamor of feet above him. He heard some shouting, as he knew the police had seen his handiwork. They wouldn't appreciate the turn of events that had caused the death of one of their own. And there was probably no chance they would be willing to take him for a prisoner. There wasn't much time now, he had to get to the bottom as fast as he could.

Vincent was now passing the second story windows when he looked up to see the silhouette of a figure pointing down at him. Before he could turn back, the figure was joined by four more like it, all seeming to have the same idea in mind - killing him!

Guns flashed in the darkness as bullets whizzed past the thief clinging tightly to his rope. His dangling body would be an easy target, and soon, one of his attackers would come to the realization that they could simply cut his rope.

Vincent did the only thing he could. He let go of the rope.

The one-story drop lasted only seconds, but the ramifications would last quite a good deal longer. He was lucky, though. The shrubbery lining the ground wall was thick, tall, and provided a reasonable amount of cushioning for his abrupt decent. But, a deadened limb of brush managed to send a jutting spike through his upper thigh, causing a considerable amount of pain.

Vincent took a heavy gulp and rolled from the three- foot bushes and onto the ground below. He was bleeding from the twig in his thigh as well as the bullet graze to his shoulder. His body ached from the fall, and his mind was exhausted from the night's frustrations. He looked up to see, in the distance, his salvation.

Pulling himself to his feet, he began a sprinting limp toward the black

Mercedes awaiting him across the street. The rain of bullets continued pouring from overhead.

Cecilia was the first out of the car to defend her brother who she could see was wounded. She exploded from the vehicle with a 9mm weapon and began to direct her fire at the security guards rounding the ground floor wall.

Luigi wasn't far behind her, and he made sure to direct the aim of his weapon towards the building's roof.

They couldn't do this much longer. In moments, radio dispatch would ensure more reinforcements would join in the fray and then, out- numbered, they would be in real trouble. They always prepared for small - scale situations but nothing of this magnitude himself. With more luck than was deserved the small van managed to enter 7th Street undetected and blend in with the surrounding traffic.

While they were not totally out of danger, and still further away from London, they had eluded capture for now. They were all alive, and they had the Manuscripta Diabolica in their possession.

The five-people seated in the van's back seat were halfway to the airport. All were a little relieved as they knew their circumstance could have been significantly worse.

Vincent was banged up, but a few weeks from now he would be fine. It would take longer than that to heal Sean's mental state. As for the rest, they were untouched- except for poor Luigi Basso's head. Cecilia had slapped it enough times to practically warrant stitches.

Sean noticed Vincent looking at his leather bag.

"Can I see the book?" he asked.

"Of course," Sean said reaching in and pulling out the first volume his hand touched, "Here it is," he smiled.

Vincent brought the book close as Cecilia and Luigi drew near as well.

There was an utter magnificence in its aged simplicity. That it had survived five hundred years amazed them further. Sean watched their faces as the turned its pages. He mused at how impossible it would be to convey to any one of them just what they were looking at. That, even though he couldn't have imagined doing what they had already successfully done, what it had taken to acquire the book, was worth their sacrifice. That this manuscript had survived an age in which fellow books were burned, and that it had survived floods, fire, wars, kings, and entire governments was not to be excluded in the imagining. Even now a new adventure had been added to the annals of its history. The thieves, looking at their prize, had no idea at all what it was they were looking at.

"It's really nice," Vincent commented, "But no way is it worth our fee. This DeBury must have more money than he possibly spend."

Sean just smiled at the three of them. What could they possibly know of its value?

Vincent then handed the book to his sister and sat back, breathing a sigh of general relief. Cecilia perused the book for a few moments.

"What do you think?" Sean said, directing his words at the woman holding the manuscript.

"It's amazing," she said. "It is truthfully amazing."

Then, an unexpected thing happened.

Cecilia lifted her head from the book and smiled in a way Sean had not expected. She did have some special feelings for him, he thought - he could see it in her eyes. Their soiree· had meant something to her after all.

Then his eyes moved from her smile to the book she was holding. There was something odd gleaming from just under the outer board of the book's cover.

Before he could ration things out, there was a flash of intense light followed by the impacting pressure of a bullet piercing his flesh.

Everything was a blur.

Sean was now doubled over in the back of the van, clutching at his stomach as if he just had the worst case of food poisoning imaginable.

Cecilia had just shot him.

More thoughts were flashing through his brain than could be picked apart and readily deciphered. What....... Why.........? There was no time to peruse questions, he thought, he was bleeding...... dying, possibly. Dear God!

Sean was lying on his back now, as he could feel the van slowing to a stop. Faces were looking down at him, but they didn't seem at all real. He could feel someone grabbing him. Luigi maybe? There was conversing in Italian. His breathing was quick and faint. He felt himself being lifted, but couldn't feel much else. A door was opening. The van's door. His eyes were rolling back.

He felt his body crash upon the ground. He wasn't in the van anymore. He was on his back in some godforsaken park. Then, something hit his chest. He felt for it with his hands. He was convulsing, sweating, dying. Life was ebbing from his body. How had this happened?

His fingers came to the items that had smacked him in the chest. The thieves had, for-some reason, tossed out his bags.

He felt inside the leather bag. There were some loose bills. His jeans. And God help him, the other book. The bastards hadn't realized he had accidentally taken two books. He tried to lift his head, but even this wasn't working. He could see the blurry image of the van as it started to pull away. He thought he could hear someone yelling an apology in the distance.

His hand drifted back to the book. He slid his forefinger toward the back pages, and with the tip of his finger, he rubbed the spot where the indention would have been if DeBury's family crest was on the volume resting in the leather bag.

Sean Wilde, lying on his back, and bleeding profusely from his stomach, mustered enough energy to Jet out a resounding laugh into the night sky. For all their efforts, the dumb- ass thieves were heading to the airport with the wrong fucking book! Meanwhile, the book scout was dying with the real one lying in his duffel bag.

He spurted some blood from his lips as he laughed uncontrollably. Death was coming for him, and he was fighting its advance with everything he had...

"Our repentance is not so much regret for the evil we have done, as fear of its consequences."

Due de La Rochefoucauld

The Necessity of Sin

"As I see it," Lucifer said, "sin is the key to everything," he said, finally bringing his awful laughter to an abruptful end. "For how can anything we have discussed have any weight without its presence among us?"

Father Koutrakos was listening intently but altogether confused. The old man sat, absent of a response. He looked out the window as if to gain some reassurance from the rising sun but it had yet to make itself present on the horizon. The sky was still just as black as if a veil had been pulled over the earth interring it to darkness forever.

"Let me explain it another way," the demon stated. "You are fond of parables, are you not?"

"Man can gain much by them if they are of a biblical nature, yes." the monk commented.

"Then I have one for you my friend. A parable."

The abbot cringed at the very thought of being called 'friend' by this beast. Yet never in a day, night, or lifetime had he had a discussion such as this. Lucifer stood and, placing his hands behind his back, began his first parable of the evening.

"Four beings stood at the edge of a cliff overlooking the vastness of earth and all those who occupied it." he said. "One's name was Salvation. One was called Damnation. One was named Death and the last, well, his name was Sin.

All but Sin were arguing their importance in the world, each believing himself to be more important than the other three.

Damnation spoke first, saying that. if not for his existence, justice could not weed the righteous man from the evil man, thus his effect was of paramount importance.

Salvation was not about to let Damnation distort the facts. He said that if not for him, there would be no reason for man to exist at all. He was the standard by which all men had to grasp. He believed himself the very key to life, and that without him, why should man live at all?

Death was angered by this. He pointed his finger at both, shaking it and saying, What is Damnation and Salvation, without the means for a human to reach either? You fools squabble with the very scraps from my table- the after - effects of my role. What is humanity if it is without end? My importance is clearly paramount, for without my offering, how would a man reach either of you?

The three belabored the point for a few more moments, when Death noticed Sin had not given his take on the matter. He just sat as if he was waiting for something, saying nothing. Death knelt down, asking Sin for his take on the matter.

Sin just smiled. He stood at the request of his brother and faced them all. 'Fools and ingrates you all must be!'

'Death, where would you have value to human existence if I were not able to heighten the fears of these lowly beasts. You would on the whole be unnecessary at all and I should think for it is in my very wages you are even given to existence at all!'

'Damnation? How could you exist if not for me? I am the very means in which the human finds you. Without my worldly offerings when the human breathes his life, there could be no means with which to even seek you. You are the least important of us all!'

'And Salvation, my poor brother. I hate that we must constantly be at war, but 1 am necessary for you as well, I fear. For why would you be necessary had I not committed myself to human decision? Why should the human seek you out if not for me and my coming to be?'

'I curse you all,' he spat. 'I have never needed any of you, yet you would not even exist without me! You argue for bragging rights you do not rightly deserve. Yet, quietly, I wait as I have always done, seeking some new design of depravity with which to offer these lowly beings.' And having spoken this to the other three, who were speechless before his words, Sin took to the air and left them forever."

"That is a fine tale, Lucifer," the monk stated, "but it does not fully explain why sin must be."

"Oh, but it does, Father!' the devil responded. "Sin has always been a necessary stage of human development, and, more to the point," he said, turning, "I believe it is why I am allowed to breath at all."

"Explain, demon," the monk stated with much inquisitiveness.

"This is my take on the matter of sin," he said, focusing himself fully on the monk. "It is my belief, if I am right. that if human life is an early stage of angelic existence, then my role, which I have become much tired from, had been purposed before my very fall from Heaven." He paused briefly to make sure the monk was well focused on his words. "That my Creator saw my coming discord, allowed it to manifest prior to the birth of the first human. and thus now has me to help weed the good from the bad. I must ration this, because on the grand scale that is my understanding, I can find no other logical explanation for my being at all. I have had much time to ponder on this manner. And centuries after you have died, I suppose I will still be pondering this. You understand me as one thing, I understand myself as something altogether different. In the end, I am no more at odds with the human than he should rightfully be with me. We are each given a role, yet in the stage called humanity, you beings are given a choice. Much as the butterfly develops from the caterpillar, so do I believe the angel develops from the human. At least, Father, that has come to be my belief. Sin is necessary because I am necessary. When the world no longer embraces me, so will sin cease to exist as well."

The monk shook his head. His aged hands, soft and more wrinkled than when this conversation began, found his brow and rubbed it profusely. He was humbled by the candor of almighty Lucifer. What the demon believed did not really matter. That he was excusing himself and his role, that fell short of being sorrowful, and that fell short of forgiveness.

"Monk," the demon began to speak again. "Sin is necessary, because life is necessary. What is a life? I have stated I have never had one so I can only have an imagining on the word."

"Again," the abbot stated, "You speak from both sides of your mouth."

"Do I?"

"Indeed."

"Forgive me, I shall slow my thoughts, they come at me all at once," the old angel stated in an apologetic tone. "Each man governs himself by his own self- appointed laws, regardless of whether or not it coincides with my Creator's law. Sin is a byproduct of this very audacious contempt of man. In every way, you are no less guilty than I when it comes to directing My Author's anger, yet you can be forgiven and I cannot. I find this grossly unfair. So here I am, before you now."

"You tried to usurp God!" the monk said.

"And you do not?" he retorted. "Each day man does what he sees fit, hoping to be forgiven before death finds him. Oh, if l could but show you the souls ablaze who even now thought themselves but a day more to live. To repent. Yes... but enough of this," he said, lifting his hand, "I can say only this, monk - one can justify any act, any decision, or any thought. As Long, Father, as he makes a home in his compass for sin. This is the very reason it is so powerful. I have watched a man kill another man and justify the bloody deed for more reasons than there are stars in the sky, yet no man has the right to take that which my Creator gives. No one," he said, slamming his fist to the table. "Sin has an unholy alliance with the mind of the human, but I am to side with the human on this fact. You see, I realize you are without the ability to fight the trappings sin offers, partly because your mind is so small. You cannot ration strength such as it would take to deny its welcoming offers. In this, we understand one another perfectly."

"There is no basis for such a permanent argument, Lucifer," the old man said, "But if man is so alone and so destitute when it comes to this matter, are we to exist on a course which, by its very design, leaves us void of love and the ability to overcome sin's very weight?"

"Your question is your answer, old man."

"What do you mean?"

"Sin has but one enemy," he stated, holding a finger to the air, "Only one."

"And that would be........ ?"

"Love."

"Love?"

"Love," the demon stated, "It is the only thing man experiences that is a genuine offering of Heaven. Nothing of Heaven is made of sin. So, there you have it," he said with a new smile. "Shall I continue my parable?"

"I thought you to be finished?"

"You thought wrong."

"Please continue," the abbot urged.

"When Sin thought himself far away from his brothers, he came to rest beside a small brook just outside a tiny village. As he plotted some new device with which to deceive and separate the small community, he noticed up the road behind him there appeared a traveler walking. He sought at once to test some of his new offerings on this being. He then approached the man asking for a name. The being said, 'Why do you not recognize me? I am your twin brother. We were separated at birth, but I can see you plain! I am called Love.'

Sin withdrew himself as his brother reached to embrace him.

'I have no twin brother,' he stated. But the traveler hung his head. 'You do not recognize me, because you cannot see the very thing you cannot be.'

Sin then asked where he was going, to which Love replied, "This village where I am to be needed soon.'

'But that is where I am going,' Sin stated.

'I know,' said Love.

'But there is not to be room for us both, my brother.' 'I know,' said Love.

'Then why will you go to the village in which I am bound?' Sin directed himself. 'I must offer my services,' Love stated, 'as I will be needed to offset your advance.'

'I see,' said Sin. 'I will not be kind. I will do what I can to damn those within.'

Love responded-'And I will do what I can to show these people you are not a means to an end.'

'Very well, brother,' Sin said turning from him. 'To the victor the spoils!' And he tarried down the road leaving Love to his lonesome. Love smiled to himself, and followed behind his brother down the path. From the spoils shall rise a victor, Love thought. And the two twins, one behind the other, accompanied one another down the path, Love having won before the two even entered the village, for he knew himself to be born one second before his brother. In their power struggle, he knew timing was everything."

The old monk found much in the demon's offering. The night had belonged to them both, it seemed. Lucifer had defied every convention in his age. His guard still up, he wished to probe deeper.

"Love," the old man began, "seems a weak offering-when one realizes the scope of sin. I should think once the talons of sin are firmly embedded, Love ultimately gives way to lust, then ultimately, sin triumphs."

"Some who are wise think that is the way of it," the demon returned, "but I have seen differently. It will take your species a very long time to mature to the point where you have some true understanding of what it is my Creator had to say. But by that time you will be so divided amongst yourselves that it will not matter much. The only thing you will have that holds you together as men at all will be love, but many of you won't even have that. Still, I can only offer you this musing, Father: I have known love. But it was a very Long time ago in a place very far from earth, and I have not felt it since the day I entered this world. This is what has made my contempt for the human so easy to embrace," the demon then paused, "There is a last piece to my parable. Shall I tell you of it?"

"Please," the monk said.

"Very well. Sin had done what he could in the tiny village, but Love had managed to thwart his complete control. Then, from out of nowhere, someone new emerged. His name was Hate, and he was without conscience. Everything touched by Love was then set upon by Hate who began destroying everything in his wake.

Love knew there was only going to be one thing that could help him save the village against his twin brother Sin and this new being, Hate.

So he traveled to his home, the realm of Heaven, and pleaded with his Creator to offer him some chance at saving these humans. Love's sister, Hope, had left the village and he was all alone to defend it- but he was losing the battle.

The Creator told Love to go and seek out Hate and Sin, and tell them shortly, He would be sending a being to the village that they would be powerless to overcome. He then directed Love to hurry back as the small town was much in degradation.

By the time Love arrived to the outskirts of the village, he saw both Hate and Sin leaving. They seemed to be upset. They seemed utterly defeated.

Love inquired to their misery. Hate looked up at him saying, 'We have done all we could yet we have been beaten.' Love asked, 'But who has done this thing?' Sin responded by telling him that a large rogue had entered the village, earlier that day, calling himself Forgiveness. He had taken the place of Hope, and ultimately, Sin and Hate. They could do no more.

Love smiled. knowing his request had been granted. Then, leaving the two, he headed off to meet with Forgiveness, for there was much for them both to discuss."

In the dimly lit room, the old monk nodded his head. It had been a good tale, he thought.

"What do you think of it, Confessor?" Lucifer asked.

"Your parable has much to offer of your point. I wonder, is it this very tale that has brought you to me?"

"Indeed it is."

"Well, demon, while your tale was wise, I have one of my own," the monk offered.

"Please, Father let us hear it," the devil said, holding out his hand. He welcomed the wisdom of man, even if he often found it beneath him.

"Very well," the old man said. He then wasted no time, as he began a tale of his own.

"In the fight for survival, a tie or split decision simply will not do."

Merle L. Meacham

Crossroads

All Sean Wilde could see was a bright light up ahead in the distance- gleaming like some illuminated lighthouse beacon that was trying its best to guide a ship through a stormy sea and on to safety. While not a ship, Sean was certainly no less than a passenger. And he was now leaving one world for the next.

He could feel heat radiating from the beacon ahead. There was no doubt- it was finally his time. Death had caught up with him. Time to cross from the world he knew to a new world. All he could hope was that this destination would somehow be better than the one he was leaving behind.

Sean could feel himself will a limb to reach for the light. He wished nothing more than to embrace it. Darkness surrounded him on all sides. He was in a vacuum. A tunnel.

Then, as if from nowhere, a figure stepped forward. Though the image was fuzzy, it seemed to offer warmth and kindness. Perhaps he was in Heaven, if there was such a thing.

"Sean?" a voice said, calling him. He muffled his speech trying to clear the scratchiness in his throat.

"D...... dad?" He returned in his mind.

"Sean?"

"Dad...." he could hear himself that time.

"'Fraid not son," the voice called back.

Sean's vision began to clear and he focused his eyes tightly to the being in front of him. Though the face was indeed kind, it was certainly not that of his father. With this finding, the realization he was not dead came to him shortly thereafter.

"My name is Doctor Thomas G. Fischman," the man towering overhead spoke again, in a cool, collective tone. "I am in charge of your care while you stay with us," he said, pausing to direct the nurse standing by his side. "Do you know why you're here Sean?" he said, bending closer.

"Not exactly.... I... uhhgg," Sean tried to sit up but a pain emanating from his abdomen caused him to fall back against the pillows beneath him. His throat felt as if it were drier than the Sahara Desert, and he could barely swallow without a hoarseness in his throat.

"I'm sorry. There's no need for you to try and speak just now, Sean," Doctor Fischman stated, "You've only recently been extubated."

"Exta....... what?" Sean said, having trouble with the doctor's terminology.

"I'm sorry," the doctor stated, "I forget to simplify things sometimes," he said with a comforting smile, "but with all the odd things that have happened since your arrival...." He paused, looking at the chart in his hands, "Anyway, there was a tube helping you breathe- in your throat Sean. You were on a ventilator and prepped for surgery last night but a very strange thing happened and I'd like to watch you for a while if that's okay." Sean answered with a succession of nods. "Good. I need to know one or two things while you're awake, so let's just have you answer with a nod for 'yes' and just turn your head to the side for 'no'- all right?"

Sean nodded.

"Last evening you were rushed in the E.R. clinging to some book. You exhibited massive internal bleeding from what had been written on your charts as a deep bullet wound to your abdominal region. There was no indication you had even a slight chance of surviving the wound," he said, pausing to clear his throat. "I happened to be the surgeon on call and I immediately ordered you to be prepped for surgery. When I entered the O.R., I immediately checked your vital signs- all of which led me to believe you were only moments from death. Your pulse was thready and rapid, your skin was an ashen tone, and your body was cool and clammy to the touch. Your pupils were not reacting at all, and blood was seeping from an obvious hole in your stomach," he paused to allow Sean some digestion of the things he was describing. He then began speaking again with a look of astonishment on his face. "When the anesthesiologist, Doctor Richard Grosso arrived, I stepped out of the room for no more than two minutes to 'scrub up,' but before I could finish, Dr. Grosso burst through the doors of the O.R. with a look of complete bewilderment on his face. He told me that when he began prepping to put you under, he noticed purposeful eye movements as well as unassisted respiration's. Then, when he glanced back to the monitors behind you, he noticed an increase in your oxygen saturation. That's when he stopped his procedure and came to get me. When I returned, your vital signs were approaching normal, your pupils were reacting, and your breathing was almost completely unassisted. I wiped the blood from your stomach and noticed that the hole that had once seemed so pronounced, was virtually nonexistent. A mere scratch - nothing more. I then called to have the x-ray we had taken of you earlier posted and I ordered a new x-ray to be taken at once. Your blood pressure began to climb, so I had the O.R. nurse wean down the vasopressors while we waited for the x-ray comparison," he said pausing for a moment redirecting the attending nurse, who seemed to be agitated with the doctor. "Would you like to know what the x-ray showed Sean?"

His patient nodded.

Doctor Fischman reached over to the table beside Sean's bed and held up the chart. Sean smiled when he noticed between the doctor's outstretched arms, there was a unique tie hanging from the man's neck. It was an image of Jimi Hendrix on his knees behind a flaming Stratocaster guitar. Sean loved the Voodoo Chile.

Refocusing on the intended object, Sean concentrated on the black and white image before him. His eyes squinted as he tried to process what it was he was looking at. The film showed an obvious oblong opacity which appeared to be lying in the stomach cavity. He was a little confused at the sight but before he could open his mouth the doctor spoke up.

"I had another x-ray done this morning, while you were still unconscious," he said pulling up yet another black and white photograph, "Notice anything odd?"

There was no bullet appearing on the film anywhere. The opacity didn't exist.

"Are you sure those pictures are both of me?" Sean said grudgingly.

"Yes, Sean. I am quite sure," the Doctor stated with authority, "They are all the same person. Would you like to help me arrive at some explanation which my twenty years of medical training cannot hope to explain?"

He shook his head as if he was in just as much disbelief as the doctor himself.

"Get some rest, Sean," the doctor said smiling, "We'll talk more, a little later when you're feeling a bit better."

Doctor Fischman sat the images on the table beside Sean, and pulled his white coat over the tie the book scout had come to admire. He then turned to exit the room but paused, turning back towards Sean and addressing him.

"Oh, one more thing," he said, snapping his fingers, "There are two detectives standing outside that would like to speak with you when you've rested up. I think they want some sort of statement from you on what happened. I have no idea what to tell them so I thought maybe you could tell us both in a little while."

Sean gulped what saliva he could. He wanted nothing to do with the cops or any questions they might be interested in having answered. No doubt they were here to make sure he was carted off to jail for his role in the Smithsonian heist. What the book scout needed was a way out of the hospital. And he needed it fast.

Resting his head on the lumpy hospital pillow, he eyed the contents of his room. Everything seemed as cold and harsh as his perspective future. Steel carts and trays lying on rollers, a television hanging from the wall overhead, and paintings from K-mart seemed to adorn the walls. But there was something else that caught his eye.

In a vinyl chair across the room rested his duffel bag.

Sean tried to sit up again, and upon doing so, noticed that the pain was dissipating somewhat. He had to get to the duffel bag.

From his arm, a single I.V. tube was still connecting him to a saline bag hanging just behind his left shoulder. He stared at the dripping motion from inside the clear tubing. This was the only thing holding him captive at the moment. Thank God there was no urinary catheter.

Sean, still in pain, managed to pull himself to his feet and come to an erect position next to the bed. The floor was cold to his feet and he stopped for a moment feeling lightheaded and dizzy. Regaining control of himself. he walked toward the chair as the I. V. bag followed on rollers behind him. His throat was dry and he turned to a tray for some comforting ice chips to ease the pain. He removed the tape pinning the I.V. catheter to his arm and freed himself from its cumbersome restraint. He then redirected himself back to the vinyl chair.

Reaching for the bag, he felt his heart jump with relief as he fe1t inside and extracted the book. The Manuscripta Diabolica was still there. The hospital staff had obviously put the volume with Sean's other belongings after they had managed to free the book from the book scout's hands. Sean eyed the book for any damage.

There were no remnants of the nights activities on the book anywhere. No smeared blood from where Sean's hands had clasped the volume. No tears in the binding. No ripped or disheveled pages. No damage at all. He sat the book down and then began to rummage through his bag.

Upon deeper inspection of the bag's contents he found his wallet, his clothes-which had been neatly folded, and what remained of his cash-about seven thousand dollars. Lady luck was smiling in his direction. Now, if she would just stay with him a bit longer.

He shoved the contents back in the bag and climbed back in the bed. He had to get free from this situation. He had to get out of the hospital. There had to be a way...........

From the nurses' station, the woman on duty, Mary Chancellor, watched as two detectives paced the hall just outside room 220. They had been waiting to interview her patient all day, but he had not been available for comment. Her head rolled back to the monitor, where Sean Wilde lay sleeping in his bed. For someone who had been rushed to the hospital with serious life- threatening wounds. he seemed to be doing abnormally well.

There had even been the word 'miracle' used by some of the hospital staff when speaking of the patient in room 220.

The woman then looked back at the officer who was closest to her. He looked a lot like Richard Gere, she thought to herself. And that's when her mind started to wonder away from room 220, and to someplace else. Perhaps to a much-welcomed midday fantasy.

Time passed, as did her mental picture of the aforementioned detective and her in some tryst on one of the empty hospital beds. She shook herself from the thought long enough to look at the monitor once again.

Her patient was missing!

She slid some papers off the table as she leapt clumsily from her chair and hastened her way towards room 220. She was a rather heavyset lady and didn't move very fast, but the look of fear on her face said it all. Her beehive hairdo was coming unraveled as she ran towards the room. One thing was ever certain in her mind- Doctor Fischman would kill her for losing his patient.

As the officers saw her approach, each sensed something might be wrong, and took the liberty of entering the room before her. When they flung the door open, the three-people cased the room but found nothing. The bed was empty. The bathroom was empty. The only thing that remained of her patient was the jar of ice chips lying on the table. Sean Wilde was gone.

The woman heard one of the officers speaking through a cell phone and it sounded like something official. The three-people left the room efforting themselves to find the missing man at once.

Meanwhile, under the bed, Sean clung tightly to the steel bars that were positioning him from off the floor. He was sweating as the pain of being in this position was taking its toll. Between his stomach and the underneath of the mattress, he supported his duffel bag. When he heard the people leave, he collapsed to the floor. The pain was intense but his plan had seemed to work- at least for the moment.

He slid from underneath the hospital bed and slipped out of his hospital clothes and began to put his jeans back on along with his T-shirt. He then began to reluctantly approach the cracked door of his room. From the small opening he could see the turmoil unfolding at the nurses' station off in the distance. People were yelling at each other and darting in all directions. He would have to wait out here until the perfect opportunity presented itself for him to hasten an escape.

Within a few passing moments, the time had arrived. Everyone dispersed the area seemingly set out in different directions in an attempt to seek out a person who was still safely in his room.

Sean seized the opportunity, and bolted from the room joining the general traffic of persons moving through the hallway. He decided to take the stairs as he was only on the second floor. Sean could see nothing stopping him from his escape from the hospital.

No one seemed to be following the book scout as he burst through the stairwell doors and entered the Washington D.C. morning.

He was free. At least for now.

Sean had managed to wander the downtown city of Washington D.C. for most of the afternoon, reluctant as to what to do with his freedom-temporary though it might be. A strong smell of coffee beans was permeating the air and he turned into a small cafe in order to rest himself for a moment.

He ordered a cappuccino from a young pimple- faced teenager who probably knew more about coffee than should be necessary for one his age, and helped himself to table nearby. Someone had left a copy of the Washington Post lying haphazardly on the seat next to him. He picked the paper up and noticed the cover story; Smithsonian Robbed/Three Dead/D.C. Police Looking For Perpetrators.

Oh, shit!

Sean sat the paper back where it was and left the smoldering cappuccino, exiting the cafe. What was he going to do now? There was no way to just blend himself back into society. No way to find some inner salvation here. He had to leave D.C. at once. Whether the cops suspected him or not, he had to get moving- and the sooner the better.

Up ahead in the distance he could see signs pointing to a bus terminal. He had to get a ticket to Boston. Get back on some familiar turf. Get to the only area of home he had ever known. Quickly, he picked up his pace to a light jog and followed the signs to the nearest bus terminal.

For Sean Wilde, this was the only way to salvation. The only way out of a situation that was worsening by the minute.

Boston
The Next Morning

The last twenty-four hours had been a time of both reflection and torment for Sean Wilde. He had a few bucks and a stolen book in the bag slung over his shoulder. But that wasn't going to amount to anything once the authorities caught up with him.

Sean looked down at the tombstone below.

He found himself before the grave of his father, Thomas Wilde.

The Bostonian bent down and placed a flower on the ground before him. He had picked the wildflower from a nearby field on his way to the cemetery. A tear welled in the comer of his left eye and strolled down the living man's cheek.

Sean was at a complete loss of what to do and where to tum. He had hoped that by coming here, he could gain some greater sense of who he was, and in what direction he should go. But all it did in actuality was make him feel worse. He was no son to be proud of, he knew that to be true, if nothing else. And in truth, that admission alone was enough to shatter him at his very core.

What he wouldn't give for just five minutes of advice from his old man. God in heaven, he thought looking skyward, Just one more conversation. The other eye loosened a tear and added symmetry to the book scout's facial water markings. He sat down on the earth that kept him separate from his father's physical remains, and buried his head in his knees.

But in the wake of his suffering, he remembered the last conversation they had had before his father's death.

In the hospital, holding his hand, the last thing his father had said to him was this: 'Son, if you're ever at a point where your back is to a wall and I can't be there to get you out, remember one thing. Remember how resourceful you are, and go all the way back to the starting line. If you get tired of who you are, reinvent yourself. That was what life was all about anyway. It was a circular cycle of reinvention. Leave the comforts of your mind and listen to your heart. That's where the secrets to the universe are kept. That's where you find who you really are and moreover - what you 're capable of becoming.

Sean dried the last of his tears and lifted his head.

His father was right. Sean had to reinvent himself. Right now, this very second.

The book scout pulled himself to his feet and found some light semblance of pride. He was resourceful, and he would need that skill to further his efforts elsewhere. Sean Wilde was going to live for both he and his father. He didn't have a clue what to do, but he did know in what direction he needed to head.

He would buy a plane ticket back to Europe and roll the dice one final time. Whatever life was waiting for him to catch up, it wasn't waiting here in America. So Sean Wilde would go find it someplace else. His reality lay somewhere across the Atlantic Ocean. And in the duffel bag strewn across his shoulder, there was enough money to get him back there.

The book scout winked at the motionless stone of granite upon which lay embroidered the name Thomas Wilde.

"Thanks, pop," he said, loud enough for the birds resting on a nearby tree branch to hear. "I owe you one."

Sean Wilde then turned from the grave and walked down a cement pathway leading through the cemetery- out onto one of Boston's bustling street comers. He held out a thumb and a nearby cab stopped, screeching before the newly inspired book scout.

"Where to, buddy," an overweight man called out as the window slid down.

"Logan International Airport," Sean returned, opening the back door of the car and seating himself inside.

As the cab pulled away from the cemetery, Sean resigned himself to leave his old persona behind. He buried the person he was next to his father's tombstone, and would leave Boston for an image and ideal of the person he wanted to become. His destiny lay somewhere far from here. He knew that much for sure. And even though the future was a haze of unknowing truths and unclear specifics, Sean Wilde was ready to embrace whatever presented itself. He had been dead once already. Time to live. Time for he and his book to roll the dice one more time.

"I don't like to commit myself about heaven and hell you see, I have friends in both places."

Mark Twain

Casa Di Fernetti

"I need your help," a voice said as the door to the rather small Italian dwelling opened. Jaco Fernetti stared at the man in his doorway with a puzzling expression. There was a familiarity about him, yes, but he could not altogether place a name to the face he was staring at presently.

Searching for some way to respond, Jaco didn't have time to speak before the man interrupted him.

"You may not remember me," the stranger in the doorway began, "And I'm really sorry if I'm intruding, but it's just... I've got nowhere else to go, and well......"

"Come in... come in, my friend," the little man said, stepping aside and bidding his guest inside. While he still didn't know who the man was, it could be said of Jaco Fernetti -he was nothing if not hospitably accommodating.

As the stranger moved into the home, he entered the main sitting area, a den possibly, the ceiling of which wasn't much higher than the top of Sean's head. The room was a bit cluttered, but not what one might call especially dirty. The whole house, from what could be seen from the main room, looked to be no larger than a small apartment. It seemed viable that Jaco was the only person living here. This was good, the stranger thought to himself, no need to involve more people in his problem than was necessary.

"Steve?" Jaco said, thinking he might have just placed a name with this face.

"Sean," the stranger said, "Wilde."

"Right, right...Sean." Jaco was still puzzled at who this man was, exactly.

"I caught a ride in your cab about a week ago," Sean said while reaching in his pocket and withdrawing the business card Jaco had given him. "You had arranged a boat ride for me through Venice, and had carried me from the airport Treviso in your cab to the city. You had given me this card and said if........"

"Yes. Yes, of course!" the small Italian said withdrawing the memory, "You were the crazy American with the money." He paused for a moment, recollecting their past meeting. "What brings you to Jaco's home, my friend? What can Jaco do for you?"

Sean sat back on the vinyl couch. He was uncomfortable. He had not wanted to ask help from anybody, and his level of trust- well, if it had been poor before, it was worse now. Still, what was the book scout to do? If he wanted to reach some aspect of closure, this was as good a place to start as any.

"Well," he began hesitating for a moment, "You told me, in your taxi, that if I ever needed anything, you might be of some help," he said reluctantly. "Well.... Jaco, I'm afraid I need some help."

"Go on, my friend, Jaco is listening." The man could see the expression on his guest's face turning somber, and realized his request was not to include an extensive 'Ghost Tour' of the city. He sat in the chair opposite his guest and resigned himself to hear what his uninvited guest had to say.

"Do you remember the business matter I was telling you about when we rode from the airport to the city in your cab the other day?"

"Si," Jaco said, lying.

"Well, it involved a character called Il Fantasma, and I......"

"Il Fantasma?!" Jaco stated loudly. "Mama Mia," he said crossing himself with the Father, Son, and Holy Ghost.

"Yeah, you know of him?"

"Everyone knows of him, yes," Jaco began, "No one has ever seen him.... He is said to be the greatest thief in the entire world," the little man said with emphasis.

Sean was shaking his head, not really sure where he wanted to begin. "I was hired to work with him... on a project... a theft.... I-"

"This thing you say is true?" Jaco interrupted.

"Unfortunately, Jaco. Unfortunately." Sean said while shaking his head, himself still in denial.

He had not wished to reveal more than was absolutely necessary. If the Smithsonian knew of their missing book by now, which was in all likelihood probable, there was no need to risk being betrayed by this man for some reward money that would surely coincide with information leading to Sean's capture.

But as bad as things had become, Sean had to trust someone.

Everything that he was now faced with or any future he might wish to have hinged on Jaco's nonjudgmental help. The book scout knew, if he was even slightly honest with himself, that he had no business being here. But, 'here' was the only place he had to turn. Jaco was his last potential friend in the world.

"Tell me everything, Sean," the taxi driver said, "Jaco is listening."

"Where to begin," he said, looking around the room. There was nothing about the room for the book scout to really focus much attention. He couldn't afford to waste any more time.

Sean, there and then, spilled the entire story. He told Jaco why he had come to Venice in the first place. What he knew of the book- the Manuscripta Diabolica- and the theft at the Smithsonian Institution. The betrayal. The hospital. Nicholas DeBury. Cecilia Conducci. Il Fantasma. Everything.

The Italian sat across from his guest with a look of sheer dumbfoundedness. He was having difficulty believing what was being said to him. It would make quite a good book, or even a movie, he thought to himself.

Still, Sean's troubles were giving the little man some much needed purpose. Jaco' s life had been nothing more than work since his wife had left him. And in truth, all he really did was sit around feeling sorry for himself. Now there was man who thought enough of him to ask a personal favor of enormous proportion. The Italian resigned himself to help if he could, but in no way was he going to become too involved. He was a taxi driver for God's sake!

"I know your motto doesn't entail getting me out of trouble," Sean stated, referring to Jaco's funny little sales pitch from before, "but my situation has become extremely complicated, and here's why." He began by verbally opening the largest can of worms he could find. "As far as I know, both Nicholas DeBury and Il Fantasma think I'm dead. This has its advantages if not for a small problem," he stated - his forehead showing the wrinkles of concern. "I have one million dollars in a Parisian bank, deposited by DeBury, but I can't get my hands on it because if I try extracting any of the money and DeBury happens to be watching that account, he'll know I'm alive. And no part of that money's gonna do me any good if I'm hunted down and killed."

"Sean," Jaco interrupted, "How do you know the money's still there?"

"I checked yesterday via the phone, when my flight to Venice connected in Paris."

"Man, that really sucks," the Italian laughed, "You're rich, but only if'n you're dead."

"Tell me a part of my story that doesn't suck," Sean smiled haphazardly.

"What else, my friend?" the Italian urged. "You tell Jaco everything."

Sean wasted no time obliging his friend.

"Right now, or maybe even already, DeBury has been handed a copy of the book lifted from the Smithsonian Institution. He will know as soon as his hand touches the book that his copy is a fake. He may tum his attention my direction anyway, wishing some proof of my death. My body should by all accounts be in some morgue in Washington D.C. And then there's the real clincher to all of this," he said, reaching in his bag, "I've got the real manuscript."

Jaco stared at the age- old relic clasped in the book man's hands. It seemed an odd thing for someone to be willing to pay that kind of money for, let alone kill a person over. But stranger things had happened. One thing was certain, this matter was decidedly becoming more and more serious the longer Sean talked. Did the taxi driver really wish to become involved?

"I know, I know," Sean said in an effort to block Jaco's mind from thinking too deeply about all he had said, "but whatever you're thinking, this isn't about the money anymore. Truthfully, it never was," he said, letting out a sigh. "I was forced into this - partly from my own ignorance, and partly because these are bad people I got involved with. These people," he paused, embracing a growing hatred, and standing from the couch, "everyone of 'em were willing to kill me! Hell, I'm sure they think they did," he ranted. "But Jaco, I'm no criminal, whatever you think." He paused to clear his throat. "I just want some fucking justice! Personally, I don't give a shit about the money!"

There was a long pause as Sean paced the room for a moment. Jaco sat quietly, digesting the American's tale- deciding what part of it he was going to believe. Sean abruptly turned back towards the Italian, sliding his hands into the back pockets of his jeans. He then began speaking again.

"I'm laying my cards on the table, though. I've got no family. And I've got nowhere I can go. There's no one I can trust. You and I are strangers, but my back's to the wall on all this shit, so necessity dictates I lay things on the line one more time. You're the only person that can help me. I don't think I'll get another chance," he said, pausing. "Will you help me Jaco?"

The Italian thought for a moment as he sat fidgeting with his hands. He had resigned himself to help if he could, but these people Sean was speaking of, they were a dangerous lot. Not the sort of people he had any business dealing with. He was happy not living in fear of losing his life.

But here was a man who was putting faith in another man he hardly knew. Jaco respected that. There was substance to this. He had not been needed by someone on a personal level for quite some time. He searched his mind for anything that might trigger a means of lending his guest some help. This was not the sort of thing one decided upon without some serious forethought. He mused at the request...

Yes. There was definitely a way he could help his new friend. But, he thought, it could definitely be questionable as to whether it was the greater or lesser of two separate evils. Still, if Sean was desperate enough...

"Sean," Jaco said, watching the man across from him slide towards the end of his couch, "I cannot help you my friend," he said respectfully. His guest slouched back down, his face showing a look of disgust. "But," he retorted, "I might know of someone who can."

Sean Wilde immediately perked back up.

Jaco stood up from his chair and walked into his small but quaint kitchen, and reached into his cupboard withdrawing two glasses, and returned to the living area with both the drinking utensils and a new bottle of Tuscan wine. The little man was undecided as to how he should approach this conversation, and where he should actually begin. He decided to be straightforward.

"Sean, my friend," he said as he began to fill their glasses, "I am going to tell you a story. You may see it as a fable, a parable, or something altogether different. What I say to you is the truth, so listen closely." He arched an eyebrow. He then began after a long sip of wine, "When I was a boy- much younger than I am now," he began licking the red liquid from his lips, "I was born, raised, and lived in Sicily - Palermo to be more exact," he corrected himself. "It happened that one day, probably about the time I was in my early twenties, that something occurred that would change my life, and my location, forever."

Jaco paused long enough for the two of them to take an additional sip of wine. He wasn't altogether happy with the thought of sharing this story, and the more the two drank, the easier it would be to conceal any inhibitions he might have with telling it.

Sean smiled after pulling the glass from his face and Jaco began again.

"You see, Sean, most of the men in my village were fishermen, and this was how I had come to make my living as well. One day, after many hours at sea, I was cleaning the day's catch off the back of my small boat which was moored in the harbor. I had returned late that afternoon, and I was the only remaining fisherman left at the docks.

"Off in the distance, I could see a man running towards the harbor. He seemed terribly frightened, and it wouldn't be long before I would come to realize the reason for his fear. He was being pursued by a group of men, secured in a brown car, with what appeared to be guns. It did not take a genius to realize this man was running for his life."

"As he ran past the many boats rocking in their slips, He made eye contact with me and I ushered him to my boat. When he entered, I told him to lie down in the bait well, and I covered him with some blankets I had well stashed in the bow of my vessel.

When the car passed by, the men inside the vehicle got out and started to check the entire waterfront for any sign, of their intended victim. It was not long before they approached me and began questioning me as if I might have some knowledge on the man they had been chasing."

"Weren't you scared?" Sean asked.

"Scared doesn't even broach the surface, my friend," he responded, "More like terrifuckinfied- beyond- imagining- pissing- in- my- pants scared, would better describe my momentary reaction at their questioning."

"Why did you help the stranger, then?"

"The same reason I am speaking to you now," he said. "My mother, God rest her soul, told me there were two kinds of people in this world - those who, in a moment of crisis, did something and those who did nothing. She raised me to be the foremost, and the truth is, I have always been the better for it. Besides," he commented, "The last thing I needed was a man's death on my conscience, because in a moment of tribulation, I did nothing."

Sean was impressed by the courage this simple man talked of possessing. Perhaps the two had something in common after all. They had both been put in a situation they could have done without. Sean urged the man to continue his story.

"Well... what happened?"

Jaco cleared his throat. "The men lightly searched my boat, but my stowaway was well hidden, and they left me to my fish-cleaning responsibilities. They continued searching the harbor for about fifteen minutes but apparently got discouraged and left. When I watched the car drive off, I helped my guest to his feet, having no clue at all what I had just done or who it was that I had lended aid."

"What do you mean... who?"

"The young man who I had shielded turned out to be Andrei di Trapani."

"Who is that?"

Jaco looked back as if the man before him was joking. "Sean," he began, "This man, whose life I saved, was the son of Don Giovanni di Trapani, the family head of the Mafioso's most powerful Sicilian organization. I didn't realize it at the time, but this man now owed me a blood debt."

Sean was floored. It seems he wasn't the only one with a fascinating story to tell. But before he could inquire further, Jaco had started talking again.

"What I did not know at the time, was that the reason Andrei was fleeing the men was because he had, only moments before, killed a member of a rival crime family. So you see, in an effort to do what I believed to be the right thing, I had only succeeded in defending another killer and gotten myself involved in some feud that was way over my head. What furthered my disliking of the event was that somehow, given enough time, I knew my name would come up as the man who aided Andrei, as these things happened in small villages such as mine. It would not be long before someone from the rival family might come fishing for me!"

"So what did you do?" Sean hoped to find an answer to his problem in the answer Jaco provisioned himself.

"Slept with one eye open that night," he said laughing, and finding humor in the moment. "No, but seriously, my friend, I did not have time to even think, for the next day two men appeared at my door, outfitted in suits that would have cost me a year's wages selling fish in the markets of Palermo. While terrified I was to be killed in some horrible fashion, they asked if I would accompany them to Trapani, Sicily. There, I was to meet with Don di Trapani, the elder."

"You must have shit yourself."

"Yes, my friend, it took two weeks just to get the smell from my house!" he said, motioning with three fingers raised instead of two. They both laughed, as they had now emptied the bottle of wine, and inhibitions were of no more concern to either of them. Jaco excused himself and made for the kitchen and bottle number two.

Returning, the Italian began picking up his story from where he had left off.

"In Sicily," he said, refilling Sean's glass, "from the time you are born, you are taught to avoid the Mafioso if you can, and one should never aspire to be called out and asked to visit with a Don. This my friend, was not a happy thing," he said, shaking his finger. He was through another glass before he started talking again. "I figured myself a dead man."

"So what did you do?"

"I got drunker than a male virgin about to fuck a two-dollar whore," he said, causing them to burst into laughter. Sean toppled right off the couch and crashed to the floor, glass and all. It was clear they had both drunk enough wine to become well past the point of caring what was said or talked about. Sean apologizing for the mishap, lifted himself off the floor and returned to the couch. As he sat rubbing the water from his eyes, he saw Jaco attempt to somber his expression.

"Sean," he began, "Seriously.......! accompanied the men at their request. Because my friend, what else was Jaco to do, eh?"

"Where did they take you?"

"Palermo, as I think I -said."

"What was it like, I mean meeting a real godfather and all?"

"It wasn't like meeting Marlon Brando, if that's what you mean," he said. "I arrived at a large villa just off the coast of Mar Torreon, and was welcomed inside, though at the time I would have rather eaten cockroaches for a week!"

Both of the men began laughing again. Clearly, it was time for bottle number three.

Trying to sit upright, Sean struggled to listen. The problem was, every time Jaco would look his way, the Italian would burst out laughing at the funny expression Sean was making while trying to be serious. Finally, after a few more moments, they both calmed down enough to reasonably focus on one another.

"I was eventually led into a large room," Jaco began, "and seated in front of Don di Trapani himself. I wanted to speak, to somehow ease my fear, but I could do nothing of the sort. I did not know of anyone in my village who had ever seen Don di Trapani, let alone spoken with him. Yet there I was. Before I could react to my situation, the Don spoke, saying to me 'You have saved the life of my firstborn son, and what I owe to you is more than any words I could offer. Anything I have is yours. Ask any favor and it shall be granted. What is it, my new friend, Don di Trapani can do for you?' he said as I tried hard to swallow. I responded with an answer of 'nothing'."

"Why?" Sean asked.

"Part from fear," he said, "Part from the fact that I simply did not wish to become entwined with this man or his *familia*. I am a simple man, Sean. All I have is all I need. I certainly did not want any more involvement than I already had."

"So that was that?"

"Yes...... and no," the man said, arching his brow. "He said if ever there came a time when I should need a service he could provide, all Jaco had to do was ask, and the debt I did not wish to have would be settled. I hastily thanked the Don, and I left."

"So how is it that you wound up in Venice?"

"Sicily is too small a place to walk around if you are in some way connected to the Mafia, my friend, so I left. I was not spending each night sleeping with one eye open awaiting some reprisal or vendetta from Don di Trapani's rival family. So I left at once and have been driving a cab in this city ever since."

"That's truly a fascinating story, Jaco."

"Yes," he commented. "But no less than yours, my friend- eh?" he said, toasting his guest. "Which brings me to my current reason for telling you my life story," he paused, awaiting the swell of a heartfelt burp, "If you would like, I shall take you to meet Don di Trapani. Perhaps, if you're desperate enough my friend, he will help you in a way I cannot."

Sean said nothing for a long minute. The laughter and the conversation had now turned in such a way as to quickly sober him up and bring about a look of utmost seriousness to his face.

Then, at once, a sense of personal reality dawned on the face of Sean Wilde. What was it about him that superseded everything else? It wasn't his ignorance. Hell, it wasn't even his knowledge of books, nor anything he had readily put his finger on. It was one fact and one fact alone; Sean was resourceful.

And in his current situation, being resourceful might mean bargaining with people with far less scruples than himself to make right his awful circumstance. Sure, dealing with the Mafia might be dangerous, even somewhat insane. But wasn't this entire situation? Yes, he thought, this might be his only way out of the fiasco that had become his life. This was his last hand at a game of poker that had gone on way too long. The house had almost taken him to the cleaners, but he had one chip left. Just one.

He would bet it all. Sometimes, he thought, one might have to tunnel deeper into a hole to find a proper means of getting out. Time to roll the dice. Time to tempt fate.

"Jaco," he said.

"Yes, my friend."

"Can you take me to Sicily?"

"This I will do for you. Yes, I will take you if this is what you want."

"It is."

"This might be one expensive cab ride. Sicily is a long ride from here," Jaco joked.

"When do we leave?"

"Tomorrow."

"Tomorrow, then," Sean said lifting his glass in the air.

"Si," Jaco said, taking a last swig of wine, "Best get some rest my friend, tomorrow's a'gonna be a long day for us both."

Welcoming him to stay, Jaco Fernetti showed his guest to a small room just down his narrow hallway and bid the book scout goodnight. Tomorrow would be upon them soon and there were many demons to overcome for them both.

"Whenever two people meet there are really six people present. There is each man as he sees himself. Each man as the other person sees him, and each man as he really is."

William James

The Abbot's Tale

"A sorrowful man was brought before his King," Father Koutrakos-said, as he began a parable that he hoped would make some impression on his uninvited guest.

Lucifer sat his opposite, rapping his fingers on his knee. The demon was attentive, calm, and quite interested in where the abbot was to take this tale of his. The old devil, with much reluctance, had come to find some semblance of respect the human before him.

That, of course, was in no way to give false adulation for the man- he was after all, still a human. And Lucifer had made clear one very direct point over the whole evening. He hated all mankind. The monk held up a finger as if he was lecturing to a child and redirected the tale.

"The King said to this man before him, 'Why doth my guards bring you hither, before me now? I am told of you, some crime has been committed.' You see, demon, the King was surprised. This was no rogue or scurrilous villain before him- it was his only son, the Prince! The man then spoke for himself saying, 'I am before you, dear father, dear King, for a terrible deed has by my hand been committed.' The King then turned towards his guards and said to them, 'What crime has this man done such that you find reason to bring him to me? What crime could he possibly do that would not escape my pardon?'

"The guards fell silent, Lucifer," the monk said, "For they were afraid to speak ill of the Prince in his father's presence. However, the Prince wasted no time speaking for himself.

"'Oh great King, oh father that gave life to my bones, I am before you guilty of hastening a peasant to his grave. I have done many deeds which, while black to be certain, have been done in youth and in ignorance. I have killed many a slave for sport and for folly. I have deflowered virgins on a whim. Aye, too have I taxed many a peasant beyond the poor wretch's means- but all because I have been unwise and foolish. My namesake hath allowed me to be spoiled and I have with it done villainous deeds. Still, I stand before the King, father, and ask your gracious pardon for I am repentant and shall do no such deeds longer.'

"With this, the Prince took a prolonged bow and awaited his sentence. The King, taken by this confession, sought some justification for his son's pardon.

"'Why bring such woe to one whom you would call father? Tell me, my son, if I should call you such, how I hast failed to give you those reasoning's that should have swayed thee from these horrible ventures?'"

Lucifer was shifting his weight, all the while engrossed in the abbot's tale.

"The Prince responded, 'Thou hast done no wrong, father. Mine are crimes of youth, of inexperience and ignorance. I stand before you as one who is full in recognition of his failures. I have sinned against this house, and I am sorrowful indeed. Forgive thy son, great King. Forgive me, I beg you.'

"The King looked at the son to which he had given life, and began to cry at the pitiful offering of condolence this man had brought to him. Where was there to be justice in forgiveness of crimes such as these, he thought. Was this in truth his son, or some bedeviled impostor prone to some horrible act at some later date? He knew not. For you see, demon, this King was a division of himself. He was both father and King to this man. How would he rule his people if he were to pass a light sentence?

"So he sat still for a period of time, and searched his mind for some response. For him, the task of forgiving these lecherous deeds could not be fairly punished if they were not weighed against the same scale of judgment that he ruled his people. So his decision fell as not that of a father- who had but one son. But as a King who had a body of people, and therefore, many sons."

"'For these crimes my son,' he began, 'You shall be broken upon the Rack. After this, then you are to be beheaded before those you have offended, for this is our law. And this is just of thy crimes.' The Prince, who had smiled with his former confession, was speechless at his father's response. He could say nothing. The King then spoke again."

"'I can, as a father, forgive you my son. Aye I would take thy very place if I but could. As King I must do right by those I govern, and likewise I must do what is punishable to these crimes. Understand this: I pass this sentence not in question of forgiveness of thy acts that have been committed, but as question of justice. For these crimes are not such that one forgives by any demand save death of him who has committed the deed. I am sorry.' Do you understand?"

Lucifer sat quietly listening and said nothing. Then the old man directed his question at the demon once more.

"Do you understand?"

The fallen angel jerked his head. He realized suddenly that the monk's final sentence had not been part of his story, but a question to the old devil. Lucifer responded at once.

"Are you saying, Father," he snarled, "That due to the nature of my crimes against mankind, I am unworthy to ask a pardon? That somehow, were I to find forgiveness, justice would not be fitted or served?"

"What I have learned this evening," the monk began, "Is that I do not believe it is my place to offer you forgiveness. For where could we hope to start with one such as yourself? Your individual crimes are more numerous than the stars!" The old man then paused. He watched the demon's head droop somewhat, and brought up another point. "Understand, this is all just my opinion of all I have seen and heard from your confessions. Never mistake the fact that you are horror's very namesake. And even if God should find some level upon which to forgive you, I should think for the good of those He governs your forgiveness should be a difficult thing to overcome. Especially from the likes of a human such as I."

"I suppose you are correct in this thinking. This has been a foolish errand," the demon said with a heavy brow.

The monk then surprised the demon. He began to offer the old beast some bleak, glimmer of hope.

"I shall pray for you regardless, devil. For though I have offered a parable of a King, we must calculate God to be much more than this. I am prone to believe, after this night, anything is of possibility. Perhaps Lucifer, even your forgiveness."

"I was well to seek you out, old man," the angel said. "You have passed judgment on me in both a fair and calculated manner. I have an answer of sorts. It will be enough for now. As I am soon to depart I would show you one last...." Lucifer paused halfway through his sentence. Something startled him, and in turn, startled the monk. The demon jumped to his feet and began sniffing the air. He looked bestial in this respect. It was as if Lucifer had no power to control his actions. Something odd was going on. He sucked in breath after breath of air- his chest heaving excitedly. The old monk, still seated, directed a question to the demon.

"What is happening? Why did you stop speaking?"

"I.... there it is again!" Lucifer exclaimed.

"What do you mean?"

"Can you not sense anything Father? There is something in the air...... growing.... stronger... I can feel a......."

"Lucifer?"

The demon stopped suddenly. His body whipped around and he marched in the direction of the monk - who was how terrified at the speed in which the demon was moving toward him. Towering above the man, the old angel positioned himself so close to the old man as to defy any personal space the monk could have hoped to have had. His words came quick and with great precision.

"I am sorry, Father," he began. "I have no choice but to hasten a departure. There is a division beginning within the religion of man. I must tend its offering at once. Forgive me this. I shall return to you and finish what I started after I have witnessed what is happening."

"Where are you to go?" the monk asked.

"Wittenberg, Germany. At once, I am afraid. But I will return as promised, for there is one more thing in which you must play host to. As it is, I am bound to the psycospheric changes in earth's atmosphere. I am willed elsewhere."

"And when should I expect you to return?"

"A fortnight. No later."

The demon then backed away from the monk and took a bow, excusing himself in a polite manner. As he turned, the old man noticed wings protrude from the back of the demon, seemingly at the will of a thought. Their discussion, for now, had come to an end. The devil walked to the window and leapt from it, dispersing his body into the prevailing darkness.

The old man rushed to the window but could see nothing from it. The sky's background was black, but well- illuminated with twinkling stars. Lucifer was no more. And even so, had he ever been?

Below the window, the old monk rested his arms on the lower window frame listening to the pounding waves below. Perhaps dawn would come, he thought. Some light would be a welcomed offering after two nights of what seemed to be nothing but darkness.

Father Koutrakos was alone now.

His demon had wasted no time in departing, and now left the old man with little more than his thoughts. The monk sat perplexed and weak. He had not emerged from the room in two days.

Food. He needed sustenance.

As he moved from the window, the abbot could feel his bones creaking inside the aging shell of a body that was his own. There was a slight air of dizziness as well.

Once more he looked back over his shoulder. What had happened to him these last two nights had been so real in the actual moment. Yet now, there was a feeling as if this 'meeting infernal' had never happened at all. His hunger was real. His weakened state was real. But there was no evidence to say he was not, in some way, mad. That the demon had been little more than a figment of two nights with little food.

And there was something else.

Behind him, just beyond the window of the library, the sun was coming up. Father Koutrakos had yet to see any sign of this glorious star in two days. Walking towards the opening, he embraced the warmth and welcomed in the coming light. Perhaps it was a sign all was to be well. There was assurance within the sun. There was also assurance within its light.

Pulling his robe tightly to himself, the elder figure of Docheiariou shuffled across the stone floor of this library and towards the large oak door that would give him leave of his current surroundings. When he reached it, he placed his hand to the wrought iron handle. His head turned to scan the quiet library once more. There was only he and his adoptive spider resting on a web. The old man smiled Iii first genuine smile since he had entered the library two nights before.

It had taken the monk little time to reach the hallway and begin his trek through the cloister.

Though the abbey was dark, there seemed to be a newness to everything he could see. Perhaps this was nothing more than a notioning. He found himself appreciating every sight- even the iron sconces on the walls. A night spent with the demon Lucifer had done this. It had made him frightfully aware of everything that surrounded him. Their conversation must have happened. It had to have been real.

The abbot had no more rounded a comer of the abbey when he noticed two fellow monks coming towards him down the hall. As they approached, he spoke softly to them, offering a greeting in Latin. When the two hooded figures heard the words, they did not respond as one would have expected. Instead, they froze where they stood.

The monk closest to him removed his cowl, and stared at Father Koutrakos.

Not wishing to seem rude, the abbot did the same, but noticed a reaction from the monks he could have never expected. The two monks facing him froze with an utter look of horror on their faces. The man furthest from him collapsed to the floor, fainting away at the mere sight of the abbot's face. The monk left with his senses fell to his knees and began wildly reciting the Lord's Prayer.

Father Koutrakos stood confounded by their behavior. He did not recognize these two by their appearance, but why were these men acting so ridiculously at the sight of their abbot? What had he done by removing his hood that should give cause to such acts as these?

Before he could verbalize some questioning response aloud, he turned, noticing the approach of another fellow monk. This man he knew, for his cowl rested on his shoulders and he could see the man plainly enough. 1t was brother Thomas Chrysostomus.

There was, however, something odd about the man. Something decidedly peculiar.

When brother Chrysostomus noticed the odd behavior of the man kneeling before the monk, he approached; But when his eyes came to focus on the monk that was standing, all color left his face and he turned white. His eyes then grew to resemble more saucer-like plates as he took a step back. The man then reached deep within himself to bring forth some verbal offering. He stumbled over his own robe but managed some speech.

"God in Heaven," he began, "This cannot be.... this..." he was at a loss for what to say.

"What is wrong, brother?" Father Koutrakos asked. "Why am I being treated so oddly?"

"Then you are no vision from Heaven? No specter from beyond the grave?"

"Why do you say such things?" the monk returned. "Is there a part of me that seems to be unreal?"

Brother Chrysostomus reached out, placing his hand on the monk. He wished to assure himself that the monk with whom he was speaking was real. As his hand fell upon the old man, he was given this necessary assurance. Behind Father Koutrakos, there still lay one man passed out completely, and one monk praying with reckless abandon. This old monk was somehow all too real.

Stepping back slowly, brother Chrysostomus rubbed his eyes, which had become wet with uncontrolled tearing. "This....is beyond imagining... some miracle," he stated still somewhat shocked. "I must... go to the others...! must show them...I," his words trailed, broken from his lips.

Reaching to his face, Father Koutrakos felt his features. "Man," the old monk started, "What is it about me that gives way to such terror on your face? Have I some ghastly mark upon me? Have I changed somehow?"

"Father," the man opposite the elder monk said addressing him, "What year is it?"

Why, this was simple enough question, the abbot thought. There seemed a bit of apprehension on his part to give an immediate response, though. There seemed to be something hidden in this agenda.

"The year is one thousand, four hundred ninety- six," the old monk said, "Why would you ask?"

By the time he had finished his sentence, the monk who had questioned him turned and began making his way down the hallway. Why, he thought, was everyone treating him so peculiarly?

Before the old man could think too hard on the matter, Brother Chrysostomus had returned with three other monks at his side. They found Father Koutrakos standing over the bodies of two men now passed out on the floor. The man who had been praying collapsed when the abbot reached out and touched him on the shoulder.

"Father," one of the monks spoke up, "Would you please accompany us to the refectory?"

"Of course, brother," the old man said agreeing. This did not dissuade him from feeling confused and maybe even a little afraid. One monk tended to those who were passed out upon the floor, while the others accompanied Father Koutrakos down the narrow corridor. The men were now headed to a room where they could converse with one another before the old monk startled the entire monastery with his appearance.

As they entered the room, the old monk was seated to a chair where he could rest. One monk concerned himself with obtaining wine for this man to drink. Another brought father Koutrakos a plate of warm bread.

When the gathering of monks were certain the abbot had been properly nourished, they focused their attention on the obvious question; where he had spent the last twenty-one years of his life. Or more importantly, how he had survived them at all.

Brother Chrysostomus was the first to speak.

"Father Koutrakos," he said, addressing the man seated before them, "I do not know of a way of explaining this," his· words began to stumble from his mouth. "But I shall nevertheless try......"

"Out with it, brother," the old man replied. He was becoming increasingly frustrated by the monk's reservedness. "Why are you all so awestruck before me?"

"Father," he said, "The year...it is... one thousand, five- hundred and seventeen." There. He said it. The words had come reluctantly. But they had come nonetheless.

Andreas Koutrakos sat dumbfounded. His jaw had dropped and he could not say a word. The bread he was holding fell from his hands to his plate, and his mind emptied itself of all thought, save one. The year. 1517.

Seeing the blanket look on the monk, Father Chrysostomus began to elaborate on what the monk was finding hard to digest.

"Twenty-one years ago, you entered the library of this place and we have not seen you since. Your absence had gone unnoticed for about eight days before a decision was made to seek you out. At once, every monk in Docheiariou was employed to search for some sign of your body. After a week of intense survey of both the inside of this monastery and the outer grounds, we had given you up for dead. The only place we could not gain access to was the library."

"Did you not try?" the elder monk asked.

"With every facet we could employ," Father Chrysostomus stated, "But even though every monk in this abbey tried to break the door down, it simply would not give way. Nothing we tried worked at all," he said shaking his head." Father, I tell you now, it was as if some otherworldly force held the door steadfast. And regardless of how hard we tried, there was to be no entry." The monk who was speaking paused just long enough for the abbot to digest what had been said. He knew if the man before him was no ghost, that these revelations were going to be hard for the man to bear. But as astounded as the abbot was sure to find all of this, the monks encircling him were having even a more difficult time. Father Chrysostomus began to speak again. "We were sure somehow you had died in the room, but without a means of entry........ well.... we consecrated the room in your memory, and began construction of a new library elsewhere in the monastery. So, you can see why our two brothers passed out when encountering you in the hall earlier."

The old monk could say nothing. He was in complete disbelief of his situation. To him, it had only been two nights ago when he entered in the library- he was sure of it! Yet here he was, twenty-one years later. His mind was both maddened and confused beyond all reckoning.

As the abbot looked at the men surrounding him, all he could see were blank stares. In each set of eyes there was a stark semblance of fear, fascination, and questioning disbelief. He knew what each wanted to know, yet he had no idea where to begin. They would think him mad. Of this he was sure.

Twenty-one years. He had gone into the library a man of sixty, and by his reckoning, left two days later as a man of eighty- one. This was far too much for one man to bear. His throat now soothed by the wine he began to stammer for speech.

"I..... I.......," there seemed no point in which to begin. He played an imaginary conversation out in his mind, but even this was not helping him.

"Easy, brother," one of the younger monks, whom he did not recognize, said. This young monk then put his arm around the old man and offered as much comfort as he could. "Relax, this will come in time," he said, "We shall tend to your needs."

"I.... am fine.... I just.... no... l...," the abbot was speaking, but short of breath. He would fight to get through this.

Brother Chrysostomus was more direct, and moved toward a specific question. "Tell us where you have been for the past twenty-one years," he begged.

Father Koutrakos had no trouble issuing a response.

He looked up with a profound expression of grievance on his face. His eyebrows were weighted and heavy. His face drooped with mental exhaustion. But nevertheless, he mustered the energy to speak the first and most truthful sentence that came to mind. Where had he been? "In Hell," the elder man said, "In Hell."

Those five monks who were present for this response drew back and looked at each other in confusion. When they turned back to address the old man, they saw he had come to rest his head on the table. It seemed that Father Koutrakos had passed out from the excitement.

Not one of the monks in attendance knew what to do or say.

> "When choosing between two evils,
> I always like to try the one I've never tried before."
>
> Mae West

Sicily

Jaco Fernetti had come home at last.

It had taken him a long time, a special reason, and a decent amount of courage to come back - to Palermo. To Sicily. But he had returned nonetheless.

The small Italian couldn't help but draw in the smell of the place. It seemed as though it had gone unchanged since he had left this city years ago. But to a child, home always has a familiar scent and a distinguished feel. Now, one of Sicily's sons had come back.

Stepping from the doorway of the small aircraft, he surveyed the landscape. Everything was just how he remembered it. Ancient. Rustic. Familiar.

Jaco turned around as if he wanted to make sure his traveling companion was still with him. Sean Wilde was gathering his things and nodding in Jaco's direction. Sean wanted nothing more than to get off the plane. He hated flying.

The two travelers had chartered a small flight that had taken them from the Northeast territory of Venice to the southernmost island of Italy. Their point of destination had been Trapani, Sicily, but they had to land in Palermo to get there. It was nice to be on the ground, each man thought to himself. The flight had been a bumpy one. And both men wasted little time abandoning the aircraft and hailing the first cab they could find. Jaco in particular wanted to get on with the business at hand. He would have loved to avoided this situation and these circumstances. He wanted nothing to do with the Mafia or Sean's predicament. Yet there was a neediness with his new friend that he found sympathy with. Sean was desperate and had no one to turn to. Perhaps this touched a nerve with Jaco Fernetti. Perhaps Sean was just grasping at straws. Whatever the case had been, he felt an obligation to help if he could. But he had resigned to do so only to a point. The first priority was to find a ride that could get them out of the city.

While Jaco set about the business of hailing a means of transportation, Sean looked around Palermo as if he was a stupefied tourist. Every destination in Italy had impressed upon him some sense of wonderment. The entire country fascinated him in a way no other place he had visited ever had before. Everything was so old, yet so beautiful and enchanting. The people were friendly and the women all seemed beautiful. Whether any of these things were true in fact didn't matter, they were true to Sean. And where he was concerned- what he told himself was all he needed to believe in. The book man was all about listening to his heart now. His head be damned.

The American paused to rub his head, which was still throbbing from the excessive amounts of Tuscan wine he had consumed the night before. It seemed like an orchestra was beating out Beethoven's Ninth symphony in his head. And to make matters worse, he had not been able to locate any means of alleviating the pounding headache.

As a car approached, Sean stepped back, allowing Jaco to address the driver in Italian. There seemed to be a verbal dispute as the driver did not seem to want to do whatever Jaco had asked of him. Then Sean saw Jaco reach for a thick wad of bills tucked in his back pocket. The driver nodded, but held up a finger as if there were to still be some conditions to their trip. It was frustrating Sean that his education had fallen short of being able to understand what was being said.

Jaco tugged at Sean's sleeve, telling him to get in the back of the car.

Once the little Italian joined him, he began to speak and explain their situation.

"The driver says he will take us only as far as a mile's walk from the Trapani Villa."

"That's fine with me," Sean said, "The walk will do me good."

"My friend," Jaco began, "I am not well," he said changing the course of the discussion. The Italian was bothered by Sean's seemingly unconcern for the seriousness of dealing with the Mafia. He looked at the book scout with a heavy brow. "This whole endeavor of yours- 'it scares me. Jaco would not do this for just anyone."

"I know, Jaco," Sean responded, looking him directly in the eye, "And I am very grateful," he said, putting a hand on the Italian's knee.

"These people we are going to meet with...... they no good people," Jaco said in way that remind Sean of Al Pacino's title role in the movie Scarface. "I am going to take you as far as the front door of the villa...... but that is all. No way is Jaco going in that place. No way." He had made the statement more with his hands than with his tongue.

"Listen, Jaco," Sean said with sincerity, "I didn't expect you to take me this far. I just needed a push by someone in the right direction; I need to see some justice. I need to know that even for a loser like me, some way, somehow, there's a light at the end of the tunnel. For me there must be a reckoning," he said. "These people, for no reason, tried to use me and kill me. Never in my life, even on the worst day, have I felt as insignificant as I do right now. My life may not mean much to anyone else, but it's all /have. And Jaco," he said, turning from the Italian and looking out the back-car window, "nobody's got the right to take that from me."

"I hear what you say my friend. But is this really going to fix your problem? I mean... would it not be better to just walk away. Perhaps you could find some work in Venice. I could help you in that way."

Sean looked back in the direction of the little man. Jaco had a look of seriousness that made Sean feel like he had finally found a true friend. He smiled. "At any time during this bullshit, I would have gladly walked away. But things have just gotten way too far out of hand. Sometimes, I think a man is just put in a situation that was never in his control from the start. Ultimately that man's gotta figure a way out for himself. I don't know that what I'm doing is right or wrong Jaco, I just don't know. But I'm following my gut this time. Not my head," he stated, "My head's gotten me in enough trouble already."

The man seated next to Sean looked up at him and smiled.

"That girl you told me about.... Cecelia I think," he began, "She betrayed you somehow didn't she?"

"Shut up. She's got nothing to do with it."

"Yes my friend," Jaco said snickering, "She seems to have nothing to do with it," he paused then started again, "Tell me my friend... was a Frenchman in the picture by any chance?"

Sean just turned his nose up and gave the Italian a stem look. The man had meant to lighten the moment, but the book man was in no mood. "This is about a book, and some people who thought my life was worth sacrificing to get it. I'm out for revenge, or at the very least, payback. It's as simple as that."

"I see," Jaco said, rubbing the stubble on his chin. "And tell me, my friend, are you prepared for what may come from all of this?"

"What do you mean?"

"You could still end up dead."

"Jaco," Sean said, looking away, "Get me as far as the front door of Villa Trapani. What happens next will be between me and God. Besides," he said, "I've got a plan."

The small Italian man sat back in his seat and said nothing else. He didn't know what kind of plan Sean was speaking of. But he hoped God might lend the poor American some help. He figured Sean could use all he could get.

Besides, there was no use trying to get his new friend to abandon his foolish ideas. Sean's ability to reason was gone. He was bent towards one end. And Jaco was worried that that 'end' might be at the cost of his new friend's life.

Sean didn't say much else, either. His eyes were looking out onto the sights of ltaly as his brain pondered other issues. In truth, he had no idea what to expect. But as he had already been dead, what more was there to be concerned about? Now was the time to focus on life and living. And somehow, he believed that there was going to be no way to do this if he couldn't end the worriment of constantly looking over his shoulder. As long as the people who had tried to kill him thought he might be alive, he could never rest. Sean had to get at least back to where he had come from. Even if that meant hustling first edition fiction on the streets of Boston.

Sean glanced out of the window and at the scenery once more. The cab, not much bigger than the one Jaco drove back in Venice, bumped noisily down the A20 highway heading west. It was sputtering toward the small coastal town of Trapani, Sicily. The unlikely pair seated in the back of the car would be at the Don's villa soon enough, he thought. Soon enough.

Sean then rested his head on the side of the car's window and fell asleep, while Jaco fidgeted with his hands on the seat next to him.

Sean woke to the car engine idling and Jaco shaking him.

"My friend," the Italian said, "Wake up. We are very close to the villa"

Sean yawned and began rubbing his eyes. There was a sharp pain in his side from the uncomfortable position his body had been cramped within the cab, but there was little use in complaining. If the driver had gotten them to the villa, it had been worth it.

"What is it, Jaco.... are we there yet?"

"Not exactly, my friend," the little man responded, "But we are as close as we are going to get in a car."

"Whadda ya mean?" Sean said, forgetting what the Italian had told him earlier.

"The driver says he not going any further."

"Oh. Yeah, right."

"You had better get your things together, my friend. We are going to walk the rest of the way on foot."

Sean looked out the window. He could see, not too far in the distance, what had to be the villa up on a hill. They had arrived on the narrow peninsula of Trapani. But they were not near the shore, they were in the country it seemed. The book scout opened his mouth, yawning again. He then reached down and pulled the leather satchel off the floorboards and from between his legs. He then opened the car door and stepped from the vehicle.

He was still close enough to the ocean where he could smell the salt water breeze in the air around him. It seemed, though_ impossible, that he could even smell the scent of fish being gutted in the harbor below them. He turned around to see Jaco speaking Italian to the cab driver. His friend didn't seem too happy.

"Let's go," Jaco said as he walked past Sean in a huff.

"What's wrong?" the book man asked.

"Nothing," he said, "The asshole in the cab didn't want to come back to pick us up later."

"Why?"

"Sean," Jaco said looking at his friend, "You just don't know how dangerous these people are. I would have never moved from my home in Sicily if I had not been in a real fear for my safety. No one wants to be involved with these people. No one."

"Well, what do we do?"

"We go to the villa on the hill up there," Jaco said, pointing to the path lined with cypress trees, and toward the rustic- looking house on the hilltop. "I figure something out later."

Sean chose not to respond. He felt bad enough for having ever involved Jaco in the first place. The last thing he wanted was for something to put his friend in harm's way. So, neither man speaking, they began to walk down the dusty Italian path, heading toward the villa up ahead. With the Sicilian sun beating down, Sean's quest for justice was just beginning. Much to the chagrin of his little Italian friend.

They had walked for no more than a mile before they were greeted by two well-dressed men, both of whom were sporting firearms, black glasses, and attitudes. As the first man approached - a skinny goon with long black hair tied in a ponytail - Jaco stepped in front of Sean and said something in Italian that caused the man to relax. Sean noticed his friend was shaking a little, but said nothing. He realized at that moment that he was already in way over his head.

The second man approached and motioned with his hands for the two of them to follow him. Jaco turned to Sean and began to explain what was happening.

"These are just guards," he said, "They are nothing but the Don's household protection. Dogs. I assure you, they are no smarter than the guns they carry, but they can kill us nonetheless."

"What did you say to them?"

"That we were expected guests of the Don."

"And they just believed you?"

"Yes."

"Why?"

"I showed them this," Jaco said, reaching in his pocket and extracting what appeared to be a medallion of some sort. "That is the family crest of Trapani," he said, pointing to the emblem on the coin-like object. "This is proof I have ties with the family. It will get us at least as far as inside the home."

Sean looked up at his friend. "Jaco," he said. "I thought you weren't going in the house."

"I wish I wasn't," he said, "But Jaco got to thinking," he began, "If I let you go in the villa alone, not speakin' Italian, you very likely won't come out. An American with no experience dealing with these people could find himself some very real problems in the home of a Mafia Don. Besides," he said flippantly, "What is Jaco going to do alone out here by himself?" he stated, turning to present Sean with his own personal dilemma.

"I was serious about what I told you last night," Sean returned, "I don't want to cause you any more trouble than I already have."

"I understand, my friend," he said, "But you really should let this go. You are only going to deepen your problems by getting involved with these people. They not so good for your health."

"I hear you, Jaco," the book man said, "But I'm not letting this go. I didn't have much of a life before, but nobody's got the right to take what little I had. Coming here... well, it's a means to an end, I guess."

"Yes, Sean," the Italian said, "But whose means and whose end are we talking about?"

Sean snickered at the Italian's attempt to bring humor to their situation.

His mind was beyond made up, and the course was set He would do what had to be done - right or wrong.

He then turned from his friend and began following the guard toward the entrance· of the villa. Jaco kicked at the gravel path and the two men said nothing else until they had come to the massive structure of stone before them.

Sean's mouth gaped at the grandeur of the building before him: It was an immense structure that made it hard for Sean to imagine that this was someone's home. The book scout could tell it was old by the flaking of paint and the cracks webbing throughout the stone exterior. Large pillars topped with ornate capitals reflected the grandeur of a time when importance was paid to the details of a building. Just the stone railway leading up the front steps and to the large entranceway must have commanded tons of earth and mortar to construct. The building showed its age. But its sheer enormity made up for any shortcoming that could be associated with it.

Jaco punched Sean in the arm in an effort to get the man's attention. They weren't here to admire the scenery. They were here to speak to the Don and get the hell out.

The three men moved up the stone stairway until they reached the front door. It only took one knock for a new face to appear, opening the large entrance to the Villa. The guard that had led the men this far then traded roles with a short, fat Italian with big lips and squinty eyes, and walked back down the path.

The fat man eyed the two visitors and flicked his wrist, motioning them to come inside. Sean found it odd that so much conversation could take place between these people without a single word being said. He watched Jaco take a deep breath before stepping a foot over the threshold. Sean laughed internally to himself. He had been dead already. Nothing really scared him that much anymore.

The entranceway was tiled with sleek Italian marble. And Sean rolled his eyes at the vast expanse of openness to this foyer. Even Jaco stopped for a look While the outside of the building had been old and rustic, the inside was as beautiful as a palace.

The fat Italian spoke in some Sicilian dialect that caused Jaco to quickly respond in a tone Sean didn't recognize. The small Italian held a hand up to Sean's chest, and spoke. "We must wait here until we are permitted to see Don di Trapani. Best take a seat over there," he said, pointing to a gold- trimmed couch seated under a solid wall in pastel colors. The book man followed Jaco's lead and sat next to him on the couch.

Sean could see Jaco twitching nervously to himself. He had been glad to have the company of the small Italian with him, even though he knew how much his partner would have loved to have been anywhere else. Perhaps Sean had made a real friend. If he didn't get the two of them killed, he thought, this might be something for them to joke about in their old age. Jaco might have begged to differ.

They were well into an hour by the time they were acknowledged again. This time the two were approached by a tall, slender individual. He was nothing if not both well-groomed and polite. His Italian came across with flawless punctuation and precision.

Jaco parlayed conversation, and instructed Sean that the time had come for them to meet with Don di Trapani.

Sean was quick to his feet. But Jaco halted his enthusiasm long enough to get a word in.

"As it is time for us to meet with the Don," he said, "remember a few things." He put a finger to the air, "First, only speak when spoken to. Second, show nothing less than the utmost respect. Bad manners have no place here," he said. "This man has killed people for far less."

"Understood," Sean said, with a look of waning sincerity.

"Be careful of what you say," Jaco spoke, "Your word is your bond. These people take that very seriously. If you promise something -you had better deliver the goods. These people can get very ugly."

"I've seen the movies, Jaco. I'll be cautious."

"Good," the little Italian said as he turned meeting the impatient stare of the slender figure who was still waiting for the two men to follow him. "Forgive me," he said to their guide, "We are ready."

The two men walked down a marbled corridor until they came to two double doors ornately carved in the old-world style. Each wooden structure held an intricate floral design. As one of the doors opened, they were greeted by yet another new face. Jaco recognized instantly that this was the family's *consigliore*, or advisor, to the Don.

As the man smiled at the two guests, Sean tried to oppress his feelings of nervousness. He didn't want the Don to think him weak. That's what he had Jaco for.

Stepping into the room, Sean was met with the magnificence of old world style. The surroundings were open, much like that of a library. This made Sean relax at once. The ceilings were coffered and the walls were paneled in oak, with shelving lined with books. His eyes then moved towards the room's center where, amidst four leather couches and some pillowy chairs, was a small elderly man sipping coffee.

He knew at once it must be Don Giovanni di Trapani.

The man looked to be in his seventies, but was well- groomed, appeared alert, and seemed to be of good health. He rested the cup on a small plate in his lap and welcomed his guests, offering them a seat across from him. Sean nor his companion wasted any time finding a seat.

The consigliore took his position, choosing to stand on the left of his boss. With everyone comfortably situated and reserved to silence, the old man began to address Jaco.

"It has been a long time since we have seen each other, my friend," he said smiling. He spoke in English as to be considerate of the American in his presence. But it was thick with Italian dialect, and it was still barely coherent to the book scout. "Now you have come to see your old friend, eh?"

"Si.... Godfather," Jaco said, fidgeting.

"It is good to see you."

"It is good to see you Godfather," Jaco lied.

"I see that you have brought someone with you," the elder man acknowledged, turning towards Sean.

"Si, Godfather."

"Tell me, old friend," the elder man said, lifting the coffee again, "I am to assume you are not here for a social visit. What is it that I might do for you?"

"My friend here," he said, cautioning every word he said while trying not to seem agitated, "needs your help, Don Trapani. I.... would ask that the favor you offered me so many years ago... well... might I ask that you offer that favor to my friend here, instead?"

The old man looked at Sean, who now felt reasonably intimidated.

"Tell me," he said, smiling at the book scout, "What is the request you would ask of me?"

Sean, while somewhat cautious, wasted no time efforting a response. Within moments, he found himself confessing everything that had happened to him over the last week to a frail, old man who held the power of a god. He accentuated every detail of the adventure, and left nothing to be imagined. As he spoke, the old man never flinched or offered any sign of change in his facial expression. He simply listened to what his American guest said while sipping his cup of coffee. When Sean came to a stopping point, Don Giovanni di Trapani had but one question.

"Sean," he said, "What would you have me do?"

The book scout sat quiet for a moment, then started with a thought. "I know at whatever point DeBury knows I'm alive or at the very least, in possession of the book, he'll come after me. I need some means of getting to him before he gets to me. It's that simple, sir."

"I wish to know more."

"Like what?"

Sean felt Jaco's foot dig into his own, as the little Italian was sending a subtle reminder in how one should watch his manners.

"I wish to know what you want me to do, specifically," the Don said.

"I have one million dollars in a Parisian bank I can access at any time. The only problem is, if I go to extract it, there's a very good chance DeBury will know I'm alive and track me down. The money is worthless to me if I'm dead," he said, pausing to catch his breath. "What I'm proposing is this: help me convince DeBury to leave me alone. And help me get even with R Fantasma. I don't want to kill anybody. I just need to know they will leave me alone in the future. For this I will split the money with you. Six hundred thousand dollars. Just help me... please."

The old man motioned to the man standing next to him, whispering something in his ear as he bent down. Sean then watched the figure leave the room as if on a mission from God himself. The old man seated looked back at the book man, then in the direction of the agitated Italian seated next to him.

"Jaco, my friend," he said, "I told you long ago I would help you with any request you would ask of me. You have never come to me, and this has disappointed me greatly. Now, you bring me this American, and I am at a loss of what I should do."

"Help him, Godfather."

"This is how I am to repay you?"

"If you feel you owe me," Jaco said choosing his words carefully, "Yes."

"Very well," the old man said turning from Jaco and now towards Sean. His language switched from Italian to rough English. "You will have what you ask, Sean," he said. "I shall provide you with four men for the task. My associate has gone to instruct them to meet with you momentarily. I will leave it up to you to instruct them on what they are to do. This I will do for the man who saved my son's life."

Both Sean and Jaco thanked the Don in unison, then turned toward the double doors that were opening presently.

The consigliore had returned with the four individuals the old man had spoken of earlier.

"I have arranged for you a small villa closer to the coastline. You can make whatever plans necessitate this 'revenge' of yours there."

"Thank you, Godfather," Sean said, feeling odd about the statement.

"This thing of yours," the old man visited, "This revenge.... be careful. It is a circular plan with often terrible results. I have learned that killing a man for these reasons quite often leads to further injustice to the person who exacts it."

"I understand."

"Good," he said, "I must rest then, for it has been a long day."

The men who were seated stood and the old man walked towards Jaco. He took the Venetian's head in his elder hands and kissed his cheek. "This thing I do for you to pay back a kindness you once did for me. I will never forget that you saved my son's life once. It seems you are on some mission to save another," he said, looking at Sean. "And you, my friend," he addressed the book scout, "Be wise in your endeavors. It will take more than the protection of my men to aid you if these people who banned you are as dangerous as you say."

"It has been an honor to meet you, Don di Trapani," Sean said, ignoring the old man's wisdom.

"Take care....... you both," he said turning and hobbling towards the doorway.

The two men eyed one another for a moment then were escorted out. Sean thought about what he was going to do as they departed the room. He would make a phone call to DeBury tomorrow morning. Then, perhaps he could set a plan in motion- one he had yet to create. Then maybe he could get back to life as usual. But he knew nothing would ever be usual again. So he would be happy to just get back to life. His life. But first, a final reckoning.

> "Where there is the tree of knowledge, there is always Paradise: so say the most ancient and the most modern serpents."
>
> Friedrich Nietzsche

The Revelation of Saint Andreas

Upon his awakening, the old monk returned to the refectory and spent the entire portion of the following day explaining his experiences to all the men of the Docheiariou monastery. They had assembled for the monk's telling of what had occurred. He explained the visitation by Lucifer, and revealed much, but not all, of what the demon had told him.

He could not explain why twenty-one years had passed, or how he had lived through them without sleep or food. But there was no mistaking the obvious toll it had taken on the elder monk. Whether the words he spoke were of madness or fact, he was urged by his fellow monks to pen the entire tale in print. They wished for their brother to construct a manuscript of the demon's words. It would be record, they each agreed, to give some explanation of what had happened to the old man.

Father Koutrakos was unsure of what he wished to do. There were still the last words the demon had spoken dancing in his head. The demon had promised to speak to him again.

Would this cost him an additional twenty-one years? Had Lucifer been out to trick him all along? There was much to think on.

If the devil had not been lying, a farce to imagine in itself, he would return soon enough.

The old monk finished his tale, and wished to be excused. His body was aching and he needed time to rest.

The other monks agreed.

The eldest of the men stood, with a cane now grasped tightly in his right hand, and excused himself. He was helped to his feet by several younger monks and they escorted the old man as far as the door.

He then brushed them off; assuring each man he was perfectly capable of walking back to his cell unaided. They obliged him, as was their station to do, and the old abbot began to make his way from the refectory back to his cell.

The monk had not made it far down the musty corridor when a voice inside began to pull him in another direction altogether. He couldn't return to his bed just yet. There was one place he had to see again.

He had an inner compulsion to revisit the library. For him, there was no choice in the matter. Someone was beckoning him along. Someone..... or *perhaps.......some......thing.*

The abbot could feel his heart rate rapidly increasing as he turned from the direction of his cell. He began to make his way towards the library. Arriving at the door, he turned the wrought iron latch and entered the room.

Father Chrysostomus had wished to follow distantly behind the old man in an effort to assure the abbot made it safely to his room without any trouble. Upon arriving at the old monk's cell, he peered through the small window slit in the door but saw no trace of his elder brother anywhere. Then his heart surged with a dreaded realization.

Please God in heaven – not the library!

He wasted no time making his way towards the direction of the library. Fate had other plans however and all he was greeted with was enough time to see the door closing behind Andreas Koutrakos. The very same door that had been permanently sealed shut only a day before. He pulled on the door with all his strength yet it would not budge. It was as sealed at this moment as it had been the day before.

He fell to his knees and began to pray for the old man on the other side. He would need every prayer, he thought, every last one.

Inside the room, Father Koutrakos shuffled about. Nothing had changed or was out of place. He felt nothing but rage. He had been tricked and in his anger he picked up a candle and hurled it across the room with all the strength his aged frame could muster.

"Devil from Hell!" he screamed, "You have done this thing to me! Robbed me of twenty-one years of my life! And for what?! Had you nothing else with which to amuse yourself?!"

"Why damn me for your own misgivings?" a voice said as a wing-like shadow began to project itself on the wall opposite him.

The monk turned as fast as his body would allow. There, crouched on the library table was the figure of Lucifer. His wings were stretched four feet in either direction from his side. And he was smiling.

"True demon," the monk began, "I allowed this thing to happen. And for it, twenty-one years hastened to the grave. I am a fool."

The demon leapt from the table and began to pace the room. The old man was coming apart mentally and he could see this all too well. Lucifer eyed the monk and began listening to the inner workings of the old man's body. The heart within the abbot's chest was out of rhythm and he could tell the other organs in his body were weak with age. Seventy-nine was an almost unheard of age for a man to live in this century.

"Reformation has begun, Father," the angel said trying to quell the angered monk and turn the discussion once more in his favor. "I have returned from Wittenberg as I had promised to bring you news of a major division which is occurring."

"What are you speaking of, demon?"

"A human, in your tongue called *Martin Luther*, has just nailed a list of demands he calls a thesis of ninety-nine dissatisfactions with Catholicism, to a door in the city. Your church it would seem has been split at the seams," he said making a motion with his fingers as if he were slicing the air. "What divisions I had spoken of earlier have already begun to take place. A major chasm opens within the world of your faith. My triumph finally begins and yet I am more concerned about you than I am about the paltry world in which you occupy. Religion is beginning to destroy Christianity. Religion *will* ultimately destroy mankind."

"I am confused," the monk stated.

"Come with me," the devil said as he extended his elongated hand, "I wish to show you something."

"Never!" the monk said pulling away. "Am I to have lost all faculty and reason?!"

"What do you fear?"

"You are *Lucifer*!"

"So I am," the devil said as he bowed and put a hand to his chest, "But I am before you as I have been always and there is no need to fear me. The thing I wish to show you will not cost you a moment of your life. It is but a revelation. A view from atop a hill, one might say."

"You must think me mad."

"I would think nothing of the sort," he quipped, "Come with me."

"I cannot. I will not. What more could you possibly offer me?"

"Watch," the demon said as his eyes became aglow.

The library began to change shape as it had done when the angel had taken the old man to the outskirts of Hell. Now, they were not in some darkened hole but on the top of a mountain that overlooked a vast cityscape below.

The monk was noticeably frightened. He clutched at his robe and began a rapid succession of quick breaths. Lucifer, towering over him, moved toward the edge of the cliff. He lifted his arm out towards the vastness below and began to speak.

"You have allowed me my confession," the angel said, "And I wish to show you a glimpse of a future as I believe it will become."

"You are neither omnipotent nor omnipresent," the monk retorted, "It should not be in your power to reveal such a thing to me."

"This is a future that *could* be – not one that shall be. Behold the world as I see it to become. Behold a realm where man has become his own god. Behold, dear monk, hell on earth…"

"Hell on earth?" the monk was confused.

"Do you remember when I told you Hell was growing, expanding, and ever changing? It is my belief that as the human matures from this age to the next, he will find no need for his Creator. Man will become his own god. Religious division will have brought this. Man's inhumanity to man will have brought this. Ultimately, the advancement of forward thought and 'Science' will bring this about as well."

The monk turned from the conversation looking to the city below. Nothing he saw seemed similar to what he knew presently. The devil continued his thought as the old man looked on.

"Love, as it should have been, will be no more. I think as Hell grows, filling its belly with the souls of your world, it will ultimately have no place to expand and it will, at some point, literally enter your existing world. The human will not see it – for Hell is deceiving. I would wager at some point mankind will have no belief in a 'Hell' at all.

"This, I cannot imagine," the monk offered.

"Take heart, monk," the demon stated lifting a finger. "I have shown you nothing." He motioned the old man to come towards him and then positioned his body in such a way that there would be no further miscommunication between them. "Look out upon the pitiful existence these people have come to worship."

The old man was silent. His own desire for knowledge had already cost him twenty-one years of his life. Yet it was his fault. He opened himself to this confession. Now, he opened himself to the revelation of a possible future. He digested the thought of moving forward. If he did decide to construct a book – a manuscript of this infernal conversation – a glimpse of the future could prove a proper ending point. A final chapter. A warning. His eyes found the demon and he followed the expression on Lucifer's face.

"They will worship their own selves," the devil stated. "And their form and dress and their appearance will be such that you cannot differentiate between which is male and which is female."

"But, as you stated before, won't the family be able to thwart you as you say it does now?"

The demon bellowed an infernal laugh that sent him into a wild display of humorous outpourings. "What family?" he said. "There will be *no* family. There will be no home. There will be no love. Mark this, monk, somewhere in your incomprehensible musings: Marriage will no longer be sacred, nor will be the idea of home in any rationing you might imagine it to be. Lust for worldly things will have replaced man's ability to see what was ever important. Objects and possessions will take precedence over human life and simple kindnesses.

Yes, I know this is true in this age, but only within a specific class of human in the future I show you now, this disease will have spread to all men. And all will suffer their individual demise by this offering;"

"This picture is difficult to imagine."

"I do not think it is, Father," the devil bellowed. "Look at this age you live in now. Kings vie for more lands and more people to conquer," he said, laughing; "as if there is some god- like right to ownership of anything my Creator has lain forth. Only a man, only a pitiful, selfish human being, would have the gall and the audacity to believe he could possess and own what was never his to begin with. Wars are fought for the dirt beneath the feet of men who will leave this world with no more than what they brought into it. And this *fascinates* me," he said with emphasis. "Watch an animal. A beast you find to be lower than yourself. Do you think it worries how much it takes possession of! Do you think at any point of its lowly existence, it has desired to fashion its existence around an acquisition of *things*- or do you think it simply concentrates on living its life? One simple day to the next."

"I believe life is far simpler for an animal than that of a man," the abbot professed. "Ah, Father, it was not supposed to be this way, though. Your species was to take pride in what was around you and share in its glory and wondrous creation. Fools!" he exclaimed. "Instead, you look to conquer each other! You look for the meaning of life, when the only reality you pitiful beasts ever had was to realize that there was never a meaning to be had - there was only life and what you choose to do with it. The human is morphing, every day of his existence, into an angel of light or an angel of darkness. And Hell, my friend, has just as much room as Heaven - perhaps even more. Life is the test, father- not the means to an end. And never think it to be a race to experience all one can before death arrives to claim you. The human of the future will acquisition as much as possible while trying to experience as much of the world as he can before death claims him- all the while living in the illusion that it was necessary. Yet one will never come to grips with the idea that the treasures that exist beyond this world so outweigh those of earth, that this would befuddle the imagining."

"What will bring this to pass?"

"Money!" he stated, "And the greed which will come with it. At least, that is what I think."

"But money only exists in the hands of the few."

"In this age, that is true, but you and I speak of a future world that will become far different from the one you occupy presently."

"Continue. Please..."

"There is little need for me to elaborate to one such as yourself on the perils of individual fortune. You have seen enough of the greed such foolish needs beget, I am sure. But in the future, men will find wealth on an individual basis that they do not presently have in this age. Some of this wealth will be real and some will be illusionary. Again, I cannot tell you what this will cause the human to sacrifice and to what depths man will degrade himself. Life will mean nothing, save the unyielding pursuit of worldly pleasures. Men will sell their souls to hell to satiate their own gain, yet the fleeting time in which their life passes will pave their place on the road to eternity. The belief in me and my Creator will, at some point, dissipate altogether."

"But how am I to imagine this? I can barely contain what you have shown me presently."

"Then behold this," the demon said as he waved his elongated hand in the air and visions began to race pass the old man.

At first, the earth around him began to change. Cloud cover moved overhead at incredible speeds. Then, as the blurry visions solidified themselves, the old man could see the Hell the demon had referred to in his speech.

In a distant land, one he did not recognize, he could see a race of men and women, all in a strange dress, moving about in a hurried frantic pace.

"Look at them, old monk," Lucifer said with disgust, pointing at the mass of people crowding the streets. “Does the human not look as if he has become his own whore? Babylon has risen in the west.”

The monk tried to dissect the images, but they were unimaginable to his mediaeval mind. The clothing. The method of transportation. The lights. They were all too much for his limited comprehension. The old man became alarmed at the sights- his mouth gaping and his eyes flexing as far open as the skin encompassing his face would allow. He could not speak nor could he breathe. This glimpse of the future, be it real or illusionary, took his mind far away and rendered him mute at that very moment

“These humans could never believe in a god nor could they imagine a devil,” Lucifer said abruptly, “They will be their own individual gods-worshipping their life and their individual desires above all else. Daily life will see to that,” he said, catching a breath. “Some will resist, I am sure, but not enough to ensure the survivability of the human race. These beings you see will do everything in their power to prolong a life they should be happy to rid themselves of. And, whether you believe me or not, these disgusting creatures will figure some way to make more of themselves through advancement in learning. This, I predict, will start the second and final war. Armageddon,” the demon said, crossing his arms. “Because as patient as my Creator is with you hopeless beasts, there will not exist enough room on his earth for more than one God.

“Imagine,” he said throwing his arms in the air, “Having a being you created from the dust of the earth throw its gift of life back in your face by trying to clone itself! Oh, I can see in your face, Father that you do not believe me, but I can also see the audacity of the human and where it is headed even clearer. I suppose,” he stated, rubbing the cleft in his chin, “then I will have my final laugh at the Creator. He will have banished me for *nothing,* because He will realize I saw the truth all along! And do you know what else, Father?” the demon said, looking at the monk with a puzzeled expression. “Father?....Father…?

But Andreas Koutrakos wasn’t listening anymore. The monk’s mind was full of things he could not possibly understand. He was grappling with the images the demon had shown him, and he was not doing well with them at all.

The old devil bent over and flashed a hand in front of the old monk.

Nothing. No eye response at all. The monk just sat in quiet repose, his eyes frozen open and his mouth a gaping hole.

"Oh, dear," the fallen angel said, withdrawing backwards, "Forgive me, Father..I should not have taken this confession so far. It would seem I have crossed the mental boundary to which a mortal man may grasp........I did not see this coming," he said, as if to apologize with false sincerity, "I…I will leave you now. You must rest from this meeting- I can see that now." The old man stared blindly back in the demon's direction, saying nothing.

"I suppose there is nothing left for me to say that will mean anything to you, my friend. But take this with you," the demon said as he stretched his wings and looked down at the old abbot. "I have never been one for games, and I came to you as humbly as I could with my confession. You sit quietly before me now, unable to answer my final request of forgiveness, and I cannot help feeling that this has been brought upon by myself. I wished to show you a future warning you might somehow pass down to generations of man to save your undeserving species, but I see this has failed as well. You are a mess, my friend," he said, drawing his own conclusions from the monk's unmoving state. "But you listened and I am grateful. Should you able yourself a return to sanity, I shall leave you with this parting thought," he directed the coming words carefully, "Hell will complete its journey to your earth, when man no longer believes in me, my Creator, or an afterlife. For me- this will be my ultimate triumph. For my Creator this will be a reason to destroy you all. I have seen the world destroyed once, and it is beyond even the words I found for you earlier. One cannot imagine His wrath, Father," the angel said, pausing to redirect himself. "Look at me. Am I not proof of it? Heed my warning and take these words and bury them deep in your soul. Perhaps they will be some repayment for your time and your sacrifice. Perhaps not. I leave you to your fate as I found you- humble and alone. Know that a demon found you, a human, worthy of life. That is as much as I can offer," he said, bowing before an unresponsive monk. "Good-bye, Father........fare thee well."

With these final words, the fallen angel vanished where he stood, leaving the old man alone to his meandering and his lonesome fate.

In the stillness of his surroundings, Father Koutrakos started to move his eyes.

> "It's far easier to forgive an enemy after you've gotten even with him."
>
> Olin Miller

The Phone Call

Cecilia Conducci was pacing the library's hardwood floors in disbelief. The words that left Sir Nicholas DeBury's mouth had the Italian woman confounded, bewildered, and momentarily shocked.

The look on her face resembled a mouse which had suddenly realized it had mistakenly dropped its guard and wound up as prey - entrapped in the claws of some skillful cat. The Italian woman could hardly grasp the concept nor remotely digest what she was hearing from the mouth of the Englishman.

"Do not play games with us, signore," the woman said, eyeing DeBury with a look of staunch aggravation. "What are you trying to say? This book... this libro we have stolen......... it is some fake?" she said, pointing to the book the Englishman had thrown down.

Nicholas DeBury met her frustration with the same look of aggravation. His face was turning deeper shades of red as each second ticked away. A copy of the Manuscripta Diabolica was in front of them. But it was unquestionably a fraudulent rendition of the real book they had been after. It was completely worthless. There had been no mark or seal on the final leaf, and the binding was eighteenth century at the earliest. A moron well acquainted with book binding, could have seen the obvious difference.

"Lessen your tone," he said with authority. "You have managed to steal the wrong book, that is all. It is as simple as that. It would appear money does not always afford one the best of services." DeBury proved he could be as insulting as he was direct.

Vincent rose from the chair where he had been smoking an unfiltered cigarette. He was becoming as noticeably upset as his sister. There was a look of exhaustion on his face and he was in no mood for DeBury to try and weasel out of the balance of payment they were due. They were professional thieves- the best in the world. They had executed the theft with precision and had procured the object they had been after. Now, this Englishman was not just accusing them of having stolen the wrong book, but he had insulted the integrity of their craft, and in doing so, insulted them as individuals. One should think twice before doing such to an Italian, he thought.

"I do not understand, signore," the Italian thief spoke up as he lifted himself from the couch and let a cloud of smoke pour from his lips. "We relied on your man- this 'Sean' person, to identify the correct volume. What you have in your hands is that very book. Whatever problem you have at this point no longer concerns the three of us."

The Italians were less one member of their team at this point. Simone Pisano, the mastermind behind the technical aspects of their criminal enterprise, had returned to Italy after the heist at the Smithsonian Institution. For reasons he had never admitted to anyone, he hated England, and he hated the English people. He had resigned himself to let Vincent, Cecilia, and Luigi deal with DeBury. He would await word back in Venice- a place he never liked to be too far from.

DeBury, though agitated with Vincent and his sister, remained calm. It was his nature to be smug and calculatingly direct at all times. This moment was no different. "That's where you're wrong," he returned, turning away from Cecilia and in the direction of Il Fantasma himself. "You did not think to check and see if he had in his possession another volume? I paid for the best of thieves. Do not think I am prepared to pay for this worthless volume you have brought me," he stated, addressing the fake copy of the Manuscripta Diabolica lying on the coffee table in front of the thief. “Obtain the book I was promised, then we’ll complete our business arrangement and I will pay you the agreed upon amount.”

Cecilia fumed with all the fury of a housewife finding her husband in bed with another woman. “Sean is dead!” she chimed. “The only thing that ignorant fool had was the clothes on his back and a duffel bag with a few lira and some street clothes. I separated our ties with a gun. I can do the same for our relationship as well, if that is what you would like.”

“Then one would assume we have a problem, wouldn’t they?” DeBury said watching her huff around the room.

”No, signore,” Vincent said, “You have a problem,” he emphasized, pointing at DeBury with the cigarette burning between his fingers.

As Vincent delivered the statement, Luigi Basso stepped forward and reached into his coat as if to extract a more convincing means of ending the discrepancy between the two groups. The Italians were not accustomed to lending themselves out for hire and not receiving proper payment for their efforts.

Nicholas DeBury remained calm. He even smirked, allowing both Cecilia and Luigi to present their weapons as he sipped on a glass of Cabernet Sauvignon. He was not use to being handled by anyone- let alone the likes of the bunch trying to threatening him now.

“I am not about to play games,” he said, swirling the wine in his glass, “Let me put things another way,” he said; “I have employed-”

De Bury was not allowed to finish the delivery of his statement. There was a sudden intrusion as Finneas Frakes entered the room.

“Pardon me, sir,” the butler said, eyeing the weapons drawn in the direction of his employer, “but it seems as though there is an urgent message for you on the phone. Shall I bring it to you?” He said seemingly unfazed at the bodily threat being suggested by the Italians and their guns.

“I am quite busy at present, Finneas,” he snapped. “Perhaps you could take a message?”

“Sir,” the butler began again, paying DeBury’s guests even less attention, “The caller claims himself to be one Sean Wilde. I should think the call to be of some importance. Shall I still put him on hold?”

DeBury smiled to himself and watched as everyone positioned about the room froze in some stupor at the very mention of the book scout's name. DeBury had a hunch Sean might still be alive, but chose not to share the reasons with his present company. If Cecilia had shot the American where she said she had, there was no way he should have survived a professional hit. No logical way, that is.

"Transfer him to the library's speaker phone, if you would be so, kind Finneas."

"Very good, sir," the thin man said as he excused himself from the room, closing the glass door behind him. Before doing so, he glanced at the beautiful Cecilia Conducci, smiling at her for a split second. She chose not to respond, but holstered her weapon instead. Finneas and his thin, pale form had creeped Cecilia out from their first meeting months ago. There was something the Italian woman didn't like about the perverted way he looked at her.

Nicholas DeBury stood from his chair and placed the empty glass on the table in front of himself. He then placed his hands behind his back and began a deliberate pacing about the room. There was momentary static from some invisibly placed speaker system on the upper library wall as he waited for the book scout to begin speaking.

"Sean?" he said, calling out to the air, and awaiting some response.

"Back from the dead," the voice said.

Cecilia's heart sank. Sean was really alive. The sound of his voice made her brother collapsed back down on the couch. He was just as confused as she was. Luigi Basso just looked dumbfounded as if he was still wondering where the voice was coming from.

"Missing something?" the voice said sarcastically.

"Hello, Mr. Wilde," DeBury said with a smile, "So good to hear from you." He was ignoring Sean's directive. "I was beginning to wonder where you had run off to."

"Oh, cut the shit," the voice said as his northern American accent resonated through the line. "I know you probably didn't expect to hear from me," Sean said, "but the damnedest thing happened after I died."

"Please tell us, Sean," DeBury stated nodding his head as if it were he who was approving the continuation of their conversation. "We are all here. Vincent, Cecilia, Luigi, and myself. What exactly happened after you died? Spare us no details. Leave nothing out."

"Well," the voice stated, "I came back! "

"How fortunate for all," the Englishman said, "Shall I alert the papers?"

"Please do," Sean said, now speaking with the same pomposity as DeBury. "And while you're informing them of my resurrection, please don't leave out the fact that I managed to acquire the Smithsonian's copy of the Manuscripta Diabolica. The real one. Not the fake one you have. Be sure you tell them I tricked some third- rate Italian thieves and sent them packing with the wrong book and their tails between their legs," he said, knowing everyone but DeBury was probably fuming with contemptuous feelings. "Oh, and don't forget the fact that /have the book you want."

"Now, Mr. Wilde......"

"And make sure Cecilia knows she was a lousy f-"

"Go to hell!" the Italian woman screamed to the air.

"Ah............. there she is," Sean said, knowing Cecilia could see him smiling in her mind's eye. "Hey," he directed his words towards her, "How's tricks?"

DeBury boldly put his hand over the woman's mouth as it opened, ready to send inflammatory remarks into the air. It was an extremely bold move on the part of the Englishman. Cecilia was really pissed.

"Sean?"

"Yes?"

"May I have my book, please?"

"Perhaps."

"What is it that you want?"

"Hold on," he said, "I'm still thinking about whether or not to part with it."

"Please, my friend...... take all the time you need."

As DeBury played games with Sean over the phone, Vincent left the couch to console his sister whose face looked as red as the noon day sun. She had been upstaged and scorned at the same time. This made her altogether inconsolable. Luigi reacted with as smart of a decision as he had ever had in his life. He said nothing at all and stayed clear of Cecilia.

"Sean.... are you still there?" DeBury asked after giving the American time to think.

"I'm here."

"Instruct me what I can do to retrieve my book."

"Okay DeBury," Sean began, "Listen closely."

"Is there any other way one should listen?"

"I'm not joking around..."

"Understood, my friend," he said, "Please continue."

"I want a meeting on some kind of neutral ground. Someplace I don't run the risk of being killed a second time."

"You pick the place," the man said, "But realize........ you have nothing to fear from me."

"Look," Sean said with a sigh they all could hear, "I've got no time for any more games, and I'm not getting in the position I was in before. We all know I should be dead. But here I am. The basic point of this is simple- you promised me two million dollars for my help when this crap started, and I want the rest of my money. And of course, to be left alone."

"A simple request," DeBury acknowledged, "And what of my book?"

There was a pause of hesitation. Then, Sean began to speak. "Meet me at Anthony Taylor Rare Books on Charring Cross Road, the day after tomorrow at twelve noon. Come alone. This deal is between you and me. Send the Italians back to their boot-shaped country. If I see them, consider the book and our arrangement null and void. Oh, and make sure you bring two suitcases each filled with five hundred thousand dollars each. We'll then make the exchange, and God willing, never see one another again."

"A respectable plan."

"Yeah, something you're probably not use to."

"Now, let's not be harsh," DeBury said. "Let me assure you now that it was never in my plan to have you harmed. That is the unfortunate hazard one sometimes crosses when dealing with individuals of a low moral compass. You have my humblest of apologies."

"Your excuses and unsympathetic bullshit mean nothing to a dead man, so let's not go down this road. I want what I was promised. And I want to never see you again."

"I shall grant you both wishes. Be assured."

"Then I'll see you on Charring Cross in two days."

"At noon. Yes."

"Good-by, Sir Nicholas."

"Good-day, Mr. Wilde."

As Sean let the phone's receiver come to rest on the frame, he let out a sigh. Making the call had been hard. He wanted nothing to do with these people or this situation again, but he knew nothing was over until it was over. He would have to finish the game and face DeBurywhatever the outcome. Three days from now all of this would be behind him. If things went his way, he would not only walk away alive, but very wealthy and free from company he hated. If things went bad...... well, there was always death.

Sean looked out the window and into the rolling waves of the Sicilian ocean. He paid little attention to the men clamoring about behind him. He had a mental plan for what they would do. And he afforded himself the next day to go over it with his new acquaintances. He had sent Jaco back to Venice earlier that day. His friend had helped him as much as Sean was willing to allow. He hoped to see the little taxi driver again. But those hopes rested on his own shoulders, careful planning, and lots of luck. Over the setting sun, he thought he could see a dove flying just off in the distance. Probably just a seagull, he thought. Sean Wilde then closed his eyes and did something he hadn't done since the death of his father. He began to pray to a God he wasn't sure he believed in.

As Nicholas DeBury took calculation of the rouges gathered in his library, he began mulling over a preponderance of ideas and how things should be handled. Sean was not living past their future meeting, that was a fact. And he would be reacquainted with his book. This was also to be fact.

Vincent Conducci turned from his sister, much more relaxed now than he had been before Sean's call. He realized the only way any of this was going to work out was if everyone worked together. It was stupid to bicker amongst themselves. They needed their remaining payment, then they could deal with DeBury their own way. Vincent was often the voice of reason within the group.

"How shall we aid you," he said, humbling himself before his employer.

"The fool wishes us to meet him along the crowded streets of Charring Cross. Here is the opportunity for us to put right our former wrong," he said, beginning to pace the hardwood floor of the massive library. "I want Luigi to remain in close proximity to me, but well-disguised in the crowds of people who will be perusing the bookstalls. Vincent," he said, addressing the Italian couple seated on the couch, "you and Cecilia stay further back, out of sight. If anything should go wrong, you will serve as our protective insurance. When Sean and I meet, he will most likely berate me with some foul language his temper is prone to administer. Once he has satisfied this yearning, we will then make the exchange. When he rises to leave, Luigi will approach from behind, and take the American out. Be sure to use a silencer on your weapon," he said, meeting Luigi's eye. "We want no trouble. With the aid of you, my friends, Sean Wilde has no business leaving Charring Cross Road alive."

"Very well," Vincent said turning from DeBury.

"Let's make no mistakes this time, my friends."

Vincent turned around addressing his employer's concern. "Sean Wilde is dead, Sir Nicholas. He just doesn't know it."

De Bury smiled as he bent over and renewed his glass with the half-emptied bottle of wine. "I think, my friends," he began rising with a full glass of wine, "deep in his heart, he does realize he's dead. He just needs our confirmation, that's all."

"Then we shall give him his wish," Vincent said, raising his own glass in an effort to toast DeBury.

"Indeed," the Englishman said, bringing their glasses together, "We shall indeed."

"Here all that live no more; preserved they lie,
in tombs that open to the curious eye."

George Crabbe

A Manuscript is Born

There was a musty odor emanating from the walls of the library, but Father Andreas Koutrakos paid very little attention to the smell. His mind was focused on the one thing that had now taken on a meaning of paramount importance- the creation of a manuscript from Lucifer's confession.

But this was not to be a manuscript like any other that had ever been created before. This would be an assemblage of words and illuminated miniatures from the mouth of Lucifer himself. A testament of sorts. A confession infernal. There would exist nothing like it in all of Christendom, and it would stand as a work of unparalleled importance in understanding the world of man from the point of view of the Devil himself. The old monk would make sure of that if he did nothing else.

It would not be a book for the uneducated or the lay person. And there was one sure way to control this.

Each chapter would be written in a different language and each initial letter would be illuminated with a different picture (there would be ten chapters total). On the frontis or the opening page, there would be a picture of Lucifer as drawn by the old monk - both in his angelic form and in the form of a demon as he had appeared. The volume would also be decorated in the finest floral patterns and pictures. He would spare no effort and take whatever time was necessary. This book would be his personal triumph, showcasing all the skills he possessed as both a scribe and skilled illuminator. He would put his very heart and mind into the matter. The creation of this book was to be his parting gift to a world he only now had come to understand at all.

The first step in the process found Father Koutrakos on his knees in the solemn darkness of the library. His hands were clasped tightly together as the remnants of slow burning candles flickered behind him. His eyes focused on the iconography around him and he looked at the wood beams overhead as if they were all that barred the monk from seeing Heaven itself. Hesitating no longer, he strained himself to pray.

His first request was to ask the being he had worshipped his whole life to imbibe his work with greatness, and to allow the completion of it before his death. He wished the work to be blessed. But even as he felt the request leave his mouth. there was some sense of being alone. That what and whom he was speaking to, was not listening. There was a strange feeling within the monk that the creation of the book was something he should not be doing. Yet still he prayed, calculating each and every word for the greater glory of the being that made him.

When he was finished, several hours later, he rose from the stone floor, his bones creaking with the simplicity of the motion. The time had come for the elder monk to assemble the things that would be needed for the project to begin.

He shuffled from the room's center and made his way to the bookshelf, swatting the thin layer of cobwebs that swayed from each tier of shelving.

He noticed, in the depths of madness that had overtaken sanity and encapsulated him in a world where nothing now mattered but the book, that there existed some void in Lucifer's absence. An emptiness that caused him to hate himself for feeling this way. Perhaps there had been some human quality in Lucifer that the monk had found a likeness with. He dare not ponder such a thought for long.

Shaking the idea from his mind, his aged hand, soft and wrinkled, reached for a stack of dried vellum parchment. He pulled the loosely placed group of pages from the shelf and shuffled for a piece that was in decent enough condition to support the weight of his well illuminated words. His goal was to find a surface that was free from the imperfections that often appeared from the drying of the animal skins used to create the parchment. None were perfect, but he came upon a piece that was smooth and pliable. This would support the title page, he thought.

He then folded the vellum into quarters, and carried the skin to the lectern on which the creational process was to begin.

Next, the old monk pricked the page with a sharp knife and began to rule the page such that each line would evenly support the text he was going to write. The process was tedious, but altogether necessary. This was to be a work of perfected style and artistry. When the book was completed, it would rival any manuscript that had ever been produced.

It was now necessary to pick the tools for which would carry the deliverance of words to the page. The monk began shuffling about for the right quill, or pen. Each was made from the feather of some large bird and he preferred to use those from sea gulls, which he had occasioned himself to collect on the beach just below the shadow of Docheiariou's mount. Lifting the quill that suited him the best, he picked up his knife once more from the desk and sliced the tip in an effort to sharpen the feather for writing. He then allowed the ready- made quill to rest on the table and set about to create the ink that would be needed for the script.

Father Koutrakos made his way towards the shelves again, where in a large jar he kept sap from an acacia tree. He brought the jar to the table and then poured its contents into the hollowed horn of a goat which had been inverted within the writing desk. Next he poured some soot from a used candle, mixing it with the dried sap. Now he had a mixture of ink which would serve the purpose of his writing.

Then, as if calculated from the very beginning, the old man did something unprecedented.

He took the sharp blade of the knife, and as it gleamed in the candle light, he ran the blade across his arm ever so gently. As blood trickled forth from his arm, he lifted his appendage over the horn which held his ink, and mixed his own blood with the blackened substance inside. His life-force would serve as a facet of the ink. He was now forever bound to the book which he was about to create. Whether an act of madness or that of artistic license, the creation of the manuscript was now underway.

The old man paused as sweat poured feverishly from his brow. He shook his upper body until the robe encasing him loosened, falling to his waist. Free from the material, and cooling somewhat, he pressed the quill to the page as a burgundy ink flowed to the parchment on which the connection was made. Images raced through the old man's mind. Images of the demon. Images of Hell. Images of mankind's demise through its own proclivitive nature to sin.

He pressed the writing utensil hard and allowed it to flow in a circular motion that would render a large letter, or capital, to the page. He then outlined the letter with floral designs and outlined compartments which would serve as guidance for the images he would illustrate on the inside. Complete focus was important, but difficult. Lucifer's words were guiding his pen, regardless of how he wished the control to be his alone.

Perhaps the confession had gone too far and for too long. It mattered very little now. What mattered was the book. This book.

In the pervading darkness of Docheiariou's sealed library, Father Andreas Koutrakos began to pen the book that would house the confession of the most villainous entity that would ever be - Lucifer, the fallen angel.

Under the flickering of only two candles, the old man hovered over the pages. He placed the nib of his quill to the parchment and began a calligraphic motioning. The creation of the manuscript was now underway.

Outside the sealed library door, Father Chrysostomus rose for the first time in two days of uncompromised vigil and prayer.

It might seem incredible to one who lives a secular life - the idea that one could spend forty-eight hours in prayer- but the monk, especially this monk, was of a far different make-up than a common individual. Each man knew God on a deep and intimate level. This, more than anything else, was the hardest to rationalize with a man of common faith.

The abbot felt exhausted and knew he had done all he could do for his friend held captive on the other side. Now it was up to the intervention of God Almighty. The force which had opened the door and resealed it again was beyond this world. And unfortunately, beyond his power to stay.

The monks who remained in prayer behind him began rising to their feet one by one. They too, were exhausted and weakened from the vigil. Each comforted one another and turned their gaze toward the large wood structure that separated them from Father Koutrakos.

Father Chrysostomus was not doing well with what had happened to his friend. He could not contain his own anger which at this time was welling out of control. As penitent as he was, he was still human. Still a man. And all men were fallible to their own compulsions of rage and anger.

The abbot began slamming the door with the soft flesh of his palms several times, exhibiting uncontrolled bursts of anger. The three monks closest to him tried to stay his rage, but he shook free and shouted some demand into the open air, directing his outburst to whatever presence held his friend and colleague prisoner on the other side.

When his hands slapped the door one last time, they stuck, as if some force held them flush to the door. He tried to move them but the door would not allow it. It was as if the tar that held the door closed now held him as well.

As he struggled to remove himself, the door altered itself. The wood began to twist and contort until it no longer resembled a door, having now shaped itself in the form of some monstrous face which spoke with authority, yet refusing to release the monk held fast to it.

"Leave- this- place!" it said in a low and grumbling tone which sent the monks into a frenzy of terror-laden confusion. Then the door returned to its flattened form, but lit itself with a red glow which scorched the palms of Father Chrysostomus as it released its hold on the abbot.

There was a strange bellowing sound of laughter each man could hear regurgitating throughout the hallways. As the confusion mounted and Chrysostomus tried to stay the burns on his hands, every candle blew out on each sconce that lined the cloister walls behind the monks.

Now cradled in the darkness, the monks closed in around each other and began a new and more purposeful vigil. One that would hope to see them through the evil that now resided in more than just this library. Shivering, cold, and scared far beyond reason, each man began to chant soft prayers in the blackness that surrounded them. God, it seemed, was nowhere to be found.

There was no way to calculate or even arrive at some understanding of just how much time had passed since he had begun, but one thing was for certain - Father Koutrakos had no intention of slowing his pace.

He had already completed the first chapter, and found himself looking back over each page and finding great pride in the illuminated quality of each illustration. The words were of gothic design and the first chapter was penned in Latin, for it was the universal language of the scholarly. One would have to look no further than the opening paragraph to grasp the inner contents of what was to be found as the reader foraged further through the book's pages.

It was named the Manuscripta Diabolica, or The Devil's Manuscript. There was no musing over that title- one could be assured of that.

The old monk, satisfied with the title page and the first chapter, set aside the writing and stood for a momentary stretch. His bones, frail now from age and stress, creaked again with such effort from the act. He then walked back to the bookshelf and selected another piece of vellum, folding it once again into quarters, and returned to his chair.

Placing the page flat, he scored a new quill with his knife and began to dip the nib into the goat homed inkwell. He noticed that his arm was now healed, as if it had never been cut at all. This was odd, he thought. Yet it was nothing to what he had witnessed in this room over the last twenty-one years.

Before he began the next chapter, he noticed he had attracted a visitor of sorts.

It was the tiny spider that he had watched incapacitate a fly earlier that evening. It scurried across the desk as if it was on some purposeful mission the old abbot was unaware of. The tiny arachnid came to a halt just beside a bundle of quills that were gathered to one corner of the table. The monk, instead of squishing the tiny beast as might be expected, decided to befriend the creature and allow it to observe his skill. Perhaps madness had found a home in the monk. Or perhaps he just was in appreciation of having the company of his new companion. However the friendship began, it was sealed with the monk's permitting the tiny beast a smile before he returned to the work at hand.

The spider seemed to watch from atop the pile of writing instruments as the monk put pen to page, and in Greek this time, began to illuminate the second chapter of his manuscript.

The old monk was completely unaware of what was transpiring on the other side of the library door. His fellow monks were now glimpsing a side of Hell he had been unable to properly describe. For them, the infernal realization of what was coming had not yet fully unfolded itself. For Father Andreas Koutrakos, Hell had unfolded itself all too clearly.

"Each morning puts a man on trial and each evening passes judgment."

Roy L. Smith

Charring "Double" Cross

Sean took a deep breath as the flame from his lighter ignited the soft tip of his cigarette. He reluctantly paced back and forth underneath a sign that read Anthony Taylor Rare Books. The time on his watch showed it was eleven fifty-five a.m. If Nicholas DeBury kept his word, he would be here in five minutes.

Gray clouds had positioned themselves above London and a thick, pervasive fog was still prominently resting in the alleyways and corridors below. For Sean Wilde, one way or another, Charring Cross Road was where everything was going to end. This had been the place where not so long ago, he had sipped tea with Anthony Taylor. This had been the place his father had brought him as a boy to experience book-hunting at its finest.

But all that had changed. Charring Cross was a different place now.

An ominous wind ruffled the book scout's un-tucked Armani shirt as he scanned the street comer for any sign of DeBury. Sean had taken enough time to shop for some new clothes while he was in Sicily, and this, if nothing else, made him feel more comfortable and confident. He looked behind him into the empty bookshelves of the boarded-up store and thought how nice Anthony Taylor had treated him when he first arrived in London, and how much he would have liked to have explored a relationship with the man. But DeBury, Sean was sure, had seen fit to kill his friend Anthony Taylor. Just like God had done to his father, so many years ago. Secretly he would have been happy to avenge them both. But today, he would tackle the easier of the two beings.

The former book scout exhaled a cloud of smoke and tried to calm his nerves. If everything went according to his plans, the meeting with his English adversary would be over in about fifteen minutes. If it didn't, well, death was a means to an end.

A trickle of rain fell from the sky and burst at his feet. Perhaps this was a dark, foretelling sign. But, it could've just been a precursor to another shitty day in London, he mused. He held out a hand as if to see if anymore would fall. He was comfortable now. He was in his jeans and a paisley shirt. Sean had even taken the time to get his left ear pierced at a London boutique. To him, it served as some rite of passage - like sailors who crossed the equator. He had been dead, and some part of that experience had liberated him.

He took one last puff on the cigarette and then pulled it from his parched lips tossing it to the ground. Extinguishing it underfoot, he now noticed the thickening groups of book hunters weaving in and out of the book shops around him. There was apprehension on his face and a degree of fear in his heart. Once again, Sean Wilde was in a place and a situation where he didn't want to be. So many meanderings played havoc with his thoughts. He wondered about all the misfortune life had brought him and then laughed to himself inside. With all that had happened, it was odd how much he was still fighting for survival. Nothing great seemed to await him in his future, but death still seemed to hold no particular allure either.

"Good-day, Mr. Wilde," a voice called from behind the book scout. Sean whirled around. He had been caught off guard.

There before him stood the individual who had been the cause of his involvement from the very beginning - Sir Nicholas DeBury. Supreme asshole of assholes, he thought.

"It's so very good to see you again," he said with abrasive gall and snobbishness.

The Englishman was well dressed, as Sean would have expected. A long trench coat concealed a bespoke three- piece suit fashioned of some dark woolen material. On his head he wore a hat that leaned slightly to the left. In his left hand there was a cane. In the other hand, he held a suitcase, which presumably held part of Sean's money.

Their eyes met with a clear understanding of what was expected from each. A simple transaction between thieves. The exchange of money for a book. Simple as that. DeBury could see in Sean's eyes a degree of fear, but unlike before, when the book scout had arrived for their first meeting. Something had changed. Behind the fear, Sean looked somewhat confident as well.

The American started to speak as the sky opened slightly, letting a light, misty rain fall upon the meeting. But before the words could come, the book scout felt a nudge of steel poke him from behind. He knew without turning around what it was, just not who was at the other end. Cocking his head to the right ever so slightly, he could see the emotionless stare of Luigi Basso looking back at him. The stature of the man was mirrored in the rain puddle collecting at Sean's feet. There was a gun poised at his back and a heartless idiot holding it. Once again, DeBury usurped immediate control. Sean did his best to keep calm, and looked up at DeBury. The Englishman, looking back at him, parted his square jaw and began to speak.

"I'll have my book, if you please, Sean."

"You must think I'm a fool," the book man responded, "I would have never been so stupid as to have brought it here. It's the one insurance policy I've got left. Call off your dog," he demanded, referencing Luigi Basso and his gun. Sean was attempting to regain some small control of a situation that was already slipping away from him.

"So you've learned a thing or two; Smart boy," DeBury returned. He then nodded and Sean felt the momentary relief as the object eased from his back. "So, my friend, tell me how we are to proceed."

Sean wasted no time in addressing the directive. "Do you have the money?"

"I do," he said. "Do you have the book?"

"Close by."

"Then may I ask what I am to do to obtain it?"

"Trust me," Sean said smiling, "Turn over the two briefcases of bills I asked for, and I'll hand over the manuscript. It's that simple."

DeBury motioned towards Luigi. The Italian stepped from behind Sean and brought over one briefcase and DeBury lifted the other off the ground. placing both before Sean. He then rolled the combination locks on each and clicked them open. Sean's eyes grew wild at the sight of the money neatly packed in each. It was like some drug deal scene from a movie. Only this was very real. The book scout tried to conceal his astonishment. He surveyed the crowds of people around the street, hoping no one was paying them any attention. There was more money in each briefcase than he had ever seen in his whole life. And there it was- real and right in front of him. Sean nodded with approval and DeBury closed the briefcases.

"These are yours, Sean, just as I promised," he said, sliding them in Sean's direction, "Now, may I please have my book?"

"Wait here."

"Where are you going?"

"I told you the book was close by. Wait here."

DeBury had little choice but to comply. It was he who was unnerved a little bit, but he could not do a thing about the situation. At this point he would do anything to have his coveted manuscript back in the hands of his family's possessions. Sean could see the over enthusiasm and did what he could to use that to his benefit.

Sean stood up, sneered in the direction of Luigi, and walked away from the table. He then made his way around the corner of Anthony Taylor's boarded up store, just out of DeBury' s sight, and retrieved his duffel bag from a place he had stashed it earlier. He then returned and extracted. the volume from his bag.

There was no denying the actuality of the book. It was The Manuscript a Diabolica. Not a fake. Not a replica. It was the real thing.

DeBury's eyes widened. His face then grew wildly animated. There was a look of madness forming almost as fast as the smile on his lips. He reached out and snatched the volume from Sean's hands as if he were hogging a toy from the other kiddies in daycare. The oiliness of the binding was soft to the touch and he knew as he sat there clasping the book that it was undoubtedly the real thing. He didn't even open the cover before looking back at Sean.

"My friend," he began sarcastically, "Do you have any idea what we have here?"

"I think I do," Sean responded, wholly unconcerned at this point.

"Imagine having a manuscript from God Himself. That is how significant this book is. Interred within these pages is the confession of Lucifer himself. A chronicle of the Devil himself. Imagine it. The only one of its kind. This book," he said, clasping it tightly and rubbing it as though it were an obedient dog, "is priceless beyond words. Worth whatever price need be paid."

"It must be," Sean spat, "You killed enough people to get it."

"What is human life when compared to this?" DeBury stated with the utmost sincerity.

"One of those human lives was mine!"

"Sean," the Englishman said trying to calm him, "You were a necessary sacrifice. A martyr for the cause. Every religion needs someone willing to lay down their lives for its continuum. What more could one who loves books do than give up his life for them?"

DeBury was nuts. On that matter Sean was decidedly certain. Perhaps money had corrupted him, perhaps it was his mother dropping him on the floor as a child. The reason for his insanity and his position really didn't matter. That Sean was not very far away from him- like, in some other country - now that was a problem. There were still questions the book scout would not let alone.

"Did you kill Anthony Taylor?"

"Yes," he responded, "I am afraid I had no choice."

"Why?"

"Because he was always getting in my way," DeBury said nonchalantly. "I had you followed from the time you arrived in London and met Mr. Dodd at the airport. When you left my house and came to Charring Cross, I was mortified by fate's attempt to draw you into his storefront, but it happened nonetheless. I have had more than one altercation with that man over the years of book collecting, and I'm sure if you mentioned my name, he had no kind words for me as well," DeBury stated as if these excuses were justification for the old book seller's death. "But allow me to put things more directly. I was not willing to allow the man to come between this book and myself. It is as simple as that. He had to go. You have my apologies."

"Now I suppose I'm in the way."

"No. But you do know more about me than I'm willing to leave alone. So you will have to be disposed of as well, I am afraid."

The look on Sean's face said it all. It's one thing to imagine an enemy trying an attempt on your life. But it's another altogether to actually have the man tell you to your face -time's up!'

Sean had no time to react.

DeBury stood, turning his back to the book scout and began to walk off. Sean could hear Luigi approach him from behind again. Shortly thereafter, a bullet entered the chamber of a small gun the Italian had aimed directly at Sean.

Suddenly, a sound pierced the air! A gun went off!

Sean's body jerked- reacting involuntarily- as if it had been he who was the recipient of the gunfire. He grasped his stomach where the bullet may have exited, but noticed there was no pain and no visible wound.

Turning toward the direction of the noise, he saw Luigi Basso grasping his chest. The small firearm he had been holding was now rocking on the tip of his forefinger, and his face was as white as a virgin's wedding dress.

Another shot sounded! This time Sean watched the upper portion of the large Italian's head detach from the nose upward. What remained of his body dropped, lifeless, onto the pavement.

Off in the distance, one of Don di Trapani' s assassins smiled at Sean from behind a building. It was his gunshot that had sent Luigi Basso to the other side. The final game was on!

More gunfire sent small pieces of pavement into the air inches from Sean's left foot. When he whirled around, he caught the image of Vincent Conducci and his sister Cecilia dispersing from the spot where they had been hiding. Smoke was rising from ll Fantasma 's left hand. He had a gun! And more importantly- so did Cecilia.

The crowd of book hunters, normally about as reserved as the average person could hope to be, began to scurry about the scene for shelter. Each tried to shield themselves from the gunfire that was surrounding them. Many of these people found release in the imaginary stories of the books they read. Now they were reluctant participants of their own adventure story. People were shocked and caught off guard. Doors to shops slammed, and above, the sky opened up, sending a torrent of rain thundering down. Even in London, this was a bit of crazy activity for mid- afternoon.

Nicholas DeBury had already begun racing in the opposite direction with the Manuscripta Diabolica safely tucked under his arm. He cradled the book as if it were his only child and the salvation of the world depended on his getting it to safety. He was heading in the direction of his limousine, knowing all the while that success was not so far away.

Not far from the scene, Vincent and Cecilia had taken cover behind two unusually large bookstalls and both started firing their weapons in Sean's general direction.

Sean was stuck in the middle of Charring Cross Road, catching fire on both sides. He couldn't find shelter and it was only a matter of time before he was going to become the unwelcome recipient of a bullet.

Without warning, a figure darted out from nowhere. The large shape managed to shield the book scout from the hail of gun fire, but it embraced a bullet from Vincent's gun at the same time. Sean fell to the ground, toppled by the weight of the man who had charged him. Coughing and scraped up, he lifted the man from atop him and rolled his limp form away. He realized immediately that the man was dead from a wound to the head. The face was recognizable. It was one of Trapani's men, Carlo Bugatti. The man's unwavering loyalty had bought the book scout some extra time.

Back at the limousine, a smile slid across the face of Nicholas DeBury. He could see before the back door of his limo come flying open as if it could read his mind and waiting for the Englishman with open arms. He turned to quickly see the chaos he had started playing out behind him, then he hastily ducked into the vehicle.

When he landed on the leather seat in back, he saw the business end of a double barrel shotgun staring him in the face. Behind the gun was a Sicilian holding it and smiling. Roberto di Veccho, one of Sean's hired assailants, was now in control of the Englishman's future movements. DeBury cursed himself for his own miscalculation.

Elsewhere, Sean noticed the dead Sicilian's gun beside the body lying next to him. He picked up the shiny weapon and began to return fire in the direction of Cecilia and Vincent.

The two Italians dispersed their momentary location as quickly as they could, keeping some distance from the pursuant book scout. It wasn't Sean they were concern about, but whoever was under his employ. That's what scared them. Neither the English book collector nor the group of Italian thieves had counted on Sean resourcefulness. They had only focused on his ignorance. They were deciding how grave an error this had been.

Cecilia turned around mid-stride and withdrew her weapon- aiming the gun at Sean. The bullet left the barrel like a torpedo, but Sean dove to the ground, causing the shot to miss him as it grazed off the brick wall behind him. Cecilia fired again, but her aim was even further off this time. The Italian woman was nervous. This was all wrong. Nothing ever went this poorly. She gave up focusing her efforts on Sean's demise and tried catching up with her brother, who was further up the street.

After she had rejoined him, Vincent and Cecilia turned down an alleyway in an effort to keep clear of Sean and take the battle from the frightened onlookers of Charring Cross. Up in the distance, a new figure appeared before the couple.

Nick Gravano, another Sicilian contemporary of Sean's, was blocking their path. He had a gun drawn and had the two thieves cornered. Sean had just entered the alleyway behind them as well. His shirt was ripped from his earlier meeting with the pavement, and he was weak, but this didn't prevent him from raising his gun at the two figures up ahead. Cecilia and Vincent were trapped with no route of escape.

Vincent dropped to one knee and took his best shot in the direction of the new face up ahead. He was far more worried about the Italian-looking man than he was Sean. The bullet left the chamber at an incredible speed, and caught Nick Gravano just above his knee as he tried to dodge the Italian's shot. Gravano made a more effective means of returning fire. And unfortunately for Cecilia's brother, his shot was a bit more successful.

The 9mm bullet from Nick's gun took out Vincent's lower jaw completely.

Il Fantasma collapsed at the foot of his sister, writhing in horrible pain. Blood was gurgling from the empty space below his upper jaw. His hands searched the air for something to hold as his weapon fell to the street. The pain proved to be intense, and Cecilia dropped immediately to his side, offering what momentary comfort she could. She cradled the dying man in her arms as tightly as she could, but he could say nothing. His whole body gyrated uncontrollably in her arms. The pain was gratuitous and unmerciful. And for Vincent, there was no way to escape it.

Cecilia Conducci was a mess. She had collapsed into a woman whose tear-smeared mascara and matted hair resembled little of the radiance and beauty she had once exuded. Her brother was dying in her arms and there was nothing she could do. In a moment, Vincent Conducci would be no more.Il Fantasma would be no more. They were finished.

The Italian woman looked up from where she had been consoling her brother and saw Sean approaching from her left. The American was moving closer but she had a feeling he wasn't about to use the weapon he was holding. Then, she quickly turned to her right and saw the man Vincent had shot limping towards her as well. She spent little time in thought. Her well-manicured hand reached down and lifted the gun she had been carrying and she pointed it in the direction of the book scout. The silver weapon caught the book scout off guard.

Sean froze in his tracks. He drew his weapon as well, but he knew his own apprehension to actually use it might cost him his life. He could see, just beyond Cecilia, his Italian friend had drawn his weapon as well, ensuring, if nothing else that Cecilia would be caught in a crossfire. One way or another, the Italian woman couldn't take them both out at the same time. Or could she?

Then Cecilia did something that surprised both Sean and Nick Gravano.

Before Sean could react, the woman looked down at her dying brother, then back at Sean. In an instant, she turned the gun back on herself, pressing the muzzle of the weapon to her temple.

"Wait!" Sean screamed as if something he could say was going to change the matter.

The Italian thief parted her full lips and smiled defiantly. Then, in the next instant, Cecilia Conducci pulled the trigger.

A momentary blast ensured this part of the game was finally over.

Cecilia Conducci's brain tissue entered the atmosphere at once, leaving the comfortable encasement of her skull. Her limp and lifeless form collapsed atop the brother she had been trying to comfort. There was nothing to resemble the beautiful woman Sean had met in Venice a week ago. Nothing but a mass of human tissue that had no business being there. Like it or not, she was dead.

Sean bowed his head. A solitary tear joined the streaming rainwater gliding down his face. It wasn't so much that he was in love with Cecilia. It was perhaps that he thought there was some chance of saving her from all this mess. From this life. She was so beautiful. Yet now the woman lay, mangled, on top of her brother. A heap of deconstructed flesh and tissue that had once been two thinking, breathing human beings. This was not the kind of revenge he had been after. When would all the death end? he thought.

When he lifted his head from the bloody sight, his eyes met those of his accomplice, Nick Gravano. The man had a bad wound above his knee, and blood was dripping from the open hole. He aided the man as best as he could, giving him a shoulder to lean on until they could get him somewhere they could bandage him up.

Another figure caught the comer of his eye, too.

He turned to see the face of Sir Nicholas DeBury staring back at him. Only this time, DeBury was at the mercy of someone else. Sean could see just behind DeBury, a familiar face at the other end of a shotgun.

"What shall we do with this one, my friend?" Roberto di Vecchio said, smiling from behind DeBury's right shoulder.

Sean stood there, supporting the weight of his friend. He could think of a lot of things they could do with Sir Nicholas DeBury. An awful lot of things...

> "Books are bound in many different styles, varying according to their age and value, and the use to which they are to be put."
>
> Arthur W. Johnson

A Clever Binding

Madness had finally embraced Andreas Koutrakos.

For the monk, there was little cause to gratify the illusion of sanity. The old abbot was well detached from the cares of the world around him. What consumed him at his deepest core was the final assembly of pages that lay spread about the table before him.

This man had committed himself to no other instruction save the completion of his manuscript. And in doing this, he had separated himself from his attention to the outer world around him. But such consumption of detail and self- removal from all else is what defines madness.

A normal man with reasonable intellect has the ability to resist the depths to which despair often gives way to the loss of one's sanity, but the monk was somehow different. He had allowed himself to converse willingly with this bit of insanity. Thus, it made a home within the man. Thought and reason had taken refuge behind the weight of utter madness.

On the table before the monk was a stack of vellum. Upon each page was illustrated and written the entire confession of Lucifer as had been relayed to him by the demon himself. It was as magnanimous as any work present in the library, for it was the testimony of the very angel who had fallen from Heaven.

The old monk placed the last drop of ink upon the final sentence and then rested his quill on the table. Each leaf and every page held the musings of the man who had compiled them. He watched as the remaining ink bled from the nib of the writing instrument and followed its flow across the desk's oaken grooves until it nearly came in contact with the spider that had been watching from the far comer of the table. The tiny bystander jumped at the approaching river of ink and glided across the top pile of parchment, as the monk watched the arachnid's tiny limbs effort the rest of the its body across the table. The soft placement of the limbs didn't even do so much as press the vellum where the little spider had trodden.

Father Koutrakos sat with his heart pounding and his eyes dilated. He was little more than a shell of the man he had been. He had been consumed by the brevity of the work before him. It had taken hold, this material, and sucked out what remained of the man who had compiled it. Such was the sacrifice of putting Lucifer's infernal testimony into words. Such was his private road to Hell.

If the old man believed the conversation with old demon had not come with a price, he could be assured now that it had. To the monk, these things were of little importance. What mattered was the work. What mattered was the book. The Manuscripta Diabolica.

What had been written on these pages was a warning for generations to come. A clearly defined guide to Hell, or Heaven, and a footnote to the Bible itself.

Yet something was still missing.

What sat before the old man was little more than an assemblage of vellum pages. They had no real form. No structured aspect of being. What they needed was to be bound. They needed a proper binding. No book could come to completion without the aid of a front cover and a back cover. How else would the inner contents be protected?

The monk lifted his body, which seemed even more decrepit than before, and began to search for some material in which to aid his task. He flipped through his supplies resting on the lower level of the bookshelf, but could find nothing in which to aid his desires. He then lifted the candle from the desk and set about looking elsewhere in the library.

The attempt was a futile one. He could find no leathers of any kind.

No calfskin, no goatskin, no skin of any type with which to begin the outer construction of the book.

But, the beauty of insanity lies not in what others see of a man, but the illusions to which the man sees so clearly inside himself. This ideal helped foster the monk's ability to think outside himself. To reach deep into his artistic scope and withdraw the only idea that seemed of any choice. He needed an outer binding. And the book could be assured he would give it his utmost attention.

Father Koutrakos allowed his eyes to fall on the object lying next to his quill. A knife gleamed at him in the candle light. The very object he had now sufficed himself to use in a new way. He reached forward, scooping the blade from its position on the lectern. And in the depths of his madness, from the very pit of his soul, he came to an idea.

A wonderfully unimaginable, horrible idea.

He now had a means of protecting the pages before him. Yet, another revelation had been revealed to him. There was no denying what needed to be done. He looked to the door which led from the library, and concluded the means in which the further construction would continue.

Just outside the sealed library door, a group of monks had maintained their assembly and vigil. Each man was upon his knees praying fastidiously for their brother held captive inside. The Devil was on the other side of that door as well, and each monk knew that keeping to their prayer was the only way they could hope to aid the beloved Andreas Koutrakos. Besides, they were afraid.

Something horrible was with each man. Something that seemed to be watching and waiting. Something without the same fears as they.

The first monk to raise his head was Father Chrysostomus.

Looking up from his crouched position, he noticed something odd about the door. It had opened slightly- about an eighth of an inch. There seemed to be no tar concoction sealing it closed.

Not anymore, at least.

He tugged at his garment and lifted himself from the floor. He was shaking but trying to dissuade his nerves. Behind him, thirty-six monks were ending their prayers and rising in an effort to join him.

Chrysostomus walked toward the creaking door with great apprehension. From out of his robe, his bony hand emerged to grasp the door's handle. A noise from behind, perhaps nothing more than a rat scurrying about in the distance, frightened him, and he wasted no time in withdrawing his hand.

Once he resolved himself to admit his own fear - fear of what lay in wait on the other side of the door- he took a gulp and raised his hand to the door again.

Where is your faith? a voice seemed to say. Where is your trust in Me?

Slowly, he began to press the door forward. The darkness before him embraced his approach as if they were long lost friends.

His bare feet stepped, one in front of the other, until that very darkness surrounded him totally. No candle illuminated the passage, and he could see absolutely nothing. His first action was to gain control of his own fear. This was not easy as each leg shook violently with every step he took. Little sounds would cause his heart to jump. But his friend had entered this room and his mind was made up that he wasn't coming out without him.

Having suppressed the terror as best as he could, he called out in the distance to see if his friend might give some return noise.

There was no response.

Then, in the quiescence of the moment, he thought he could hear a soft whimper coming from a corner area of the darkened library. It was a soft, delicate sniffle perhaps. But it sounded human enough. The mumble, however slight, was reassurance.

The group of monks had crowded the doorway behind him, but none had ventured inside the room with him. Chrysostomus turned to the man closest to him and beckoned him to disconnect a sconce from the wall and hand it to him at once. He could do nothing but falter in the darkness without some form of light to guide him onward.

A monk, Nickos Calloskus, returned to the doorway, and handed the sconce to Father Chrysostomus, placing the object in his right hand. The abbot then turned and, shown the burning light before him, stepped further into the room. He held the object above his head to light as much of the foreground as possible.

The eeriness of the room was somewhat overbearing and Chrysostomus could feel his legs becoming heavy and weak. There was little he could make out, save a large bookshelf to his right. He then heard a cracking noise under his foot, and looked to the ground, where he saw he had stepped on a quill, snapping the object in two. He chose not to acknowledge the feathered writing tool and kept about the business at hand. He motioned himself still further into the darkened chamber.

He turned back for a moment, only to realize the monks who had gathered at the door had still resigned themselves to stay where they were. No man seemed apt to follow behind the abbot. He then turned from their fearful gaze and walked on.

The mumbling was growing stronger now and seemed to be emanating from a specific direction of the room. He was far enough in the room now to where the window was giving him a light clarification of moonlight. Following the beam to the floor, it seemed as if there was a man lying crouched in the darkness.

His need for resolve outweighed his fear, and he quickened his pace in the direction of the figure.

As he approached the window, he held out the sconce and gasped in the darkness. His loose hand cupped his gaping mouth by no control of his own. The sight left him speechless. Tears welled uncontrolled in each eye.

He fell at once to his knees and shook all over, trying not to drop the sconce.

Those monks who stood in the doorway behind him rushed willingly forward as if the consolation of their beloved Chrysostomus outweighed their fear at that very moment. As they crowded to his side they were now able to digest what he was bearing witness to.

Father Koutrakos was lying in a corner, just below the window. His body was propped up against the library walls and his arms lay loose at his sides. He was naked from the waist up, and a red robe was crumpled around his waist. His eyes were widened and dilated like large saucers. His lips seemed parched and curled inward, exposing the black emptiness of a mouth that bore no teeth. Drool slid from one corner of the gaping mouth.

This alone was a terrible sight. But the image of their brother's face is not what had caused the men standing above to shun their eyes and turn away. There was something altogether more horrible.

From the monk's neck to his waist, in two ragged strips, the outer layer of skin was missing completely. It was as if his upper torso had been peeled like the outer layer of an orange. Father Koutrakos's skin had been stripped from the layer of muscle that had held it to his body.

Beside the old monk, lying in the palm of his right hand, was a small knife covered in blood and matted hair. Looking back at the old monk's body, the men could see the bright red layer of exposed tissue where the skin had been, and a pool of blood neatly collecting off to the side of the elder monk. As horrible of a sight as this was, what furthered the torment was the fact that the man before them was still alive! Though they were sure he was far beyond the limits of conversation, he was mumbling incoherently.

The sight of their friend and mentor exposed in such a way, caused many of the monks to rush from the library and find individual consolation elsewhere. Father Chrysostomus kept his status. at the feet of his friend as did the few monks who remained. He was in the throes of trying to console himself.

The image usurped the compass of his moral fiber and he found himself having to withdraw for a moment. He lifted himself from his knees with the aid of two monks, and withdrew back to the empty pit of the room behind him.

The two monks which had aided him then bent down in an effort to try and aid the bloody monk lying on the floor. Each hated himself for being reluctant in their willingness to touch his body. Sure they had witnessed horrible executions in their former life, but there was some self -effacing horror to this scene. Each man had to think, even if only for a moment, the idea that this man, in the throes of madness, could have possibly done this to himself. It was a horrible thing to imagine.

As Father Chrysostomus wandered lightheaded in the darkness, the light from his sconce fell upon a new sight.

Alone sat a lectern in the other comer of the room. Motioning towards the desk, the elder monk brought the light closer to his side so he could see the object of prominence sitting upon it. It was hard to focus properly, due to the effort it was taking to shake the image of his friend lying behind him.

There, among hand prints of blood and hair, sat what appeared to be a newly constructed manuscript.

It was not the book itself that grabbed his attention, but what had gone into its assembly that so befuddled his imagining. He knew instantly how it had been constructed- and this caused him to weep involuntarily at its sight there upon the table.

Father Koutrakos had bound the book in his own skin.

The old monk had assembled the outer layer of his book with the outer layer of himself. The book and he were now one. The old monk had become his own book and, from the look of things, he had done so with his own hands. It was as unthinkable as it seemed unimaginable.

Chrysostomus reached out to the book, but something stayed his hand.

Perhaps his fear of the object was mixed with the abject horror that his friend's very self was part of the volume's construction... But even this could have been a poor excuse. It was altogether something greater, and he knew it.

If Father Koutrakos had told his fellow monks the truth earlier, (and Chrysostomus felt sure he had) then there was some evil to what lay on the table. Some relic of Hell had found its way to Docheiariou.

Still, he had to pick it up.

What existed on the other side of the newly -bound cover of skin must have been of extreme importance to Father Koutrakos. And that thought alone caused him to reach out again.

Chrysostomus' fingers found the volume resting upon the top layer of skin ever so lightly. He seemed to expect something to happen by touching the book, but nothing did. Lifting the book from the table, he noticed the enormity of the volume. Moreover, there was a fact of morbid reality that stood out as well. The skin of his friend had taken unusually well to the binding process. What caused him to recoil was the oiliness of the outer tissue and the blood collecting in small points of the volume. This process must have been painful beyond belief.

The old man then opened the cover.

The first page showed a block illustration of the library he was standing in presently: the monk at his desk, and what appeared to be two angels behind him- one beautiful, the other, a demon. He then read the first words that followed the large illustration:

Manuscripta Diabolica

or

The Confession of Lucifer, fallen Angel
Where it is hereby put forth the confession
of the first angel to fall from heaven as was
told to me between the years anno Domini
1496 to 1517

Father Chrysostomus dropped the book from his hands and brought them to his face. This was all too much for him to bear.

He turned from the desk and wiped the light oil and blood smear from his hands, rubbing his hands on his robe. He looked to his friend who was being cared for by the monks. He then walked towards the man bending down and aiding the others.

He knew it was far too late to help Father Koutrakos.

Blood loss and sheer madness had done far too much damage already and the consequences of not knowing how long he had been in this state were reflected in the weakening motion of the old man's limbs. He mumbled only a short time more, then looked to an icon on the wall.

Father Andreas Koutrakos pointed to the painting in a last hopeless motion. A smile formed on his wrinkled lips.

Chrysostomus followed the direction of the old man's mumble and outstretched arm until he could see the icon hanging from the wall as well. It was an illustration of Christ ascending to Heaven.

The old man's arm fell from the air and his body collapsed into the arms of his friend. Chrysostomus then bowed his head over the limp head of his friend and began to weep incoherently. He could do no more for the monk.

There, in the darkness of the library, Father Chrysostomus cradled the bloodied body of his friend. Father Andreas Koutrakos was now dead, and the world had become a lesser place with his passing.

"I shall tell you a great secret, my friend.
Do not wait for the last judgment, it takes place every day."

Albert Camus

A Final Reckoning

Nicholas DeBury was now on his knees. Behind him, looming above, was a very dangerous assassin anxious for an order to pull the trigger of his shotgun. What was so odd about the Englishman was that he didn't seem to be concerned for his own safety or what was happening to him. He simply held the Manuscripta Diabolica tightly to his chest, keeping silent and watching as Sean approached. He was waiting for the American to say something. Anything. He flinched, feeling the large barrel of a shotgun firmly edging between his shoulder blades. This was not familiar territory for DeBury. He was used to being the aggressor. But all that had changed. Now, he had found himself in a uniquely uncompromising position. The position of helplessness.

Sean Wilde, on the other hand, had never felt more confident in his life.

But this feeling didn't concern him that much. He had just witnessed the death of two people he had not-been properly prepared to deal with. Truthfully, he had not intended for things to get this far out of hand. But the fact was, these events had never been in his control to begin with. At least that's what he told himself. DeBury had held the cards, the playing table, the dice and the casino. Now Sean had taken control of them all. The book scout was sick of his game and wished to finalize his own ready-made conclusion.

Before addressing DeBury, Sean turned to the assassin, Roberto di Vecchio. The Sicilian was standing behind the Englishman with a sinister smile on his face. Sean noticed the man seemed to have no qualms with the idea of separating his captive's head from the rest of him with one well- placed pull of the trigger. But whatever Sean's decision, the resolution needed to hasten itself before the police arrived.

"Say the word," di Vecchio said, with a thick Italian drawl, "And he dies right now."

Sean looked at the assassin and then back at DeBury, who seemed altogether unfazed by what was happening to him. One thing prevailed in the forefront of Sean's mind- that he had seen enough death today to last him two lifetimes. However unscrupulous DeBury had been, and regardless of what this man had put the book scout through, Sean could not order the man's death. This would prove too much for his conscience to bear. Besides, it wasn't who he was. Sean was no killer.

And then there was the book to consider. The Manuscripta Diabolica.

In DeBury' s hands, Sean could see how tightly the man was clinging to the object that had started this whole fiasco. How much death had it caused? How much needless suffering had been propounded by DeBury' s need to possess it? Every aspect of its existence seemed to confound Sean's imaging.

In truth, DeBury looked as if he was preparing to take the book with him to the grave. And with one nod from Sean, the trigger-happy Italian could easily make this probability a part of reality.

Sean looked down at DeBury, shaking his head. The Englishman remained quiet, still saying nothing. He looked up from the book he was holding, watching the rain pour overhead. He could see water sliding in tiny streams off the face of the man controlling his fate. Off in the distance, the three men standing in the alleyway could hear the sounds of belated police sirens approaching.

"Why did it have to come to this?" Sean asked, as if any answer

DeBury could give would somehow give logical reason for the events that had taken place.

"Sean," the man on his knees began, "There is still so much you don't know. So much that escapes your simple understanding."

"Explain it then!" he barked. "Make me understand why so many people had to die so you could gain possession of that book!" Sean said, pointing at the volumous work in DeBury' s rain- soaked hands.

"You and I haven't the time," he said with an agitating response, "Order my death or set me free. Just make a bloody decision - neither of us needs to spend the rest of our lives in prison," he stated, referring to the ever-loudening sounds of the approaching police sirens. Roberto di Vecchio was not amused with DeBury' s commanding tone and placed the barrel of the shotgun deeper in the Englishman's back.

"I want my life back!" Sean demanded through the downpour, "I want a life back."

"No one is preventing you from having it, Sean."

"I can't spend the rest of my life looking over my shoulder- wondering when you'll send one of your people from out of the shadows to end it."

"Sean," DeBury started, needlessly trying to wipe away the rainwater from his eyes, "I have what I want," he said, looking down at the book ion his hands. "My plan did not go exactly as I might have wished. But I have my book. That is enough. I'll have no need to bother you anymore. You have my word."

"Up till now your word's been worth absolutely nothing," Sean said as he stood, there dripping in the afternoon rainfall.

"Then kill me," DeBury said with little hesitation. "What I have said is all I can offer."

Sean looked down at the man who had instigated all of his troubles. A part of him wanted to see this man die. It would be justifiable. But he was no killer, however much he may have wished otherwise at that moment.

Sean reached in his pocket and withdrew a small silver oblong object and flashed the device before the wide- eyed DeBury.

"This is a tape- recorded confession of you admitting to killing Anthony Taylor. It was in my pocket when we met for the exchange just a few minutes ago."

"Clever boy," DeBury interrupted.

"I've got this for insurance," he said, waving the recording device in the air, "and the remaining money to help with a new life. All you have to do is leave me alone. Don't ever seek me out. Ever." Sean backed up slightly, "Regardless of what you've done to me, I don't want your death on my hands. But if you come for me, I'll make damn sure these men seek you out and I promise this tape will find its way to the police."

DeBury nodded. "We understand each other perfectly, Sean. I think we are much alike, you and I."

Sean was quick to address the book collector.

"You and I are nothing alike," he snapped. "The only thing we share is an appreciation for old books, you condescending asshole- nothing else!"

Sean allowed DeBury to stand, ordering the man behind him to step back. Roberto wasn't in the least happy with the decision, but lifted the gun from DeBury's back, and let him come to his feet. DeBury was soaked from the rain but still smiling. Sean, looking at the book in the book collector's hand, noticed that the rain water wasn't dampening the pages whatsoever. The water simply ran off the book's cover, un-fazing nor un-altering the item in anyway.

"Tell me, Sean," DeBury asked, "How did you survive your gunshot wound?"

"I.... I haven't had time to really think about that... I......"

"Cecilia is...." DeBury paused to draw attention to her bloody carcass lying in the street, "was... a professional. She should have easily killed you with that shot to the gut. Yet, six days later here you are in London- as if nothing happened to you at all."

"I'm alive, and I've got the pain of the memory," Sean said, "That's enough for me now."

"Is it?"

"Yeah, asshole, it is."

"And you aren't just slightly curious as to how your wounds healed so fast?"

"What are you getting at?"

DeBury lifted the book in his hands skyward, as Sean watched the rain bounce off the cover. "You are alive because this book was in your possession."

Sean looked at the man with a blank stare, as if DeBury was losing his mind.

"What are you trying to say?"

"This book has a supernatural foundation, Sean," DeBury began. "One no one has ever been able to explain nor categorize. On its inner pages lie the confession of the Devil himself. But the outer binding has been fashioned with the skin of the man who wrote it. An honest- to- God saint."

Sean just stared back, unable, or perhaps unwilling, to fashion some response. He hadn't really paid too much attention to the first thing DeBury had said, only the last part. The part about the binding. The part about it being human skin. This might explain the oiliness he felt when he first touched it. But it wouldn't have been oily after five hundred years. No way possible.

"The combination of saint and sinner give the book an unusual power all its own," DeBury said, pausing to catch his breath. "No one has ever been able to explain how or why it exudes supernatural gifts....... but it does. It healed you, Sean. It saved you from death, because it found a worthiness in you. Just as it caused the death of the pirates who took it from its resting place in Docheiariou on Athos so many years ago. It has been talked of in secret societies, that this book is alive somewhat- seemingly passing judgment on all who are in possession of it," he said, looking down at the manuscript once more. "This book is a living entity. The words of Lucifer. An angel of death and judgment for all who possess it."

"You're out of your mind!" Sean said, scoffing in an atheistic tone.

"Am I?" DeBury paused. "Look who has been in possession of the volume. Adolph Hitler, Napoleon Bonaparte,........... shall I continue?"

"I've had enough of this," Sean said, "I'm a simple guy who could use a very large drink right now. If 1 tried to digest any of what's happened to me over the last week, I think I'd go insane," he stated, turning from DeBury and his ranting. "What I know is that I'm alive. And I plan to get back to life. If you believe any of what you've said, my advice is to get as far away from that damn book as you can get. God only knows what kind of judgment it would pass on you!"

"Oh but I plan to study it- to harness its power," DeBury said. "Imagine what could happen to the person that unlocked its secrets?"

"To Hell with you and that damn book," Sean said, brushing him off. "Just leave me alone. Understood?"

"You have my word, Sean."

"If you come for me," the book scout said while shaking his finger in the direction of DeBury, "The man behind you will come for you," he spat. "And try not to forget- I have your recorded confession to a murder."

"We understand each other perfectly, my friend," the Englishman nodded.

"Consider the final victory to be yours. I'll not pursue you again. My life on that."

Sean didn't concern himself with whether or not there was honesty in the man's voice. He could already feel a weight lifting off his chest. And that, for now, was enough. The book scout turned to the man who was standing behind DeBury and nudging him with the muzzle of the shotgun.

"Let him go....... let' s get out of here."

The assassin was dumbfounded. He was unaccustomed to leaving a job unfinished. And his personal desire to kill DeBury was paramount in the Sicilian's mind. "Signore.........?"

"No questions," Sean fired back. "I can't live with his death on my conscience. I know that now. Leave him. Let's get the money, and get the hell out of here."

"As you wish," di Vecchio sneered reluctantly.

The assassin then walked over to his friend and fellow accomplice, Nick Gravano, who was on the ground nursing his wound from Vincent Conducci' s weapon. The Sicilian helped his friend to his feet, took one of the briefcases Sean offered him, and headed in a northeastern direction, where the car they had arrived in would aid in their departure.

The Sicilians had dispersed the scene rather quickly, leaving Sean alone in the company of Nicholas De Bury.

DeBury smiled at Sean as he tucked the Manuscripta Diabolica under his arm. The two men seemed to stand there looking at each other for some time as if neither individual needed speech to relay what the other was thinking. Words were of little use to these men now.

Suddenly, the rain quickened its ferocity, bouncing off the ground like tiny bullets being discharged from a machine gun.

One thing was now certain. Each man knew he would never see the other again. Ultimately, DeBury had gotten what it was that he had been after all along. The book was in his possession at last, and the cost to him had not mattered in the slightest.

And there was something else that gave Sean a degree of reassurance.

The book scout could tell that DeBury had found a respect for him. At least, enough to convince himself that the Englishman was going to leave him alone.

The police sirens were just up the street. London traffic had held the authorities up just long enough for the men to disperse, but they would arrive at any moment.

Sir Nicholas DeBury excused himself, and turned from Sean, cradling the Manuscripta Diabolica in his arms and hurrying toward his limousine that was idling close by. The American watched the Englishman until he had climbed in the back and closed the door, and then watched the car pull off, obscuring itself in the London traffic. Sean Wilde then looked up at the gray sky above, then back at the sign that read 'Charring Cross Road.' There was no hope of grasping all that had taken place in the last few days, and he wasn't going to even attempt to try. He was alive. And that would have to suffice.

The book scout lifted the remaining briefcase, and quickly dispersed down a nearby alleyway. If he didn't get out of London fast, he would not have the opportunity to spend either his new wealth nor would he enjoy his new freedom. The prison system was rough everywhere.

As he ran through the alley, Sean couldn't help but breathe a sigh of relief. Hopefully one adventure was behind him and a less hazardous one was going to begin. He smiled as he thought he might find work in some new field.

Stamp-hunting was a possibility. He needed something much safer than book hunting, he grinned to himself.

As with anyone who had been given a second chance, both Sean's life and an uncertain future lay ahead. What he did with each, was now decidedly up to him.

"According to the state of one's mind, a departure is either a relief or the reverse."

Victor Marie Hugo

A Parting Eulogy

Docheiariou was empty today.

This was not because the monastery had been abandoned. It was because each man who called the monastery home had now gathered before a large mound of dirt on a hill just behind the place they each called home. They had assembled to pay their final respects to a friend and mentor, and to offer a blessing that might accompany their brother to heaven.

The island of Athos was still- as quiet as it had ever been. No birds squawked overhead, and there was no rumbling in the sky above. All that remained for the common ear to hear was the stillness of the landscape and the light, soothing breeze· from the Aegean Sea.

The entire human contents of the monastery had gathered around a tapestry of sadness and regret for the passing of one of their own.

A small mound of black dirt, marked humbly by a small, hand- made wooden cross served as the final monument to a man who had meant so much to the community here on Athos.

But the monks were not the only beings convening for the funeral procession. Something else had come to join in the fray.

Lucifer was here as well.

The old demon was completely invisible to those congregated around, but he had come to pay his respects. He appeared in both a mixture of both his pleasing form and his demonic state. His body was beautiful, but present were horns, hooves, and black, leathery wings. He was a visual representation of his two selves. And he seemed honored to be in attendance.

The demon weaved unnoticed in and out of the gathering horde, toward the grave itself. He cared nothing for the human epitaph being given by Father Chrysostomus. What he was focusing on was the actual mound that held the mortal remains of Father Koutrakos. Walking past the mounded earth, he came to find respite on a nearby rock, and looked up to the sky above. Toward the Heavens. Toward his former home.

"A fine day for a funeral," he relayed to no one in particular, "Don't you think?" He redirected the last statement in the direction of the grave. He knew well there would be no response. No reply from the man resting within. Still, it didn't stop his desire to hear himself speak. "I must avow my appreciation for your commitment to my tale, Father, but there was no reason to take the construction of the book so far," he said, referring to the monks binding technique. "Did we reach a conclusion- you and I?" he said, crossing his arms and beginning a purposeful march about the grave. "Am I forgiven, do you think? Or will your death be hung over my head as well? Ah.......l suppose it is of little matter. You allowed me time for my confession, and you have the gratefulness of a repentant angel. Still...," he said, arching his brow and bringing his forefinger to the air, "I must confess to you that I do not feel forgiven." He looked down at his hoofed feet. "Oh, I know...l know," he began, "You would probably say something self-righteous like 'You are the devil! What do you expect!' and of course you would be right............ as often you were. But I hope you saw more to me than just some evil being bent on the never- ending temptation of you insufferable human beings."

Having said this, Lucifer strolled over to where the monks bad gathered and joined them in a sorrowful chorus of Latin chants. He gave the appearance of wishing to express a more tear- soaked offering for the passing of Father Koutrakos. But this didn't last long. And he began talking loudly among the men even though they could neither see nor hear the demon.

"Help me understand these men, Father," he yelled. "They have assembled for your death as if it is sorrowful, yet you have only passed on to your angelic form- death being the absolute necessity of angelic development. Do they not realize you are far better than you have ever. been?" he stated, shrugging his shoulders. "What am I saying?" he said, throwing out his arms, "Humans understand nothing, and they corrupt everything." Lucifer then put his arms behind his back and left the crowd. "Human life is such a joke, Father. The progressive state of all living things is that they live and then they die, but then, of course, you know this," he said, looking at the mound of earth. "Yet all humans search for a mystery where there exists none. The great secret of Life is that there is no secret at all! Your species understands so little of the fleeting time in which life passes and the eternity which lies in wait. There exists no real comprehension of what lies beyond the grave, does there?"

The old angel stopped at the foot of the wooden cross marking the dead monk's grave, and bent over as if he was whispering so none could hear. No one could hear anyway.

"Do you know what they did with your book?" he addressed the emptiness of the grave. "Father Chrysostomus placed it under lock and key in the newly constructed library, at the other end of Docheiariou. He was adamant in his attempts to destroy the old library where you and I conversed. And all this just because I was there. Speaking with you. Confessing my sins, as it were." Lucifer then bowed his head, shaking it from side to side. "He should sanctify the room instead. If he only knew what it took to stomach being there........." When the beast looked up, his black eyes caught hold of a dove flying by on the wind. As it flapped its wings, the demon spit on the earth below his feet. "Oh, please...." he said, as if he was bothered by the heavenly messenger. The demon then stood on the very mound of dirt that interred the old monk and began a recollection.

"We had a moment together, you and I," he stated, as his wings fluttered behind him. "Look," he said talking to the grave, "No change." He was rubbing his horns now. "We must assume I am still among the damned. Oh, unforgiven am I," he stated, feigning the mockery of passing out. "It seems, Father, that I am to play the hand I have been dealt. But," he said as he peered down at the wooden grave marker, "never think for a moment that I did not find some worthiness in you. For a human, you were among the most deserving of my Creator's gift of life. So, in the honor of you and your willingness to hear my confession, I will grant your species this gift," he said, looking skyward again, "I will stay my hands from the human. Never again will I labor myself to cause these indigents harm." He pointed to the body of monks chanting over the grave. "As I confessed to you during your life, they will do more harm to themselves in the days of the future than I could ever hope to accomplish by myself alone. Perhaps in this I can find forgiveness by myself. Perhaps not. At any rate, I have found little understanding in the behavior of man with what time I have spent with them. My ultimate destiny is the true mystery, I suppose. God only knows........ right, Father?............. Father?"

The demon knew there would be no response. Father Koutrakos wasn't with him anymore. But after years upon the earth by himself, he was not above amusing himself in his own way. The old demon then pitched a small piece of rotting wood, no bigger than the palm of a man, onto the mound of dirt before him. As the small object hit the earth, it became visible to every monk standing nearby. Lucifer began speaking as one of the monks grazed by him in an effort to bend over and pick it up.

"This is a small token from Golgotha, Father," he said. "It is a piece of the upper beam that your 'Christ' was nailed to. If it matters, it was located just below his left hand. Take this gift as a consolation prize for your sacrifice," he said, turning from the grave. "No doubt these monks will make you a saint when they realize it appeared at your tomb. They will think it an offering from the Creator above. A relic from Heaven. Yet you and I will know where it came from, won't we?" the demon said, looking back at the grave. "In the end, Father, where man is concerned, there is always just me, and just them. Just us. Justice. Seems only fitting............."

As the monk beside Lucifer grasped the small piece of wood, something he was unprepared for happened.

As his young hand came in contact with the item, his surroundings altered at once. No more was the monk on the recognizable home of Athos. He was somewhere different. Unfamiliar. Old. Ancient.

He was surrounded by Roman centurions. But they were not looking at him. They were focused on the hill a few yards away. When the monk focused his eyes in the direction that they were looking, he fell to his knees. He then emptied the contents of his stomach onto the ground.

Before him, only a few feet away, he saw the man he had spent a lifetime praying to hanging naked from a crossbeam. There and then, every conviction he had ever doubted was instantly confirmed. Tears flowed uncontrollably.

By touching the piece of wood, he had transported himself back in time. He was bearing witness to the very crucifixion itself. His mind was not prepared for the reality of the sight and he dropped the object screaming before a crowd of monks gathered around him on Athos.

As the other monks rushed to his side, offering what aid they could, they all noticed his hair - black as pitch only moments before - was now as white as newly cleaned linen. And moreover, he was utterly inconsolable. When they grasped his hands in an effort to provide aid, they noticed something else.

Blood was seeping from his palms. And blood was seeping from his brow-line. The young monk was exhibiting physical signs of being crucified. He had received the stigmata for picking up the small simple piece of wood.

A wiser monk reached down to pick up the piece of wood with the lower portion of his robe, for he had realized the mental anguish that might accompany touching it with his bare palm.

Off in the distance, Lucifer was on his rear, laughing.

"Ah, Father," he called out, addressing the dead monk, "I miss you already. Where shall I go without my 'Father Confessor'?" He paused the outburst long enough to rest his right arm on his knee. He then allowed himself to ponder the spiritual existence of Father Koutrakos. "One can suppose the secrets of the universe are at your fingertips now that you have passed this world. You must also realize how simplistic life really is when the idea of it is compared to the infinite time to which you keep company now. Be honest, old monk," the demon said with a sneer, "Even you must pity human existence now."

But the grave didn't answer the old serpent.

An ocean breeze sent a chill through the demon and caused him to turn and look in the direction of the gathering monks. It seemed to him that two of the men were having to physically support the unfortunate soul who had come in contact with the relic Lucifer had placed at the dead man's grave. This caused a smile to form on the demon's face. The devil then took to his hoofed feet, standing, while not taking his eyes from the monks as they assembled like ants, following single file, shuffling in the direction of the monastery below. Yet one monk remained.

Father Thomas Chrysostomus was still hovering over the grave when the last monk departed the scene.

Lucifer studied the last monk, as he seemed to be mumbling a few offerings to himself. The human then bent over and placed a small flower on the grave of his beloved friend; After this exhibition of sorrow, the man then made the sign of the cross over his chest, and turned to leave the sight.

As he passed by the invisible demon, Lucifer stuck out a hoof, tripping the elder man and causing him to fall to the ground.

Father Chrysostomus looked dumbfounded as he scanned the area around him. Nothing seemed to have caused the fall. There were no branches or half broken roots jutting from the earth. Nothing that should have caused him to fall. He wasted no time coming to his feet even though his old age caused him somewhat of a hindrance.

Then, the old man noticed an uneasiness about him. The monk arched a brow as if he could feel the presence of something else with him. Something.......... otherworldly. But he shook free of the feeling, owing the fall to his own stupidity and miscalculation. He then turned from the grave of his friend and hobbled down the hill in an effort to join up with the monks who had already made their way halfway back to the monastery.

Lucifer, on the other hand, returned his attention back to the lifelessness of the grave.

"Well what did you think, Father?" he said to the dead monk. "The depth to which I can keep a vow lies within my own ability to resist temptation," he said smiling. "Forgive me. I am not one for hypocrisy."

The fallen angel then leapt from the ground, batting his leathery wings heavily against the air that surrounded him. Soon, he was in the sky where he was most comfortable.

The world below him was a vast marketplace of human detritus. Nothing would make the fallen angel happier than to bear witness to all manner of debaucherous activity that he could find. There was much he could learn from the depravity a human would allow himself.

For all manner of human life, Lucifer would resign himself to never be that far away.

> "Time gives all and takes all away; everything changes, but nothing perishes."
>
> Giordano Bruno

Epilogue

Venice, Italy
The Present

Jaco Fernetti heard a knock at his door, and wasted no time racing from his kitchen to answer the sound.

The Italian hadn't long been awake, and was cooking breakfast when the knock came. He was anxious, even hopeful, that it would be his American friend telling him all had gone well. He wanted reassurance Sean Wilde was alive, and that the American indeed had the life back he so desperately wanted.

Unfortunately, Sean wasn't on the other side of the doorway.

Two large, well- dressed men were standing in his doorway blocking the light and the street behind them. The small Venetian stepped back and tried to control the pounding in his chest- but it wouldn't slow down. He had never had visitors that looked like these men before. These men were Sicilian. And it didn't seem to matter that they were slow introducing themselves - he seemed to know at once that he was in trouble. At that moment, Jaco forgot all about his American friend.

Sweat began to form on his scalp, and he braced himself for what was coming next. He knew, without a doubt, he was about to die.

"Jaco Fernetti?" the figure closest to him asked in a way that seemed to be less of a question and more of a warning.

The little Italian passed every possible response in his mind, but settled on the most obvious. "Si," he said with reluctance.

The largest of the two massive men stepped forward with little concern for whether or not the man was going to invite him in. He then lifted an object from his side, thrusting it forward in Jaco's direction. The small Italian got so scared he screamed as if the man was drawing a gun. He could hear the other large man begin to snicker in the background.

It was only a briefcase.

Jaco looked at the square object and then at the man holding it, then back at the object once more. There was a significant element of confusion between the two men. When the well-dressed man holding the briefcase realized this, he spoke up.

"This is from Don di Trapani," he said with a Sicilian tongue. "He instructed us to deliver this to you personally," he said, setting the briefcase on the floor of the dwelling. Jaco was shaking way too much to have ever reached out for it by himself. "You are not to seek him out, but accept this as a token of his thanks. *Capire*?"

"S...... Si...," the frightened man said as the two men waited only for an acknowledgment of the gift. Jaco watched them tum, leaving his home-each chuckling to themselves with a smile on their faces.

A million different thoughts raced through the Italian's mind.

This could be a bomb. Or a warning of some kind. Even a trick from some rival familia.

Jaco Fernetti soaked up what willpower he possessed and crept toward the object resting on the floor of his home. He could wonder all he wanted, he was going to know absolutely nothing until he opened that briefcase. If it was bomb, then he was dead - end of story. But there was always a chance...

The cab driver rushed toward the briefcase and clicked the gold latch. The object parted in the middle and its contents poured all over the floor of his modest home.

What spilled out was money. And lots of it- all in British Sterling. About half a million pounds, from the looks of things.

The little Italian noticed a note attached to the inside of the briefcase, and he ripped it from the tape that was holding it fast.

> ***Thank you for saving the life of my son***
> ***I hope this makes life easier for you***
> ***It is the least I could have done***
> ***Please consider my debt to you re-paid***
>
> ***G. Trapani***

The note was from Don di Trapani himself. The old man had sought to set things straight with Jaco Fernetti, even though it had been unnecessary. And he had done so in spades.

Jaco sat in the doorway of his modest home surrounded by brand new, crisply minted bills. He lifted them in the air, unbelieving that they were here, and ·that they were his.

He was rich.

The small Italian opened the door of his home as if to thank the men who had just been there, but saw no evidence of them anywhere. They had vanished. All that stared back at Jaco Fernetti were the bustling canals of Venice and the dawn of another beautiful Venetian day.

He then looked to his beat- up taxi sitting on the street and walked toward it, rubbing his chin. The little car was a mess.

Might be a good time to get the car a new paint job, he thought.

Paris, France
The Present

Sean Wilde was sipping coffee and sliding some of his new antiquarian acquisitions on a book shelf in his store. He had been glad to finish the story of the Manuscript a Diabolica the night before, and had tucked the manuscript of his tale in a safe place in his upstairs flat.

What held his attention now was his store and the books inside. And he had spent much of the day pricing a few of his latest acquisitions, finally getting them put up for sale.

As he continued the task, the door to his small shop opened, and a well-dressed couple walked in. They seemed to be American, by their mannerisms, and the store's proprietor stopped what he was doing long enough to greet them and ask if they needed any help. The woman said nothing- looking as though she was bothered by having had to come in the bookstore at all. The man, however, seemed all too willing to speak. He held out his hand introducing himself to Sean.

"My name is Sian L. Gibbs," he said as Sean reached for his hand. "I am a book collector from America." Sean thought the first name a bit odd.

"Pleased to meet you," Sean responded, releasing the man's hand, "Anything I can help you with? Are you looking for a specific book?"

"Actually, I am," he said, pausing and looking at his feet. "I am looking for a book entitled Dios de la Inquisition. Have you ever heard of it?"

"To be honest, I try to keep up on as much as I can, but that's not been a book I have ever heard of," he said, "No. I can't say I have." Sean was eyeing the man with a curious expression on his face.

"Don't worry," he said. "Few people have heard of it. It was written in the middle ages by an educated layman who tried to make a record of the Spanish Inquisition's bloody tribunals in Spain. There exists only one known copy, as all editions were either destroyed by the Inquisition, or lost to time's uncaring hand. The thing about the book is that it contains a detailed account of one of the key figures of the Inquisition - Tomas de Torquemada."

Sean took a step back. "If the book's that rare there is little chance of me coming across it," he stated. "You might do well to watch an auction house or something like that. I'm just saying you'll probably have better luck that's all."

"Actually," the man said, rubbing the unshaven stubble on his chin, "I was hoping I might make you a proposition."

Sean's heart sunk for a moment, but he said nothing. Then, the man looked back up at him and began speaking again.

"I've heard you used to be a pretty resourceful book scout," the stranger began, while Sean Wilde just listened with his heartbeat becoming more and more rapid. "Getting more to the point, I'd like to hire you out to find this book. I can pay you a significant sum for your troubles and I'll front whatever money you need to hold onto you're shop while you search for the book, but understand I would really like your involvement if possible."

Sean Wilde smiled at the absurdity of the request. The former book scout had enough money in the bank to sustain him and any offspring he might have for life. He had a small Parisian book shop and a nice little loft just above it. This man was insane if he thought Sean was going on some fool's errand again. He had had enough dealings with crooks and madmen on his last caper to last him a lifetime. No need to put himself in a position like that again. Besides, he wasn't Indiana Jones, for Christ's sake!

Still........... something was tugging at him, the way a bottle of alcohol beckons a drunkard happening by a liquor store. He resisted temptation as best as he could, but there was nothing that could stop the words as they passed from his brain through his lips.

"Tell me more about the book," he said.

Trouble just seems to find some people.

London, England
The Present

Sir Nicholas DeBury sat in front of a raging fire gently turning the fragile pages of the large book sitting in his lap. He was maddened with the beauty of its illustrations even though he could read very little of the words written in the book.

But there was no mistaking what lay before him. He had the one true copy of the Manuscript a Diabolica. His family's possession had finally come home.

Behind him, the butler Finneas Frakes had entered the room, pushing a serving tray. Upon it were several glasses, a wine bottle, and some various cheeses and crackers. The slender figure stopped the silver cart just behind the couch where DeBury sat groping his new acquisition.

"Will that be all, Sir?" Finneas said in a proper English tone.

"That will be all, Mr. Frakes," DeBury returned. He never took his eyes from the book for a moment.

"Very good, Sir," the butler said, excusing himself and turning from his employer, walking towards the glass entranceway of the library.

But an odd thing happened.

Instead of shutting the doors behind him as he left, the slender man closed the doors before he exited the room, leaving himself alone with DeBury in the library. He then turned and walked back to where the Englishman was seated as if he had forgotten something.

DeBury could hear nothing save his own heart beat each time he turned a vellum page.

His eyes widened as he held the book close to himself. There was a part of him that couldn't believe it was actually in his hands. The words, though DeBury couldn't read all of them, seemed to leap from the pages. This book was the only one of its kind, and as future days passed, DeBury would do what he could to translate the writing he didn't understand. Perhaps then he could channel whatever power the book possessed, and use it to his own end. Nothing else in the world mattered right now but what lay in his lap. One could say the man was so entranced by the brevity of the work - that he was completely clueless to what was happening around him.

Just then, the Englishman came to the last page of the book. It was set off from the rest because there was no illustration or fancy outline of the page. It was just simple red ink that sat out from a white background of parchment. The words that were written were in perfect Latin and they were much easier to read than any other passage of the book. He read the Latin aloud, as it was written, then sounded off in English;

Teneat Qui Librum
Tum a Libro Judicetur

"Let him who holds the book; Then by the book, be he judged." A simple message, DeBury thought, from a superstitious monk.

DeBury was startled by the sound of something making a noise from the silver tray behind him. He motioned toward the direction of the sound. When he turned around, his heart sank deep into his bowels.

Finneas Frakes had lifted the small knife from the block of cheese resting on the table, and was holding it in his hand and smiling with the most sinister grin DeBury had ever seen.

Then, within the confines of the Englishman's library, his butler began to change shape.

There was no amount of rationing to make the man holding the book believe what he was witnessing. DeBury opened his mouth to scream but the shocking reality of what was transpiring before him rendered him speechless. He was frozen to his chair- utterly motionless.

Horns slid from Finneas's temples, curling as they came forth. Wings, sleek like those of a bat, unfurled from his back. He seemed to be snarling and laughing all at the same time. DeBury didn't look down, but could hear the clapping of what sounded like horse hooves against the wooden floor. The being that had once been Finneas Frakes hastened over to where he was seated. Then, the beast- this aberration of nature, began to speak.

"Let him who holds the book be judged............... nice touch, don't you think?" the creature commented. "I added that myself when I returned to the monastery and found what Father Koutrakos had done to himself," He added. DeBury could say nothing. Thoughts raced through his mind, but words were wholly absent. The terror on his face said all that needed to be stated. "Oh, come now, my friend, don't you think after five hundred years my story could use a new, more modem binding?" the demon said, holding up the small knife, "One more in touch with the times? I'm quite the book smith, and I promise," he said, looking around the room then back at the terrified man seated before him, "I'll make the new binding as nice as any you have in the room....and besides, I've always wanted to know if I could do as good of a job at stitching skin as the old monk did with his own," he said, pausing and moving closer to DeBury. "Now hold still...... I've got a feeling this will probably hurt somewhat............."

The screams that resonated from the library of Sir Nicholas DeBury were more like that of a beast than those of a man. But such is the pain caused when flesh is stripped from a living, writhing human being.

Mount Athos
Docheiariou Monastery
1518

There was no evidence anyone had ever ventured into this room.

What had once been a library, a place of repose and sanctified book making, record keeping, and cataloging, was now little more than a shell of its former purpose.

The room had now been boarded up for some time by the order of the monastery's acting abbot, Father Thomas Chrysostomus.

Though it sat empty and void of human consort, there was still activity taking place.

Within a profusely intricate web, a tiny spider was gliding effortlessly, but with decisive precision, towards a newly captured victim. It had trapped a small fly, which it felt writhing in its netting. Though the beast struggled and fought valiantly for its freedom, all that it succeeded in was trapping itself tighter in the sticky encasement.

The arachnid was positioning itself to further entrap the beast and suck its blood for nourishment. The spider raised its legs and placed its abdomen close to the tiresome bug- who had all but tired itself out with its ceaseless struggles.

As the spider began to dispense with a bit more webbing, an unexpected thing happened.

A dove, no bigger than the palm of a man's hand, flew in from the library's open window and lapped the spider from his web and gobbled the little creature down its throat. The beast that had only moments before been predator now had become prey to something greater than himself. Such was the nature of all life. Such was the encroaching compass of death.

The small bird seemed to survey the emptiness of the room for a moment, then lifted itself from its position atop the empty bookshelf, and flew out the window.

Below him, Athos rested comfortably in the Aegean Sea, as it had all the days before. All was normal, it seemed. The monastic republic was at peace once again.

*******************_finis_*************************

About the Author

Chuck Maier is a self-employed business owner, artist, bibliophile, and writer. He has traveled Europe and spent a lifetime in pursuit of his artistic voice, creativity, and spiritual awakening. He is the father of two beautiful girls. He currently lives in Columbia, South Carolina.This is his first novel. He can be found at ChuckMaierArt.com

www.ingramcontent.com/pod-product-compliance
Lightning Source LLC
Chambersburg PA
CBHW030822310726
48980CB00006B/592/J